CASTLE MINERVA
and
THE HIDDEN FACE

"A blessed companion is a book"—JERROLD

CASTLE MINERVA

and

THE HIDDEN FACE

*

VICTOR CANNING

THE COMPANION BOOK CLUB
LONDON

To
MY WIFE

Made and printed in Great Britain
for The Companion Book Club (Odhams Press Ltd.)
by Odhams (Watford) Limited
Watford, Herts
S.257.ZSA.

CONTENTS

*

CASTLE MINERVA

CHAPTER I

THERE was a light cold rain falling as I came down the road out of the pass. It would freeze during the night and I knew that any climbing the next day would have to be handled carefully. Across the wide valley the gentle slope of Moel Siabod rose out of the misty rain like a stranded whale. Moel Siabod, Snowdon, Tryfan, the Carnedds . . . the lovely Welsh names and the lovely Welsh hills; just to get up here for a long weekend gave me a lift and a freshening of the spirit. It was a far cry from morning chapels, the smell of chalk and changing rooms, and the trapped look of boys floundering in a morass of French irregular verbs. I like my job. I liked being with boys and watching them develop into young manhood, but by mid-term I was always ready for a break. Up here the wind blew all memory of school away, and the strain of setting my body against the steep rock faces brought that liberation of the spirit which every man needs now and again if he is going to keep on top of his job.

I kept going through the rain, happy, and with that growing tiredness of the body which is a form of contentment. At that moment I wasn't asking for anything. I was over thirty, reasonably ambitious, and interested in my work. I imagined I could see the shape of the future, and I liked what I pictured. One day I'd be a housemaster, perhaps a headmaster. I'd be married, have children and then I'd have to make my vacations more orthodox, bathing and sailing, not trying to feed still the old war-bred appetite for strange places and people. A good future. But right then I should have had the sense not to compliment myself about it. The future maps itself.

Below me the lights of the inn showed up through the rain. I began to anticipate the comforts of getting out of wet clothes, of soaking in a hot bath, of the large whisky before dinner and the leisurely pipe afterwards in front of the bar room fire.

But for me that evening there was more than comfort in store. I got in, bathed and changed, and went down to the bar and there, unexpected, sitting in a corner was the one man in all the world whose company I would have asked for if the gods had given me the choice.

Colonel Francis Drexel, D.S.O., M.C. He got up and came

across to me, his movements dancing, brisk, terrier-like; the iron-grey hair crisp, short cut; the lean, weather-tanned and worn face smiling; a small, dapper man full of life and still, for all his near sixty years, as hard as nails.

He grabbed my arm and said, "David. . . . Well, if this isn't luck!" Apart from us there was only the barman in the place and Drexel's voice echoed about the room joyfully. It was the old voice, the old tone and with it—the grasp of his powerful fingers on my arm—all the old magic.

"When did you get in?" I asked.

"Couple of hours ago."

"I didn't know you used this place?"

He laughed, called to the barman for a couple of whiskies, and went on, "David, I was climbing up here before you were born. And I'll still be here when you're dead." He stood back and looked at me and then with a snort said, "Still can't get used to you in those damned civilian clothes. You looked better in uniform. You still buried in that damn school?"

"Still there," I said, smiling. "Happily interred." And as I spoke I was thinking of the times in the past when this man had scared hell into me, of the times he had forced me to the edge of breaking but never over. He had taken me as a young officer—Captain David Bladen Fraser of the Gordon Highlanders —with the mist of Edinburgh still in my hair and had put me through the rolling mill of the Mediterranean and the Near East. He had helped to turn me into a man, and I knew that after the war he had hated to see me go back to itchy-bottomed schoolboys with minds like colanders.

He tossed his whisky back and ordered two more.

"Tomorrow," he said, "we'll climb together. How's the old knee-cap?"

"It's all right as long as I watch it." As I answered each of us was thinking the same thing I guessed, both of us years back in the past.

He said, "We'll do the Milestone Buttress or maybe some of Idwal Slabs. I've been in Berlin for three weeks and I want to get the smell of frustration out of my nostrils."

I didn't ask him what he had been doing in Berlin. I had more sense, but there was an ugly bruise and a few cuts on the side of his face in a pattern that only a knuckle-duster can raise. I knew because I had used one in his service before now. But no questions: Colonel Francis Drexel, a hero to the public, a war-time legend, and still in harness. I wondered if the Foreign Office or M.I.5 ever pensioned off their people.

I said, "You'll have to go easy with me. I have to pick my climbs these days."

"Nonsense. For a six-footer you're carrying too much weight. I'll take it off you. The kind of life you lead makes people fat and complacent. How the hell do you stick it?"

"Because I like it. Don't let's begin that all over again." This was an old argument between us. We lived now in different worlds. I had touched his during the war, but now I was back where I belonged, with the kind of job millions of men have to do, nine till five, boring sometimes, but with a purpose behind it and pleasure in it. Only during my vacations could I slip into something like his kind of life. With me a little excitement went a long way. With Drexel it was food and drink. The world had a place for both of us.

"Wasted," he said. "A good man wasted. However. . . ." He finished his whisky, and then in that abrupt way of his said, "Married yet?"

I laughed. "Not yet. No takers."

"Not surprised. Don't find your kind in vicarage gardens, or at school bun fights. I've tried marriage twice and it doesn't work. Not for me, anyway. Suppose I'm not at home enough." For a moment I thought I caught the hint of regret in his voice.

He tapped his glass for the barman to fill it again and I think it was then that I noticed the change in him. At first I thought it was something to do with the way he was drinking. Then I knew it wasn't. He always had drunk hard. It was an all over something. There was a strain on him. He looked much the same, the hardness, the trim compactness, the tight rebellious mouth of a schoolboy, the restless eyes full of visions and fire . . . but something was gone. His laugh was no longer as easy as it had been. . . . And then I saw it. He was showing his age. Just that. He was being worn down and, because I had so much affection and respect for this man, I was suddenly resentful of the anonymous service which was doing this to him. He had been in harness too long. No man should have to go on being a hero, a colourful public figure, after fifty-eight. It was time he slowed up and took things easy.

But change or no change, the next day on the towering Idwal Slabs, he scared the hell out of me. Ever since my cracked knee-cap I've had to go carefully, and anyway going carefully is the best bet in climbing. But Drexel climbed as he did everything else, with one hand on death's shoulder for support. And there was a grin on his face which I knew was for my benefit. It was a challenge and I had to take it. It was a bright, clear March day with a freezing cold wind and a thin layer of ice on most of the rocks, and more than once I said to myself, "Fraser, if you don't want to break your neck put your pride in your pocket and get down below." But I didn't. Where he went, I went, and that was like the old times.

When we stopped to eat our sandwiches at midday, Drexel passed over his flask and I was glad of the nip of brandy. We were sitting on a wide ledge, our feet dangling over space. Reaching out around us was the great bowl of the purple and green hills, and far below the thin line of the road running past the tip of Lake Ogwen, its surface foam-lined with breakers from the boisterous wind.

Drexel said, "You still go well." He waved his hand at the view. "Wonderful, isn't it? Free of all the muck and stink. A man can breathe."

"You go too fast," I said. "You'll break your damned neck one of these days. This afternoon I lead."

He tossed a sandwich crust out into space and watched the wind take it. Then after a little silence he said quietly, "You really like being a schoolmaster, David?"

"Of course I do. The war's over long ago. My kind have to go back to work."

"You seem to get about in your vacations if what I hear is right?"

"That's what holidays are for."

"What are you doing this Easter vac.?"

I felt in my windbreaker for my cigarettes. "Flying to East Africa. Tanganyika."

"Going to wipe up the Mau Mau?" he grinned.

"No. Going to look for some of the lost property of the Queen of Sheba."

Even as I spoke I could feel the excitement rise in me. Drexel had it out of me in no time. Three of us were going and the school was prepared to give me a few weeks extra exeat. A thousand years before Christ all the islands off the coast of East Africa had formed part of Sheba's great empire of Tharish. We were to explore the island of Songa Manara, an island so far untouched, its thick jungle hiding the ruins of great palaces and traces of a long dead civilization. It was something I had always wanted to do, something which, in an odd way, meant a lot to me. Work by itself isn't enough. A man has got to have a few dreams even if they never become real. But this dream was going to come alive. We were taking an old movie camera and everything was being done on a shoe-string. It was something that had been in my mind for years.

Drexel said, "You talk as though it were pretty important."

"It is."

I couldn't go into it more with him. Some things you have to keep to yourself. The whole Songa Manara thing might cause quite a little stir . . . the film we should make, the possible discoveries, and the book to be written. Though we were doing it for its own sake, in my profession these things count. They make a difference when a housemaster's job is going, and later. . . . Well, the competition is keen, but it's no good being a schoolmaster unless somewhere in the future you see yourself running a show of your own.

He didn't ask any more questions. But he was no fool and I think he understood. He stood up, flipped his cigarette into space and said, "O.K. You lead. Knee all right?"

"Fine."

We roped up and started again and, frankly, I took the easier pitches. Behind me Drexel was very silent, which was not like him. But it was good to feel him there. Once on a stretch of loose shale my knee gave me a twinge and the pain took me back. . . . I had a swift picture of myself lying in the desert sand, the flies thick about the wound in my knee, the sun like a brazen gong and my head spinning with fever, and myself knowing that when the sun went down so would I. . . . And then Drexel coming back, out of nowhere, unexpected, risking himself for me, and never a moment of doubt in him, bullying me into courage and strength, half-carrying, half-dragging me for a couple of days. From that time every second I lived I owed to him. That's the kind of debt a man seldom gets the chance to repay.

When we stopped for a breather, he came up alongside me. He stood there with the wind shrieking over the ragged edge of the rocks behind us and the sun making the ice shine on the spurs below. He stared down into the valley. After a moment he said, "This Songa Manara thing could mean a lot to you?"

"Well. . . . Yes." His question was quite unexpected.

He nodded. Then suddenly he turned to me. His eyes were troubled. The lean, ageing face was very still. He said, "David. Meeting you up here was no accident. I came up after you."

"You did!" I was surprised and my voice showed it.

"Yes. I had to talk with you, David . . . I need your help. I need someone I know, someone I can trust absolutely."

I said, "You know that if there's anything I can do for you, you've only got to ask."

"That's why I hate doing it."

"Rot. Get it off your chest. What is it?"

Then abruptly, he said, "No, I can't do it. Get moving." He waved me on and I had to go. But now the thought that he wanted something from me and wouldn't ask stirred me up. I tried him once or twice as we climbed but he waved me on.

Finally we made the top of the climb and unroped on the short turf. As we started to walk around the top to find the easy path down to the lake, I swung round on him.

"If you want something from me, you've a right to ask for it," I said, and I heard my voice angry and determined shredding into the wind. "I'm not moving until you tell me."

He was a long time answering and I could sense the struggle in him.

"I don't want you to go to Songa Manara," he said at last. It was so unexpected that for a second a voice inside me cried out against it. But only for a second.

"Why not?" My voice showed nothing except curiosity.

"Because I want you to do a job for me during the Easter vacation. Not such a colourful job, though it may have its excitements. But it's a job that means a hell of a lot to me."

In that moment as I faced him I knew that if I put off my Songa Manara trip now the chance would never come again. That's the way life goes. I stood there and if I hesitated it was not because there was any doubt in my mind, but because one wants a few seconds to kiss a dream goodbye. No, for me the choice was never in question. I owed this man my life. I admired and respected him and I knew his qualities. So up there on the Welsh hill I let the Queen of Sheba go out of my life. Drexel wanted me and that was enough.

I said, "I'll do it."

"Thank you, David. I knew I could rely on you." He started to move on round the shoulder of the hill. On the valley road below a green bus moved slowly like a shining beetle.

As I walked beside him, I said, "But why have you picked me?"

"There aren't so many people in the world you can trust absolutely, David. This is your job."

"What is it?"

"Private tutor, companion. In a villa I've taken near Banyuls-sur-Mer on the French coast close to the Spanish border. A month on the Mediterranean this April."

It sounded dull compared with Africa.

"Tutor to whom?" I asked.

"You'll know when you meet him. You speak his language. That's another reason for it being you."

"I speak five languages, including a little Welsh."

He grinned. "You won't have to brush up your Welsh."

"What questions am I allowed to ask?"

"Any you like. Though I may not answer some. Everything is confidential at this moment."

"A large Foreign Office seal on it?"

"In a way."

"Where do you stand in all this?"

"I'm on the Army retired list. A private citizen. But the F.O. will come in at a point and then I shall be their agent. I can't go into that now. As far as you're concerned I employ you privately. Five hundred quid for a month's work."

"I don't want any money."

He shook his head. "I know what you're giving up. Don't tell me you couldn't use five hundred."

I didn't argue with him.

17

CHAPTER II

THE place the Colonel had taken was called the Villa Maruba. Calling it a villa did nothing for it. It was a largish, square building with the stucco flaking off it. The green window shutters were blistered and weathered pale by the salt wind and all the rooms smelled as though their only inhabitants had been penitents in damp sackcloth. Moving about the place, whenever I came upon a gleam of sunshine I used to walk around it as though it were a hole in the floor. Outside, day after day, there was plenty of sunshine. In the house it became something alien and suspect.

But I could see why the Colonel had picked the house. It stood just off the road between Port-Vendres and Banyuls-sur-Mer. A tall wall ran along the road face and down to the sea on either side of the garden. Along the top of the wall was a *cheval-de-frise*. The only way to look into the grounds was by climbing the vine-covered slopes on the far side of the road. The wall, I was sure, had settled it for the Colonel. The garden was a wilderness of tamarisk and oleander bushes, weed-grown paths and, at the sea-edge by the boathouse, a clump of pines whose shade was patrolled by red ants. Close to the house was a dry concrete pool with a fountain in the middle. The leaf-littered bowl was the haunt of lizards which fed on the flies that were attracted by the hot concrete. Coming up from the sea I used to see the house through a great shimmering wave of heat haze from the pool.

For the first week I stuck fairly close to the place, bathing, reading and letting the sun work into me. Brindle looked after me. Brindle had been Drexel's batman and then servant for years. 'A moon-faced yokel from the leafy lanes of Kent', was how the Colonel had described the Brindle who had first come to him thirty years before. He was no longer moon-faced. He was a square solid-looking man in whom the blood seemed to have thickened sluggishly. Every movement he took made me think that he was fighting against the onset of immobility, and what had been yokel in him was now shaped to a close, silent nature and a dog-like devotion to Drexel.

The first time I had any real conversation with Brindle was about a week after I'd arrived at the villa. I was down by the boathouse watching the sea. A large, wolf-hound kind of dog was with me, lying in the lee of the low wall below the pines. This one, a bitch, was free all day. Two others were let out at night. After a week of the wall and the dogs and the waiting I was beginning to get curious. During the war, when I had worked with Drexel, there had been some things I never had understood. Maybe because Drexel himself never had the full truth. But always the Colonel had given me and the others enough to soothe our natural itch for information, enough to make it easy for us to close our minds to demands for more. Since Wales I'd seen him twice in London at his Grosvenor Square flat, but so far he had given me no more than that I was to be companion to someone and was to keep my mouth shut about it.

Brindle came down the path to me, carrying a tea tray, his slippers making lazy conversation with the loose gravel and fallen pine needles.

As he poured the tea for me, I said, "Is the mail in yet?"

"Yes, sir."

"Nothing from the Colonel?"

"No, sir."

I chipped away at his hard mahogany. "Do you know where the Colonel is?"

"No, sir."

"Do you know what all this is about, Brindle?"

Brindle took a deep, slow breath and just saved himself from turning to wood and then said, "The Colonel's affairs is the Colonel's affairs, sir." If there was any emotion in his voice it was of reproach.

I ignored the reproach. "Do you know when he's due to arrive here?"

Brindle handed me my cup and then holding the sugar basin said, "One or two lumps, sir?"

"One. And don't be so po-faced, Brindle. You know a damned sight more about this whole affair than I do, don't you?"

He put sugar in my tea and then, straightening up carefully so as not to crack the bark that was growing on him, said, "At the moment, yes, sir."

I knew I wouldn't get any more than that from him.

I said, "I think I'll walk to Banyuls after tea. Can I bring anything back?" Brindle did all the catering and cooking and I used to see him going off in the morning on a bicycle to do the marketing.

"No thank you, sir."

He went off and I sat there and finished my tea. It was hot, wonderfully hot for the beginning of April and a little way up the coast I could see part of a private beach that belonged to some holiday orphanage home. Children in funny red bloomers and straw hats were shouting and running about, and a covey of black and white nuns looking like magpies were fussing around them. It was a good feeling, sitting there in the sun, facing the sea with the grey and gold coast line spread out on either side of me and the white-topped crests of the Pyrenees behind me. I didn't even think about Songa Manara much. Time slipped by without making a ripple.

I walked into Banyuls along the road, carrying my light jacket over my arm. This strip of coast reminded me of Cornwall, sparse and bare. There was no great height to the cliffs until you got down past Banyuls and on to Cerbère and the Spanish border. The afternoon had a bright, hard, metallic ring. I liked the neat rows of vines with rags of young leaf showing, the stone walls and the twisted blades of the tall cactus clumps. Some *Ponts et Chausées* men were working on the road just before Banyuls, hard, dark-skinned fellows, and one of them was singing in sudden lusty snatches as though his blood were too hot for his body and his spirits hard to hold down.

I left the road just before it began to curl down into Banyuls. I went out on to the level spread of headland, past tiny patches of garden with dried bamboo fences that protected the rows of lettuce, beans and arum lilies, and then came down through the old part of the town. Banyuls was two towns. The first part was like Clovelly; little cottages clinging to the sides of stepped and cobbled streets. But it had a lot of things not found in Clovelly; a warm smell of garlic, fennel and charcoal, enormous geranium growths and foaming cascades of petunia and bougainvillea washing down over the high garden walls on which hung cages of pigeons, bantams and rabbits. There was a smell of fish and wine, of poverty laid out under a sun which took the mildew and despair out of it. The women sitting at the open doors were mostly old and the men with their backs against the walls mostly asleep. They looked as though they had been sitting and sleeping for a hundred years.

Coming down through this part I could see the sweep of the bay ahead, the long curve of sand, broken by the Banyuls stream where it snaked out of a growth of tall bamboos and under an iron bridge to find the sea. Along the curve, facing the dusty road, was the other town, pure Mediterranean Margate, cheap cafés and bars, two or three hotels, a *rond-point* for dancing, a couple of garages and over it all, at this time of the year, an air of waiting for the season to begin. At the far end of the bay there was a pinkish looking hotel and the tall block of the Arago Aquarium.

About a dozen women in black dresses were scraping up the dead seaweed from the sands and burning it. The smoke went up in brown columns and then the off-shore wind took it and spread it in a fine canopy. Along the road between the dancing platform and the bridge long, tan-coloured lengths of sardine nets were spread. The men and women mending them looked up at me curiously as I passed. A young man with a suitcase came up to me and said he would be delighted to sell me a pair of espadrilles. I said he wouldn't and passed on. But I knew he would be waiting for me when I came back, and I knew that if I came here often enough he would end up by selling me a pair.

I walked right along the length of the sands. I knew where I was going and, as I got nearer to it, I felt the return of an old and familiar excitement. It's a thing aquariums do for me. Plymouth, Brighton, the London Zoo, Naples, Monte Carlo. . . . Since I was a boy I've never lost the joy that comes from the first movement into those shadowed vaults where great green panels let me stare into another world.

This place was something to do with the Marine Biology department of the University of Paris. Some of the building was still under construction. As I went up the steps a party of students came out; young men, in brief shorts, with long legs and heavy boots, festooned with nets and specimen tins, and girls in thick skirts, stout, workmanlike jumpers and gay head-scarves. I stood aside to let them pass. There were so many of them that I pressed back against a dusty run of boarding above which rose scaffolding where workmen in paper caps were plastering the face of the building. They rushed out into the road, shouting at a blue bus which had drawn up outside the pink-faced hotel. One of the youths put an empty specimen bucket on his head, couched his long-handled net and charged at the bus, defying it to move until they were all aboard. Their laughter went sailing up into the air and I grinned. In every class there is a buffoon. I watched the loaded bus grind around the corner and away towards Cerbère.

I paid my twenty francs and went in. The well-known company greeted me with a green silence. The moray eels, the spider crabs, the starfish and anemones; the shoals of brill and bream like drifting clouds of birch leaves, the surly jewfish and the fastidious golden dories. I wandered round, feeling about twelve years old. And come to think of it, maybe that was why I liked such places. They took me back to a state of suspended, innocent tranquillity.

After about half an hour I became aware of the other people in the place. There were five of them; an elderly couple, then two men who must have been officials since they were standing by a door at the far end of the aquarium discussing some alteration to a partition, and lastly a woman. There was a large, open pool in the centre of the place and she was sitting on the low concrete wall that surrounded it. There were under-water lights in the pool and as she was immediately above one I could only see her in silhouette. There was something about the way she sat, as though she were posing, yet bored and longing to be free, that interested me. Maybe the fact that I couldn't see her very well made me want to have a clearer view. I moved round, and as I did so she, too, moved. Not much and that was her trouble . . . not enough to be casual, but just enough to keep me in sight. Years in the army in Drexel's special jobs had grafted into me the anemone-instinct which contracts when other eyes watch every movement. I tested her: changing position and waiting for her reaction. She was still nothing but a shape, but after each move of mine I saw the pale frame of her face turn in my direction. I walked so far round the tanks that she had to change position so that she could keep me in sight. After a time I went over to the open pool and stood there, about three yards from her. There were a couple of turtles and some dogfish moving sluggishly about the water. The woman turned away from me. I still couldn't see her very clearly in the gloom. She wore some kind of loose coat. The twist of her body brought her legs out towards me and they looked strong and well formed. Her hair was dark and fell loosely back into a gentle curl about her coat collar. But her face was hidden now. She sat there, and something about her pose, as she leaned on one hand and stared at the pool reminded me of an illustration in an old fairy-story book of mine. I could imagine she was waiting for one of the dogfish—though in the story it had been a carp—to come to the surface holding in its mouth a golden mirror. And that was odd, for until this moment it had been her covert interest in me which had made me come to the pool. Now, I forgot that, and was interested in her. I pulled out a cigarette and lit it, risking the sign at the door which said—*Défense de Fumer*. And I stared at her back and all the time my mind was wondering what there was in the twist of a woman's shoulders and legs that could evoke such a clear desire as the one that was running through me. I

22

wanted to go and sit beside her and say, 'You'll never get your mirror back. Come with me and forget it. You can look at yourself in my eyes. . . .' Then I took a smart kick at the compassion that was leaping up in me like a dog anxious for a walk. What do you do to cure yourself of always inventing happiness for people who probably are quite content with their lot?

The two men went out of the door at the far end of the aquarium and slammed it loudly behind them. The noise was like a pistol shot in the long, dark stretch of room. The woman started and her hand moving away from the concrete pool wall knocked to the floor a black handbag which had rested there. It burst open and a scattering of small objects rolled over the floor towards my feet.

I squatted down and began to gather some of them up. And now I was smiling to myself for, despite the noise of the door, the action had been transparent. She had even had to move her hand well out of its normal line of withdrawal to knock the bag over. I didn't look at her, but she was there, crouching opposite me collecting her things. I picked up a lipstick, a cigarette lighter, a small bill clip which was empty and two loose keys. There were also five or six of those wrapped sugar lumps they give you in French cafés with your coffee, but she got to those before I did. Why should a woman carry sugar in her handbag?

I stood up and handed the things to her.

She said, *"Merci bien, monsieur."*

I told her it was a pleasure and wondered where she would go from there.

Speaking in French, and fiddling with her bag, she said, "There is something wrong with the clip. Whenever I drop it— it goes off like a bomb."

"Maybe I can fix it?" I reached for the bag.

"Oh, no, no, no . . . !"

I smiled at the way she said it and also the movement, the bag drawn up in both hands against her breast. My bet was that the clip was perfectly good but had been left open deliberately. I could see her better now; a long, not unattractive face, solemn until she spoke and then full of a wonderful animation and, unless it was the gloom, she had the largest, darkest eyes I'd ever seen. But it wasn't the way she looked that held me. It wasn't in her voice, soft but touched with a faint hoarseness, or in the way she held herself. It was the way she was; playing a part, and not very well, and under that something else. I didn't get it then. Though I tried to put a word to it. Frightened? No, it wasn't fear. It was something else. A forcing of herself towards some point she

23

hoped never to reach. . . . In a few seconds a jumble of sensations flashed through me and none of them really rang a bell but I could feel that many of them came close to doing it. And because she did that to me I suddenly didn't want her to go. It suddenly seemed important that I should know more about her. Never before in my life had any woman raised this kind of feeling in me. None of them. This was new.

But she went, and that puzzled me like hell. Why knock her bag over, start something with me, and then go away?

She said, "Thank you again. You've been very kind."

She turned. I saw the loose coat swing back, had a glimpse of a white blouse and she was walking away. I stood there watching her move to the door. And then I realized something. When she moved she was sure of herself as though all thought and emotion went from her and the body took over, strong and with a beautifully controlled grace. But when she stood still something came sweeping back into the mind and she was near to grieving for her lost mirror.

I sat on the pool wall and finished my cigarette. A small boy came in with his mother and, tiring soon of the fish, began to run round the pool pretending he was a jet plane. The noise he made echoed through the place madly. Since the war I'd lived with boys and I knew that once they got the wind up their tails there was nothing to do but avoid them. I stood up to go and my foot hit something on the floor by the pool wall. I bent down and picked it up. It was a small silver flask, no bigger than a lighter, and what used to be called a *vinaigrette*. I flicked the top open. There was a wisp of scent in the air. I put it in my pocket and went towards the door. It had been in her bag. She couldn't have gone far and I could easily catch her up. I didn't know why but I was glad that I had an excuse to go after her. I didn't even ask myself whether the thing had been left there to give me just that excuse.

When I got outside, at the top of the steps, I saw her. She was coming back, moving quickly up the rough path by the scaffolding. When she saw me she hesitated. I raised a hand in signal and she stopped, waiting for me to come down.

Even without the pure accident that waited ten seconds ahead, it would have been just the same. Everything was written into that moment. With some people, I guess, these things are like taking a correspondence course; six months or a year before you know your way around. Sometimes you never get anywhere. Hell, who can say how it happens with other people? You just know about yourself. You drift into a green cavern, not caring much about anything, not even unhappy . . . you just drift in and all you see is the line of a back and shoulders, the curve of a woman's leg as she stares at nothing in a pool and something begins to fight for life inside you. And then you come out into the sunshine, with the wind taking the dust from the road and making it dance in tiny wraiths, and the woman is still there. She stands with the wind against her body and her face is raised towards you and her black hair is loose and soft and you don't even see her as a human being but just as the thing, the point, a thin, trembling note you've never heard before, and like an explosion inside your breast the something fighting for life has broken out, free and mad with the tingling of new blood.

I went down towards her and, as I did so, I heard the men on the scaffolding above suddenly shout, a wild, desperate noise and with it a growing, grating sound. I looked up and I saw the bucket and rope, a great bucket full of plaster that they had been hauling up, and the two of them grabbing at the slipping rope, and then the whole thing out of their control and the bucket plunging downwards straight for her.

I jumped and my hands found her shoulders and the impetus of my body took us both crashing into a small recess under the scaffolding. The bucket smashed into the ground a couple of yards from us, the plaster spurted up in a great brown fan. I felt the wet flick of its spray on my hands and neck.

I was pressed against her, my arms round her. Her face was close to mine and I could smell the scent from her and knew it was something I would never forget. She was scared. So was I. One always is after a thing like that. We stood close together while the men shouted and flapped above us like a couple of hoarse crows. The fear went from her face and she smiled, not needing to say anything, each of us feeling the other's heart racing, and she worked a hand gently upwards against my breast and with an infinitely slow, gentle touch she rubbed at a plaster mark on my cheek. And with the movement her lips came closer to mine and I kissed her as gently and slowly as her fingers had touched me. But it was like no kiss I had ever known, no anguish of body or mind behind it: just a drawing together in recognition and then as she moved away the sound of her breath like the faint sigh that comes as a page of a new book is turned.

The foreman came down and apologized. He and his man fussed around, brushed us, offered wine and cigarettes, told us how it happened and then told each other how it had happened, and then said how good we were to take it so well. Monsieur was English, of course, which explained it and mademoiselle was *très courageuse,* and in the middle of it all the blue bus came rattling down the hill to the pink hotel and before I could do anything she had put her hand in mine, looked at me and then was running towards it. She swung aboard just as it began to pull out. She stood on the step and gave me a wave and I waved back, but I made no attempt to follow her. I didn't have to. I knew I wasn't going to lose her. Both of us would come back because the moment when she had been in my arms and our lips had touched carried inevitability with it. It was from this moment that I began to think less and less of Songa Manara and the Queen of Sheba.

CHAPTER III

THERE was reaction of course. The greater the fantasy the harder common sense will come shouldering its way back at some point. The point with me that day was just after I had been tackled about buying espadrilles again as I had come out of the chemist's shop where I'd bought myself some razor blades. Going up the hill out of the old town common sense came back with a rush, and from there on until I reached the villa I did everything to knock it all out of myself. It was rather like playing squash rackets with myself. The racquet was common sense and the hard, black ball was fancy . . . call it what you like. I smacked at the ball and it came back to me. I knocked and slammed it around and waited to see what would happen, but always it came right back at me.

Things don't happen like this, I told myself. You're bored with being cooped in the villa, and you're subconsciously angry because you don't know why you're here. Arguing with yourself is the most exhausting thing I know. The mind frames question and answer, accusation and defence at the same time. I must have walked that length of road like a man in his sleep. I didn't know the woman. There was nothing special about her. She talked as though she were just getting over a sore throat and, if she did move well, she was in fact a little short in the body. And her hair wasn't as soft as I had first thought. There was a suggestion of thready strength in it. I tried to kick her out—and was even a little angry that she should seem important enough to warrant all this effort. I could push her away so far, but then she stopped and nothing would move her. So then I thought about the hand-bag and the clumsy acting. Maybe I could scare her off with that. What was behind all that? Something to do with the Colonel —or some other ploy of her own? For a time I favoured the Colonel angle and thinking about this I began to find common sense taking more room in me. I had something in trust from Drexel and it was important to me not to fail him. I knew only too well that when one entered the circle at whose centre the Colonel sat, then an automatic readjustment had to be made in one's assessment of the smallest trivia, the casualest meetings and words. Drexel was no fool, no matter how melodramatically he seemed to act. He used mystery and anonymity stripped of all zest or idle play-acting because that was the surest way to keep alive. Other men dealt in potatoes and ready-made suits, filed correspondence and totted figures. Drexel's life was just as precise and regulated. Only in his world if a bird sang it was almost bound to be in code. . . . Was she part of that world? If she were I could mistrust her and my feelings about her. For the time being I was back in that world and I had to obey its rules. I got some comfort from this. I could push her away, but I still had the feeling that I could not keep her away for long. Even in Drexel's world—the world which, tough as he was, had begun to wear him down—there was room for. . . . I knew the word, but at the moment there was a taboo in me against saying it.

It was beginning to get dark as I went into the villa grounds. The three dogs came rushing up to eat me, but I stood fast and let them see they were wrong, but I still found nothing warming in this last-minute-recognition act of theirs.

Brindle served dinner and it did something to offset the damp and gloom of the dining-room. There was nothing yokel about his cooking. There's a talent buried in each man somewhere. Brindle had found his in cooking. No matter where he was or what food he had he could produce something that no one else could. The first time I'd known him work a miracle was in Yugoslavia, high on the grey *karst* above Spoleta, when all he had had was a handful of walnuts, flour, water and a chunk of fat bacon. Drexel had always refused to eat rough soldier fashion and he had wasted no sympathy on Brindle because he had had to do the cooking flat on his stomach to avoid sniper's bullets.

I finished a bottle of Montrachet with my cheese and then as the Sèvres clock on the mantelpiece struck ten when it should have struck nine, Brindle brought in the coffee on a tray. As he set it down, he slipped a crumpled envelope over to me.

"The Colonel asked me to give you this, sir."

I picked up the envelope and began to work the flap loose. "And I'll bet he said today and at nine o'clock precisely."

"Yes, sir. Will you have black or white?"

"Black." He knew I took black but he always asked.

When he was gone I pulled one of the table candles towards me and read the note. It was in the Colonel's neat, renaissance-like script.

There is a motor launch in the boat-house. Brindle has the key. Within the next four or five days you will receive a telephone call from the British Consul at Marseilles. If he says 'Go ahead' you will that same evening rendezvous cargo-boat *Roi Bleu* three

28

miles due East of Cap Cerbère at 22.30 hours. Signal three torch
flashes, five-second interval between groups. If no message
from Consul await my arrival.

I read it through twice and then burnt the paper in the candle
flame, dropping the ashes into my coffee cup.

Early the next morning I got the key of the boat-house from
Brindle and went to have a look at the launch. It was a beautiful
arrangement of mahogany and chromium plating. I took her
out and the song her powerful engine made was specially com-
posed for those in the upper-income brackets. She was fast and,
although there was only a smooth swell running, I could feel
that she would be seaworthy. I went down past Banyuls until
I could see Cap Cerbère edging out of the low shore mist.
Inland the great sweep of the snow-capped Pyrenees shouldered
roughly against a pale blue sky. And now that I had had some
word from the Colonel I was content to let my curiosity ride.
He had left England two weeks before I did and he might be
anywhere.

I came back faster than I had gone out, giving the launch
full throttle and singing to myself at the whip of wind and
spray in my face. In the boat-house I filled up the tank
and then handed the key back to Brindle. He didn't say a
word.

Later I walked into Banyuls. In the confusion of the falling
plaster bucket I had forgotten to give the girl back her silver
flask. I wanted to return it, but more than that I wanted to see
her again.

I went and had a coffee at a small café called *Aux Bons Enfants*.
It was in the Place Mairie, well back from the dancing platform,
and shadowed by three tall plane trees. There were a few green
tables and chairs on a strip of concrete outside. A tall three-ply
cut-out of a man in chef's clothing holding in one hand a large
fish and in the other a card with a list of sea-food stood by the
door which led into a low bar and dining-room. It was a sad,
slightly crumbling place and the proprietor seemed to have no
help, perhaps because the season had not yet started. He was a
big, pulpy man who looked as though he had been left out in
the rain and at any moment would collapse into a heap of shapeless cloth and cardboard. He sat on a chair by the door and read
a tattered copy of *Paris Soir* and now and again he raised his
head and stared at the sea indignantly as though it had just
made some offensive remark to him.

After a time my friend of the espadrilles found me. He came
up cheerfully, carrying his battered brown suitcase and insisted

on showing his wares. He covered the table with coloured, rope-soled shoes and chattered away, not trying to force a sale, because he knew in the end he would get me. I gave him a cigarette and he told me that his name was Jean Cagou and that in a couple of seasons he hoped to have enough to open a shop either here or at Port-Vendres a little farther up the coast. He was about twenty-two, brisk and glossy as an olive-fed starling. He said that, in addition to espadrilles, if there was anything else I wanted he could get it for me.

"N'importe quoi, m'sieur—je peux le trouver."

I told him there was nothing I wanted and quite rightly he didn't believe me.

As we talked a motor-cycle drew up alongside the café. It was a Norton and had a GB plate. A plumpish, elderly man in a cloth cap and a light raincoat got off it and sat down by the door. The proprietor gathered himself up from his chair and went to take his order. He was English, but he ordered breakfast in French, a hard, stiff, badly-accented French as though each word was being dragged unwillingly from his memory.

Jean Cagou at once gathered up his samples. As I left I could hear his cheerful, excited voice going into its sales talk with the new arrival.

For the next two days I walked into Banyuls, morning and afternoon, hoping to see the girl. But I never did. I saw Jean Cagou and I became quite friendly in a monosyllabic way with the proprietor of the *Aux Bons Enfants*. The Englishman was there, too, in the mornings having his breakfast. I think he knew that I was English but he never tried to make my acquaintance. The most he ever did was to look up at me as I sat down, stare for a moment, nod, and then turn back to his food. He was a man with a good appetite.

Although I still hadn't got to the point of admitting to myself that my intuition that I should see the girl again was wrong, I did on the third morning rebel against the thought of going into Banyuls. I went and sat by the dried-up fountain in the villa garden and read. It was some French novel I'd found in the house. But I remember nothing about it except that I got more and more annoyed with it. The old bitch wolf-hound came and lay in the dust by me and scratched away at her fleas, and gradually for no reason that I could think of I began to get depressed. It seemed as though I had been washed into some backwater of time and nothing was ever going to happen to me again. There was only the ugly villa, gloomy and echoing as a tomb, and outside this fierce, unseasonable heat that pressed down over everything. I got up and chucked a stone at a lizard on the edge of the fountain pool and missed it.

And then I was out on the road, walking towards Banyuls. My feet had to go somewhere. I had to create for myself the illusion of progress.

I'd gone half a mile, I suppose, when I heard a motor-horn behind me. I stopped and turned. An old army jeep painted a dark blue, battered and very dusty, drew up alongside me. Sitting in front were two men and behind, alone, was the girl.

The two men looked at me and, while they did not smile, it was clear that they knew about me. She smiled, and I saw her teeth, small and very white, against the warm tan of her skin.

"You are going to Banyuls?" she asked.

I nodded.

She patted the empty seat beside her.

"We will take you. I am glad we have found you."

I climbed into the jeep and sat at her side and we went off with a quick spin of the rear wheels that sent a cloud of dust up behind us. It was only a short ride and not more than a dozen words passed between us. I sat there feeling a little embarrassed, not because of her but because of the two men. They gave me the impression of having picked me up and dumped me aboard as though I were a crate or package of merchandise.

In the bottom of the jeep were a couple of harpoon fishing guns, a face mask with a breathing tube and a pair of rubber webbed feet. The girl, seeing me look at them, nodded towards the man who was driving and said, "George is mad about under-water fishing."

The depression that had been with me was gone. I felt neither lonely nor lost and it was nothing to do with the men. It was her. Just sitting beside me. The way she sat and let her body sway to the movement of the jeep seemed to say something to me. She wore a green summer frock with thin white stripes and her hair was caught back with some kind of clasp at the back. Her arms and legs were bare and she wore white sandals. Most of the time she stared straight ahead of her and I could see her profile, strong and thoughtful; but at the same time I didn't feel she was at ease. Her hands were clasped over one knee and I could see the long fingers moving with a slow restlessness.

We pulled up outside the *Café aux Bons Enfants* and the four of us sat down at a table. It was then that she introduced me to the two men and I got a good look at them. I don't know whether it was anything to do with my feeling for her, some touch of jealousy starting early, but I didn't like either of them.

Perhaps like and dislike weren't the right words. The men were wrong with her.

It was the one she had called George who made the most impression on me. His other name was Sarrasin. I'm tall and fairly well built, but he made me feel small. He was well over six feet tall and with a body that was all bulk and muscle; hard, but not ungainly. He wore his short, dark hair *en brosse* and he had a large face, deeply and pugnaciously cut, a rough, unfinished face like a sculpture's first block with all the power of the original material still harshly apparent. His voice was slow and heavy and all his movements, though they had grace, showed economy. He was full of strength but, I guessed, never wasted it. He wore a pair of faded, blue canvas trousers, a yellow singlet and a loose grey jacket. His shoes were no more than a flat leather sole with a toe-piece and thongs that were tied around his ankle.

He ordered the thick dark Banyuls wine for us all and, while we waited for it, made a little speech of thanks to me for the service I had rendered Sophie. Sophie Orbais was her name.

I pulled the scent flask from my pocket and handed it across to Sophie. "You left this in the aquarium."

"Ah, yes. I was coming back to look for it when . . . it all happened."

I wondered whether the moment of hesitation and then the last three words meant to her what I felt they meant to me.

The proprietor came up to us with the wine. Whenever I saw him with a tray and glasses I felt that the weight would tear his limp hands from his arms. We drank to each other politely and while she and George and myself just sipped at the syrupy wine, the other man, Astar Paviot, finished his glass in one movement and sighed. He was small, mean-looking and seedy. One could have collected a hundred of his type from the *bistros* of Marseilles in an evening. He had thin brown hair with a touch of grey over the ears, an unhealthy looking face, the chin too pointed and the eyes a little red as though they were weary of the weight of the pouchy skin beneath them. He didn't look too clean. His suit had once been a smart grey with a fancy stripe and, I felt, had been made for another man. He was a man it would be very hard to like; a man with a shabby spirit, and nothing immediately wholesome about him except his hands which were strong and lean, the fingers full of an unexpected grace and beauty, the nails astonishingly well kept.

The talk didn't flow very easily between us. They puzzled me because they didn't seem to fit together properly; the girl and these two. Sophie said very little. George Sarrasin complimented me on my French and Paviot said I reminded him of a British officer he had worked with in the Resistance. We talked about this officer and the war years, but though I was alive to the possibility I don't think he was pumping me for any information. I'd told them I was staying for a holiday here. Over all I couldn't detect in anything they said the slightest sign that they had any real interest in me except that I had done Sophie a service. And that, since I was sure she had knocked her handbag over by design, made everything seem odder.

We sat there under the shabby plane trees. There was a large circus poster plastered around the trunk of one of them and I could see Jean Cagou, case at his feet, sitting with his back against it. The Englishman, who had been at the café when we arrived, finished his meal and went off on his motor-cycle. And suddenly all conversation died between us. It didn't last long, maybe half a minute, but there was a weight and deliberateness in it which made me feel that it came from design. This was no pause while angels walked over somebody's grave, but a point reached and then a silent gathering of forces for the new move. I looked at Sophie. She was watching the women burning seaweed on the beach. Then she turned a little and saw me. She smiled but so absently that I knew her thoughts were remote and, from the swift tremor about her mouth as she looked away, I fancied the thoughts were unpleasant. Astar Paviot was tipped back in his chair, his face up to the sun, half a cigarette dropping at the corner of his mouth. He seemed to have gone into a trance. George Sarrasin had taken a penknife from his pocket and was shaping a piece of cork for a fishing float. I was on the point of making an excuse to go when he stood up. The movement brought Paviot's chair tipping back to earth and Paviot was at his side.

"All right, Sophie. See you at four?"

George put his hand on her shoulder and squeezed it and then, with a look at me, said, "*Au revoir, monsieur.*"

Paviot echoed him. "*Au revoir, monsieur.*"

And there they were the two of them walking towards the jeep and I was left with Sophie. I saw them gather up their fishing gear from the car and then cross the road and disappear among the beached fishing boats on the pebbles of the little cove below the old town.

I said, "Where are they going?"

She said, watching them, "They take a row-boat out to fish. It will be this afternoon before they return."

33

"What about you?"

"I do not like to fish. Sometimes I have been sick, even when there is no sea."

"They just leave you to amuse yourself?"

"Generally. I go for a walk. I read." And then, unexpectedly, she turned and smiled at me and said, "You sound a little angry about it. Don't be. I prefer not to go." And the smile was the warm, natural smile that she had given me under the scaffolding. It was as though the moment they had gone some new life, new personality had come back to her.

Bluntly, out of a protective affection which was strong in me, I said, "Who are they?"

She had a right to resent this, but she said quietly, "They are my friends . . . good friends. We are at Argelès for a holiday but they prefer the fishing here."

Argelès-sur-Mer was a resort about half-way between Banyuls and Perpignan.

*　　*　　*

We spent the rest of the day until four o'clock together.

I didn't arrange it and I'm sure she didn't. We just drifted into it without ever acknowledging that it was going to happen. We didn't talk a great deal. She was one of those comfortable people whose silences are happy and restful, and, for myself, I was glad just to be with her. We bought ourselves a bottle of cheap Roussillon wine, a length of salami and a loaf and walked down past the Arago Aquarium and then up the twisting road towards Cerbère. After a time we went down across a barren cliff-head, close carpeted with thyme, marjoram and silvery-leaved rock roses, to a steeply enclosed cove. We found a flat rock above a deep pool of jade and turquoise water and sat there talking about small, unimportant things. If you'd taken each moment of the afternoon apart and examined it there would have been nothing special about it, nothing that somewhere in the past could not have been matched, but altogether it was like no other afternoon I had ever spent.

After lunch the wine made me drowsy and quite unashamedly I went to sleep. I think she did, too. When I woke up she was sitting close to me, looking down at me. I blinked my eyes to cut down the sun glare. She smiled at me and her eyes were deeper and darker than ever. I put up a hand. I don't know whether I meant to take hers, but her hand was in mine, a firm, strong hand but with a warm gentleness to it that seemed to reach right into me and I heard myself saying, "When I came and stood by

34

you in the aquarium do you know what you made me think about?"

She shook her head and the sun through her loose hair was broken into a thousand bright points of light.

"A fairy story. You were the princess who'd dropped her favourite mirror into the pond and in a moment a magic carp was going to bring it up to you."

She was silent for a moment. Then she said, "You've got the story wrong. It wasn't a mirror. It was a golden ball. The princess had lost her golden ball."

"Mirror or ball. It doesn't matter. I just wanted you to have it back."

She didn't answer at once. She looked down at me and I felt her fingers escape from mine and then touch the back of my hand and finally close softly around my wrist. And then she said very deliberately——

"You are a very kind man, aren't you? A very good man?"

It was said almost simply, almost childishly, and came from her with a sincerity and meaning that had the curious effect of shock in me. At once I seemed to have acquired a responsibility for which I was completely unworthy.

I was embarrassed and I laughed and then seeing the watch on my wrist, said, "Hullo, it's nearly four. We must be getting back to your friends."

She changed at once, and I wished to hell that I hadn't said it. With a few words I'd brought her back into another world and it wasn't a world she liked. I knew it and I hated it without understanding it.

We walked into Banyuls and George Sarrasin and Paviot were waiting by the jeep. I refused a lift from them. I made no arrangements to meet her again, but as they drove off she half-turned in her seat and waved to me and I knew she would be back. I walked along the cliffs to the villa, remembering the change which had come over her face.

I was having a drink before dinner when the telephone went. It was from Marseilles giving me the go-ahead to rendezvous the *Roi Bleu* that evening.

CHAPTER IV

IT was nine o'clock when I went into the kitchen and got the boat-house key from Brindle. He was drinking cocoa and listening to the B.B.C. on a portable radio. As he gave me the key he also handed over a small silver-plated flask.

"What's this?"

"Whisky, sir. Just in case you have to wait longer than you think."

It was a mark of affection. It also proved that, at this moment, he knew more than I did of this business. I had an idea that Drexel probably told Brindle everything. The man was a drawer into which he stuffed all his secrets for safe keeping.

I went out into the garden and stood there for a moment while the dogs came up and inspected me. It was a warm close night with little wind and I felt hot in the sweater I had pulled on. The dogs followed me down to the boat-house and the bitch whined a little as I went aboard. I think she was getting fond of me.

I took the launch out, the engine well throttled down so that it made only a gentle bubbling sound, and kept the lubber line of the compass running East and West. I had worked out that if I made five miles due easting and then turned south and ran down ten miles I should be in the position the Colonel wanted me. Fifteen miles and well over an hour to do it was easy for the launch. When I made my rendezvous I should be outside the international limit and practically dead on the Spanish-French border. The only light I allowed myself was from the panel board, so that I could check the patent log and the compass. There was a fair bit of smuggling along this piece of coast and there might be a customs patrol boat. I didn't want to attract attention.

The night was like rotten velvet, a soft, unresisting fabric which fell away before the sharp bows of the launch. Away on the starboard side, down towards Banyuls I could see the little red navigation light that stood on a tripod in the middle of the bay. There were other lights too; a firefly cluster where the Banyuls fishing boats were making out to sea, acetylene lamps flaring at their bows, and a light from the rocky point by the Arago Aquarium. And all along the coast there were the bead-

36

strung lights of the various towns and then the scattered sharp points from individual houses and farms on the hills behind. But the night itself had swallowed sky, land and sea. There was only this amorphous velvet pricked haphazardly with yellow, silver and red.

After a time, away to the left, I picked up the flash from the lighthouse which stood at the entrance to Port-Vendres harbour and I saw that the log read two miles. I sat there with my hands gently on the wheel. In the old days this kind of thing had carried excitement and danger, a heightening of instinct and sense that reached back into the primitive hinterland of one's ancestry. War, a world at war, flags, sacrifice, backs to the wall, *dulce et decorum est pro patria mori*. . . . In those days it had all meant something. But not now. There was no true excitement in me. Each generation grows out of its own war, turning away gladly to the rows of potato plants and the piles of exercise books. But the war went on just the same, carried by people like Drexel. I thought of the book he had written just after the war. He had a surprisingly mature and sensitive way of writing. Ethiopia, Arabia, Persia and the Mediterranean and Adriatic areas . . . an Odyssey into which now and again I had come. Some of his acid comments had raised questions in the House of Commons but the whole thing had blown over. He was the hero-type, the kind the public had to have to make their morning papers palatable and their comfortable lives bearable. I knew because I was the public and I loved him. Perhaps my love was prejudiced, knowing the man personally and owing him so much. I remembered him coming back over the long sand drifts, myself quiet with the final despair and not even roused by the bullying, vigorous cheerfulness of the man. The bullet had cracked my right knee-cap and he'd dragged and carried me for three days, given up his water and his strength to me, cursed and insulted me, but had kept me going. I owed him everything from that moment of return. The only way to repay that kind of debt that I knew was with love. I loved the man and was unashamed to use the word to myself. In a little while I was going to see him again and, if there was any excitement in me, it came from that thought.

I made the rendezvous by a quarter past ten. I set the wheel so that the launch just eased around in a slow, gigantic circle. At half past ten I began to work the torch, keeping the flashes seaward. Three flashes and then a five-second interval. Each flash made a little gold shaft across the velvet and the monotony of counting the seconds to myself made me a little drowsy. On this kind of job I knew it was no good worrying about time. It was an element to be ignored.

I thought about a lot of things while I circled round, leaving just enough of my attention on the job, and the rest of me wandering about, having what my brother would have called 'a good old think'. His 'good old thinks' had come to an end on the Normandy beaches. Eventually I found myself thinking about other women I had known and then comparing them with Sophie. Why was it that when she had touched my hand it had been warm and friendly but without any magic? Magic was the only word I could put to Sophie and it was a poor word because it wasn't what I meant. There had been times in the past when I had told myself I was in love. But telling myself so and even believing it hadn't made any difference. I wondered if I was in love with Sophie, and immediately I knew I wasn't going to answer that because there wasn't any answer. The question itself was inadequate. The poor, tired old phrase seemed to have no meaning against the reality that had sprung into existence inside me. Love, as I knew it, was a literary sensation and a sunlit tableau; maybe that was the result of being a schoolmaster with English Literature as a first subject, potted biographies of Shelley and Byron spooned out to a row of healthy little savages who were listening more intently to the buzz of a blue-bottle on the window or the quiet snigger following some inky note making its rounds of the desks. Love; pastoral, lyric, shepherds and shepherdesses, *When as in silks my Julia goes,* resin-flavoured Greek wines. . . . But now I was beginning to feel that the real thing, which demanded another name, was harsher, more sudden, like the sear of fusing metals. I sat there thinking about Sophie and after a time the warmth of my thoughts was chilled by an insistent question. I began to ask myself what Sophie could be doing spending a holiday with two men like George Sarrasin and Astar Paviot. Who was she, what was she and what was her real interest in me? The men were wrong and she did not seem to fit any life they had. The next time I saw her, I decided, I would be less vague and diffident about these things. There should be question and answer.

My thoughts were broken by the distant thud of a boat's screws. *Chump, chump, chump* it came across the water, like the muffled beating of a hand on a door. A green navigation light swayed low down away on my port side and then, faintly below it, came an answering flash to my torch.

I headed the launch towards the light. After a time, almost over my head, a deck flood-light came on and the high, clumsy bows of a tramp steamer rose sheer before me. I swept down past her, turned and came up again under the stern. It dipped and rolled and I saw the words, *Roi Bleu, Marseille*. As I came alongside and threw out a couple of fenders, a rope ladder was dropped from the deck and lay banging and swinging against the rusty plates. A rope came down, hitting the foredeck with a smack and I hung on to it. Voices shouted above and in the dim light I saw faces peering down. A small figure in a raincoat and beret came down the ladder and jumped past me, moving to the stern of the launch. Then I saw Colonel Drexel. He came down the ladder rather slowly, dressed in an old army greatcoat and wearing a white cloth cap. I noticed that his left hand was bandaged, though he seemed to have the use of it.

He dropped into the launch at my side, put his arm round my shoulder and grinned.

"David."

That was all he said, but it was enough. The word and the touch and everything that meant anything between us wrapped up in them. His breath smelt of whisky, a strong, masculine smell that fitted the night and the movement of the boats and the massed faces peering down. Someone shouted and two pigskin cases were lowered. Drexel took them and passed them astern to our other passenger.

The deck flood went off and in the darkness a heavy voice called down——

"*Au revoir, Colonel. Nous finisserons le bouteille un autre jour.*"

"*Au revoir, Didi,*" Drexel called up.

And then as I swung the launch away into the darkness the heavy voice came faintly across to us——

"*Bonne chance. . . . .*"

I said to the Colonel, "Speed, or gently does it?"

"Speed."

I opened the launch up and she tore through the velvet with an angry ripping sound and behind us a great curve of phosphorescent wake flared against the darkness.

Drexel ducked behind the wind shield and lit himself a cigarette and, as he came up, he shouted against the wind——

"Everything all right at the villa?"

"Yes. What's the matter with your hand?"

"Just a graze. Messy but not serious."

"Anyone seen it?"

"Yes. In Cairo. It's all right."

I glanced back. "Who's our friend?" I shouted.

"Later. Let's get home. Can't talk with my mouth full of wind and spray."

We were about half-way back when I heard the sound of a mouth-organ behind me. I turned. Our passenger had moved up closer in the well of the launch and was playing gently to himself. He looked up and smiled at me over the instrument. I saw his face touched by the light from the dash panel. Anyway, I knew now what language I was supposed to speak. A young face, dark-skinned, a hawk-like nose, high cheek bones and deep-set steady eyes.

The Colonel seeing me turn shouted——

"Know him?"

"No."

"Should do. You went to his father's funeral."

I began to have an idea then, but I still wasn't sure.

No more was said, but our friend played dance music softly all the way in.

*   *   *

Brindle was waiting at the boat-house for us. He took the cases. I stayed to lock up the launch and when I got up to the house, past the dogs who were barking themselves crazy over the newcomers, there was no one about. I went into the stuffy, uncomfortable lounge and poured myself a whisky. The Colonel joined me after a while and got a drink for himself. As he turned back to me he tossed a key across.

"Here."

I caught it.

"It's the key of his bedroom—next to yours. I've got a key as well. He's locked in at night and during the day one of us must always have an eye on him."

"Is he likely to give us the slip?"

"No. But other people would like to get their hands on him."

I sat down, took a drink and waited. I knew he was going to enjoy this moment and I had no wish to spoil it for him. A walled villa, dogs loose at night, keys, a wounded hand . . . it was all in the Drexel tradition; cloak and dagger stuff for most people, but for Drexel, I knew, it would make sense, hard common sense.

The Colonel, relaxed now, rubbing one thumb over the curve of his whisky glass, said, "Remember Saraj?"

"I do."

The room was suddenly full of hot strong smells, of bright sunlight on a dusty square noisy with Arabs crowding around

40

stalls, and I saw a great grey plug of a harbour fort at the entrance to a blue-water bay and the shark-fin sails of dhows beating in from the sea. Saraj was the seaport capital of Ramaut, a small, independent Arab state on the Trucial coast where the Persian Gulf met the Indian Ocean. The Colonel and I had spent six months there as members of a British mission during the war, an interesting but uncomfortable time. It was there that I had improved my knowledge of the Arab language. I had an easy almost glib talent for picking up languages which impressed people.

"Have you been keeping your finger on Arab politics?"

"A little." I knew the funeral he meant now, and went on. "This is one of the sons of King Akhdar who was assassinated just before we reached Saraj?"

"The elder son. Prince Jabal Akhdar. He's not quite sixteen. The only other brother is nearly fifteen. Until Jabal is eighteen the state is being run by a Regent."

"I remember him. Shiek Ahmed ben Fa'id. A first-class louse." It had been one of those goodwill missions dictated by strategy. Saraj would have made a good refuelling point for the German raiders in the Indian Ocean and that was the way Sheik Ahmed ben Fa'id saw it until we arrived and Drexel got to work on him. Even then goodwill had not prevailed until we had a destroyer in Saraj Bay.

"A louse, but a clever one. When Jabal's eighteen he can take over the country. That's the constitution. But when he's sixteen, then by tribal law he's no longer a minor. He becomes head of the family. It's a nice distinction—and an important one for a lot of people."

"When is he sixteen?"

"At the end of this month. That's why Ahmed ben Fa'id didn't want him to go back to school in England. He wanted him in the country at that date."

"Why?"

"Because he wanted to make sure that Jabal, as head of the family, didn't sign an important document. As long as he had his hands on Jabal he was safe."

"And Jabal?"

"He wanted to come back to school. He wants also to sign the paper. But he knew what would happen to him if he stayed there and tried to sign it. The boy's got his head screwed on. He has an idea who was behind the assassination of his father. It could happen to him. That would have left his brother—who is entirely under the influence of the Regent—to become head of the family in a year. His brother would have refused to sign the paper."

It was not hard to understand. It was the kind of situation that was fairly common in most of the Arab states from time to time. But I wasn't deluding myself that Drexel and the Foreign Office were breaking their hearts over the injustice and savagery. Any reason they had for interference would have a cash or military answer. Goodwill, protection, spheres of influence . . . nice phrases with no altruism behind them.

I said, "What is it? Oil?"

Drexel finished his whisky, and as he levered himself up to go and refill his glass, he said, "Yes. The original concession was granted by the Akhdar family in 1933 for twenty-one years. It's purely a family affair. Nothing to do with the State, though the whole population of Ramaut lives by it. Just the same as in many of the other Trucial states. The concession is due for renewal next month. Jabal wants to renew it. Sheik ben Fa'id thinks otherwise. He has ideas about nationalization. It's a kind of bug going round the Persian Gulf just now. Maybe they caught it from us. Anyway, his real reason"—he turned back to his chair and his mouth had a sarcastic twist—"is decently capitalistic. Ben Fa'id feels he could shovel more money into his own pocket if he had nationalization. Not that he isn't doing pretty well for himself as it is."

"Who's got the concession?"

"Anglo-Media."

"And you've got Jabal."

"Sure. I've put up with that damned mouth-organ for over a week."

I looked at Drexel's bandaged hand.

"Was it an Ahmed ben Fa'id bullet that mucked up your hand?"

He shrugged his shoulders.

"Always some little thing goes wrong."

Something about the way he said this marked an uneasiness in him. Instead of sitting down he began to move around the room, restless, touching a piece of furniture, an ornament. He was worried and I saw no reason why he should be at this stage.

"What about the government, the Foreign Office? They're behind you, aren't they?" I said it with some idea of easing the strain in him, but it had the opposite effect. He swung round and the lean, lined face was full of contempt.

"At the moment they know nothing—officially—about it. You've no idea how it goes, David. Sometimes I feel absolutely played out by this kind of thing. . . ." It was almost a cry and it went straight to my heart because it was so unlike him, revealed that in him which until now I had never suspected was there. There is a weakness in us all which time and trial slowly weathers free of our surrounding strength, the bare, crumbling rock that comes up through the turf as the years wash away the top-soil. I think he caught something of my feeling, my shock, for he went on quickly, angry now rather than pathetic, "I've no official standing. Nothing in writing. No firm promises. Just hints, hints, hints and everyone knows damned well what is meant, and everyone knows damned well that the last thing any Whitehall stooge it going to do is to commit himself even unofficially until it's absolutely safe. I'm the game-cock that's shoved into the ring."

"But they know you've whipped this boy out of Saraj so that he can sign the concession in London?"

"Yes. The cipher people should be decoding the message about now. But the point is that if anything went wrong while I was about it—then it would be my responsibility. I'd just be a common kidnapper. But once here—then they take over. Prince Jabal is in France on his way back to school."

"You've got no worry then. You're here."

"Oh, the innocence of the man! It'll take 'em at least four or five days to take over."

"I see. I suppose they'll want to get Sheik Ahmed ben Fa'id's reaction first?"

"He's no fool. He'll see right through the scheme, but he'll fall in with the diplomatic game. Or pretend to. But he'll start thinking and acting. That's why until the F.O. boys take it up officially we have to keep Jabal's presence here a secret."

"I don't see that anything could go wrong. And, anyway, the Government and the oil company are going to be very grateful to you."

Drexel laughed. "The gratitude of governments has never kept down the size of my overdraft. As for the oil company, they think I'm a public servant. I save them thousands and maybe they'll send me a couple of cases of whisky at Christmas. And later on I shall have to fight like hell to get expenses from the Treasury. Hire of a launch, they'll say. Why not swim? Watch dogs? What is all this? Five hundred for this Fraser chap? Really, couldn't you have got him for two? Termites, that's what they are."

There was a silence between us for a while. If we'd still been in the army; if I'd still been under discipline, a captain who just took orders, I don't think he would have shown himself to me so clearly. But things were different now. I was hired by him, it was true, but the real bond between us was friendship and perhaps a touch of reverence on my side and because of that he could let himself go, knowing that anything spoken in this room would never be uttered again outside it. He was doing a job and like any clerk or shophand he had a right to blow off steam. He could do it safely with me, and perhaps with no one else. I sat there and I was angry for his sake, bitter against the strain in the man, resenting the dark moments he had to live through. I could imagine what had gone on in Saraj, imagine the patient organization that had gone to getting Jabal out; the plane in the desert, the dhow in the Red Sea, the long, hot camel marches and then the quick furtive move into Cairo and so on to the *Roi Bleu* . . . and Drexel was nearly sixty.

I said impulsively, "Why the hell do you go on doing this kind of thing?"

"Why? Because there's nothing else."

"You could retire. Raise chicken."

"On what I've saved?" He laughed suddenly and sat down. I could see that his mood had changed swiftly. He was back with himself. "No, no, David. You know why I do it, and I know. I suppose I bloody well like it. But I do wish these poops in Whitehall had some little idea of what it all means."

I said, glad that he was over the peak of his resentment, "Why couldn't they handle it differently? If Jabal wants to sign the concession and the Regent has shown he would go to the lengths of killing him to stop it, then why the devil doesn't the Government step in and kick the Regent out of Saraj?"

Drexel roared with laughter. "David, you're preposterous! This isn't the war or 1901. The Persian Gulf's no longer a British lake. Trouble? Send a cruiser and a detachment of marines? I wish they would. But the new diplomacy doesn't know how to kick the arses of people like ben Fa'id. Interfere openly in the affairs of an independent state that owes everything it has to British capital? Protect our own interests by open force?"

"Well, if I were ben Fa'id I'd scream through the Press that Jabal had been kidnapped."

"He won't do that. He's much too clever."

"Why won't he?"

"Because if he admitted Jabal had been kidnapped from Saraj, it would be admitting that Jabal wasn't safe there. He doesn't want anything out in the open. Least of all does he want

44

to show his hand over this oil business. There's quite an opposition party out there . . . you might call it a Jabal party."

"They helped you get the boy out?"

"Of course. But that's all we need from them. In time the oil concession will be renewed in London and Jabal will go back as ruler. We don't want to start a civil war out there. Neither does ben Fa'id. That's why he will pretend the prince is on his way back to school and make no mention of kidnapping."

"But that won't mean he's given up."

"Not on your life. He'll do all he can to get hold of Jabal before he gets a chance to renew the oil concession. That's why you and I have to move carefully. If we lose Jabal now—we'll never get him back."

"Well, what's you next move?"

"Have another whisky and then go to bed. Tomorrow I shall drive to Marseilles and get things moving through the British Consul. He's been briefed. He'll look po-faced and pretend he hasn't, and within twenty-four hours we shall have Benson down here."

"Who's Benson?"

"A Foreign Office poop who envies me my exciting life and has a bank balance that's always in the black. Lucky man."

He had the whisky and went to bed. I sat there for a while after he had gone, and I was wishing that he hadn't had the whisky. He'd always been a hard drinker but his strenuous living had offset it. I had the impression now that he was drinking, not to relax his abundant energy, but to dull some pain in his spirit.

CHAPTER V

I HAD breakfast with the Colonel the next morning. Brindle took Jabal's breakfast up to his room. The Colonel was a different person, relaxed and cheerful, and eating like a horse. It was a thing I'd forgotten about him; his enormous appetite. He even alluded to his mood of the previous evening.

"Take no notice of it, David. It's a reaction after I've carried a thing off. Just feel I want to raise the roof. Does me good, I suppose."

I saw him off. He drove an old Bentley with an open tonneau. The car had been locked in the garage by the villa gates. When he saw my eyes going over it, he said, "I've had this fifteen years. Usually keep it in Paris. Brindle drove it down." It was just his sort of car, open, splendidly shabby and powerful.

When he was gone, Jabal and I went out in the launch. We took her seawards a couple of miles and then anchored while we bathed. I liked him at once; a lean, finely built youth with short, slightly curly black hair, and he had that assurance and quiet reserve which was pure Arab. Inside him, I felt, there was already a man, and a man, I was sure of this, who could be ruthless not only because the pattern of his life demanded it, but because it was there already in his nature. He joked and laughed, swam and played his mouth-organ. We talked about his school and the orchestra he had organized there and how he played also the drums and the saxophone (I had met this passion for modern jazz in the Eastern breast before, as though it were a kind of short-cut, an easy way into the mood of Western life), but, although no reference was made to the real nature of his presence here, there were moments when he was silent and brooding. I knew then that he was back in Saraj. One day Sheik Ahmed ben Fa'id was going to regret the trouble he had given Jabal.

We talked sometimes in Arabic and sometimes in English, but his English was good and I realized that Drexel had not offered me this job because I could speak Arabic. It was good to think that he had wanted me for myself, wanted someone whom he liked as well as trusted.

After lunch Jabal went up to his room to sleep. I went with him to lock him in. I felt a bit like a jailer and to shed my own embarrassment, I said, "I'm sorry about this."

He smiled at me. "It is necessary." Then the smile going, leaving his face suddenly grave, he went on, "You are a good friend of Colonel Drexel?"

"I like to think so."

"Such a friendship is an honour. He is a man."

I locked him in and went down to Brindle. I told him I was going for a walk. The Colonel had left his key with Brindle and I asked him to keep an eye on Jabal when he let him out.

I did not go into Banyuls. I turned off the road and went across a field of vines to the sea. I found a little dip in the low cliffs, a hollow full of a tall, flowering rush-like plant which I thought was amaryllis. It was common in the district, but maybe it wasn't amaryllis. I lay down with my hands behind my head and stared up at the sky.

I must have dozed off and been in a light sleep. Something wakened me and for a moment I rested with my eyes shut, my lids a red curtain between me and the sun. Then the redness darkened and I felt the movement of a shadow across my face. I opened my eyes slowly.

Sophie was above me, standing between me and the sun so that I could see the outline of her body through the silk dress she wore. It was a firm, beautiful silhouette, and the sight of her there, immobile, looking down at me, seemed right and expected, for in my light sleep I had been, not dreaming, but thinking about her in wide, lazy splashes of thought which had little definition. Seeing her now, definite and steady above me, carried the mood and thoughts into a warmer, more cogent existence.

I said, "Hullo, how did you get here?" and my voice was lazy with sleep still as I reached up a hand to her. She came down, kneeling beside me and the light airs playing over the amaryllis brought me the scent of her perfume.

She said, "You were asleep and you were frowning. Why?"

I laughed gently, playing with her hand. "Maybe because I was dreaming or thinking about you and I wanted the real person." I remember that I hesitated over the French, making a decision between saying '*la vraie chose*' or '*la vraie personne*' and finally, swiftly deciding for '*personne*'.

And then she said something which I was beginning to realize was characteristic of her. She had little small talk, at least not with me. She gave me the impression that she already knew all the trivial facts that were to be known about us and that somewhere time was running out and each word and sentence had to count. Or perhaps that was my impression and I credited her with it, too.

47

"The real person? The real thing? How do you tell? Can you touch it? See it? And when you find it . . . how do you keep it?" She laughed and then went on quickly so that it was almost as though she hadn't spoken, "There's a beetle crawling over your collar."

She leaned forward and picked it off and her face was very close to mine so that I could see the small creases of her lips and how the line of lipstick near one corner of her mouth was delicately blurred, and her eyes were deep and still like a polished, smoky marble, only there was none of the coldness of marble in them and the depth was not darkness but light in the way that a summer night can be luminous.

I said, "You know it because you know it." And I knew what I meant and I knew that she knew. "And you don't have to try to keep it because it's not a thing that can be taken away from you."

She may have said more and I may have answered her. I don't know because from that moment neither words nor time had any meaning because the thing that was between us, and then was us, was outside words, outside English literature or any other literature, unrelated to any space or dimension I had known. I knew only that now it was here I recognized it as the fire recognizes flame, the snow recognizes cold . . . the element without which we are never ourselves.

She lay in my arms with her face against my neck and her body under my hands was trembling gently and then still, and all I could see was the line of her shoulder and part of the pattern of her silk dress, a green leaf spray with a red berry against a yellow background and I saw how the overprinting of the red berry and the green leaf colours was offset a fraction of an inch from the pattern outline. Perhaps because this said to me that the material was cheap . . . I don't know . . . it raised a great tenderness in me. I wanted to gather her up in my arms, to walk away with her, away from Banyuls, away from whatever it was that brought the look into her eyes when I said it was time to go back to George Sarrasin and Astar Paviot . . . to carry her away from everything she and I knew. Maybe this was love, maybe this was what a lot of people possessed, but the protection and tenderness in me raised an arrogance that said this was ours and for us alone and that it had never been before and could never be again with anyone else.

For a long time I held her, my Sophie with the dark, unravelled hair. The sun was hot upon us and the bees and flies noisy in the amaryllis blooms around us and, perhaps, the beetle that had

48

been on my collar watching from the shade of some granite chip, black, green and iridescent and never to be forgotten by me though I had never seen it.

When she did move and lay back, shielding her eyes from the sun, the movement brought the opening of her dress apart where the top button was undone and I saw the smoothness of her right breast. Above it, just under the shoulder, was a dark bruise. I put my finger tips to it and kissed it and then, as I sat up, I was angry in a way I had never been before.

"Somebody hit you," I said.

She shook her head.

"Somebody hit you."

I'd been bruised often enough myself. I'd fought often enough, given and taken bruises, and I knew the mark of a fist on flesh.

She sat up. The trapped, apprehensive look was in her eyes again, the wanting and the not wanting.

"Who was it?"

I waited and eventually she said, "George."

I kept my anger down now, but I was going to have it all.

"Why?"

"He wanted me to do something I didn't want to do. He has a quick temper, but it means nothing."

"A bruise like that. What the hell did he want?" And then I saw it. "Was it something to do with me?"

"Yes."

She was making no defence. Just answering, her voice without any shades of feeling.

I didn't have to have finesse. I wanted the truth and meant to have it, and I knew that she could take anything I had to say.

I said, "Is there anything between you and George or Astar?"

"Only business."

"You knocked over your bag on purpose in the aquarium?"

"Yes."

"To get to know me."

"Yes."

"Why?"

"They told me to. They want something from you. At first I didn't mind . . . but later it was different. You know why."

"What do they want from me?"

"It is difficult to explain. They live . . . we all live . . . from one day to another. They because they like it, and I . . . because it is something that has happened to me and I cannot yet shake it off. Around Banyuls, you must have heard, there is smuggling. Things coming over from Africa and then up and down the coast

49

between here and Spain. And you, you have just what George wants. I was to get to know you and to ask you to do this for them. This morning I tried to refuse. . . ."

"They're in that racket, are they? What do they want?"

"They would pay you. . . . At the villa where you stay there is a launch. All you have to do is to leave the key in the boat-house door one evening and take it back the next morning. I do not ask you to do this. I am telling you what they want." She was silent for a moment then she put out her hand and took mine. "David. . . ."

It was the first time she had used my name and with it all my anger went.

"They're a lot of bastards. I've got to get you away from them."

She said nothing to that. She didn't have to say anything; but her hand held mine tighter.

"What do I tell them?"

"Tell them I said they can go to hell. They won't take that as a final answer. But I want time to think . . . about us."

I was thinking, too, about Drexel and Jabal. I was in no position to charge off and square up to George Sarrasin. For the moment I was tied to the Villa Maruba.

I stood up and pulled her up with me and put my arms around her.

"They know nothing about us?"

"No."

"Then don't let them, Sophie. In a little while I can fix it . . . a little while."

"I can wait . . . waiting is no longer important."

I kissed her and we walked to the road together. She went back towards Banyuls and I went on to the villa. But before we parted I said, "You can tell me what it is, the thing that holds you to them?"

"Yes, but not now. After this afternoon, I am not ready. If you had not seen the bruise I would not have asked you about the launch today. There is only one thing I want to remember today. . . ."

I didn't force her, though I felt I could have done. I didn't want to because I was wishing, too, that I had not seen the bruise. But I walked back to the villa promising myself that sometime I would have the pleasure of leaving my mark on George Sarrasin.

On the way to the villa I thought the whole thing over and, though I now knew what they were after, there were certain aspects which worried me. I could see that if they were smuggling then to hire a launch publicly would be to draw attention to themselves, particularly if they were people in whom the police were likely to take an interest. Our launch would be ideal for them. I saw clearly, too, that I was under an obligation to tell Drexel all about it. I didn't think it had anything to do with Jabal—but it might. And not to tell him would have been stupid. My decision to do this was strengthened by a small core of suspicion which I could not disperse that somewhere, somehow, the whole thing was a little too pat and convenient. The only thing which was natural and unplanned was my relationship with Sophie. That stood apart from everything else.

I meant to tell him that evening. I had dinner with Jabal and afterwards we played a game of chess which ended in a stalemate. It was midnight before we went to bed and the Colonel had not returned. Brindle sat up for him. I heard his car come in and the dogs barking about three, but it was too late then to get up and bother him.

I was up at six the next morning for I had promised to take Jabal out for an early morning swim. I pulled a towelling dressing-gown over my swim-pants and then turned to get the key of Jabal's room among the stuff from my pockets which I had emptied on to the dressing-table. I couldn't find the key. I had a moment of panic as I ran along to his room, but he was there. The door was locked and I could hear him playing his mouth-organ softly, waiting to be released.

I went along to the Colonel's room. He was still thick with sleep and when I asked to borrow his key of Jabal's room he slipped his hand under his pillow and flicked it across to me and was back in sleep before I had left the room.

Jabal and I had our swim about a mile off shore. The water was as smooth as treacle with faint trails of morning mist curling lazily over it and the surface was marked with a wonderful pattern of slow currents and colours. Its beauty was lost on me. Most of the time I was worrying about my key.

Back in the villa as I went along to my room, the Colonel called to me. The door of his bedroom was half-open and he was standing before his dressing-table, brushing his hair.

"David . . . I was half-asleep when you came in. What's all this about your key?"

I crossed to him and put his key down on the dressing-table. "It seems to have disappeared."

"What?" He turned round quietly, at once alert. "When did you have it last?" There was the beginning of crispness in his voice.

51

"As far as I know late yesterday afternoon."

"Who locked him up last night?"

"Brindle. He came up with us and while I was fumbling for my key he got out yours. I've looked everywhere in my room for the damned thing but I can't find it. I must have dropped it somewhere. . . ."

He was looking fixedly at me and I could see his eyes had begun to take on a touch of the God-damn-you expression.

"You're not the kind of man who drops things."

"I didn't think I was. . . ." I could feel the hesitation in myself and a kind of stupid, schoolboy guilt which made me wish I had sat up for him last night and told him what I had wanted to have him know. He saw that, too, for he knew me, knew the shades that could take a man's voice and face.

"Cough it up, David. Something's on your mind."

I told him then, about Sophie and the two men: everything except the real thing that lay between Sophie and myself because that, at the moment, wasn't something I wanted to share with anyone.

At first I thought he was going to take it calmly.

"No one knows we are here," he said. "There's not even been a news release about Jabal leaving Saraj. I don't know. . . . Maybe you're right. This coast is thick with smugglers. Maybe it's just a coincidence."

Then he paused and his face went hard and I saw the quick flick of his eyelids as he went on thinking, his mind surveying the whole panorama of possibilities and not liking the view. When he spoke his voice was a familiar echo from the past, the voice of the man who drove hard and demanded obedience to the point of fanaticism. "You're a bloody fool, David. I'm not paying you five hundred pounds for a picnic. You should have known you had to keep to yourself. You should have known we can't afford to take any risk."

I didn't mind being reprimanded. I'd asked for it.

"I'm sorry," I said and, if there's any phrase more inadequate than that one I don't know it.

He exploded. "Sorry! I don't care a damn about that! Jabal's dynamite. He could blow up in our faces any moment. Don't you see—until the F.O. take him over—everything's got to go right. It's got to go right!"

And then, though I was to blame, I couldn't help but see the difference in him. In the old days he didn't blast you to hell. He looked and said a few words and there was gall and worm-wood, contempt and yet understanding in them, and then he left you to sort out your own punishment while he went on to a consideration of practical measures to put things right. But this cry . . . *It's got to go right* . . . was full of strain. It was an old man complaining that he couldn't carry the same load, the hero losing his vigour to uncertainty. Hearing it, I hated myself for bringing it on him. I wanted everything to go right for him. And, although I was the immediate cause of his distress, I had the odd feeling then that our positions were now reversed. No matter how inadequate I was, I was now responsible for him. I had to protect him and see that this thing he had started came through without any hitch. He was a name and a power in the public mind. He was the principle of valour and adventure which men and women had to have displayed for them to make them forget their own smallness; a hero who could not afford to fail. So I didn't mind when he said—

"What about this woman? Could she have lifted the key from you?"

"It could be. But I don't think so."

He looked at me queerly and I wondered if he had detected anything in my voice.

"All right," he said, turning away and slipping into his linen jacket. "Benson from the Foreign Office should be here today sometime. We'll check on these people just to be sure. I can't afford to neglect anything. Ben Fa'id would pay a fortune to get Jabal back and cut his throat. I don't care a fig about the oil side of it—that's an F.O. business and just my job. But I like the boy. And you do, too. Nothing must happen to him."

And then he did the thing which he always could do with me, lift me out of purgatory and take me back into the sunlight and warmth of his own friendship. He put his hand on my arm and squeezed it. "Don't be such a casual, friendly bastard, David —not when you're working for me. You should have given that trio a wide berth the moment you saw they were interested in you. However," he laughed, "who am I to tell someone to steer clear of a pretty girl? I still have that kind of trouble."

We all had breakfast together and the thing was not mentioned again. But afterwards he kept Jabal company and I think he did so because he knew what I would want to do. I went off, along my old route of the previous day, looking for the key. I searched around in the little dip where Sophie and I had been but I couldn't find it. I asked myself frankly, kicking out all emotion, whether I thought Sophie had taken it. But I couldn't accept that. I went down into Banyuls in the hope of seeing her. I was unlucky. I had a drink in the *Café aux Bons Enfants* and when Jean Cagou came and chatted to me, I asked him about the three. He should have know anything there was to know about anyone in this district who had anything to hide. He knew nothing about them. I borrowed an old copy of the *Guide du Pneu Michelin* from the café proprietor and telephoned the only three hotels listed for Argelès-sur-Mer, *Plage des Pins*, *Commerce* and the *Lido*. There was no one of the names Orbais, Sarrasin or Paviot staying at any of them. But that proved nothing much. There would be plenty of small *pensions* not listed.

I walked back along the road so far and then, still worried about the key, I went over the vineyards to the dip again and had another look. But there was no key. Instead of going back by the road I kept along the coast track towards the villa and, about a quarter of a mile before I reached it, I dropped down between a break in the low cliffs and found myself in a small valley through which ran a dried-up stream bed. One side of the stream was lined by a narrow, sandy patch of cultivated ground laid out with melon plants and young tomatoes. The runnels of sand between the plants were still wet after the morning irrigation from a stone well which stood at the head of the patch. There was a plot of marguerites over which a cloud of yellow and black butterflies lifted and danced. Beyond the stream was a small clump of pines, the bottom of the trunks hidden in a growth of myrtle and broom bushes. The cliff path went up by the pines and as I passed them I heard someone groaning from the direction of the bushes.

I forced my way through the bushes and found myself in a little hollow. A small tent had been pitched under the trees and alongside the tent stood a dusty Norton motor-cycle with a GB plate. A piece of string, tied to the kick-start of the motor-cycle, ran across the ground and then into the tent. As I stood there another groan came from the tent.

I moved round to the front and looked in. The Englishman whom I had seen in the *Café aux Bons Enfants* was inside. He was in a sleeping bag and sat up as he saw me. Although he looked doleful and unhappy I had to smile. His pyjama jacket was open and his hands were clasped across his stomach. He was plump, not very big, and at first sight gave the impression of coming to pieces, of being scattered in parts around the untidy tent. His false teeth were in a glass at the head of the tent. He wore a soft, light brown toupee with a curl and central parting that reminded me of a chairman of an old-time music hall. The toupee was cocked a little to one side as though he had slapped it on carelessly as he heard me coming. His clothes were scattered all over the place.

"You in trouble?" I asked.

"Yes. Crab." Despite his condition his voice had a boom in it, a kind of public-house voice, the voice which is uplifted in withering sarcasm above all others at a football match.

"Crab?"

"Yes. Shouldn't eat it but I do." His voice sounded miserable, but I couldn't believe he was. There was an incorrigible twinkle in his eyes, a beaming, good-tempered air about him that seemed to suggest that he found life a joke, even when its kicks were turned against himself. He reached out for his dentures, slipped them home, and then, eyeing me up and down, went on: "Seen you at the *Bons Enfants*, haven't I? You English?"

"Yes, I am. Can I do anything for you?"

"A nice cup of tea might save me from dyin'. What I really need is a new stomach." He belched loudly and then, as he raised a hand to thump his chest, I saw that the string from the motor-cycle was attached to his wrist. He saw me look at it, and went on, "Safety precaution. Don't trust these foreigners."

I laughed and began to sort out his methylated stove and tin kettle to make him some tea. I wanted to help him because there was no doubt of his distress but also I was interested in him. I felt I had already let the Colonel down once. Nothing was going to pass me now. This man—as I prepared the tea he told me his name was Dunwoody, Leslie Dunwoody, from Walthamstow, London—had chosen himself a spot quite close to the villa. He might be a genuine camper, but he might not.

"Have you been here long?" I asked.

"Nearly a week."

"You enjoy camping?" He didn't seem the type at all to me.

"Not bloody likely! But it's all I can afford. Travel is the thing I like. You live in Walthamstow, mate, and you could understand that. Travel—broadens the mind. Wish it would leave the stomach alone, though. Very nice of you to do all this."

I handed him a mug of tea. He sipped at it and then said, "I was headin' for Spain, but if I start having these turns I don't think I will." He belched again more gently and went on, "The 'eat from tea is very mollifying. I'm grateful to you, real grateful." He closed his eyes and became a picture of comic bliss.

"You'll be all right," I said. "There's nothing wrong with you that tea or bicarbonate won't cure."

He nodded.

55

"Crab. Any kind of shell-fish. Also oil. Can't stand anything cooked in oil. Limits you, you know, when you're abroad."

We talked a little more and then I left him. I got back to the villa in time for lunch and I told the Colonel about him. As far as I could judge there was nothing wrong with the man, nothing to arouse suspicion, except one thing and that could easily have been put down to his condition. He hadn't asked me my name, though he had given his own, and neither had he asked me what I was doing here. When I put this point to the Colonel he said—

"I'll wander over and have a look at him."

He did that afternoon. I was in the garden with Jabal when he returned. We were lying sun-bathing by the boat-house. As he came down by the pines I thought his face looked reflective, almost care-worn. But seeing us he smiled.

"He was asleep, David. What a mess that tent was! Never been in the army, that's clear. But he looks harmless to me."

He sat down and smoked a cigarette, and then after a while he said, "I've had a 'phone call from Benson. He's at Perpignan and wants me to go up and see him. He thinks it wiser if he doesn't come here. I shall go off after tea."

CHAPTER VI

COLONEL DREXEL left in his car just after four o'clock. Perpignan was about an hour's drive away, and he told me that he did not anticipate that he would be late back.

I was having a drink before dinner, waiting for Jabal to come down, when the telephone in the hall began to ring. I didn't do anything about it, expecting Brindle to answer it. But he must have been in the garden, for it went on ringing and eventually, grumbling to myself, I got up and went out.

A voice speaking in French said, "Is that Mr. Fraser?"

I said, "Yes. Who is it?"

My question was ignored and the voice went on, "Sophie tells us that you are not happy about our suggestion."

"What Sophie tells you is right."

It was Sarrasin, and I saw no need to let any friendliness into my words.

Sarrasin laughed.

"Naturally, you have to be cautious. I understand. However, you need not worry. Just leave the key in the boat-house door tonight. No one will ever know anything. And you will have made some very easy money."

I said, "Go to hell!"

The door from the kitchen quarters to the hall opened at this point and Brindle's head and shoulders appeared. He raised his eyebrows stiffly and I waved him away. He drew back like a tortoise into its shell.

On the other end of the line Sarrasin was saying: "About the money. Of course in a few days we shall make a deposit in your name at any Crédit Lyonnaise you name. Say at Perpignan?"

"You say what you like. But keep away from this place. Tonight, or any night!"

"You sound angry."

"You pick things up fast."

He laughed and went on quickly, "Such a small thing to do. Tonight, then? No other night will do. You understand these things——"

The man was taking no notice of me.

I said fiercely, "Look, Sarrasin—get this fixed in that wooden head of yours——"

57

There was a laugh, followed by the words, "Tonight . . ." and then the receiver was replaced.

I slammed the 'phone down, and I didn't understand the thing at all. I might have been talking to a stranger on a crossed-line.

I went back to the lounge. Why the devil should they think I would help them? Why persist when I made it clear that I wouldn't? And why give me warning that they meant to come? They could come along secretly any night and break into the boat-house. Their only risk would have been from the dogs. There was an oddness in their behaviour which confused me. It was like trying to untangle a mass of thread and knowing some-where there was the one loose end which needed only a jerk to make the whole thing come unravelled. I spent half an hour trying to find the loose end and couldn't. Jabal came down and switched on the radio. He sat with a glass of orange juice listening to a talk on bell-ringing from some British station. He was absorbed enough to make me think that his great hobby was campanology. In a way, I was irritated that he could sit there so placidly while I became more and more convinced that subtle forces were gathering around him, that somewhere something was going wrong.

In the end I went out into the hallway and got on the telephone to the British Consul in Marseilles. The Consul, of course, was not in. It took me five angry minutes to convince whoever it was on the line that there was such a person as Drexel—though I knew damned well that he knew all about the Colonel—and another two minutes of exasperation to get it into his thick head that the Colonel was meeting Benson in Perpignan, that I didn't know how or where to reach him but if Marseilles could do this I wanted the Colonel to ring me at once. In the end I got a promise that this would be done if possible and the last word I heard was . . . 'irregular'. It was a situation I knew well. Secrecy and pretending not to know things you know damned well, and the anonymity of the telephone are all very well so long as things go to plan. Let anything slip, and then it takes ages to get into another gear and another frame of mind. I knew perfectly well what would happen. In fifteen minutes Marseilles would ring back the villa and ask for me. They would then ask me if I had just spoken to them. I was rather looking forward to that moment.

From the telephone I went into the kitchen. Brindle had the radio on, too. But his choice was dance music, very soft and sweet. I surprised him humming to himself but he went wooden the moment he saw me. He was gutting and cleaning fish for dinner.

I said, "Are there any arms in the house?"

He looked at me and there wasn't even a flicker of surprise in him. "You mean guns, sir?"

"That's it."

He cut the head off a bream and flicked it into a pail at the side of the table.

"Two, sir."

"Let's have one."

I think then for the first time in his life he wanted to step outside his part and ask 'Why?' He looked at me steadily for a moment and then he slowly bent down and drew open the table drawer. He handed me an old service Colt .45, but before he did so he wiped his hands on his apron, broke the gun and spun the chamber.

I took it and saw that it was unloaded. Holding the gun gave me a queer sensation, not the old feeling of being an inch bigger all round and better prepared for what might happen, but another feeling . . . of going back and not wanting to go, of myself this time stepping outside the part I'd picked for myself.

The revolver was beautifully kept . . . cleaned, oiled. I wondered how Brindle got it through the Customs when he came abroad. Drexel probably arranged that.

"Ammunition," I said.

Brindle put his hand into his back trouser pocket and then tipped six bullets on to the table. I picked them up.

"You was always inclined to pull a little bit to the left, if I remember, sir."

"I was."

I tossed the Colonel's key of Jabal's bedroom—the only key left now—over to him.

"You'll lock our friend in tonight. Then we'll take turns to sit outside the bedroom until the Colonel gets back."

"Are we expecting trouble, sir?"

"Maybe. You'll want the other gun. You don't know how I could get hold of the Colonel in Perpignan?"

"No, sir."

"I don't want Jabal to hear about this."

"Quite, sir."

At that moment the telephone went. It was from Marseilles. When I confirmed that I had indeed telephoned before, the voice was instantly helpful, passing smoothly into the next gear. If the Colonel could be found it would be done. In the meantime

59

was there anything that could be done that end. I had to say no.
I wasn't even sure what I was going to do myself or whether
there was any need for anything.

For dinner Brindle gave us the bream grilled, a beautiful
côtelette de veau, a cheese soufflé and a bottle of Chateaux
Margaux 1949. I ate well but I hated to leave the wine practically
untouched.

I started a game of chess with Jabal as Brindle brought the
coffee. My mind was not on the game and he beat me easily.
I think he knew then, from the wine and his victory, that something was in the air, but he asked no questions and I liked him
for that. He was a good boy, happy to be by himself or with
other people, never demanding but with no false modesty. It's
a thing you find in people who inherit dark destinies and learn
how to live with them . . . this powerful reserve and force, a
mixture of patience and strength which marks them with a rare
dignity. Even with his few years he had it . . . and it had made
a man of him already.

He went up to his room at ten and, with Brindle, I saw him
locked in. I left Brindle up there, squatting on a cushion, his
gun resting on his legs. Anyone else might have brought a book
to read, or a pipe to smoke, but not Brindle. He sat down, gave
me a look and a nod, and that was it. He would sit there now,
unsleeping, until he was relieved. As I left him, I said, "I shall
be in the garden. If there's any trouble you'll hear the dogs bark."

I put on a sweater and went out into the garden and sat in
the shadows on the edge of the fountain. It was a point from
which I could watch the front of the house and also the landing
steps before the boat-house.

I sat there thinking of George Sarrasin and Astar Paviot. They
might well be small-time, bungling smugglers . . . but they
might not. I had to guard against that risk. And from them I
began to think of Sophie, wondering what had brought her into
their lives, no matter what they were. She was no innocent, raw
girl. I had never imagined her like that. There must be a lot of
things behind her . . . but what they were had little importance
for me. She was the thing. She and the life which had flashed
into flame between us.

It was a lovely night. Warm and soft and an occasional current
of air as though somewhere a curtain was swinging gently. The
stars were so bright that I almost expected them to blow their
filaments. And sitting there it all became a little unreal . . .
and I distrusted that at once, because I knew it was nerve
tension, the hair rising on the back of the neck. From the far

side of the house where there was a gum tree, a nightingale began to sing too theatrically to be true. And the waves down by the landing steps lapped musically until the sound became words, a tune . . . a chorus of sweet-voiced peasant children I had heard somewhere performing at Christmas for *Monsieur le Curé*

> *Mon beau sapin*
> *Roi des forêts . . .*

A late lizard scuttled among the dry leaves of the fountain, I sat there for an hour. And then, the noise growing slowly, I heard the unmistakable sound of oars knuckling against wooden rowlocks. A few moments later I saw the boat; a dark shape about fifty yards offshore and coming up from the direction of Banyuls. I got up and, keeping to the shadows, went down to the landing stage.

As I went, the dogs which had been wandering around the garden came padding up to me and followed me down growling softly. Just as I reached the landing stage the boat turned towards the shore. By the light of the stars and a pale crescent of moon which had just begun to lift itself clear of the mauve stretch of sea, I could pick out the people in the boat.

George Sarrasin was rowing. He was dressed in something that looked like a dark-coloured track suit. In the stern was a man I had never seen before, a short, nondescript-looking creature in a light raincoat and a beret. When the boat was a couple of yards from the steps George pulled round and it rested there, swaying gently. George's white, slab-like face turned full towards me and I saw him throw a leg across the thwart so that he now sat comfortably astride it.

"*Bonsoir, monsieur,*" he said.

I said, "Sarrasin—this is private property. Keep off it."

He nodded a little, as though he were considering this point. Then he said, "It is very hard to do business with you."

"Not hard. Impossible."

As I spoke I brought the Colt from behind my back and the faint moonlight slid in an oily ripple along its barrel. The boat drifted a little further inshore.

George looked from the revolver to me and again he shook his head. "You would use that?"

He sounded a little sad as though we were friends and I had affronted him. And I was hating every moment because everything was wrong and out of place. I had the feeling that he wasn't caring a damn about me, that he was absolutely sure of

61

himself. It was a feeling that I'd known before; the fine sense which tells you that your adversary has a card up his sleeve and doesn't care if you know it.

"I'll use it," I replied, "if you make it necessary." And I meant it. Behind me was a powerful backing, Drexel, the Anglo-Media Oil Company, and eventually the Foreign Office and possibly the French *Bureau des Affaires Etrangères*. A bullet in George Sarrasin would cut no ice with them if he were interested in Jabal . . . and I was becoming more and more convinced that he was.

George said, "You are making a great mistake. However, since you are determined. . . ." He leaned forward to take up his oars. And then, a fraction of a second too late, I realized that this was the moment of the trump card. I had been waiting for it, wondering how it would come, trying to foresee it, and the mistake I made was anticipating subtlety. There was a whisper of noise behind me and I swung round towards the shadow of the boat-house. Part of the shadow moved, crowded in on me and something smashed at my head. I went down like a log and the last thing with me was the sound of my own breath, forced from me in a sob of angry futility.

*   *   *

It must have been a good hour later before I came round. I felt stupid and muzzy and I lay for a while staring up at the stars through the pine branches, not really aware of myself or of what had happened. The bitch wolf-hound came and whined about me. Slowly I pulled myself up. My legs felt like rubber, and, the moment I was upright, I was sick. I felt better after that, but light-headed still and I had the extraordinary sensation of being divorced from my body, of watching it move erratically up the path to the house and of wanting desperately to get back into it and communicate urgency and concise understanding to it.

In the house the lights were burning in the hall and up the stairs. At the top of the stairs lay Brindle. He was sprawled out with his automatic close to his hand and was groaning gently to himself. I went past him and along to Jabal's room. The door was open and the room was empty. It was then that I came back to myself, my outside self overlapping and then fitting itself to my stumbling body in the way the images are brought into focus in a camera.

I went back to Brindle but he was still out and I could see that he'd taken a crack over the head, too. I turned him over and loosened his collar and was about to go to the bathroom to

62

get some water for him when the telephone in the hall began to ring.

Going down the stairs to it as quickly as I could the movement made my head swim and I must have taken longer than I imagined. The incessant *ring-ring-ring* made me irritable. I picked it up to hear the Colonel's voice.

"David? Why did you want me? Has anything happened?"

I said, "Where are you?"

"Perpignan."

"Then get back here, Jabal's gone. . . ."

At the other end I heard him swear, not with anger, but with a note of sick despair, and then came his questions and I told him as well as I could what had happened.

I said, "What do you want me to do?"

Crisply, taking control now, pushing down whatever he was feeling, and I could guess even in my state at the anxiety that was with him, he said, "Stick there and wait for me."

I went up to Brindle again, hauled him along to his room and put him on his bed. It seemed to take me ages. I bathed his face with water and made him comfortable but he was still out. Then I went down to the lounge and got myself a drink. I gave myself ten minutes with it and then I could rest there no longer. I was beginning to be myself now and a lot of questions were hammering away in my mind. I got up and went down to the boat-house. The launch was in its place and there was no sign of the row-boat. I made my way up the path to the road-gate in the villa wall. It was wide open. As I came back to the house the dogs joined me and, thinking of Brindle upstairs, Brindle who must have been taken by surprise, I suddenly realized that the dogs hadn't given him any warning. It was something I didn't understand at all. Even when I had gone down to Sarrasin the dogs had only growled softly.

In the lounge I fixed myself another drink and sat there trying to sort things out. Jabal was gone, and the conviction beat in my mind that it was my fault. I seemed to have done everything I could, taken every precaution, but the whole thing had gone wrong. I was confused and sick at heart because I knew what this was going to mean to Drexel. He'd picked me, relied on me and I'd let him down.

I must have dropped off to sleep. When I woke it was two o'clock and Drexel was standing in front of me with another man whom I soon learned was Benson. Outside the dogs were barking and I guessed that there were other people about.

Drexel was grim and efficient, as I expected him to be.

Whatever he was feeling underneath he was not showing it. Benson was a tall, shadow-like creature behind him who said hardly anything.

Drexel fixed my head. Whatever had hit me had been blunt, not making much of a cut. While he did it he made me go through my story, asking a question now and again. When it was over he said, "All right. Now you get some sleep."

He came up to the bedroom with me and I wanted to say something but there was nothing I could say. Inside I was dried-up and miserable and, although he hadn't said a word of censure, I had the feeling that he was gone from me; that something between us had been broken.

I dropped off to sleep, hearing the telephone ringing and the sound of movement and voices throughout the house.

CHAPTER VII

I WAS awake by nine o'clock the next morning. I went along to the bathroom and shaved and showered. I wasn't feeling too bad physically, no worse than having a bad hangover. It was a fine morning, calm, bright and not yet hot. Through the open window I could see the wall gate. There was a *garde mobile* standing by it and I could see his motor-cycle parked on the path. By the garage was a long, low Citroën car.

When I got back to my room Brindle was just leaving. He had set a breakfast tray on the table by the window. He looked all right except for a wad of plaster just behind his right ear.

I said, "How are you, Brindle?"

"All right, sir."

"We both bought it, didn't we?"

He grunted something, but it was just a noise. Nothing in it for me.

It was then that I got my first suspicion that something new was in the wind for, despite his usual dourness, his manner carried no recognition that we had shared anything the previous night.

If two people get cracked over the head they have something in common. Brindle was miles from me and, before I had time to say anything more, he made it clear that he was only the instrument of a new influence.

"The Colonel's compliments, sir, and he would appreciate it if you kept to your room until he calls for you."

He was gone before I could question him and I was left wondering what the hell all this was about.

It was an hour before Brindle appeared again and said the Colonel would like to see me. Drexel was in the lounge. When I went in he was standing by the window and there was another man sitting at a small table close to the fireplace. Drexel asked me how I was, and then introduced me to the other man. He was a Monsieur Didier, a Commissioner of Police from Marseilles or it may have been Perpignan because at that moment I wasn't really listening. I was watching Drexel. He had changed since last night. The strain was on him clearly now. He looked older and there was a greyness about his skin which I had never seen before. As a boy I had known my mother to be worried by things outside my comprehension or kept from me (our finances had never been very sound and she had had a brother who had caused her constant trouble) but, even so, a child, recognizing anxiety in an adult, is distressed by his own ignorance. I felt like that with Drexel now. I could not say he was avoiding me but he was making no movement towards me.

I said, "Is there any news?"

"No. Not so far. Though we've got things moving." He came across the room, one hand rubbing his chin, his eyes on the ground and he might have been talking to himself. "There's been a Press release from Saraj that Jabal left a week ago for London via France. That's Sheik Ahmed ben Fa'id playing ball, of course."

"Do you think he's got hold of Jabal?"

"Possibly. But there's still a chance to find him. Benson and I have decided that the Press must know about this. It'll help the police in their work. But we've got to get agreement from London and Paris first. I only hope it doesn't take long."

He halted suddenly and beat a fist into his palm and said, "I can't understand how anyone could have got on to us so quickly. There's been a leak somewhere." As he finished speaking he raised his head and looked at me and I knew then what he was trying not to think. It was like being hit in the face. I took the shock hard, and heard my inner self saying 'He can't think that! He can't!' But I knew damned well that he did, or was coming to it.

I was going to say something but he forestalled me.

"David, I've told Didier all you told me, but he's got some questions to ask you." He paused and momentarily he smiled, for the first time, and I knew it was to cover his embarrassment. "Didier's a policeman and he's got his job to do. Don't get your rag out if you don't like some of the questions."

He did not have to warn me. I knew what was coming and had already told myself that it wouldn't help me or Drexel to get angry.

I sat down and looked at Didier and said, "Go ahead, monsieur."

Elbows on the table, Monsieur Didier rested his chin on tented fingers and stared at me. His friendly, brown eyes were troubled now and again by a nervous flutter of the eyelids. He had short, stubby fingers, not too well kept, as though he did a lot of gardening. In fact his whole appearance made me think of a gardener, solid and middle-aged. His bearing was slow and patient as though he knew neither the seasons nor human beings

66

were to be forced if you wanted good results. He had a trick, too, of cocking his right cheek forward, possibly to conceal the hearing aid he wore in his left ear.

He said, "The three people you have described—you say they made your acquaintance by design?"

"They did."

"You told the Colonel nothing about them until you lost your key?"

"I was going to tell him." It sounded weak and made me angry with myself.

"It strikes me as odd that, after your refusal to co-operate, they so conveniently warned you they were coming."

"I think it's odd, too."

"We agree. In fact I don't think there is any truth in the story."

"In *their* story," I corrected and I was beginning to see how difficult it might be to hold my temper. For all his friendly brown eyes this man did not have any interests of mine at heart.

"In their story. Or—could it be in yours?"

"They damned well came for the launch, didn't they? They also cracked me on the head—and Brindle."

"I was coming to that. How do we know they came for the launch?"

"I saw them."

"But no one else."

"Brindle?"

"He saw no one. He heard a noise from the stairs and going to investigate was hit from behind."

"Someone hit him and me."

"True. At the moment I find the whole thing very confusing. Can you explain, for instance, why they should come for a launch which you had already refused them, and why they should conveniently telephone you and tell you they were coming?"

"It sounds absurd."

"I'm glad you agree."

"But it's damned well true."

"Maybe, but we have only your word for it."

"Brindle heard the telephone go."

"He heard the telephone, but that might have been anything. A wrong number or a different message from the one you have told us you received."

I stood up and looked at Drexel.

"Look, Colonel, why don't you both come out into the open

67

and say what you think." I couldn't keep the bitterness from my voice.

"Take it easy, David. See it from our point of view. The whole thing's a muddle and we're trying to get it straight."

Didier ignored the passage and went on——

"Can you explain why the dogs shouldn't have barked when these strangers entered the grounds? That at least would have given Brindle some warning."

"I don't know. I've been puzzled by that." I had a fresh hold on myself. I wanted to help Drexel and if this would get us anywhere I was prepared to force under my own feelings. But it wasn't easy.

Didier blinked at the ceiling for a moment, then said, "The key you lost. Do you think it could have been stolen?"

"Well I suppose it could have been."

"It was—or else fortunately found for it was used to unlock Jabal's door last night."

"Didn't they take a key from Brindle?"

"No. After you left him he hid his in the cistern of the water closet in the bathroom. It was there this morning."

"Well, I know nothing about that. I can see what you're driving at. You think I may have helped these people in some way. Or even arranged this. I don't blame you for examining that angle—but it's just too bloody fantastic for words. I took every precaution I could. I tried to get in touch with the Colonel. I phoned Marseilles. I armed myself and I put Brindle on guard."

"And despite all that—Jabal was taken."

I could have kicked him in the face; he said it in such an unctuous manner, the petty triumph of an official.

"Maybe Brindle's in the thing with me, too," I said sarcastically. "We knocked one another over the head to give ourselves good alibis."

"You could have done." There was no shaking him and I suddenly wanted to laugh at the absurdity of the situation. But he went on quickly. "What I would like to know is which of you washed up the coffee cups. Brindle says he didn't."

"Coffee cups?"

"Yes. There is no sign of struggle in Jabal's room. He may have been drugged before his room was entered. The coffee cups you both used after dinner were in the kitchen washed."

I turned to Drexel. This was getting beyond anything I had expected and I wanted to see the same recognition of its absurdity in him as there was in me. "Colonel—are you with him in this?"

He came over to me slowly, biting his lower lip and he put his hand on my shoulder.

"David, I'm not anywhere. I've got a bomb in my hands which is about to go up unless I act quickly. I'm not interested in anything but the truth and, by God, I'm not accepting anybody's word unless it can be proved. Do you think I like standing by and listening to this? But I'm not stopping it, not if it gets me an inch nearer the truth."

For the first time in my life—and then it was only for a fraction of time and left me ashamed—I found myself against him. With anyone else he could be like this, but not with me. I owed him my life. He was my friend. If I gave him my word then he was in honour bound to accept it. God, it sounds old fashioned, but there's all truth in it. I was angry with him, and sorry for him because he was letting me down. And then it was gone and there was only compassion. He was old and his career was shredding before his eyes, and I loved him for his weakness as in the past I had loved him for his strength; and I knew I would do anything for him—even put up with this.

There was worse to come.

Monsieur Didier blinked, wrote a few notes and then, without looking up, said, "Last year while you were in Turkey you spent five days in gaol?"

"What's that to do with anything? I was on holiday. It was a passport mix-up."

"You do some very odd things in your holidays, Mr. Fraser?"

"Why not? We all need a change from our work."

"You are not a rich man, Mr. Fraser?"

"Of course not. I'm a schoolmaster."

"Maybe you'd like to be something different. Maybe you'd like to have money?"

"Who wouldn't?" I was very weary of him now, but not angry, and I let all the life go from my voice. "Monsieur Didier—you're chasing the wrong hare. I'm a schoolmaster. Not a kidnapper. I can't stop you thinking what you like. But don't think I don't understand what's in your mind. Maybe I should help you." I heard my voice taking on a strange bitterness. "I speak French fluently. I worked for a short while in the French resistance movement which you know had many crooks in it. Some of them I still know. Some of them, no doubt, live in and around Marseilles or Perpignan or who-cares-where. Give me ten minutes and I could make a stronger case against myself than you could. But give me ten centuries and I'm still fool enough to think that nothing could ever make me betray Colonel Drexel!"

I didn't look at Drexel. I didn't want to. I kept my eyes on Didier and very quietly the bastard replied, "Your dossier which Mr. Benson of the Foreign Office has supplied states that at Oxford you were an active member of the O.U.D.S. Even the police can be fooled by an actor."

But not even that could touch me.

I said calmly, "Why don't you get out and look for Jabal instead of sitting on your backside wasting time with me?" And I said it in the same tone that I might have remarked on the weather, not caring a damn how he would take it. To his credit, he took it well.

He gave me a little nod, and said *"Touché."*

He got up and looked towards the Colonel who was standing staring at both of us as though he were watching some scene from a play, something that wasn't touching him, his mind busy and far away.

"Colonel Drexel, maybe Mr. Fraser is right. We are wasting time with him at the moment." Then he turned to me. "You will oblige me by staying in this room. Later today I should like you to come to headquarters with me. From our photographs you may be able to identify some of these people with whom you are acquainted. Also . . ." and now for the first time the edge of a threat crept in, "we shall be able to go on with our talk and possibly reduce the confusion a little."

He went out and the opening door showed that there was a *gendarme* outside. Drexel lingered for a moment. He came close to me and then, unexpectedly, his face cleared and he smiled, really for me this time, and said, "No hard feelings, David. It's just that the whole thing is slipping through my hands like sand."

"Forget it. Didier doesn't understand. Don't worry about me."

I think he wanted to say something else, but it wouldn't come. He punched my shoulder affectionately and then left me.

I sat there alone in the room and it seemed damper and gloomier than it had ever been. For once I was almost in a mood to enjoy it. I turned my back on the sunshine outside and stared at the fireplace which was covered with a great spread of a cheap, paper fan. I had a lot to think about. I could see how a fairly good case could be made against me for carelessness, though even so I couldn't really accept this myself. And, in a way, I could see that Didier might have the beginnings of a half-baked case against me on the score of aiding or even planning Jabal's abduction. But, however he was going to look at it, I could not feel any real apprehension and after a time I found that my thoughts had gone to Sophie. Just where she stood in all this confusion I wanted to know more than anything. She had told me that Sarrasin and company were smugglers and wanted the launch. This was a lie. They had come for Jabal. But did she know it was a lie? I wanted the answer to that desperately and I knew why. If the thing which had come to life between us was what I thought it was, then I knew it had no place in it for a lie. If she had known they were going to take Jabal then all she had brought to me was false. And this I was not going to believe unless she herself proved it to be so. Drexel could make a mistake about me, even begin to give credence to an absurd suspicion, but I could not find it in myself to be suspicious of Sophie. I could just not do it. There had to be an explanation. The only one I could think of was that Sarrasin and company had started off as smugglers and then in some way had learned about Jabal and had seen the rich possibilities of kidnapping. They could make a deal with either side—with the Regent, though this would mean the end of Jabal, or with the oil company and British interests. Drexel had been forced to use other people in getting Jabal out of Saraj. He had travelled up through Cairo. There was the crew of the *Roi Bleu*. There must have been fifty opportunities for leakage of information.

I sat there mulling it all over, and outside in the hall I heard the telephone go constantly and a parade of different voices. Brindle brought me some lunch but there were few words between us. After lunch I was allowed to go for a stroll in the garden, but I can't say I enjoyed it with an *agent de police* keeping a strict two yards behind me. A wind had got up, a fierce, whippy touch of tramontane blowing out of a clear sky and raising the dust in my face. I was glad to go back to the lounge.

The hours went by. I read all the magazines in the place and finally finished up with a battered cookery book which had found its way in there. I remember reading a recipe for *escargots à la bourguignonne*. I shut my eyes and repeated it to myself, knowing I would never forget it. Maybe that's why I was good at languages. I have a facile, visual memory. I can look at a railway time-table and remember the details months later. And if anyone said to me what was I wearing on the 4th July two years ago I could go right through the list. Recipes, trains, clothes, useless junk. . . . *Faites d'égorger des escargots en les faisant bouillir dans l'eau où l'on a mis deux poignées de cendre de bois.* . . . 9.21 a.m. from Tunbridge Wells Central station for Charing Cross: Saturdays only; arrive Charing Cross 10.23 a.m. . . . A Donegal tweed jacket, blue shirt, collar a little frayed, blue tie, grey flannel trousers. . . .

I must have gone off to sleep. When I woke it was dark outside and Drexel and Didier had just come into the room. Drexel was fixing himself a whisky and he brought one over for me.

I took it and stood to drink it.

I said, "Well?"

"No news. We've combed Argelès-sur-Mer for your three birds. No one knows them. Your espadrille seller—Jean Cagou—remembers you with them but he doesn't know them. Nobody knows them. Also nobody hired a row-boat from Banyuls last night and none is missing."

"And Jabal?"

"Not a trace."

Didier, carrying a black brief case, came forward. I could see he was not approving of this conversation.

"Colonel Drexel . . . I must get back. There is much to be done."

Drexel nodded and he held out my light raincoat to me.

"Better put this on, David. This wind's making it a bit chilly."

I had the feeling that he was sorry for what had happened that morning; that he was trying to make it up to me, reaching out again to draw me closer to him. But he knew and I knew that it could never be the same. We had both taken a step forward and away from each other. I would still go to hell for him. But now, instead of worship, there was understanding; instead of faith a compassionate logic.

As I slipped into the coat, I said, "What do I do about getting back?"

He hesitated too long before he answered, "Benson and I will be coming in later. We'll see to you."

It was as good as saying, "I don't know how long you'll be kept by Didier. I don't know what's going to happen to you."

Outside the wind was blowing strongly and the sky was suddy with little clouds. I got into the Citroën, which was driven by an *agent de police*, and sat in the back with Didier. A *garde mobile* on a motor-bicycle went ahead of us along the road to Port-Vendres. He must have been an impatient man for he was soon far ahead of us and then eventually lost to sight.

I said to Didier, "Where are we going?"

"Perpignan." His tone was clear enough, and I did not have to be hit over the head to make it obvious that he was in no mood for conversation with me. The talk, I knew, would come later.

And maybe the hit over the head. I sat there, disliking him more and more.

We went down the steep drop into Port-Vendres, and along the quay front. One of the North African steamers was in, her decks a blaze of light. She was white and beautiful and stirred something inside me, the thing which was always moved at the sight of a boat. With a bitter irony I thought then of Songa Manara. I had given all that up—for this. I kept my eyes on the boat, staring past the stolid Didier. I suddenly thought how good it would be to get aboard her or any other ship and watch Europe sink over the stern . . . the desire to get away was strong in me that instant for I felt too much caught up and involved and—to be honest—uncertain of myself. Only one thing I would have asked and that was that Sophie should come with me. I didn't want to be alone any longer.

I sat there as we swept down on to the long straight bamboo-fringed road to Perpignan and thought about Sophie. And I found running in my head a phrase of poetry which though it came straight out of Eng. Lit. third year syllabus—God what ages away the school and the feel of chalk on my fingers seemed! —had in it a great deal of what I felt for Sophie:

> What I do
> And what I dream include thee, as the wine
> Must taste of its own grapes.

Parse it, take it apart, write it in paraphrases . . . but it wouldn't mean a damn thing unless once in your life that high note of recognition had vibrated in and around and through you.

I don't know where we were on the road when I saw the torch flash from ahead. Beyond Argelès-sur-Mer, I think, but not as far up as the point where the road crosses the River Tech on its way to the sea.

Didier muttered something to the driver and the man slowed. I think he thought as I did that it might be our *garde mobile* signalling. Then the headlights picked up the figure of a man in the road centre, the torch swinging in slow arcs from his hand. *"Qu'est-ce qu'il a?"*

There was no answer, not in words; only an incredible swift-ness of movement and manoeuvre that left both Didier and myself helpless. The nearest I got to doing anything was a half-move of my arm towards my door handle and the word, shouted in surprise: "Paviot!"

The driving door was jerked open and the *agent de police* was

pulled out. As he was dragged into the road I saw Paviot's arm
go up and then down and, although the darkness hid it from me,
I could tell he held a knife. The driver sighed and then gave a
scream that died into a whimper. Paviot let him drop to the
ground and slid into the driving seat. At the same moment, the
doors on either side of Didier and myself were jerked open.
George Sarrasin, the lower part of his face masked, slid in and
forced me over, his hand holding a gun against my ribs. On the
other side of me a small figure in raincoat and beret, his face
masked, too, held a gun on Didier and a rasping voice said:
"Out!"

Didier was grabbed by the arm, pulled out, and then forced
by the gun in his back to move to the side of the road. He stood
there with his hands raised. Above the wind I heard his voice.

"Fraser . . . you won't get away with this!"

I did not get his meaning then, and I was given no chance to
reply. Paviot turned the car in the road with two long backing
and filling movements. When he was round, the man with Didier
gave him a push that sent him over the road bank into the ditch,
and then came running to the car. He jumped in alongside Paviot.

The car drove off at top speed back along the road it had just
travelled. There was nothing I could have done. Not a thing.
It had been a dark pantomime with no part in it for me except
to watch. Behind us I knew there was an *agent de police* who
would be lucky if he were not mortally wounded. Before us was
the white ribbon of road and around me these three.

Sarrasin relaxed the pressure of the gun on my side. Almost
to himself I heard him say, "Beautiful." It was a sigh more than
a word, a lingering breath of pleasure.

Angrily I said, "What the flaming hell do you three think
you're doing?"

Sarrasin turned his great face towards me, an unsmiling solemn
slab of flesh and then heavily he said, "Don't talk. Don't make
trouble." Calmly he began to untie the scarf he had worn over
his face and which had now slipped into a noose around his neck.

I sat there, silent.

Paviot whistled thinly to himself as he drove. We went back
as far as Argelès and then swung right-handed away from the
coast. They made no attempt to hide their route from me. We
were speeding now along the road to Le Boulou and for a while
I wondered if they were heading for the Spanish border. Wherever
they were going I told myself that it would be dangerous for them
to remain on the road long in Didier's car.

We were some way out of Argelès when the car stopped.

74

Watching the speedometer and checking the time on my wrist-watch, I made it about ten kilometres. That would be about half-way to Boulou. For the moment, I was glad to leave the big issues. I wanted time to come to that. I kept tabs on the small things like distance and place. So far I knew where we were.

The car stopped without any instructions from George Sarrasin. Paviot got out of the driving seat and the other man slid across and took his place. Paviot opened my door and motioned me out. I obeyed and Sarrasin came behind me with the revolver.

I heard Sarrasin say to the driver: "Take it as near Perthus as you can and then ditch it. Don't try to be brave."

I knew what that meant. Le Perthus was beyond Le Boulou and on the border. If the ditched car were found there it would look as though we had gone across the Spanish frontier.

The car went off, its tail-light wreathed with a plume of exhaust gases. Sarrasin hustled me along into the side of the road and Paviot produced a long length of rope from around his waist. He tied it about himself and then, leaving a working length, looped it round my waist and passed the spare end to Sarrasin who fastened it about his own middle. We were roped like climbers. It would be difficult for me to break from them.

Sarrasin said, "Keep going and don't give trouble. It will serve nothing but unpleasantness."

I said nothing because I had nothing to say to them. I didn't understand what it was all about and for the moment I wasn't bothering. All I knew was that I meant to give them the slip as soon as I could. In the Army they had taught that if you are taken prisoner it is easier to escape in the first hour than the second. Every hour and day that passes makes escape harder. I knew this was true.

We began to climb by a small path through a plantation of young fir trees. The ground was slippery with loose needles. Very soon we were crossing a rocky plateau and the path dipped into a narrow valley. The wind was dead in our faces and I knew we were moving north. The young moon was up now, slipping in and out of a patchwork of small clouds. I saw that the far side of the valley was terraced with vines and away to the left I thought I could make out the shape of a house, probably the cabin of the *vigneron*. I put my hands in my raincoat pocket and plodded after Paviot. Behind me I could hear the even breathing of Sarrasin. The raincoat had slit pockets that allowed me to get at the pockets of my jacket. I got hold of my penknife and opened it. They should have searched me.

At the head of the valley slope the path got rougher, twisting through patches of tall white heather and a tangle of broken boulders. Leaning forward to the slope I brought my hands out of my pocket and holding lightly to the rope about my waist I cut into it. In a few moments I had sawn through the loop. With my left hand I held the two ends together. All I had to do now was to wait for the moon to go behind a cloud and then run for it. I was in good condition and I felt that if I got only a short start I stood a chance of losing them. I cocked an eye up to the sky. A largish cloud was scudding up towards the moon. I waited, plugging forward, and there was a growing edge of excitement in me. Fifteen seconds, I thought, and the moon would be covered.

"Paviot." It was George Sarrasin.

Paviot stopped and looked back, and I half-turned too. Sarrasin came up close to me and I saw him look down towards my left hand which was holding, and hiding, the loose ends of the rope. He had his revolver out and he said evenly, "I was a fool. We should search you."

I took a chance. I kicked out at the revolver and threw myself sideways. I missed the revolver and fell and he was on me like a cat. He had that combination which is rare; a big man with the gift of speed. He came smashing on top of me and his weight drove the wind from my body. I didn't try to shake him off. He straddled over me, his knees gripping my sides and behind him was Paviot and I could see the knife in his hand. There was nothing I could do except curse myself for not having tried to escape in the first five minutes. I might have made it.

"You have caused trouble. *Eh bien*, you wish for unpleasantness."

Sarrasin smacked my face with his open hand. It was a hard, fierce blow but less painful than insulting since he used his open hand, showing his contempt. From that moment I began to hate him, and it was a warm, comforting vigour inside me. I lay there and I think he contemplated hitting me again. But he changed his mind.

They went through my pockets as I lay on the ground and then, tossing my knife into the bushes, they roped me again. We went on, and I knew that so long as we were roped I was not going to have any chance with them.

And as I walked, roped between them like some slave, I could feel my face smarting from the blow. It was the same hand I thought that had struck at Sophie and bruised her. George Sarrasin, I thought; full of strength and vigour, who didn't care

76

whether it was man or woman he struck, who breathed 'Beautiful' when a knife went home. . . . How I hated him, how I warmed myself with the hope that one day I should be free on my feet with a chance to get at him. I'm a Scot and we're good haters and I hadn't felt like this for years. I was almost happy as I looked forward to the moment when I could get at him. It was a wonderful, unchristian feeling and I nursed it tenderly.

CHAPTER VIII

THERE was that about these two men which slowly began to impress me. Putting a word to it was difficult. It was a combination of strength and resolution, not fortitude because that had too much of a crusader shine on it for them. The essence of their appearance was seediness and shabbiness, their setting small, smoke-filled rooms, unmade beds, bar-tops marked with pernod and bock rings. Looking at them I should have said I could place them; Paviot was straight from Marseilles, from La Canebière, and Sarrasin a boxing booth slugger from some travelling fair. But I began to feel I was wrong. They were both as hard and fit as apes. After two hours of some of the roughest cross-country work I have ever done they were almost unmarked. They knew how to move in the dark and they knew how to travel economically sparing all useless effort. They spoke only once after the frustration of my attempt to escape.

We crossed a high meadow, the wind taking the thin grasses like smoke, a smell of wild thyme and basil rising from the crushed turf under our feet. At the head of the meadow, the narrow path we were following led away to the left.

Paviot stopped and turned round to Sarrasin.

"The path, or over the top?"

Sarrasin said, "Over the top. By the path we might meet someone."

Paviot said, *"Merde"* to no one in particular and was off again.

Against the sky ahead of us I saw the sharp line of a peak. It took us an hour to make the top and there we rested in the lee of a boulder while Paviot smoked a cigarette and I kept him company. No one spoke. Sarrasin sat by himself. He was wearing a loose black sweater and tight knee breeches and about his middle he had a wide leather belt with what looked like a large silver buckle worked in some intricate design. I couldn't see clearly what it was. Far away and below us—a good fifteen miles, I thought—was a great night stretch of the coast laid out, a dark hem of land embroidered here and there with faint whorls of light from small towns and villages. I wondered what was happening below there. An *agent de police* probably dead. Didier snapping out instructions, and back at the villa Colonel Drexel and Benson working out this fresh complication.

As I went I was working it out myself. I understood now what had been in Didier's mind when he had shouted to me from the roadside. He had decided that I was not being taken away by force, but that I was being rescued. From his point of view it would seem a reasonable interpretation. And now I saw that from Sarrasin's point of view—if he were the brain behind the abduction of Jabal—it was also a convenient interpretation. It gave the impression that I was not merely involved in this affair but had possibly organized it and, when my innocent front had begun to fail, had signalled for help. Sarrasin, Paviot . . . for a moment my mind almost said Sophie, but I checked myself . . . were unknown to the police. Now they had me they could shelter behind me. But that was only a beginning. A hundred following questions stirred in my brain. The most important, since a man is a fool if he doesn't put the highest value on his own skin, was what was going to happen to me—and to Jabal. I hadn't thought of him much, but now I started to. I liked the boy very much and my anger against Sarrasin grew as I thought of what would happen to Jabal if he were sold back to Sheik Ahmed ben Fa'id.

Some time after we had passed the peak and had made three or four miles down the following slope through groves of cork trees. we came out on to a rough cart-track flanked on one side by a dry watercourse and on the other side by a thick belt of trees, oak, beech and birch with here and there the lacy white plumage of an acacia showing against the shadows. Some way down the road we swung right-handed into the trees and then came out into a small clearing. To one side of it was a small cabin with an outside veranda, the whole thing reminding me of a country cricket pavilion. As we went up to it Paviot gave a low whistle.

The door opened and a golden wedge of light struck across the veranda. Someone stood beside the door and we clumped up the wooden steps and into the hut, still roped. For an instant I had a childish desire that all this should be a dream, that really I was just coming back to the Climber's Club hut at Helyg after a long day over the Carnedds. . . . I suppose I must have been more exhausted with our night trek than I had imagined.

I didn't take in the details of the hut. I just stood there while Sarrasin cleared the ropes from us, and I saw that the rough table held food and a large flask of wine.

Sarrasin nodded to the table and I sat down. Somewhere behind me the door closed, and then he was saying:

"You go well. You are used to the hills." Not a question but a statement and his tone a compliment for which I had no need.

And then I saw Sophie. She came from the door to the table and, lifting the flask, poured wine for us. She wore a wind-breaker and a rough skirt and her thick, black hair was caught up carelessly at the back with a ribbon. She put a glass before me and I looked at her. She made no sign. I might have been anyone sitting there.

She half turned to Sarrasin, reaching past me to pour wine for him, and she said, "You have been quicker than I thought."

"Things went well."

"Good."

"Our friend here travels fast. He gave a little trouble once. But after that. . . ."

He laughed and she smiled easily as she handed him his glass. They talked over my head, as though I had no existence. Then she moved to attend to Paviot.

Paviot took his wine from her, raised the glass in a salute before drinking, and said, "Coming over the hills. It is like the old days, eh? Night work puts an edge in a man. Makes the taste of a poor wine good."

I tossed back my wine, feeling it rough and stimulating against my tiredness, and turning to Sarrasin, I said, "Now we've time to breathe perhaps you'll tell me what all this is about? You've got Jabal, you've got me—and you've killed a policeman. You're doing fine."

Sophie said, "Have some more wine. There is also bread and ham." She wasn't even looking at me. She bent over the table and began to slice a large ham. A hateful doubt crept into my mind. I loved her and I had faith in her, but this was the moment of trial and at such times a man is victim to his darkest thoughts. I tried to push them away. I believed in her. She would never betray me, and the force of my emotions came up in me with a great surge of anger directed against the others. It was more than I could hold.

"Come on, Sarrasin!" I shouted. "What is all this about?"

He looked at me and smiled. "You are angry. Don't be. In time you shall know all that is necessary."

He spoke so placidly, was so damned sure of himself, that it made me lose control. I jumped to my feet. I didn't know what I was going to do or say. I didn't get a chance anyway. I saw the miracle of swift movement which was Sarrasin's pride. He was up and his revolver was out and levelled at me, and on the other side of the table Paviot, lounging back, had his knife ready. I don't know how he got it out so quickly. It seemed to have

80

materialized in his hand. He sat there, tipping his chair back, a dog-like grin on his face. In jumping to my feet I had hit the table and Sarrasin's glass had gone over. The wine spread over the rough-grained wood in a dark pool.

"Sit down and be sensible," said Sarrasin.

Sophie got a rag from somewhere and began to mop up the wine. And then it happened, the thing I had been waiting for. She was close to me and for a second, hidden from them, her hand touched mine. Just a touch and the swift movement of an eyelash as she straightened up. And it was all there, all the love and faith between us, and I knew that never again would I question them. There was a great shame in me that I had ever doubted them.

"Go to bed, Sophie," said Sarrasin.

She moved to the only other door in the room. As she opened it she paused and turned towards Paviot. Outwardly she was dead to me again. Calmly she asked, "Did you kill a policeman?" She might have been asking if he had watered the geraniums, put the cat out or remembered to pay a bill, her voice just touched with that hoarseness I knew so well. But underneath the acting, the indifference, I knew there must be anguish, anguish for an unknown policeman and anguish for me.

Paviot shook his head. "I pricked him, no more. Our friend here exaggerates. Understandably, he is a little over-wrought."

She stood there and I loved her. She was with them, but she was for me. I didn't like the part she had to play, didn't understand all that lay behind her prudence, but I did understand the truth that was between us and it gave me hope and strength.

For a second her eyes were on me then she went through into the other room, closing the door on us.

Sarrasin said, "If you do not wish to eat and you have had enough wine, you should sleep." He nodded to a mattress that lay on the floor against the far wall. There was another mattress close to the door of Sophie's room.

I got up and went over to the mattress and he went to the main door and bolted it. I sat down on the mattress and was suddenly aware of my stiffness and fatigue. Maybe because of the long trip over the hills we had just made, I suddenly recalled my meeting with Drexel in Wales. For his sake, and gladly, I had given up the dream of Songa Manara. The choice had brought me trouble, but it had also brought me Sophie. The rough and the smooth . . . the fascinating unpredictable future. Once I had seemed to have it all mapped out. Now I was groping in the dark.

His back to me, Sarrasin said, "Tomorrow you shall have better quarters. Also, monsieur, take my advice—don't give any trouble. We are well able to deal with it."

As he turned and faced me, I remembered the bruise on Sophie's shoulder. I said, "If the chance comes I'll cause trouble. All I hope is that you're at the other end of it!"

Ignoring me completely, he went on, "Paviot—you sleep first. I watch."

He sat down by the table, hoisted his legs on to it and folded his arms across his chest; big, solid, all man, with a close-cropped head like a Roman gladiator, a Spartacus formidable with brutality and intelligence.

Paviot dropped on to his mattress and I lay down on mine, loosening my shoe-laces to ease my feet. I closed my eyes and I could hear them breathing. I hadn't behaved very well. I should have matched their sureness with reserve.

I woke once or twice during the short hours that were left before daylight. Each time either Sarrasin or Paviot was awake and watching, and the oil lamp on the table was turned low.

* * *

Sophie, humming to herself, made breakfast for us the next morning. We had coffee, fried eggs and then peach confiture on bread. I had one over-riding thought; to get away. Paviot did not eat much, but George ate enormously. I was reminded of Drexel's appetite. Thinking of Drexel was unpleasant. He was carrying so much. Not only the collapse of his mission and the loss of Jabal . . . but now he would have my disappearance as an extra load. No matter how much he had let me down before Didier, I knew he would feel responsible for anything that had happened to me.

After breakfast Paviot and George just sat outside the door on the veranda where they could see me, and Sophie moved around the hut packing things away. I wondered where we were going from here and I knew I would not find out by asking.

A couple of hours after breakfast, I heard the sound of a car engine. I went to the door. Sarrasin put his arm across it barring my way but not stopping me from looking. Paviot went down into the clearing and from behind me I heard Sophie say:

"Who is it?"

"Gerard and Fargette," answered Sarrasin.

At this moment not one but two vehicles came into the clear-

·ing from the track beyond the trees. One was a small Fiat, shabby and dusty, and the other was one of those large wine tankers which they use in the Roussillon for transporting cheap grade wines. In England they use the same type of thing for petrol and milk. They stopped outside the hut. The man who got out of the cab of the wine tanker I knew. He had been in the row-boat with Sarrasin and he had driven the Citroën off last night. I had not realized before how small he was. Little more than four feet with rather sticking-out ears and a screwed-up, monkeyish face, an old-young face. He had some slight deformity of the left leg for he walked with a quick little lilt always to the left as though there was a large stone in his shoe.

The man from the Fiat was an individual whose chief characteristics were worry and dandruff. Although I wasn't going to like any of these people I felt vaguely sorry for him. He came across with quick, short steps to Paviot and in a low voice began to talk to him, shaking his head, rolling his eyes and now and again patting one hand against his forehead. I could almost see the dandruff falling from his stringy grey hair on to the dusty shoulders of his baggy blue suit. He must have been about sixty, thin-faced and white and everything suggesting that he had been shut away in a cellar too long. Worry, I decided, would probably kill him in the next five years.

He was ticking Paviot off about something and it was so much water over the mill-wheel as far as Paviot was concerned.

Then he came pitter-patter up the veranda steps and was greeted by Sarrasin.

"Bonjour, Gerard. Tout va bien?"

He rolled his head and, even if things had been going well, it was clear that as a matter of principle he would not admit it.

"It's this dirty Paviot. Why can't he watch his hands?"

Behind me I heard Sophie's voice.

"Is it the policeman?"

"Yes, it's the policeman. They think he'll die."

I heard Sophie's breath drawn in sharply.

George said heavily, unconcerned, "We all have to die. Paviot was handicapped by the dark."

Then Gerard saw me. At once I was a fresh worry but he remembered his manners. He gave me a nod and said:

"Monsieur Fraser. You have, I hope, been treated well?"

I shrugged and he gave a suspicious glance round him at George and Paviot. I said, " 'Treated well' is a nice phrase. But I suppose you would call it that. What's the tanker for? We haven't run out of wine."

83

He thought the joke was in poor taste and maybe it was. Not talking to anyone in particular he said, "We must go. . . . I do not like this openness. One never knows . . . some forester, a boy. Fargette, open that thing up!"

I saw Fargette climb to the top of the tanker and begin to unscrew the wing nuts that held down the large filler cap.

Sarrasin seeing me watch this operation said, "That is for you. It is a good way of travelling incognito. A little stuffy perhaps."

He touched my arm and I moved towards the tanker with Paviot on one side and Sarrasin on the other. So far they had not given me a chance and they were not giving me one now. The revolver and the knife were out in the open. Gerard fussed on ahead and I heard him call to Fargette:

"You've got the little air thing fixed? He must breathe." It was nice of him, I thought, to want me to go on breathing.

Fargette grunted and half raised a hand as though he were brushing away a fly. Gerard must have been hell to live with. I had met his kind before. Underneath the fuss and anxiety—and maybe the cause of it—was a clear-sighted, cold intellect, taking in so much more than other minds did of any situation. If he had been a fool he would have had no respect from these people. They might brush him off but they did as he said without question. As I climbed up to the top of the tanker, I heard him direct Sophie and Paviot to travel with him in the Fiat. I suppose I could have refused to climb up and lower myself down into a space little bigger than a barrel but, as that would have meant a crack on the head and being tossed into the thing, I preferred to go under my own steam.

When my feet touched the bottom my head was still out of the small trap door. Fargette gave me a wink and said, "You will have to bend your legs, monsieur. You will not travel well. However, it will not be unendurable."

I said, "The best wines never travel well."

He roared with laughter, was reprimanded about making a noise by Gerard, and then began to screw me down, but I could hear him chuckling to himself. Somehow, it was comforting to find someone who would laugh at a poor joke. Of them all I decided I disliked Fargette least.

From my watch, which I checked getting in and getting out, I know I was in that tin can for two hours, but how far we went or how fast I could not possibly judge. Cooped up there, jolted from side to side in the darkness, I lost all sense of speed or direction. For all I knew we might have been travelling round and round a bumpy circuit. In fact I imagined we were for I swear we kept on hitting the same bump, slewing round the same sharp corner time after time. I did not like it. Even though I knew it was going to end and I should see daylight again, I found it hard to hold down my claustrophobia. By the time it was over I was bruised and shaken and, I think, a little drunk from the wine fumes.

I think Fargette and Sarrasin must have expected this for when we stopped and they released me, they helped me down to the ground and stood by me, holding an arm each. I shut my eyes against the sunlight and the spinning world and then cautiously, as things began to steady, I opened my eyes. The first thing I saw was a magnificent tree covered with purple blossoms. It was like a great fountain, foaming with colour. Although I knew its name, at that moment I could not recall it.

I took a couple of steps forward and my guards released me. The giddiness went rapidly. Looking up above and beyond the tree I got my first sight of Chateau Minerve, though it was not for a long time that I knew its name. That morning I only got a jumbled impression of it. It was a yellow-grey plug of towers and battlements, of steep walls cut by narrow windows. . . . It should have had banners flying from its highest tower, and knights and fine ladies strolling across the neat parterres. A gravelled causeway spanned the moat which ran around it; but the moat was dry and full of shrubs and flowering cherry trees. We went through a large gateway into a courtyard with a well in the centre. Behind the well was a large marble statue of Minerva, the goddess of wisdom, wearing a helmet and carrying a shield. She was severe-faced and seemed to frown at me and I told myself she had a right not to like me. I wasn't doing very well in her subject. A large vine covered one of the walls of the courtyard. We entered a hallway that echoed to our footsteps like a museum. I noticed suits of armour, old paintings and weapons and a fine stretch of Persian rug. Monsieur Gerard and Paviot were there. They watched us pass as though we were another party looking over some ancient monument, but at the last moment Gerard had to impose his concern on us. He called:

"See that he has everything, for shaving, clean clothes." And then, as we were going up the stairs, "And yes—cigarettes, also. He must be comfortable."

We went up three floors. He must be comfortable, I thought. It was odd. That—and the fact that Sarrasin had his revolver on me, and Paviot his knife to hand, and both ready to use their weapons if I made any trouble.

We stopped in front of a large oak door with an enormous lock and two heavy bolts top and bottom. Fargette opened it for me with a quick little hop-skip, gave the suggestion of a bow, and waited for me to enter. I stood there, looking across a great room to a wide window which opened on to a rectangle of pale blue sky. At that moment, from somewhere above us, faint but unmistakable, I heard the sound of a mouth-organ. The tune was a favourite one of Jabal's. Something about *Frim Fram Sauce. . . .*

> *I don't want fish cakes and rye bread.*
> *You heard what I said.*
> *Waiter, please serve mine fried,*
> *I want the frim fram sauce. . . .*

Sarrasin gave me a little push and said, "He is very musical."

I said, "Monsieur Gerard probably insisted you should bring his mouth-organ to make him comfortable."

The door was shut, locked and bolted on me and I heard Fargette laughing.

CHAPTER IX

CHATEAU MINERVE, except for the fact that I was locked in my room most of the time, might have been an hotel and myself a guest anxious for seclusion and rest, too shy or toffee-nosed to use the main dining-room, and having all meals sent up. I had a room which seemed as big as Piccadilly Circus and the likeness was increased by a black marble statuette in the middle of it. It was not Eros, but a grinning-faced faun in woolly pants. Part of the room had been partitioned off and converted to a bathroom and toilet. The water from the hot tap was boiling and whenever I turned it on I could hear the pipes singing and bumping in the walls. There was a four-poster bed with faded green silk hangings and a silver-thread counterpane. Over the open fireplace was an oil painting of some forbidding eighteenth-century bishop in mitre and full canonicals. He was holding up a disapproving hand at the faun statue who obviously didn't care a pagan damn. On one of the other walls was a painting of a sad-faced, anaemic-looking woman with a tower of white-powdered hair and unnaturally high, rounded breasts from which the paint was flaking badly. At the end of the first day I knew practically every detail of the room from the number of tiles on the floor to the places in the red and gold wall-paper where the pattern had not been properly matched when it had been put up.

There was one window and this I was free to open; but it offered no liberty. The chateau was perched on the top of a high crag that overlooked a deep river gorge. Below me the walls fell sheer for about sixty feet and below that there was a steep cliff face for another hundred feet and then a broken, boulder-and-tree-studded slope so sheer that the trees looked as though they had no time for anything but the business of hanging on. There was not a road or a house to be seen . . . just the dark line of river below and then a sweep of wild mountain country. I could not place my whereabouts at all, except that the country was obviously Pyrennean. For all I knew, we might be over the Spanish border.

Fargette brought me my meals that first day, and there was always Paviot or Sarrasin waiting outside in case I tried to jump him. We had no conversation.

During the afternoon Monsieur Gerard came in to check that I had everything I wanted. They gave me clean linen, another jacket and a pair of trousers, shaving gear, some books to read and a carton of *Lucky Strike* cigarettes. But, most astonishing of all, before he went Monsieur Gerard produced a bottle of whisky, *Vat 69*.

"It is to be hoped, monsieur, you will give no trouble. We do everything we can for you. . . . Please behave, and in the end you will thank us."

I was left wondering what the hell to make of that. His anxious, almost pathetic manner had a strange effect on me. It was hard not to believe that I was the one who was at fault and they were being patient with me. Being locked up in a room for hours can produce an exaggeration in the thoughts, I'm sure if I had told him that I wanted *Players* instead of *Lucky Strike*, or *White Horse* whisky instead of the other, he would instantly have done something about it.

My last meal was brought at five and after that I saw no one until morning. But around six—and I was to notice this in the following days—I heard the sound of a car leaving the chateau. From six until the morning the place seemed strangely quiet and empty, except for the passage-way outside my door. By listening I could hear the slight movement and sometimes the breathing of a watcher outside.

Monsieur Gerard came along early the second day and asked me if I had slept comfortably.

I said, "I'd be more comfortable if I knew what all this was about."

I saw at once that I had shocked him. This was a fairy story, and there was a spell over us. Remarks like that could break the enchantment.

"Monsieur . . . in time, in time." He wriggled his fingers through his patchy grey hair and I felt I wanted to go and give him a brush down, pat his shoulder and tell him not to worry. That was one part of me. The other was cold, logical, still trying to work all this out, still wondering what their plans were for Jabal and myself, and not for one moment accepting anything he said as the truth. People who are prompt in their use of knives are ruthless, but people who use knives on policemen are more than ruthless; they either have to be very sure of themselves or desperate. None of these people struck me as being desperate.

"Who's getting Jabal?" I asked. "The Regent or the oil company?"

"Monsieur . . . !"

I really had broken the spell. It seemed to me that he turned and ran from the room, like Cinderella as the clock struck twelve, but all he left behind was a smell of tobacco, coarse *Gauloise Bleu*.

It was this second day that set the pattern for the others to follow. Not long after Gerard had gone Fargette opened the door and tipped his head to me to come out of the room. Paviot was waiting outside. The two of them stood a little way from me and although neither of them showed their weapons I knew they were there, warm with the touch of their palms, and ready for use.

I said, "What now?"

Fargette, who seemed to have more natural cheerfulness than any of the others, answered, "You are free to take some exercise. But, be wise, eh?"

I took him at his word. I was puzzled, but not ungrateful at being allowed to leave my room. I went down the main staircase and across the hall into the courtyard. They followed me, not too closely and not deceiving me by their casual manner.

The courtyard was full of sunshine. As I crossed towards the main gate into the gardens I looked up at the statue of Minerva. I don't know whether it was some trick of sunlight or whether seen from this side it was some vagary in the sculpturing, but she seemed to have a softer, kinder aspect. When I had first seen her she had frowned, disapproving of me; now she was indulgent and understanding.

I was almost at the gate when a door banged away on the left. I turned and saw Sophie move quickly across the court towards the hall entrance. She looked at me and then quickly away.

I soon found that some parts of the grounds were closed to me. If I tried to move down a path that led towards the boundaries of the grounds then either Paviot or Fargette would move up ahead of me or they would call a gentle reprimand. It was all done unhurriedly, almost off-handedly, and anyone watching us would never have guessed that they held hidden guns and knife ready for use if I proved intractable.

There was a little terrace to one side of the chateau, a stretch of gravel set with iron chairs and tables and overlooking the gorge. Behind was a wide camomile lawn with a large ornamental pool in its centre. We sat down at one of the tables after we had walked around a bit. Paviot rolled himself a cigarette and ignored me, but Fargette was quite ready to talk. I think that first morning we talked mostly about films. He was a great cinema-goer and loved romantic, musical films. Now and again when I got a chance I tried to pump him or slip in a question which might give me something more definite to go on, but he just screwed up his monkey face, pushed his tongue in his cheek and said, "*Vietato entrare, signore.*" It was the only thing he gave away about himself, that he spoke Italian as well as French. Paviot sat there listening to us, tipped back in his chair, eyes half closed against the sun, seeing how close he could let his ragged cigarette droop to his chin.

We had been there about fifteen minutes when there were footsteps on the gravel behind us. I slewed round, smiling to myself as I saw how my movement brought Paviot's hand to his pocket. Sophie was coming towards us with a tray.

She looked fresh and very lovely, in a white blouse, a green skirt, and with a bloom on her bare arms and legs where the sun touched her skin. I felt my love rise inside me like a bird taking flight.

She set down the tray. Coffee and biscuits. She might have been a waitress and this a high-class country hotel. Even though I was sure of her, the whole set-up puzzled me and I would have given anything for the chance to be alone with her, to find out what it was all about, to learn what held her to these people and what their plans were.

Paviot said, "What is for lunch?"

"A cheese soufflé and then cutlets," she replied.

Fargette nodded approvingly, began to pour my coffee and said, "Sophie makes a cheese soufflé like a summer cloud. I taught her how." He touched her on the arm affectionately.

She smiled at him and then, as she turned away, her eyes met mine. It was all I needed. I watched her as she went back to the chateau. And even in the midst of this confusion and inimical politeness, I found myself glad that I was here, near her. I didn't know what was going to happen to me. There was a barrier between Sophie and myself, but one day—and the chance must come—I was going to break through.

At that moment there was the sound of a mouth-organ. It came from high up, thin and not very clear.

I looked up and back to the chateau and in a few seconds I had picked out Jabal. He was leaning over one of the crenellated battlements of a tower and gazing down at us. Just behind him I thought I could make out the head and shoulders of Sarrasin.

I raised my arm and waved to him, but though I could see

he was looking at us, he made no acknowledgment. Maybe, I told myself, at that distance he did not recognize me . . . but I did not believe this.

I finished my coffee, trying to fit all this together; the way they were treating me, this chateau . . . the whole confused business—and I got nowhere.

Just before lunch they took me in. I got the other side of Minerva's face as I crossed the courtyard. Cold and severe and obviously contemptuous of me for not being able to work the thing out for myself.

Sarrasin brought my lunch; a big, relaxed figure in a dirty singlet and canvas trousers. He said not a word to me, but his eyes were on me the whole time. We had no need of words. We knew exactly what was between us. One day, if we were lucky—and I am sure we would both regard it as luck—we should be loosed against each other. It was an unspoken, private understanding and we neither of us wanted to be disappointed.

If the morning had been strange so was the afternoon. I lay on my bed most of the time and for about two hours just after lunch the most puzzling noises echoed through the place. They seemed to come from the courtyard. I could hear people laughing, unrestrained, hearty laughter, and after a time I could even pick out the laughs: Sophie's husky but feminine and finishing in a little trickle of sound, Sarrasin's booming away and occasionally a short, gasping noise that might have been Gerard or Paviot. And with the laughter came the sound of dogs barking. Again and again the barking broke out, excited, frantic, then came silence, and then again the laughter and the barking. After a time there was no sound of dogs, but only voices and a persistent *thud, thud*, then silence, then *thud, thud,* then voices and silence again to be broken by more *thuds*.

At five Paviot brought me my evening meal.

Without any hope of an answer, I said, "Why don't they let me down to join in the afternoon fun?"

To my surprise, he pulled his knife from his pocket and with a glance at Fargette, who stood by the door, he said, "I wish they would." He laughed, flicked the knife open and ran his finger down the blade. Fargette flapped a hand at him, made an angry sound in his throat, and Paviot put the knife away. Then he picked up my empty tray and was gone.

An hour later I heard the sound of a car starting and then the chateau was silent, except for the quiet breathing of whoever was on guard outside my door.

It was a long time before I got to sleep that night. I didn't know what the hell it was all about. Quite clearly, I decided, they had probably rented this chateau for a hide-out while they held Jabal. None of them gave me the impression of belonging here. They would have rented it obviously under false names and with enough doubling back to prevent their ever being traced. But why were they holding me, giving me this quasi freedom? I knew too much about them to make it safe for them ever to release me. That meant they had to dispose of me. Why not do it right away? For the moment, since I sensed it was remote, I could not concern myself with my eventual fate—though Paviot's little act with the knife had for a second or two brought some reality into my situation. Why let me know Jabal was here, even see him, and . . . a hundred questions floated in my mind keeping me awake. That they had incriminated me with the police I could see, but after that. . . . Why all this? I had served my purpose.

The next day did nothing to make it any plainer. I was let out and this time I had Sarrasin and Paviot for guards. I took my stroll, was served with coffee and chocolate biscuits on the terrace, given a short serenade by Jabal—it was *Red Sails in the Sunset*—and then back I went to get the cold side of Minerva's face. Sophie had brought the coffee tray and for a few moments, ignoring me, she had stood chatting to Sarrasin, something about the charcoal brazier in the kitchen and a blocked chimney pipe that sent the fumes back to her . . . and I might have been a ghost. That afternoon there was the same hullabaloo from the courtyard and then at six the noise of the car starting, and then silence.

The following day I tried a few variations. Instead of going down to the courtyard I turned and began to make my way up towards Jabal's quarters. Gerard and Sarrasin were with me. In no time Sarrassin was on the stairs ahead of me, his face wooden, his great body blocking my passage.

I said, "I just wanted to put in a request for a favourite number of mine, *Lazybones*."

Gerard took my arm from behind, clicked his tongue like an old woman calling a hen, and down I went with them. Minerva gave me her going-out smile. Outside I tried to go round to the other side of the chateau, but again Sarrasin was in my way, and in the end I finished up on the terrace. When Sophie brought the coffee, I said to Gerard, "I'd much rather have an *apéritif*."

There was no surprise in me when he told her to bring out a bottle of Dubonnet and some ice.

I sat there sipping at my drink, and eventually Jabal came out, but I don't remember what he played for the thought had suddenly occurred to me that men who are condemned and wait for the day of execution are indulged. Any whim of mine was to be granted. The prisoner's last breakfast.

The afternoon was the same as always; laughter, barking dogs and that uneven *thud, thud.*

And so it went on. I often contemplated making a break while I was in the garden, but I knew I would not get five yards before I should have a bullet in my leg. There was a low wall round the chateau grounds and beyond this a rising slope of hillside thinly covered with cork oaks. A narrow, dusty roadway ran up to the iron gates in the wall, but I could see only about half a mile along it and then it twisted out of sight behind the hill.

But the truth was that it was Sophie who held me there making no attempt to escape. I could not go without talking to her, without having at least a few moments alone with her. Day after day I watched for my chance but I was too well guarded.

Then on the morning of the sixth day she came to me.

*   *   *

My door opened and she came in with the breakfast tray. I saw Fargette stand aside for her to pass. Then he gave me a wink and closed the door. Always before the door had been kept open.

Sophie came across to me and put the tray down on the table by the window. I stood to one side of it and, as she straightened up, she took from under her arm a bunch of newspapers and dropped them on to the window seat.

She said, "Papers."

Automatically, I said, "Thank you."

And there we were looking at one another. Her face was no longer a conventional mask. She was alive again, looking at me, knowing it was me. I saw the movement of her shoulders and breasts as she breathed and there was something laboured in the rise and fall as though she were conscious of unseen pressures bearing heavily on her.

I looked towards the closed door, thinking of Fargette.

She saw my look and understood it. It was curious how we were both held back by an odd embarrassment. It was as though years of separation lay between us and we had to get to know each other again.

Then, in her funny hoarse voice, the words seeming not to

93

come from her but to be diffused into the room from no fixed source, she said, "Fargette is my friend. . . ." Then urgently, the movement in her towards me already beginning, she went on, "Oh, David . . . I had to come."

But already I was reaching for her. The love that was inside me broke free. It was like an animal, a panther, swift and powerful, flashing out of the darkness into the sun, all light and strength and undying beauty.

"Sophie!" I cried. My arms were out wide and there was a sob in her throat. She came to me and was inside my arms and my hands were in her hair and her body was shaking, and I was happy and mad, angry and foolish, and nothing had any meaning for me except that she was there. I heard her voice full of my name and then moving into a torrent of words which slowly took meaning.

"That first night in the hut. . . . How could I trust myself to look or speak . . . to give anything to you. . . . And the stupid wine all over the table and you standing there. . . ."

I said, "I understood. I never doubted you." And it was true, for deep down there had never been any doubt.

She laid her cheek against mine and her voice came low:

"For them you have to be nothing to me. . . . Even now I'm full of fear."

I held her away from me gently and kissed her. I was like a boy who had got more than he expected on his birthday. I wanted to shout my happiness to the world. And then I said slowly, forcing myself back to a practical world:

"You never knew they were going to take Jabal?"

"No. Not until it was too late to warn you. I thought it was smuggling."

"What are they going to do with him?"

"Ransom him to the oil company."

At least that was something. It would only be money involved and Jabal would be safe.

"You must get out of this, away from them."

She freed herself from me and I knew what her answer was going to be. She looked as she had done the first time I met her, afraid, held down by her own weakness and fears.

She said, "I can't. Not yet. Believe me, David. You must believe me. Everything will be all right and we shall be together. . . . Nothing can happen so long as they never know what we are to each other. If they knew, they would never trust me. They would do something."

"To you?"

"Yes. They have so much as stake that they will take no risk."

"But Fargette already knows you are here."

"He is my one friend. I trust him."

"And me—what happens to me? You must help me to escape."

"No . . . no . . . that would do no good."

I looked at her not understanding.

"For God's sake, Sophie! I must get out. And you must go, too."

"No, David." She was adamant. "Please believe me——"

"You've got to help me. Why shouldn't you?" I reached for her shoulders to shake courage, sense, I-don't-know-what into her. But at that moment the door opened and Fargette put his head in.

"You said five minutes, Sophie. You want George to knock my teeth in?"

He stood there, his hand on the door, the other holding a revolver. As she went towards him I followed. He held the revolver a little higher and said, "Stay where you are, monsieur."

I watched her go and, at the last moment, she turned briefly and her eyes were on me, warm and dark and bottomless.

The door slammed. I heard lock and bolts go home. And I stood there. I don't know how long I stood there but it seemed imperative not to move until life was fully with me again. And when I did move I knew that nothing was going to keep me here. I was going to tear this place apart and be free, and I was going to grab Sophie from the middle of whatever dark web held her and take her with me. I didn't care what she was or what she had been or what she had done. All I knew was that she was mine. All romantic poetry made sense and I was in danger of jumping out of the window to try my new wings on a flight to the nearest *gendarmerie*.

*　　*　　*

I ate breakfast; surprised at the appetite I had, and then began to read through the papers. Not even they took the edge off my new optimism, though they should have done. There were copies of the London *Daily Mail* and *Daily Express* and from Paris *Le Figaro* and *Le Temps*. The news had broken that Prince Jabal, staying in France on his way back to school, had been kidnapped and that his tutor, David Bladen Fraser, while being taken to Perpignan for police questioning, had been either abducted, too, or rescued by his accomplices if, as it seemed, he had had a hand in the organization of the kidnapping. This line did not surprise me. Some of the papers were more definite about it than others. The English papers were very cautious what they said about me for fear of libel cases. But the French boys just let themselves go. There was no doubt in their minds. I was a kidnapper whose well-organized plan had come apart a little at the seams. One of them even said I had knifed a policeman. The *Daily Express* had an article about me written by an old army friend. It read like an obituary.

All over France the police were on the look-out for Jabal and myself; but it was thought that we had gone over the border into Spain or by this time were well away on the high seas. No destination was given. *Le Temps* had an article about Ramaut and the oil industry, but nowhere was the real political situation discussed and I could guess that government pressure was keeping the real truth hidden. There was no mention anywhere that the oil concession was due for renewal soon, and the reason for the kidnapping was felt to be mercenary. I could see how my abduction by Sarrasin had given strength to that point of view. I had also given Sarrasin and company a wonderful cover.

The most disturbing news item for me was a small stop-press paragraph in the *Daily Mail* which said that the policeman driver of the Citröen had died in a Perpignan hospital of his wound. Not only kidnapping, but murder, was at my door.

More than ever I wanted to get out of this place and clear myself. That morning as I took my stroll in the grounds I went over all the possibilities of escape. I could see no way of making it. If I could talk to Sophie again, she might help me. But I had a feeling that she would risk nothing that might give away our relationship. If I escaped with her help she would have to go with me. . . . I had a conviction that she didn't want me to escape; that out of love for me, fear for herself and loyalty to the men she worked with, she had seen some easy compromise in the future and was content to wait for it. Anyway, I fancied that the opportunities for me to talk to her again would be too few and distant to be of any help. I wanted to get away now.

After lunch I went all over my room, examining it. I had done this before, but I did it again. In a chateau like this part of the wall might easily have been boarded up to cover some old doorway. There was nothing. The walls were solid and the open fireplace, I knew, was never used for the chimney had been bricked up. For a time I wondered if I could get to work on the bricks and pick them away. It would take days to do this with

96

a fork or a knife and I felt pretty certain I would be discovered before I had finished the job.

I went to the window and looked out. It was not the first time I had leaned over the ledge and looked at the drop. Twelve feet below the window the face of the chateau was broken by a weathered cornice nearly six inches wide that ran along for about twenty yards and then disappeared as the front of the chateau angled back at a corner. What there was beyond this point I did not know, but I guessed that there was more of the chateau before the final turn was reached which would bring me out above the moat with a small drop to the rising ground of the gardens. I could get down to the ledge easily. I could walk the ledge. Not so easily, for it was weathered and crumbling and clearly unsafe in places. But it could be done and without more risk than an afternoon's climbing on Idwal Slabs. But I could only walk the ledge so far. A few feet to the right of the window a great length of the cornice had fallen away completely, leaving a gap about six feet wide. It was a gap that could not be jumped for I should be spreadeagled against the wall without room for such a manoeuvre. I knew that if I could cross the gap I would take the risk of what lay beyond. I leaned out of the window, staring at the break. What I wanted was a plank to place across it to give me one foothold.

I turned back into the room. If I started breaking things up Fargette would hear and come to investigate. I had already considered one of the planks from the window seat, but they were only about four feet long and ran back into the wall mortar. The only other things were the wooden columns that supported the canopy of the four-poster bed. They might be long enough. I might be able to detach one of them, but they were round and would roll the moment I put my foot on one. The picture of myself slipping and the drop that waited was something I didn't care to think about.

I spent the afternoon roaming about the room, poking my head out the window and eyeing the cornice and then coming back and staring at the bed. The pole would roll. It was madness. If I wanted to commit suicide all I had to do was to jump out of the window.

But I kept coming back and looking at the canopy supports. They were thin at the top and thick at the bottom. That would make the roll more certain.

Fargette brought me some food around five. I had no appetite for it. I was getting the feeling that it was today or not at all. This place had enchanted me. A heavy spell had been over it and me but now I had to break it or live for ever under its charge. I was a new man, restless, full of desire to get out of this place.

I smoked and finished the last of the whisky in the bottle. It was not enough to give me courage or rashness. I felt depressed. It grew dark and I switched the light on. And in the end I went to the bed and began to examine one of the supports just to prove to myself that I couldn't, anyway, get it off without a lot of noise. The top, I saw, was just socketted in to one of the canopy runners. The bottom. . . . I couldn't see how it went because of the mattress and bedcovers. I gave the mattress a heave over at the bottom—and there I had an immediate choice of six fine lengths of stout planking each about eight feet long.

I stood there knowing that luck is something you make for yourself. The bed-frame was a great shallow box, eight feet by four, and the base of the box on which the mattress fitted was made up of loose planks, just like the old army bedboards at the beginning of the war before things got soft. Good, stout, inch-thick oak planks. I decided to leave that night as soon as it was late enough.

CHAPTER X

IT WAS past midnight before I left. For two hours I had had everything prepared and I sat in the window seat smoking and watching the night. The moon was up behind the chateau somewhere so that the whole wall-face was in dark shadow. There was a blaze of stars and a warmish light wind. Below me was the grey and purple depth of the gorge and, very thinly, I could hear the sound of the river over its bed. I had been thinking about Sophie, wondering what it was that kept her tied to these people, and wishing that I had had time to ask her far more questions than I had. Also, with the thought that I might with luck soon be free, I was thinking of the coming interview with Drexel and Didier. I had a lot to tell them. Enough easily to convince them that I was innocent, but there were still elements in this affair which had me puzzled. Today, for instance, I had not heard the car leave. Neither had I heard the usual noise of laughter and barking from the courtyard. I was sure, too, that there were people in the chateau for until late I had heard them moving about. This had never happened before and, although I found a reason for it, it still left me in the dark. I worked out that today was Sunday. Why should things be different on Sunday—except that they usually are?

I had said to myself that I would wait until one. But at half past twelve I could stand it no longer. I had to move.

I half closed the window and wedged a chair on the window seat so that it rested against the lower part of the frame. To this I tied a rope length which I had made from the bed sheets and covers. The plank I tied to my back with cord from the curtains. It was an uneasy, awkward fit but it was the best I could do. I had trouble backing out of the window because of the plank. It hit me on the head and got in the way of my feet.

With one hand on the sill I gradually took the strain of my body with the other hand on the rope. The chair creaked and groaned, but it held. Then I had both hands on the rope and went down gently. They were good, stout, linen sheets and I felt happy so long as I had my hands on them. A rope is a wonderful comfort when you have a long drop below you. My feet touched the ledge and I slowly let my weight on to it. It held but I knew I was not going to have any comfort from it.

It was as crumbly and rotten as sandstone. It was dark in the shadow of the chateau, but the only eyes I needed were in my hands and feet. I reached out with my left hand and got a hold in a crack between the crudely cut blocks of stone. I waited for my breath to ease back to normal and then let go of the rope with my right hand. It was the most reluctant farewell of my life. The sheet swung away and then came back, brushing against my face. It didn't want to leave me. That went for both of us.

I found a hold with my right hand and there I was, spread-eagled hundreds of feet above the river, and the plank, unevenly balanced, came between my legs and tapped gently against the wall. Slowly I began to work my way along. I had a great temptation to go quickly. But I kept this down, moving one foot, one hand at a time and letting my weight gradually shift, testing each hold.

I made six feet and then, finding good hand-holds, I rested, letting the strain go in turn from each arm and leg. It was bliss. And then, from above me and to the right, I heard the clatter of something falling. I knew at once what it was. The chair had fallen back from the window seat. I knew exactly how much spare rope there was, and I knew that now, even if I went back, I would never be able to reach the end of it. I was out here and there was no return by my window.

I stood there with my face against the bare stone and I was frightened. I felt sick and hopeless. At the back of my mind had been the thought, hardly expressed but a comfort to reach for if I needed it, that at any time I could go back. But there was no going back now. And then I was angry, angry with myself and everything that had conspired to put me into this position. Anger is the best antidote I know for fear. But it needs watching.

I went on, too quickly, too violently, and suddenly a great flake of stone broke away from under my foot. For one moment I was clawing at the wall-face with a leg swinging over space. The board on my back hit the wall between my legs and then pivotted and crashed against my head. I swung out sideways and then back again. Somehow I got a hold and found my footing. I pressed myself against the stones and my breath was something between a sobbing and a whine. But it did the trick. I was sober; free of anger and fear. From that moment I became an automaton, allowing myself nothing but movement and keeping my mind blank.

I came to the break in the cornice. I did not trust the broken edge. I banged it with my foot, not wanting it to break back when the plank was on it. It held. For the other side I could make no test. I worked the plank around so that it was between me and the wall, one end resting on the cornice between my feet. I untied it from my waist and then worked a loop of cord to the end above my face. It was a manoeuvre I had done fifty times in my mind as I had sat up above. To my surprise it worked without a hitch. Holding the bottom of the plank in place with my left foot I let the top slip away from me along the wall-face, controlling it with the free cord from the loop in my right hand. It went down gently, a slow-moving radial from my left foot. It spanned the gap, edge upwards, and I tipped it over with my foot.

By the time I had finished every muscle in my strained body was trembling. I rested until the tension eased down.

I reached out, took a new hand hold and then slid my left foot out on to the plank. It sagged a bit and I heard the board grating on the broken edges. I moved my other foot on to it and then inched along.

I was in the midle of the plank, taking all the strain I could on my arms. The board grated and sagged beneath me and I was talking to myself, growling between my clamped teeth, "Don't hurry! Don't hurry!"

I forced myself to move more slowly, feeling my Adam's apple knocking in my throat like a faulty ball-cock.

I got over and I was myself again. The plank moved as the last strain came off it. It slipped and fell away into the darkness, but I never heard it hit anything. It must have landed in bushes or a treetop. I didn't care. I was over. What happened behind me was of no importance, for there was no return. My future lay ahead, along this rotten strip of ledge. It was good to have a future I could measure in minutes not years. I felt more capable of handling it.

Although my movements were automatic, I was free to think now. I got to the point where the wall-face angled back on itself. A gargoyle decorated the turning point of the cornice. It was some kind of animal, its head covered with bird droppings. I turned the corner and was in moonlight. And I could see what lay before me. The wall ran back and then out again, forming a sharp V. The other side of the V was in darkness and I could not tell how far the ledge went. I was sweating now and it was odd how the warm night breeze seemed cold to my skin. My fingers were cut and scratched from the rough holds I took and I could feel my right kneecap complaining about this work. That made me smile, for I remembered the army doctor who had fixed me up years ago when a bullet had cracked the cap for me.

'Climber, eh? Then don't ever trust it too long on a sticky traverse.' He should have been here now. The whole ledge was one long traverse. And the kneecap brought Drexel into my mind . . . that was the time he had saved my life. Maybe now—if I got away—I could repay a little of that debt. He'd get Jabal back . . . save his pride and reputation. I knew just how much he hated failure, just how much he needed the stimulus of success . . . it was food and drink to him, to all heroes. A jerk of pain in my knee drove Drexel from my head. . . . If my knee gave way now. . . . I tried not to think of it.

Four yards beyond the corner there was a window above the ledge. Just high enough for me to reach the sill and pull myself up. I could see too that the window was open, though the room beyond was in darkness. I wanted to go in. I told myself that I could easily find a way down through the chateau . . . but I didn't believe it. I rested under the window with my hands reaching up to the stone sill. It was a good hold and comfortable. All I had to do was to pull myself up. But I wouldn't. I was outside the chateau and I meant to stay outside. If I went back something would go wrong . . . the strength of a fetish takes little from reason. I rested and went on.

But I might have saved myself the trouble. When I got into the apex of the V I saw that the cornice finished. The out-running wall was bare and smooth. I wasn't even glad that I had an easy trip back to the window. I had made a decision not to use it and now it was being forced on me. I don't know what it was. . . . Perhaps the strain of being hung out there over that dark gorge with the black spikes of firs and pines reaching up for me and the lisp of the distant river shivering through the night. . . . Maybe I was a little light-headed and open to any omen or token of luck . . . but I knew I didn't want to go through that window.

However, fetish, desire, want or not-want, I had no choice. I went back and I hauled myself up. I swung my legs into the room and I sat there, staring at it, with my bottom hanging half over the drop outside. I didn't take in the room for a while. It was enough to sit with my muscles relaxed and take deep, sweet breaths of air without fear that my expanding chest would push me into space.

Nearly half the room was flooded by moonlight. And now I began to take it in. It was large, a cross between a study and a sitting-room. There was a big leather-topped desk, very neat and no papers on it. One wall was lined with books and against another was a wide, deep cupboard, an Italianate looking affair with painted door panels cut with open grill work at the top. Chairs, a round table with a bowl of fruit, a tall glass case full of china and a very fine spread of Savonnerie carpet from which the moonlight took all the colour, and then a tall Chinese screen that half-masked the doorway . . . a pleasant, reserved room, I thought.

I gave my knee a quick massage and then I started for the door. So far as I could determine this room was on the floor below mine. As I passed the round table, I stuffed an orange and an apple in my pocket, like a boy at a Sunday School treat. My throat was parched.

I was almost at the door when I heard the sound of voices and footsteps outside. Then, as a switch was thrown in the corridor, a thin edge of light came under the door.

I thought: this is it; this is why you shouldn't have come in through the window; and I started back. But as I went I was looking for alternatives to the open window. Now that I was in, I didn't want to go out again. The Chinese screen was no good. It was too near the door. I went to the cupboard and opened the first full length door. The space inside was taken up with shelves for linen. Hastily, as I heard the footsteps coming closer, I tried the door on the other side. There was a full length cupboard except for a small shelf at the top, a kind of cloak and hat place. I reached up and found the shelf was loose. I slipped it down and stepped inside, pulling the door as close as I could get it.

I was there with about ten seconds' grace when the room door was opened and the light switched on. I stood there and I found that I had a view of practically the whole room. On a level with my face the cupboard door panel had been cut into a fretted design of leaves, flowers and birds through which I could look.

Monsieur Gerard came in first. He went and stood by the round table and he was a pathetic sight. He was in a shabby old dressing-gown and bast slippers. The gown was made of grey feathers or towelling or something queer and he looked like a picture I had once seen of a young gannet, beaky nosed and big-eyed with worry. His whitish tufts of hair sprung upwards where he had run his fingers through them. But not in a hundred years would he ever feather up into any pleasing appearance.

He called out, half to himself, "Why does he come at night? Why at night? Why at all, and why at this time? It's wrong and it's dangerous. . . ." He beat one hand against the other and he was a bad advertisement for would-be kidnappers to join his school.

It was Sarrasin he was talking to. He came forward into my view and quite obviously he had not been roused from his bed. He was wearing a neatish grey suit and polished brown shoes.

He said, "Shut up!"

But he said it without any force, as though he knew it would produce no result.

Gerard began to pick at the end of his dressing-gown cord.

"What's he doing? Why doesn't he come?"

Sarrasin laughed. "He's having a drink downstairs. And he's talking to Paviot. At this moment Paviot is feeling very uncomfortable."

"And in a moment we shall."

"What does it matter? These things happen. He told me to get you up." Sarrasin went and sat on a corner of the desk and began to play with a paper knife. If Gerard was worrying his head off, it was clear that George Sarrasin was completely unruffled.

He said, "Karimba was much better today. But I don't get much time yet."

"And you won't until this is over. Then you will have time and money. Santa Maria . . . there are so many things we shall be able to do then with the money. Everything is falling to pieces and we have to take the cheapest . . . that's no way to get anywhere. All my life I have wanted to do it big and——"

"Yes, I know. Do not tell me what you have wanted to do. We shall do it. Attention . . . here he comes."

Sarrasin looked at Gerard and he smiled. It was not the kind of smile that would have encouraged anyone.

"Try not to enrage him," said Gerard.

"Idiot. It is already done," answered Sarrasin unconcerned.

I stood there, cramped in my cupboard, watching the room through my fretwork and I had forgotten my own predicament. Most of what they had said was double-dutch to me. Who was Karimba? Sarrasin's girl friend? But most important, for I guessed from the reference to Paviot that it was something to do with Jabal's kidnapping, who was this person that Gerard feared so much?

There were quick, energetic footsteps coming down the corridor. Then the door, which I could not see, opened and was slammed shut again. And then into my field of view came a man; a shortish, alert figure in an old raincoat, the collar turned up, and carrying a soft hat in one hand.

He went up to Gerard and he stood in front of him, angry, spoiling with fury, and he said:

"Damn you! When I give an order for something to be done I want it done my way! My way! Do you hear? And only my way!"

Cramped in my cupboard, I watched through the fretwork and I saw the glint of light on Sarrasin's paper knife as he played with it. I saw Gerard, seeming to wither and shrink before the blast of words, his thin hands plucking at the fluffy material of his dressing-gown, saw the sheen on the fruit in the bowl and on the blood-red spread of leather on the desk-top; and despair and hope, certainty and uncertainty warred in me.

It was Colonel Francis Drexel.

CHAPTER XI

I HEARD Gerard say, "But, Colonel, it was an accident."

I thought Drexel was going to strike him.

"I told you there was to be no violence!" The words were shouted, venomous. "Why the hell didn't you watch Paviot? You know what he's like with a knife. You——" he swung round towards Sarrasin and the skirt of his raincoat brushed against Gerard, who started back as though he had been burnt. "You were there. Why didn't you control him?"

Sarrasin dropped the paper knife, stood up and said calmly, more than calmly . . . the touch of insolence in his voice, "Paviot with a knife is his own man. What does it matter anyway? The policeman is dead and will recognize no one."

"I don't care a damn about that! Dead or alive it doesn't matter. What matters is that I said it was not to happen! If we're going to pull this off—things go my way! My way! Do you hear?"

There was a note in his voice I had never heard before, the shrillness of almost hysterical anger.

That was the moment when hope died in me. Until then I hadn't been sure. Drexel was devious and unfathomable in his ways. Until then I had been feeding my hope with thought that he was here on my side, that he was my Drexel . . . the knight in shining armour, playing some dark role. But not now. I stood there and felt sick, knowing that the policeman's death meant nothing to Drexel, that he saw in it only trouble and the fact that his plans, whatever they were, had been mishandled. I remembered then the reluctance that had been in me to come through the window. I felt cold and empty, drained of all life. And in my mind was only a wild regret that I hadn't slipped from the cornice into the oblivion of the gorge for I knew now that there are some things which, at any price, are better not known.

"But even so, Colonel . . ." Gerard drifted forward, one hand fluttering up to his loose hair, ". . . you should not come. Not here. It is dangerous. . . . Oh, so dangerous. . . ." His voice trailed off in a half-whisper.

"Stop whining to me about danger. I came to make you see that if you don't do as I say you'll put us all in danger."

106

"But someone might have followed you . . . seen you."

"God! Why do I have to rely on such an old woman? No one followed me. I'm on my way to Paris for a few days. I left my car on the other road over the hill and walked here."

"You go to Paris to see our friend about the arrangements with the oil company?" It was Sarrasin.

I shut my eyes. And I wished I could have shut my ears. I didn't want to believe what was happening. And if I had felt sick when they talked about the policeman, that was gone. I was filling with anger now. Anger, not against any person, but against the whole dirty sweep of things passing before me. It was all I could do to stay there. This was Drexel, my friend, the man who had once saved my life at the risk of his own. It was too awful. I was left with nothing but contemptuous rage. I could shut my eyes to put him out of my sight, but his bitter, almost hysterical, voice rasped in my ears. He was nothing but a sordid, unscrupulous kidnapper. It didn't matter that I could, even then, find reasons for his degradation. I had in me only an anger that was like an unbearable pain. His voice rang in my ears and there was a quality in it of meanness and fine frenzy, the edge and strain and stress of a man dedicated to a purpose created out of his own baseness and weakness.

"Yes. I'm going to Paris. And if there's any more nonsense, I'll cut down your share."

"Not my share!"

I opened my eyes. There was the room again, jig-sawed into crazy sections by the fretwork. Gerard, drooping and worried, was by the table and Sarrasin was standing a few feet from Drexel, not intimidated by him.

"Not my share," Sarrasin repeated.

"Be careful how you speak to me." Drexel's body stiffened and his voice was strange to me. There was a new passion and strength in it, and I hated it as I hated him and the thing which had happened to him. "You're in my hands—all of you."

Sarrasin shook his head. I hated him, too—that went way back, but against my feeling for Drexel it was now colourless. I could even like him a little for not fearing this man. At least he was understandably animal, a strong body, and greedy appetites and no scruples as to how he fed them. He was simple.

"No, Colonel." Sarrasin's face was unmoved; he was like a tower. "You are in our hands as much as we are in yours. So do not say things like that. We have followed your plan as well as we can. The policeman was an accident . . . but of no importance. The rest is as you said. Your friend is here safe. Jabal has seen him about the grounds, walking free, and he will think he is behind all this. But if there is any talk about cutting shares—then I do not promise to keep to the plan. There is another. It would be easy to slit your friend's throat and send Jabal back to the Regent where he will never talk. In fact, all along I have felt that the best plan."

It was a long speech for Sarrasin and each word came deliberately, full of weight and a little awkward as though he were unused to marshalling his thoughts into open speech.

"You are not paid to think." Drexel was pressing him hard. "You're paid to do as I say. Do as I say and everything will be all right."

"Yes, yes . . . if we do as the Colonel says it will be all right. That's so, isn't it, Colonel?" It was Gerard, poor, fluttering Gerard.

And that was odd. I would have said that I had enough on my plate; that alive or dreaming there was only room in me for one emotion, the angry disgust centred on Drexel. But part of my mind could hold Gerard and pity him. I was sorry for him because he was so lost. He was eaten up with worry from his own rashness. More than anything he wanted reassurance. Sarrasin had no weakness. And the weakness in Drexel had been turned into a perverse strength fed by his own cupidity. But poor Gerard had nothing, only an echoing, fear-haunted spirit.

"Don't be a fool." Drexel brushed Gerard away. "Of course it will be all right. In a couple of weeks we shall have the money. Nothing will lead to us and Jabal will be free, and everything he says will incriminate Fraser more."

"And Fraser?" Sarrasin was smiling. "You really trust your plan for him?"

"Of course I do."

"It sounds stupid to me. It leaves too much to him."

Drexel swung round, quick, terrier-like, all the hardness and vitality of the man working in his face and movements, and he came past the cupboard, pacing the floor, and I knew he must be holding himself in now, goaded by the calm opposition in Sarrasin. And there he was, not three feet from me, with all my future in his hands.

"It's the only plan," he snapped. "Fraser is my responsibility. Keep your hands off him. I know him and I know how to deal with him. When he comes round, he'll be at sea, on his way to South America, and there'll be two thousand pounds in his case. He won't come back. I know him as I know my own hand. I'm giving him a fresh start, a new name, money—and too much against him in Europe for him ever to show his nose here again."

Hidden there, silently watching this hideous scene, I began to understand so much . . . how Drexel had at first made me look careless, how he, Brindle, and the others had muddled me up until I looked criminally involved, and then the final move of rescuing me from Didier. My comparative freedom at the chateau was explained. Jabal had seen me, marked me down as a kidnapper and when he was free who would doubt his word that I was criminally involved?

I stood there listening . . . and the whole thing was a fantasy with cold truth and reason behind it. It was like suddenly discovering a new room in a house you know well. You can't believe it. But there it is. And inside the room is a stranger who looks like yourself. And you suddenly see that this is a you that you never suspected. Drexel had a blazing belief in everything he had said. And, in a moment of intense clarity, white-hot because it was born in the heart of my anger, I could see how right he was. He was telling something about myself that was true. What would I do if I woke on some tramp steamer with money, with a valid passport in another name, and with a new future ahead of me to weigh against all the weary complications and tortuous explanations and accusations that waited in Europe? For two days I would be mad to get back and clear myself. But after four or five, I would have counted the money and have known South America nearer and have been saying, "Oh, what the hell?" Going back was too much bother—and what would it get me? Already the newspaper publicity had pronounced me guilty. Professionally I would have to fight prejudice, and I would have Drexel and Jabal against me. I wouldn't have a chance of clearing myself. God, Drexel knew me, and how well he had worked it out, so that even his treachery was a favour to me. I suppose that was how he could do it, how he could stop himself from thinking about my feelings towards him. He was doing me a favour for which I would thank him. Part of my anger turned against myself for knowing that what he said was true.

But Sarrasin believed in one way only of making a man silent. "I would cut his throat. Cheaper and safer."

Drexel said nothing for a few seconds. He stood there, taut, strung up, a shabby figure in the grease-splotched raincoat, his tanned face wooden, lips tight-stretched across his teeth and his eyes were bright with a fierceness I had never seen before. Then he pulled an automatic from his pocket and he levelled it at Sarrasin.

Sarrasin made no move. But his eyes were measuring the

distance between them, the animal body was tensing and, without fear, he was feeling chance and time balance against the possible moment of attack. Only Gerard gave an anxious little cry that was wasted on them.

"Put one mark on Fraser," said Drexel icily; "put one foot out of line and I promise to fill your guts with lead. You and all the rest."

I suppose I should have been glad that he could feel like that. But I wasn't. I didn't want his protection now that the friendship between us had been killed. I stood there, staring out at them.

"As long as I get my money——"

"But of course you will get it. . . ." Gerard moved to Sarrasin and made a flapping motion at the Colonel to put away his automatic. "The Colonel is a clever man. His plan will work and we shall have the money. . . . Please, it is silly to show all this emotion. Bad feeling between us is unnecessary." He patted Sarrasin on the arm. "The Colonel says no violence. He is right!"

Gerard knew his Sarrasin. Maybe this was not the first time he had had to handle him. For a moment I thought Sarrasin was going to persist. Then, abruptly, the tension went from his body and he shrugged his shoulders. The expression he used for a smile touched his face and he said slowly, "All right. If the Colonel is sure. He wants to spend his money in peace. So do I. If he has no fear of Fraser—then why should I?"

They had settled it cosily at last. Would I or would I not let them down? The Colonel was right. I would not. I did not listen clearly to what they talked about now. It was a dry, leaf-skittering sound against the hammer of my thoughts. No fear of Fraser? How wrong they were. Two hours ago when I had been safely locked up the plan was perfect. Beautiful . . . all the little things that had happened at the Villa Maruba; Drexel, or Brindle, I guessed, pinching my key. Sarrasin, Paviot and Sophie making my acquaintance . . . everything ticking over nicely for Drexel. He was not going to hurt anyone. Jabal sold to the oil company. I wondered what price they had set. High, if they could afford to give me two thousand. Me—set up for life. (The successful kidnapper Fraser collects his money and disappears.) And Drexel back to his London flat, to a retirement with honour and luxury; and the others—what little dream world had Gerard and the rest planned? But, whatever it was, no one was to be hurt. No wonder Drexel was mad at the death of the policeman. It had spoilt his plan, the essence of which was to have been non-violence, and it had made it awkward for him to see himself in the role of a beneficent patron. It was all I could do not to take a chance and walk out there and then and begin to kick the heart out of him. If I nursed the hope that one day I would come to grips with Sarrasin it was only an idle pipe dream compared with the passion that filled me now to come up with Drexel and be free to speak and act. Sarrasin had made me feel unchristian. Nothing new. Drexel made me feel lethal for the first time, and I was anxious to be blooded.

When I came back to them, they were moving out of the room. The Colonel was returning to his car. He'd left it on some road over the hill. He didn't know it but I was going with him.

I suppose because now I had the whole thing in my hands practically, I should have been cautious. But there was nothing of finesse in me. I'd come back through the window knowing that I shouldn't. Come back to break my heart over a dead faith. If it sounds hyperbolic it's because it was. Strong emotion, the final dirtiness of the human spirit can't be eased by under-statement. Not by me, anyway: schoolmasters with English literature as their subject are seldom laconic. There was no need for caution. All the bad luck coming to me had arrived cash on delivery.

They went out, leaving the light on and the door open. I gave them one minute and then I left the cupboard. Outside, the corridor was empty, but I could hear their voices from the hallway at the bottom of the stairs.

The top of the stairs was in darkness. But below, the hall was dimly lit. They stood there for a while, talking, and I moved down the wide stone steps and found shelter in the shadow of one of the suits of armour that lined the steps at intervals. Hidden there, I waited. I knew exactly what I was going to do. There was no choice. I was going after the Colonel. I was going to be face to face with him. He was going to know I knew and when all that had been cleared from between us he was going to know that I meant to throw him to the crowd. The shout of the crowd in praise of a hero is one thing, but against the noise that goes up as the dishonoured hero falls it is no more than the sigh of stale air from a pricked balloon. I didn't like myself for it. I never would like myself for it, I knew. But in that moment I knew I was going to do it. And having settled that, I felt free and my mind eased its pace and for relief began to take little trips up side paths. I thought of Brindle. Didier had said my crack over the head could have been part of an act. He had the wrong man. Brindle had played that part. And I saw how Brindle's love for Drexel was stronger, stranger than mine. He had been able to follow him anywhere without question. But love was the wrong word for it: Must be. It was sorcery. In the past I had felt the spell myself. . . . But not now. There was not even the finest drawn hair-thread of sentiment remaining between myself and Drexel.

I heard the door shut and then footsteps of Gerard and Sarrasin coming up the stair. Gerard was doing all the talking, quick, fluttering words that set up echoes in the lofty stairway which beat like bats' wings against the dark vaultings.

"Oh, dear. Oh, dear . . . how nearly you provoked him. Why? Why do you do these things? You know his ways are good, but always you set up against him."

"He is English. I dislike him."

"Stupid. Look at him and see him as money. We need it so we do as he says. Oh, la, la . . . tonight we are as poor as crows. But soon." Then, his tone changing, unexpectedly hard and brittle. "That Paviot. Maybe it is his throat should be cut. He causes this trouble."

"No man takes a knife to Paviot." Sarrasin laughed, and they were passing me, hardly seen, a disturbance of the dark air rather than form.

Their voices echoed away from me and then all was silent. I went down into the hall. The outer door to the courtyard was unlocked. I slipped through it and keeping in the shadow of the walls made my way to the arch that led to the causeway over the dry moat. Minerva was white and softened by the moonlight. She gave me the gentle side of her face. But I didn't want it. There was no charity in me. Cold, hard justice was my want. I was after Drexel and there was not a sliver of compassion in me. War-like and stern—that was the Minerva I wanted as a girl-friend. I hurried on for I did not want to lose Drexel. I need not have worried. As I edged into the gateway, I saw him.

The gravelled space beyond the moat was bathed in moonlight. At the foot of the causeway a ragged plume of shadow was cast by the large tree with purple blossoms which had been almost the first thing I had seen when I had been helped out of the wine tanker, a large, splendid tree rich with flowers.

Drexel was standing just on the edge of the patch of shadows. From the movements of his hands and arms I could see that he was filling his pipe. I watched, waiting for him to move on. He struck a match and one side of his face came up in livid yellow colour. Faintly on the night breeze I caught the fragrance of the tobacco smoke coming to me. It was a smell I knew so well and instantly it evoked a hundred pictures of him in my mind, and none of them was wanted. Each one was a bitterness now to me.

He tossed the match away and began to move across the gravel and as he passed under the tree, I suddenly remembered its name, and that too was a bitterness for me: *l'arbre de Judas*. The Judas Tree.

I went after him and I knew now that whatever risk I had taken in the house, I could take no risk with him. His eyes and ears would serve him well. One wrong move and he would be prickly with suspicion. His whole life had conditioned him to walk watchfully.

He did not go down the drive to the gate. He went right-handed across the camomile lawn and through a small shrubbery. I kept well behind him, marking his passage by the slurred foot-steps on the dew-heavy grass. He climbed the wall and disappeared. I gave him headway and then climbed it at another point in case he should already have sensed he was being followed. He was about a hundred yards ahead, moving up the sloping cork-tree studded hillside and I had to admire the way he followed his instincts. He went from one patch of tree shadow to another and there was never a sound from him. Thin on the air behind him was the trace of his tobacco smoke.

I followed him. From the top of the slope the ground dropped away down a rough hillside to the bottom of a small valley. The far side of the valley was steep and wooded with young birches and pines, and here and there I could see great shoulders of rock face thrusting out from the trees. I let him get into the wood before I started down the open slope. There was little cover for me and he might well turn in some break of the woods and look back to see me. But now I did not care. We were out of sight of the chateau and had the night and the woods to ourselves. A large white owl came drifting across the slope and from somewhere in the hills a night-jar screeched. It was good to be out and away from the chateau, to be moving somewhere and to know what I was going to do. I think I was calming down a bit, too.

There was a narrow, deep-cut of stream at the bottom of the valley. I jumped it and the soft thump of my feet on the far bank stopped the calling of the frogs. Where Drexel had disappeared into the trees there was the beginning of a small path. I followed this and, as I went, I took out my Sunday-school treat apple. My mouth was parched and I ate it greedily.

Someone had been working in the wood, cutting down the young birches and sawing them into small lengths which were stacked in piles in some of the clearings. They were posts to be used for staking the vines. After a time the path swung out to the right and then went steeply up over a shoulder of one of the big rock outcrops. For a while I had to use my hands to climb and in the bright moonlight I could see the marks of Drexel's passage, the disturbed earth of the path, the long smears on the dew-thick turf; and steady in my nostrils was the tang of his tobacco.

When I came to the top of the great rock I stopped, my head on a level with it and survey the flat plateau carefully. I didn't want Drexel to surprise me. The surprise was to come from me.

It was a wide, flat space, dotted with myrtle bushes and here and there the tall, straggly growths of wild white lupins. Away to the right the rock broke away in a ragged fall of about fifty feet towards the trees banking the lower slope of the valley. To the left there was a dark palisade of pine trunks. Drexel's footsteps ran evenly marked on the short wet grass right across the plateau to the trees on the far side.

I pulled myself up and began to move across. I was almost on the far side and about to enter the trees when I heard a movement behind me. A voice said:

"Turn round and come back with your hands up."

I knew the voice and I knew what had happened and had to concede admiration for the man. In some uncanny way he had sensed he was being followed. That can happen. Just as in a crowd you can be aware of someone's eyes on you. He had gone right across the plateau, his steps a marker for me, but once there he had doubled back through the surrounding pines to the left and was now behind me.

I raised my hands slowly and turned.

He was standing a few feet out from the pines, the moonlight full on him. Against the tall trunks he looked smaller than usual, a pygmy figure full of threat. He had pushed his soft hat back from his forehead, the pipe was still in his mouth and his right hand held his automatic.

I began to walk towards him. When I was four feet from him he said:

"That's near enough."

I stopped. Cautiously, no expression on his face, strangers for the moment with nothing between us except the waiting tinder of violence needing only a spark to set it going, he circled round me and I felt him come up behind me and his hand ran skilfully over my clothes. I knew better than to try anything then.

I heard him step back and then he came round to my front and halted a wise four feet from me.

He took the pipe from his mouth, slipped it into his pocket and said:

"All right. You can lower your hands."

I dropped my arms and reached to tuck in the loose material of my shirt that had pulled about my waist in raising my arms.

At once, he said, "Keep your hands in the open."

Then after a pause he said, his voice old and patient, "Do as I say, David, and you won't regret it."

It was odd how my name on his lips meant nothing. Always before he could touch me with my name. Not now. It was just a sound.

I said, "You've finished arranging my future. This is where I take over."

CHAPTER XII

WE stood there against the dark pine trunks and overhead there was a sky with stars and moon and needing only a trio of painted angels to be pure *quattro cento*. The air was sweet with night scents and the breeze was soft on my hot face. It was a good night, but not in my calendar. There was nothing good about it for me.

I picked up the wreck which had been our friendship, the broken, splintered mess of it and I began to throw the pieces away. Turning out an old drawer or a junk room there is always something to make you linger, to rouse nostalgia, to bring the hot sting of remembered goodness and happiness into the eyes. Maybe that's why that kind of job is never finished. But there was nothing like that here. I cleared the broken, useless junk from my heart without a qualm, without feeling except the anger which was cold and controlled in me.

I said, "You saved my life once. I wish you'd left me there in the desert."

He jerked a little, as though I had flicked at his face contemptuously. I didn't have to tell him anything, or explain anything. It was all in my face.

He said, "Turn round and start back for the chateau."

"No."

"Start."

The automatic came up a little and I saw it tremble in his hand.

"No. You can't tell me what to do. You played at God, but that's forbidden, and it's over. You took me and you arranged my life. South America and a new start. You took your reputation and the love people have for their heroes and you would have used them to pay your wine bills, your tailor and to give you a rich old age. But the game's over."

"Shut up!"

He came a step forward. I kept my eyes on his face and it was the face of a stranger to me. A hard, lean, tormented face and the eyes almost colourless in the moonlight, the pale blue washed away; cold, white eyes. I saw his mouth move as though he talked to himself, as though inside he was answering me; and I knew what was happening to him because it had happened to me an hour before. He was beginning to hate me. He was

116

beginning to throw me away . . . but it was harder for him because for his own sake he would have liked to save it all, to have kept the comfort of his godlike interference with my life to off-set the future he had ahead.

"Give me the gun," I said. "You're finished."

He laughed and it was like the coughing sound a sheep makes at night. "You're a fool," he said. "A bigger fool than I thought. I'm not finished. I'm just beginning. But, by God, if you get in my way I'll finish you. I don't know how you found all this out, but what have you got to grumble about? No harm's been done. Only good. You were never really happy as a schoolmaster. In your heart you've always wanted a fresh start. But you're too loose-gutted ever to have done anything about it. I went out of my way to put you right."

"Thanks for worrying about me. And what about the policeman? You gave him a nice future. You gave his wife and kids a nice future!"

"I never planned that. Things went wrong!" But he wasn't thinking of the *gendarme* even now. He was thinking of himself, of his precious plan.

I said, "If you play God, you mustn't let things go wrong. Give me the gun."

"This is my plan and it's not going to fail! I've waited years for this chance!"

He wasn't talking now. He was shouting. It was horrible. Out there on the moonswept plateau with its bare turf and clumps of myrtle, perched high up over the valley with the wind rattling gently at the black seed-pods of the lupins, there were the two of us, both full of hate but mine now pale and tired against his. It was pure nightmare and if there had been a price within my power to pay to stop it, to put the clock back, I would have paid it. But there was no going back. I stood there listening to him, and my eyes went from his face because it was agony to watch the spirit that moved there. He was not talking to me any more. He was talking to himself, to his *alter ego*, to the spirit which had possessed him and, while it would have been easy to say he was mad, tormented and warped by his past life into this new creature. I knew he was not mad. He was naked and I didn't want to look at him. He was being himself; his full self, showing the dark and savage side of his nature; the evil principle, which in all of us must be held down and disciplined, now clear in the light and vibrant with a fierce vigour.

"It's not going to fail! What do you know about me? What do you know about what goes on inside here——" he smacked at his chest, and if it had not been tragic it would have been funny. "For years I've been a hero. I've walked the tightrope and risked my life. I've put my hand in the fire and held it there. I've seen everything I had when I started slowly destroyed. I had ideals and I let them roll in the gutter to serve a handful of officials. I had pity but I killed men who didn't even know my name or that death was settled for them. I had health and I saw it go . . . malaria, typhus. The man who stands here now isn't the man who started out." He paused, panting; his breathing an anguished sound across the still night.

"I hate your guts," I said. "Do you hear? It's me. The man who was your best friend saying it. I hate your guts."

"Don't throw your hate and your disgust at me," he shouted. "I did that to myself years ago. And what have I got from it all? A few pence, the niggardly thanks of the Foreign Office. What *have* I got? A good name on one side and on the other a mass of debts. A rich past and a miserable future. . . . To hell with that! To hell with you! I'm going to have a future. I'm going to have money. I'm going to have my name and a rich retirement. I've earned it in a thousand shabby ways. I'm going to have it. Do you hear? And, by God, I'll finish anyone who gets in my way!"

His left hand came up to steady the one with the automatic and I saw the soiled linen of the bandage he still wore round it. I could have cried for there was that happening inside me which I could neither welcome nor hold down. I didn't want it, but it came. It was as though I saw all of his life laid out before me . . . and the misery of it tore at my heart. He had taken too much from life. It had battered and warped him. He'd given so much of the good in him that now only the bad remained. And because of that, because I could see how it had brought him to this moment, what he had done to me was unimportant for the real evil lay in what he had done to himself. In that moment I had nothing but compassion for him but I would not give it full life. I could not.

He said, suddenly calm, "You've got no choice, David. You're going back to the chateau. Even now we can arrange something. One day, maybe, in South America you'll thank me."

"I won't go to the chateau."

"I shall count five. After that I shall shoot you in the leg. You'll lie here until I get help to carry you back."

"You can do what you like," I said. "But it won't save you."

He began to count and from the tone of his voice he might have been checking off stores in a quartermaster's office.

"One.

"Two.

"Three."

I listened to him and I knew what I was going to do. When he said, "Five," I was going to jump and he was going to shoot. He might get my leg or my heart in the movement. I was not fool enough to have no care which it was, but there was that in me which left no choice. Sometimes we can only go one way. We have no choice.

He said, "Five."

And I jumped for him. I saw the spurt of flame, felt and smelt the quick reek and sting of powder like a handful of dust thrown suddenly into my face. I did not know it until later but the bullet passed between my left arm and my side tearing away and scorching the stuff of my jacket. I got my hands on him and we both went down under the momentum of my body. As I hit the ground he slipped sideways from me and clubbed me across the forehead with the snout of the automatic. But even as it hit me, my hand went up to his wrist and I held on as we twisted and rolled across the plateau.

For all his age he was strong and wiry, and his smallness made him difficult to hold. We struck and battered at one another, our heels tearing up the short turf, our bodies crashing through myrtle and lupin, and all the time his face was close to mine and his breath was hot against my neck and cheek. There was no word, no cry from us except the short, desperate sigh of throat and lungs for air. I bent his wrist back, putting all my strength into it, and sometime or other the automatic went because suddenly I realized that he had both hands free and tight about my throat. He hung on to me like a terrier gripping a large dog. I shook him and pummelled him and tried to rise but he held me down and we thrashed around, sometimes myself on top and sometimes Drexel. And the curious thing was that somewhere some part of me stayed aloof, wanting no share in this. It was an indecency which sickened me. It was like a son fighting with his father. That I should lay hands on Drexel was unthinkable. If anyone had ever told me I would I should have said that it was not in the nature of my hand to strike him. But the other me was there on the ground now, hitting out, savage, feeling his flesh beneath the shock of my fists and taking his violence, too, on my body. His hands tightened against my throat and I knew that, whatever plan had been formed in his mind when he had ordered me to return to the chateau, he had only one thought now. If he could kill me he would. I got an arm locked across his throat and forced his head back. I saw the stubby line of his jaw, the thin grimace of his mouth and a wet splash of earth against his cheek. He jerked his knee up and drove the little of breath that was with me from my lungs and, at the same moment, he rolled, his body arching and straining. I went with him and the next instant we were falling together. It was no clean fall.

We went down through space and then our bodies crashed into loose stones and we slid, still grappling one another, for a few feet and then fell again. A great circle of hillside seemed to whirl round me. I saw rocks, a swift cascade of stones and then a blur of bushes, and then I knew we had gone over the edge of the plateau. We struck the steep slope again and he was torn from me with the shock. I saw him whipped away as though he were a puppet roughly jerked by some hidden wire. And at the same time I fell into a great cool well of shadow. A monstrous rocky fist drove up from the darkness below me and punched into me with a force that was robbed of pain by the immediate blackness that engulfed my mind and body.

* * *

When I came to, the sky was grey and purple with dawn. Somewhere a bird was singing incessantly and I lay there and let myself get irritated by the noise. My head ached and I was thirsty. Thirst was like a beast in me and I knew I had to do something about it. I shut my eyes against the ache in my head and at once it got worse. I opened them. A small spider with a white cross on its back was spinning an untidy web between two twigs of the heather bush under which I lay. I watched him. At a guess I should have said his heart wasn't in the job. He kept resting and taking time off to polish his white cross with a pair of his back legs. I got irritated with him, then. And I think I must have gone off again. But I couldn't say for how long. It might have been a minute or an hour.

When I came back again I was still thirsty, but I was sensible enough to do something about it. I sat up and found a squashed orange in my pocket. I sucked at the pulpy mess and felt better.

I stood up, feeling my body creak with strain and ache as though it were a badly contrived machine, a contraption of loose cords and stiff leather straps.

I was standing at the foot of a drop of sheer rock twice as tall as myself. Above the rock was a loose drift of stone, held in places by thin grass tufts and bushes. I could see the long score our falling bodies had made across it. Above the loose stone the side of the rock out-thrust went up, strewn with boulders and more bushes. Looking at the rock face I remembered Drexel.

I turned, searching for him, and saw him at once. He was lying about five yards from me, right up against the base of a tree. He was sprawled on his back, his raincoat torn and open, one arm flung out and the other folded under his head. He had a deep cut down one cheek and his mouth was open in the stupid laxness of one who sleeps and snores. From his throat came a curious low sound as though he were complaining at some horror seen in a dream. I bent down and shook him gently but his eyes were shut and he gave no sign.

I stood there, not knowing what to do, fighting off the haziness which still kept sweeping over me. Then I saw his soft hat which had fallen from the plateau with us and lay now some distance from him. And I remembered the stream at the bottom of the valley. I picked up his hat and went away, down through the pines.

When I reached the stream I knelt down by it. There was a pad of moss under my knees and I felt the dampness work up from it into the cloth of my trousers. I leaned over the water and saw myself. There was a gash on my forehead where the automatic had hit me. My face was filthy with earth and stone dust. I frowned at the face, not liking it, not liking the hollowness of the eyes or the dirt and fatigue written all over it. The frown made me wince with pain as the dried blood of my forehead gash pulled with the movement of skin. I drank, filling myself with water and then I shoved my head under. I began to feel better. I found my handkerchief, wiped myself, and then tied it around my forehead where the blood had started to flow from my wound again.

I filled the soft hat with water, plugged the ventilation holes with my fingers and hurried back to Drexel. I got some water down his throat and the rest I used to bathe his face. His breathing evened off a bit but he still made no movement. I went over him anxiously—there was no past for me then; only this moment and his motionless body. So far as I could tell he had nothing broken, but I saw now that there was an ugly bruise under his left ear.

I went down for more water and poured it over his head but he still lay like a log.

For the moment I did not know what to do. I lit a cigarette and sat on a stone beside him, smoking and looking at him. I wanted five minutes, a clear, unhazed five minutes to think, in the hope that I should know what to do. I didn't know, there and then, what to do because I was myself so much involved. This really was a job for Minerva, and I guessed she would have had trouble deciding which face to show, which line to take . . . the wisdom of the law, hard justice, or the wisdom of the heart, Christian forgiveness . . . ?

I don't know how decisions are made. Sometimes the mind in its wisdom puts two and two together and it makes four. Sometimes the heart, with no faith in mathematics, just takes over and impels one to inexplicable charity. Sometimes they both work together. But whatever it is, there is the one thing, the thing which is yourself, the needle point of the ego on which every desire has to balance perfectly or be discarded. Half the time we may not know the balancing and rejecting is going on. All we know for certain is that we suddenly stand up acknowledging what we must do in order to live with ourselves. Disregard that moment and no peace remains.

Sitting there, I suddenly knew that I didn't even want five minutes and a clear brain. I knew it now and maybe I'd known it when I brought the water to him. What he had done to me was nothing. It had been purged up there on the plateau. What he had done to himself was paramount and he would have to live with it. But I knew that I wanted him to live with it alone. I wanted no other man to know it but myself and if it could have been wiped from my knowledge I could have wanted that. I wanted to save him from everyone but himself.

The person I had been last night was a stranger to me. My real self sat there on a rock, smoking and watching him. And I knew I could not throw him to the wolves. Once the decision was made, I saw other advantages, but even though one of them concerned Sophie none of them had any true part in my decision.

How to do it was a problem and I knew I was asking for trouble. But this time it would be my own trouble.

There was a clatter of stones from above. I looked up. A man had come over the edge of the plateau and was working his way downwards over the loose stones. He lowered himself over the edge of the rock-fall and climbed down it awkwardly. Then he came across to me. I knew him but it took me a little while to place him.

CHAPTER XIII

IT WAS Mr. Leslie Dunwoody, the Englishman with the motor-cycle who had been camping near the Villa Maruba. He came across to me, rolling a little on his short legs, a half-length leather jacket belted tightly round his ample waist and a black, fur-edged motoring helmet cocked a little to one side on his head, the chin straps flapping loose. Anything he put on his head seemed to slide sideways, and as he came over I wondered whether he wore his toupee under the helmet.

He stood in front of me and he smiled, the red, soft baby face beaming with pleasure and his eyes twinkling. Life seemed a great joke to him. . . . Well, that was one way of looking at it.

He said, "You all right?"

I nodded.

He looked back up the slope of rock and went on, "Nasty fall—even when you've got company for it." Then, looking back at Drexel, he said, "He's not so good?"

"No. I think he's got concussion."

"Wonder you didn't both break your necks. Funny way, if I may say so, for friends to carry on." Then with a shrewd but still humorous glance at me, and I could fancy him hugging himself with the pleasure of being in on all this, he said, "You're Fraser, aren't you? The great kidnapper."

"I'm Fraser." I was thinking hard, wondering how much he knew, and how much I could depend on him. He had walked straight into my problem and unless I got his co-operation I was going to be in a mess. He did not give me the impression of a man who would be difficult to handle. I said, feeling the ground, "How do you come to be here?"

With a casual frankness, he answered, "Followed him when he left Banyuls last night. Waited around by his car and then I heard a revolver shot. Took me a long time to find you both. Tell you the truth, took me a long time to make up my mind to look. Didn't want to get mixed up in anything. But curiosity finally killed the cat, if you know what I mean."

He took off his helmet and I saw that he was wearing his Edwardian toupee. He mopped his face with a handkerchief.

"Why were you following Drexel?"

He shook his head. "Not important at the moment. Thing is—we ought to do something about him."

I stood up and I moved closer to him. I think for a moment he was suspicious of me for I saw the half-stir of his body to draw back. But he stood his ground and I liked him for that. He had courage and not for one moment did the twinkle go from his eyes. I don't suppose he knew how to make it go. He would go on twinkling all his life, life's joke never palling on him.

I said, "Look—I'm in a jam."

"You are. The police want you. Fact is, if the telephone had been working they would know where you are now." He paused and scratched at his chin. "It's funny that. If it had worked, I'd have done it. My duty and all that. But now I'm here, talking to you . . . seems different."

"What telephone?"

He seemed surprised by this.

"The one in the chateau, of course. Blimey, what do you think I did when I found you both? Went for help of course."

"Where?" But I knew.

"Big chateau over there. But there ain't a soul there. Not a soul. And the 'phone doesn't work. So I came back here."

I knew what that meant. They had discovered my disappearance and thinking I was on my way to the police they had cleared out of the Chateau Minerve. I didn't stop to go into all the implications of that, but I did see that if they had left the chateau the last thing they would do would be to come back. They had probably rented it furnished for this operation. All I had to do to give me some grace to work out my plans was to go back there. My only problem right now was Dunwoody.

I said, "I'm in a jam, but I assure you that I've done nothing wrong. I want your help. Later, I'll explain everything."

He did not answer for a while. He stood there looking at me and then his eyes went to Drexel. I could hear the flies buzzing about the flowers and bushes as the morning sun strengthened and I had a curious hope . . . no, certainty. With a French peasant I would have had real trouble. But this was an Englishman, as English as Walthamstow, and he was obviously a man with a lively curiosity, not one to be off easily.

He nodded suddenly and then said, "That's it. Talk later. Got to do something about him first." He moved towards Drexel and I could have taken him in my arms and hugged him.

"We'll carry him to the chateau," I said.

"Lucky he don't come in the same weight class as me," he said. "Come on then." But as he bent down to take Drexel's legs he suddenly twisted his head round to me and his face was comically serious as he said, "Let's have this straight, though. Don't try any fancy tricks with me. I can look after myself. Also," he played it as a trump card and with a smile that flooded his face, "I got his automatic. Picked it up when I was looking for you."

I didn't reply, because the answer was in my face. I took Drexel's shoulders and we lifted him.

It was a bad thing to have to carry him the way we did. I realized that. But there was no alternative. Although I was pretty sure that he had broken no bones, I couldn't know whether he had internal injuries and the rough passage we gave him would do that kind of thing no good.

I didn't think much on the way back to the chateau. All my mind was concentrated on carrying Drexel, on easing the jolting and swinging as much as I could.

Dunwoody surprised me by his strength. For all his round-ness and plumpness he kept going, a dumpy Shetland pony of a man.

He was right about the chateau. When we got there it was empty. In the hallway the lights were still burning. I wondered when they had missed me. I tried to remember if I had left the cupboard door open when I had quitted Gerard's room. If he had gone back there, full of worry after Drexel's visit, he might have noticed it and felt impelled to check on my safety. For all I knew he might have noticed the apple and orange missing from his table bowl. Anyway, miss me they had, and now we had the chateau to ourselves.

We undressed Drexel and put him to bed in a room on the ground floor. Dunwoody, who said he had had some first aid training, went over him.

"Concussion," he said. "He'll come out of it, but I wouldn't say when."

We left him, still mumbling a little to himself, and I locked the room door. Dunwoody cocked an eye at me, but I offered no explanation then.

I said, "What about his car and your motor-cycle?"

"They're on the other road. I can bring them round. Means two trips. Or we could go together?"

"I don't want to take the risk of being seen on any road yet. I don't want his car to stay there, either."

"All right, I'll fetch 'em." And then as he turned to go, cheerful and willing, he paused and said, "I ought to go down to the police, you know. It's me duty."

He may have been teasing or he may have wanted to test me, to be sure that I was set in whatever plan I had.

I said, "I don't want you to do that. Not yet, anyway."

"All right—but you got to promise to keep me out of trouble."

"I will."

He put his hand into his pocket at that and he pulled out Drexel's automatic.

"Here, you take this."

I did, but I could not help saying, "You trust me that far?"

He said brightly, "It ain't just that. You come into this house and it don't take a telescope to see you've been here before. It's empty now, but maybe your friends . . . or whatever you call them . . . might come back. You'll feel better with that. Besides"— he grinned and patted his toupee straight—"it ain't a question of trust. Got a gun of me own. Never travel abroad without it."

He was three hours making the two trips. He came back first with the motor-cycle and when I said, "Can you manage the Bentley?" he replied, "Drive anything on wheels," and was off again, his short legs twinkling, a Tweedledum quite happy without a Tweedledee. Watching him go, I realized how grateful I was for his company and help. I'd been alone a long time. It was good to talk to someone other than myself.

I searched all over the chateau, but there was no one in the place. I went into every room, every tower and cellar. It was easy to see which had been Jabal's room. It was a little round, monkish kind of a cell in one of the towers, and he had amused himself by writing in pencil the pedigrees of his kidnappers all over the walls. He didn't know their names, but his characterization was clear enough. It was done in Arabic, colourful, fluent abuse, and I was sorry that it hadn't been done in French so they could have read it.

I found the kitchen, a long, white-tiled room on the right just inside the courtyard portal, and I opened a tin of chicken soup and warmed it up. I took it into Drexel and tried to get some of it down him. I think he took some but most of it dribbled over his chin. However, he seemed to have a better colour and he was breathing easier and I think that for a moment his eyelids flickered as though he were trying to come back. I did not worry over-much about him. He was hard and he would pull out of it.

I went back to the kitchen and found some food for myself. While I was eating Dunwoody came and joined me. We made some coffee and carried it outside into the sunlit courtyard and sat on the seat by the wall. We didn't talk right away. We just sat there busy with our own thoughts and waiting for the right moment to begin.

I stared across at the statue of Minerva and it was hard to get my thoughts sorted out. Odd irrelevancies came popping into my head. Minerva was wisdom and she looked pretty serious about it. But if I went round to the other side of her, she'd be different: a kind, understanding creature. No help at all. I didn't want any double-faced woman. I wanted to know which was the true Minerva. True wisdom was what I wanted at this moment and it was hard to come by. One thing about her, I thought, was that she wore her helmet with a more natural carriage than Dunwoody wore his. *Invita Minerva* . . . that was an echo from some drowsy afternoon in form and not one of the boys a damn bit interested. *Invita Minerva . . . against the grain.* I remembered now how it had come up; the use of Latin tags in English composition. To do something against the grain, or something for which nature has not fitted you. Horace, *Ars Poetica* 1.385. That was my card index memory.

But the thing I wanted to do now was in my nature, the trouble was to find the right way the grain went and to go with it. What I wanted to do was to pull Drexel's chestnuts out of the fire. He was in my hands and he would have no choice but to do as I told him. But if I knew what I wanted to do, I was far from certain how to do it. The ways and means were beyond me at the moment. A great deal depended on how much co-operation I could get from Dunwoody. I sat there trying to sort it out. Drexel wasn't the only person I was concerned with. I was thinking, too, of Sophie. If this thing could be hushed up she would be untouched. As far as the police were concerned if the full truth came out she was as guilty as Drexel or any of the others. I sat there becoming more than ever convinced that the truth must not be known. I wanted it hidden for Drexel's sake, for Sophie's sake, and so for my own. With Drexel's help there must be some way of tracing where Gerard and the rest had taken Jabal. If I could get Jabal back I would talk to him like a Dutch uncle and I felt I knew him well enough to bet on his playing the game my way. Drexel and I between us could cook up some story of his having rescued me and Jabal from the chateau but that the kidnappers had got away and we had no means of identifying them. It would work, I knew. Drexel's word, and my word and Jabal backing us up. . . . No one would doubt us. And even if they did there would not be a damn thing they could do about it. But how was I to find Jabal? Drexel might know where they would have taken him. They obviously had

had to act on their own initiative when they had discovered my escape. Gerard was probably sick with worry at this moment. Particularly as he thought Drexel was on his way to Paris for a few days.

My more immediate worry was Dunwoody. What was I going to tell him? I'm a fair judge of men and so far he had impressed me as a reasonable sort, no fool, and certainly not hide-bound or stiff with rectitude. In the end I decided to tell him the truth. At least as much as I thought he ought to know. I would say nothing to him about the relationship between Sophie and myself (that belonged to me and I didn't want him to have cause to think it might be my real reason for covering up for Drexel).

If my plan did not work—if for any reason we could not get Jabal back, I didn't know what was going to happen. We could still cook up a story to keep Drexel cleared. Gerard would get his ransom money and Jabal would return. Jabal had no idea, I was sure, that Drexel had organized the kidnapping, and if he pointed an accusing finger at me I could clear myself by proving I was framed and Drexel would say he had rescued me. But I did not let myself think much about the plan failing. It had to work.

It was at this point that Dunwoody said to me:

"Who is that old girl?"

I said, "She's Minerva. The goddess of wisdom. She's supposed to have been born, fully clothed and full grown, through the left ear of Jupiter."

He said, "Obstetrics have altered since those days." And then with a grin, he went on, "She ought to wear her nightdress inside that coat of armour. Warmer that way."

I said, "Why were you following Colonel Drexel?"

For answer he fished inside his open leather jacket and produced a rather dirty card. It read—

The Dunwoody Detective Agency
Discreet
Confidential
Divorce Work a Speciality
Ex-Metropolitan Police.

In one corner was a North London address.

I could not help it. I laughed. Anyone less like a detective than Dunwoody I could not imagine. But that's how it should be.

I said, "You were never in the Metropolitan Police. You're not tall enough."

"True. That's me brother, Albert. He really runs the business. I'm the second hangman."

"How does this tie up with the Colonel?"

"His wife. The second one. She wants a divorce and he won't give it to her. Too busy to bother is his line. But she was sure he wasn't behaving for all that. So here I am. Must say I haven't got anything to put in the old notebook so far."

I knew the Colonel had this kind of trouble. In fact I'd heard long before I left England that he had separated from his wife.

"How did you know he was going to be at the Villa Maruba?" I asked.

His eyes twinkled. "You should be in this business. From you, of course. Or rather, your landlady."

I remembered now that I had given my address to my landlady in case anything had gone wrong.

"And how did you know about me?"

"Take nothing for granted, do you?" But it was said kindly.

"Not at the moment. I've got too much on my hands. But I'll be equally frank with you in a moment."

"Fair enough. We been watching the Grosvenor Square house for some time. Saw you go there twice and then the Colonel hops it and we can't find him. So we did a routine check on you. If I may say so you've got what I would call a gabby landlady. Told me your address and all about you."

"And so you came to France? Just on the strength of my address?" I did not know this man and I had to be careful. I had to be sure. There was irony in it for if anyone should have been suspicious it was he.

"Not as easy as that. Albert was all against it. Wild goose chase, he said. But then he's not a romantic man, and he didn't need a holiday. I am and I did. So I talked him into it. I was right, too. Except that there weren't no lady. But, correct me if I'm wrong, I've an idea I've tumbled into something much more interesting?"

I said, "You have. I'm going to put myself in your hands."

He looked down at his pudgy hands as though he was not sure whether he wanted them full of me.

"I've said my piece. Let's hear yours."

I hesitated for a moment. It was hard to begin and now the time had come I was suddenly full of doubt, not doubt of him, but of the whole plan. Putting it into words was going to make it sound quixotically stupid. Some trick of sun and shadow on Minerva's face seemed to make her frown and I knew she wasn't on my side. I knew what she would say and probably in Horatian metres, "Don't be a clot. Go straight to the police and let Drexel take whatever is coming to him." That was wisdom. Something told me that we don't live just by wisdom. It doesn't warm any heart.

I plunged. I told him the whole story, except the pieces about myself and Sophie. He was a good listener. Never asked a question and, as I talked, I could see that he was with me. I began to realize that it is a heart of gold that puts that kind of twinkle into a man's eyes. He heard me right through and when I had finished he was silent for a while. He sat there with his fat lips pursed, making a little nodding motion of his head that caused helmet and toupee to slide. He stood up and thrust his hands in his trouser pockets and took a few steps up and down. Then he stopped in front of me.

He said very soberly, "You ain't going to like me for this. But I got to say it. In fact I got to say two things. And you ain't going to like me for either."

"I like you already," I said. And I meant it. Not just because I wanted his help. "You can say anything you like."

"All right. One. You're a bloody fool. You'll never pull this off. You should go right to the police."

"I can't do that."

"Sure?"

"Yes."

"All right. Good enough for me. Now—two. I'll string along with you on one condition. If it comes off I want a hundred pounds for my trouble and a fair share of any reward money going."

I stood up, and my heart was lighter than it had been for many a long time. I was with him and I understood him. In fact, I told myself, if he hadn't asked for money, if he hadn't kept one eye on the main chance, I should have been uncertain of him.

I said, "It's a deal."

He grinned and said, "And a bloody silly one. But then, I was always one for a crazy deal. Well, all you got to do now is to avoid fifty thousand police looking for you—and pretty soon for the Colonel, too—and find Jabal. That shouldn't be difficult for a superman. Ask me and I'd say you'd better invite Mrs. Minerva over to make up the quorum."

With that he walked back to the kitchen and very soon I heard him rattling the dishes as he washed up from our meal. And, although I had no idea what to do at that moment, it was somehow comforting to hear him in there. I was not alone.

I sat there and I wondered how long it would be before the

130

Colonel came out from his coma. So far as I could see there wasn't a thing I could do until then.

That afternoon while Dunwoody sat with the Colonel in case he came round, I poked about the chateau again. It would have been hard to say exactly what I was looking for, but at the back of my mind I began to have a conviction that somewhere there might be one solid piece of information that would help me enormously. The thing I had to know, of course, was where Jabal had been taken. To answer that it was obvious that I had to know all I could about Gerard, Sarrasin and the others. And the curious thing was that I felt that between them all there was some exceptional bond. They were not so much individuals but a group and wherever one was would be found also the others. Even Sophie came into this enclave.

Ignoring the main facts of the kidnapping and my own framing . . . all of which were clear enough now to me . . . I went back over the small details which still puzzled me for in them—perhaps undeservedly—I felt there lurked the other truth I now had to have. I think I was doing this because I was half afraid that the Colonel might be too long coming round, or that when he did he would refuse to co-operate or might not be able to offer much. In that case I would be on my own. That being so it was wise to act now as though I were on my own.

I had already gone through his clothes. But he carried nothing which seemed to help me; money, keys and in his wallet only the usual dog-eared junk of letters and club membership cards that men hang on to. There was even a very old letter from me asking for a character reference just after I had left the Army. On the back he had scribbled in pencil the draft of his testimonial. I had never seen it before and I smiled at one sentence in it and wondered how the School Governors had taken it. 'A man of high intellectual integrity and one whose personal qualities are outstanding. In my opinion he will be wasting himself in the teaching profession, but that's what he wants to do—and he takes a lot of stopping.' Loose in an inside pocket was a small piece of paper that did seem to have something to say but I could not fathom it. It was just a short list of figures and numbers.

PE	2 — 7
PV	9 — 11
LB	12 — 14
BM	16 — 21

It meant nothing to me unless it was the key to some code, or the letters might be initials, but the only one that seemed to fit anyone I knew was the PV which might have stood for Paviot. The first and last set of numbers had an interval of five between them, and the middle two an interval of two. It was a neat pattern which inclined me to think it was some code key. Even so, it gave me no help. In additon it was so crumpled and dirty it might have been in his pockets for months.

I went down the gravelled drive as far as the lodge gate, following the telephone line to see where it had been cut and as I walked in the sun I tried to marshal everything neatly in my head . . . the things which I did not understand.

Why hadn't the dogs barked when Sarrasin and Fargette had come that evening to carry off Jabal? They always barked at me when I came in, but that evening the old bitch hound by my side had done no more than growl softly as the boat came inshore. The only answer I could give to that one was that Drexel had got the dogs from Sarrasin and Fargette originally and the dogs, knowing them, had kept quiet. Which led to the next point.

Here in the chateau there had been the afternoon noise, dogs barking, people laughing, and that distant, hollow *thud, thud.* In my walks around the grounds I had never seen a dog, but I knew now that there had been dogs here for behind the kitchen there was a run of kennels and all the signs pointed to the recent presence of animals. Something told me that the dogs were important. What were they, hunting dogs, watchdogs?

Something, I was sure, held all these people together. I recalled Gerard talking to Sarrasin. 'Everything is falling to pieces and we have to take the cheapest . . . that's no way to get anywhere. All my life I have wanted to do it big. . . .' That didn't sound like a man who just wanted money for itself . . . money was a means to feed some ambition. But what?

I didn't achieve anything except to pile up a stack of questions which just confused me.

Just this side of the gates I found where the line had been cut. However, I made no attempt to put the wire right. I had no need of the telephone yet.

I returned to the chateau and went over it again. This time I made more discoveries, probing and poking and getting into a state of mind which reminded me of the days when I used to do *The Times* crossword puzzle, priding myself always to do it in less than sixty minutes flat, and finding myself looking at the last empty space, the clue hammering in my head and knowing I had the answer there . . . just over the border of memory, so near and so far, but knowing that in a moment it would come flashing into sight.

Only this was no crossword puzzle. This was Drexel and Sophie, and my own arrogant determination to put things right. Or as right as they could be. A shabby knight-errant, I thought, in a ripped and scorched tweed jacket and dirty flannels. But I was not sure even whether I was acting out of chivalry or self-interest. I didn't care much. If self-interest was the reason I'd settle for that. I just knew what I had to do.

In Gerard's room the only thing I found was in the wastepaper basket. It was a small page, torn from a loose-leaf pocket book, stuck right through with a pencil, crumpled and smelling of the cigarette dog-ends that littered the basket. On it in a tight, hard hand which might have been Gerard's since anxious, fretting people often write concisely, taking a pleasure in dragooning their words even if they can't control their fears, were a few notes in French:

> Sunday. Karimba. Cut nails.
> I. Myna   3000 frs.
> Golden-eye   2150 frs.
> Remember money due on Arab.

Here was Karimba again, from whom the others took their cue. Was Karimba an Arab? Man or woman? I. Myna and Golden-eye meant nothing unless Gerard was a betting man and they were race-horse names with the amounts he had lost or won. Cut nails left me floundering. And what money was due on what Arab? Did this refer to Jabal?

Going over the chateau it was clear to me that they had taken the place furnished. Except for their unmade beds they had left little sign of their occupancy. In a closet opening off the hall there was a large and dirty celluloid collar hanging over a corner of the mirror. Sophie's room I knew at once because it was full of her perfume. I stood there looking at the bed in which she had slept and suddenly she seemed to be in the room with me. I wanted her more than I wanted anything at that moment. I didn't care a damn what she had been or what she had done. I didn't care about the past, about morality, right or wrong, about anything except the future and the force in me to pluck her from whatever tangle held her and to carry her away with me.

There was a small white button on the floor which had pulled from a dress or a jumper. I picked it up and put it in my pocket. It was good to have something which had been hers on me. It was silly, I knew, but if that was the way love took one then I believed in it and didn't care who knew my silliness.

I went down into the courtyard, had a word with Dunwoody on my way and strolled around trying to sort things out. The Colonel was easing into a quiet sleep but he was still as communicative as a log.

I walked around so many times that I shouldn't have been surprised if Minerva had told me to shut up, that I was making her giddy. And then, a little way up from the kitchen door, I saw something. I had my eyes on the ground. Maybe when I'd passed the spot before I had been staring moodily ahead. On the gravel, quite close to the wall which at this spot was made up of a smooth run of planks forming part of a lean-to coal store for the kitchen, was a scattering of cigarettes. But they were very odd cigarettes. None of them was complete. Most seemed to have been cut in half or to have had the last third cut off them. The pieces lay about the ground quite haphazardly and were clearly not cigarette-ends dropped from some waste-paper basket for none of them had been smoked. I picked a few up and saw that they were a very cheap brand. The thing beat me. I glanced over at Minerva. But she was no help.

CHAPTER XIV

I was getting nowhere fast. The Colonel just lay as good as a corpse on his bed and did nothing to help us get soup or brandy into him. Maybe it was the wrong treatment for concussion.

Dunwoody and I knocked up a meal of sorts in the kitchen that evening. I was not very good company because there was too much on my mind, mostly a feeling that time was going by and that time was valuable. From a map he had Dunwoody showed me the situation of the chateau. We were dead in the middle of a hilly triangle of country which had for its corners Le Perthus, Le Boulou and Amelie Les Bains. It was well over forty kilometres back to Banyuls-sur-Mer.

As we ate I gave Dunwoody an account of all the things I had discovered. He was a professional detective. If anyone could make anything of them, then he should. But he shook his head.

"Your only hope is the Colonel," he said. "By tomorrow morning maybe he'll be round."

"I don't like sitting here doing nothing."

"Neither do I. What is more, Albert's going to have a few words to say when he hears about this."

"You aren't going to tell Albert a thing about this. This is between us."

He did not say anything for a while. He just looked at me, chewing away at a piece of brown bread he had spread thick with Brie. Then reaching for a glass of wine, he said, "All right. I understand how you feel. If Albert was to cross me up the way the Colonel did you . . . I know how it would be. I'd kick his guts out first and then do all I could for him."

We found a bottle of whisky—I should think it was part of the store got in for me—and helped ourselves liberally to it before we went to bed. Under the influence of the whisky I began to let things slip from my mind a bit. Dunwoody was good company and his professional stories were very funny.

That night I slept on a mattress in the Colonel's room. I spread it on the floor close to his bed so that if he came round I could get to him easily. I went off to sleep easily. Dunwoody had found himself a bunk in one of the other bedrooms.

It must have been well after midnight when I was awakened. I got up and switched on the light. The Colonel was sitting up in bed with his hands against his forehead and he was moving his head slowly to and fro. The movement and the fact that his eyes were screwed up tight gave me the impression that he was suffering from a frightful headache. He probably was.

I sat by him, and reaching for a glass of water from the bed-table, said quietly, "Here, drink this."

He opened his eyes and quite normally put out his hand and took the glass. He drank it all in one long movement and I saw the rise and fall of his Adam's apple against the leathery skin of his throat.

I took the glass back. He sat there staring straight in front of him and his eyes had that bright, out-of-this-world look which I remembered from the time long ago when he had come a cropper from his horse and lost his memory.

Very gently, I said, "How do you feel?"

And very quietly he replied with a scurrilous Arab phrase which answered my question but was quite untranslatable.

I said, "You're at Chateau Minerve. You're all right. I'm looking after you."

He said, dully, "Who the hell are you?"

I said, "I'm David. David Fraser."

He frowned at this and it was clear that I meant nothing to him.

I went on, "You know who you are, don't you?"

He said nothing. Then he shook his head. It was uncanny and disturbing. I'd known this kind of thing before and in a way I understood it. But, even so, something turned over inside me unpleasantly as I sat there with a Drexel who was out of touch, not only with the world, but with his own personality.

I said, "You're Colonel Francis Drexel and I'm David Fraser, your friend."

I could say that last and still mean it. I was his friend. I was for him whether I wanted to be or not. I was beginning to understand that friendship isn't something you come to the end of easily.

He said, "I wish this room would keep still." And his voice was suddenly guttural as though the words wanted to slip back down his throat all the time. He dropped stiffly to his pillows, lay there for a while with his eyes open and then was asleep.

I let him be. I kept the light on and stayed awake for maybe two hours, but he showed no further signs of coming round. In the end I got back on to my mattress and dropped off.

Dunwoody woke me about six with a great mug of steaming

coffee. He was a good soul. Just having him around did things for me.

I told him about the Colonel's waking up in the night.

He said, "That's a good sign. Today, maybe, we'll get some sense out of him." He went over and stooped above the Colonel. He was still sleeping. He shook him gently by the shoulder but there was no response. He rolled back his lids and looked into his eyes.

I said, "The last time he took a bang like that he had amnesia for two days."

He shook his head at this. "Let's hope he cuts something off his record this go. Funny box of eggs the brain. Albert had a chum who started to drive himself mad about fire. Couldn't smoke, couldn't strike a match, a flame or a light drove him to a jelly. He was headin' straight for the nut house. Then they took a bit of bone out of his skull, relieved some pressure. . . . You should see him now. Don't care a damn. Smokes in bed, burns holes in his sheets and suits, and he's been black-listed as a bad risk by every fire insurance company in the City. But he's happy. Took a job on the London Fire Brigade."

I laughed, not believing a word of it, but knowing it was meant to cheer me up.

He took over and I went off to have a wash and a breather. There was a radio in the kitchen and I switched this on while I was having a second mug of coffee. I got the news from Paris. It mentioned the Jabal disappearance, but there was nothing of importance. The French police were working away at it. Apparently Drexel had not been missed yet, or if he had the police were not letting it be known. I wondered how Didier was making out.

I went back to the Colonel's room. As I approached it I heard the sound of someone talking and a swift hope leapt up in me.

But when I went in the Colonel was stretched out flat and Dunwoody was sitting in a chair by the bed.

"I thought I heard someone talking," I said.

He grinned. "So you did. Trying a new treatment. I sit here and I keep saying aloud, 'Come on. Wake up, you old bastard! Wake up!' Thought maybe it would reach down into his subconscious. You never know."

I said, "If he doesn't make sense by lunch-time I've got to do something. I can't sit here for ever."

"If he don't come round there's only one thing you can do."

I knew what he meant.

"That's the last thing I want to do."

"You're going to be bloody unpopular with the police if you do have to go to 'em in the end. They won't like the wasted time."

"I couldn't help them much, even now. They've got a description of all the men, except Gerard. And as long as Drexel's unconscious, he's no good to them."

"You're the boss."

I began to feel that even though Dunwoody was going to get a hundred pounds, win-or-lose, he was forming the opinion that I was playing a poor hand. I hadn't even got one card that looked like a winner.

The Colonel did not come round by lunch-time and I started to ask myself seriously if I should give it all up and go to the police. By all the rules it was what I should have done; but every instinct in me was against it. I told myself that by hanging on for a while I was not doing anyone harm, and the chance might come to clear up the whole mess tidily. Jabal was safe enough for a while. The worst that was intended for him was ransom and a return to safety. It would only be when Gerard failed to get any word from Drexel—and that was a few days off yet—that he would start to panic. What he would do then, I didn't know. He might turn Jabal loose. . . . I tried to believe this, but at the back of my mind I was worrying that he might do far worse. However, I had some days' grace yet.

But no matter what I told myself, I began to worry. I was in the unhappy position of wanting to do the wrong thing for the right-to-me motives. My common sense fought against my instinct.

I mooched around, coming back now and again to look at the Colonel. He lay there, sleeping or in a light coma, and he was useless to me. I began to feel angry towards him. He was the man I wanted to help and I could do nothing without him. I wanted to shake him into life. More than once I was on the point of sending the whole thing to hell and going for the police. I only had to get into the Colonel's car and the thing would be done in an hour. I even went and sat in his car; testing myself, knowing I only had to reach out a hand for the switch. But I couldn't do it. Not even if I painted for myself a picture of Jabal with his throat cut in a few days' time when Gerard found himself alone without guidance or instructions. But I still could not touch the switch.

Dunwoody went off on his motor-cycle during the afternoon to get some provisions for the kitchen. He did not bring much back and I could guess why. He didn't think we were going to be here long, but he said nothing.

That evening we had no whisky, but we finished a flask of wine he had bought. When it was time for bed, he insisted on taking his turn sleeping with the Colonel. I found myself a bed in a small room overlooking the courtyard. Before leaving Dunwoody for the night, I made up my mind suddenly. It was no good drifting.

Standing at the door of the Colonel's room, I said, "If he doesn't come round tomorrow, I'm going to the police. I'll give him until the evening. After that I've finished playing around."

Dunwoody pursed his fat lips and then said, "If it had been me, I'd have gone today."

I went up to my bed and for a while I stared out into the courtyard. There was a moon and Minerva looked cold and distant. I had no affection for her. Tomorrow, maybe, I was going to be wise and without pity—like her. I got into bed and had a hard time persuading sleep to come.

It must have been well on towards morning when I woke. I was suddenly alert and I knew that I had not come out of sleep naturally. I sat up and listened and away in the distance there was the faint drone of an airplane. I wondered if it had come over the chateau and disturbed me. During the day quite a few aircraft came over and I guessed we must be on some airline route. But at the back of my mind I did not believe that I had been awakened by the machine. I got up and went to the window. The moon was gone and there was a greyness outside like the belly of a tabby-cat. A little scud of mist was floating over the surface of the courtyard and Minerva rose above it. She would. She rose above everything. I disliked her more than ever. I thought I saw something moving in the mist, but the mist itself curled and lifted gently and might have been an enormous blanket held on the backs of a slow-pulsing crowd. Mist can play hell with a suspicious mind. Sentries have wasted thousands of rounds of ammunition mowing down the attack of advancing mist.

But I was uneasy and I went down. I walked around the courtyard and out to the gravel space under the judas tree. There was no one about and far away the first cock was jabbing away at the morning to waken it. I came back and, switching on the light, looked in on Dunwoody and the Colonel. They were both asleep. I had to smile at Dunwoody; false teeth in a little glass and his toupee balanced on the knob of a chair. The Colonel was snoring unattractively and he looked grey and old and really not worth bothering about. That I thought was the trouble with life, half the things we bothered about weren't worth it. I took this banal thought back to bed and slept soundly until the sun was up and striking hot through the window.

When Dunwoody came into the kitchen where I was making coffee, he said cheerfully, "Well, this is the day."

He made it sound like the morning of a school treat or an important cricket match.

"You're glad?"

"I think you're doing the right thing. He's showing no signs. Tell you what I'll do, too—I'll cut that hundred to fifty. I don't feel I've earned more. After lunch, too, I'm going down the village to send Albert a telegram. He'll be worried not hearing from me. All right by you?"

"Yes. If we've got no sense out of him by then."

I sat with the Colonel that morning, but there was little hope in my mood. Not even when he woke up. He just lay there with his eyes open, staring in front of him. I talked to him, tried to bring him back, but when he did answer it was in a stupid, confused way and he was obviously lost in some other world. I began to wonder whether he was not more badly injured than I thought. I tried not to tell myself that the kindest thing I could do would be to get a doctor to him. After about half an hour I could see the fatigue cloud his eyes and then he was sleeping again.

I was not going to get anything from him. That was clear. Not that day. And today was my limit.

After lunch Dunwoody got on his motor-cycle to go down to the village—it was about six miles away—to send his telegram. As near as damn-it I got on the back with him, but even then something held me back. I had said I would wait until the evening and I felt tied to my limit. Dunwoody looked at me and I knew what he was waiting for, but I waved him off and he went down the roadway, bouncing like a fat elf on the powerful machine.

Ten minutes later I was glad I had not gone with him for I came across something which made me feel that my luck was turning. I went back into the kitchen to clear away the lunch things. I washed up our few plates and knives and forks. We'd had mortadella sausage and a salad Dunwoody had made. There was a kitchen garden full of stuff. The bin for scraps stood near the sink and I was just going to toss into it some bits of skin from the sausage when a splash of coloured paper in the bin caught my eye. It was well down at the bottom and the paper was damp. All I saw at first was the head and shoulders of a tiger snarling, arresting in orange, black and red. I bent down and retrieved it. If I had any reason for doing it then it was an idle one. My mind was in a dull state, the colour attracted me. I spread it out on the sink board. It was a largish handbill, splotched with damp and grease as though it had been used for wrapping food.

I stood there, staring down at it. Across the top was a large banner: *GRAND CIRQUE PYRÉNÉEN.* Underneath was a picture of four performing tigers in a cage. Three of them were seated on high stools and the fourth was flying through the air towards a paper hoop held by a herculean character in a leopard skin, waxed moustaches and glossy black hair. Underneath the picture were a few lines of the usual exaggerated circus advertising stuff, and then in a small box the legend—*Visitez-le a Banyuls-sur-Mer le 16-21 Avril.*

But the thing which held my eye and in some way began to stir up my dulled mind was the lion- or tiger-tamer person. He was magnificent. And around his waist, to hold his leopard skin, he wore a belt. It was the belt which said something to me. It was a black belt with a curious-shaped buckle. The reproduction was bad and garish, but it was clear enough to wake my memories and I knew where I had seen a belt like this. Sarrasin had worn one on the night I had been abducted. And this man might easily be an idealized picture of Sarrasin, plus waxed moustaches and a black wig.

Why not, I asked myself? Long ago I remembered thinking that Sarrasin was a boxing-booth type from a country fair. But an animal trainer in a third-rate circus was just as good. All these people, I had told myself recently, belonged to a group. Why not a circus? And if they did that would account for the strange silence about the chateau at night when I had been kept here. They had to go off to their performances. Only on Sundays—when they changed pitches or rested—would they be free of that. And there *had* been one day when the chateau had not been silent during the evening. And what more likely if they were coming up here each day and bringing food with them that they would wrap it in a circus handbill?

I did not stop to think about it any more. It was a chance, and a good one, I felt. At once I knew I was not going to the police until I had tried it. There was a calendar in the kitchen. The Banyuls-sur-Mer dates were the 16th to the 21st April. Today was the 18th, a Wednesday.

I started to get ready at once. Dunwoody could stay here and look after the Colonel while I went to Banyuls for the performance that evening. Banyuls was just over forty kilometres—twenty-five miles—away. There was an old bicycle in the shed by the gates and I could make the distance on that easily. In the staff quarters behind the kitchen I found a beret and an old pair of blue workman's overalls. It was no good thinking of using the Colonel's car. The police knew that too well. And if I were dressed as a working man, then Dunwoody's motor-cycle with its GB plates was out of the question . . . anyway, I was not pressed for time. The main thing was to keep clear of the police. The last thing they would expect would be to find me riding a bicycle. They saw me as the clever, well-organized kidnapper tucked safely away in some retreat until my plans had worked out.

I looked fairly natural in the overalls, but I decided against the beret. One thing an Englishman cannot wear convincingly is a beret. I found instead an old motoring cap of the Colonel's in his car, mucked it up with grease and dirt, and pulled that on. I don't know what I looked like, but certainly not myself.

I was all ready to go when Dunwoody returned. I told him of my discovery and the chance I was going to take. I could see at once he did not like it.

"I don't say you're not on to something. But the police'll pick you up. Let me go."

"But you don't know these people. I'll be all right. And if I'm not back by tomorrow morning—you go to the police."

He argued for a bit, but in the end I persuaded him.

"All right. But take your revolver with you—and watch yourself."

He came down to the lodge gates with me fussing cheerfully. He wanted me to take his motor-cycle but I was against this. For all I knew the police might have a line on him and be watching for his machine. To take it as far afield as Banyuls would be madness. Besides, I had plenty of time and I was looking forward to the ride. I put Dunwoody's map in my pocket and off I went.

The simple fact of moving, of going forward, did things to my spirits. I was not thinking too much of what I should do if I established that Gerard and company were at the circus. That could wait. All I knew was that once I found them I would have a chance of tracing Jabal, and when I knew that then Dunwoody and I—and Drexel if he was able—would make a plan of action.

It was bad cycling country, up and down hill the whole time, but I was in no hurry. I had worked out a route on the map which would eventually bring me by the back road down into Banyuls. I had no wish to show myself on the coast road.

As I cycled along I remembered the scrap of paper I had found in the Colonel's wallet. I pulled it out and examined it and I knew the circus was not going to disappoint me. I realized now that it was a list of the places, with dates, at which the circus was playing that month. BM was Banyuls-sur-Mer; PE—Perpignan; PV—Port-Vendres, and LB was Le Boulou. Drexel had the list so that he would know where to find them at any time during the month. I wondered how Drexel had got to know them and why he had brought them into his plan. Cirque Pyrénéen meant that they probably played a circuit that covered the central and southern part of France. From Perpignan down the coast and then right across to Biarritz and maybe up as far as Bordeaux. . . . And then I remembered that at one time Drexel had been dropped in France for work with the resistance movement and that he had come out over the border into Spain. Maybe he had met up with Sarrasin or Gerard then.

Some ten miles short of Banyuls I was thirsty and went into a small estaminet called *Le Point du Jour* for a drink. It was in a hamlet of about six houses perched just below the bare, rocky shoulder of a hill. An old woman in man's boots and with her hair drawn back in a tight bun from her ancient face served me with a *blonde bière*. On one of the walls was a poster for the circus. It was the same as my handbill only larger. I asked her about the circus. I was the only one in the place and she had kept me company to see I didn't steal anything, though there was nothing in the place that would have fetched five hundred francs. She told me, grudgingly, that the circus came through these parts once every two years. She hadn't seen it herself, but her grandson went. He also went to the cinema in Banyuls once a month. She seemed to think he was too fond of entertainments and was still grumbling about him when I left. I felt I was on his side. He probably broke his back fourteen hours a day hoeing and tending the vines on some mountain slope and then had to help run the *Point du Jour* at night.

CHAPTER XV

I TUCKED my bicycle away in the lee of a stone wall a couple of miles outside Banyuls and started to walk towards the town. I came to it by a footpath that led down the long flank of a hill behind it. I stopped half-way down the hill and made myself comfortable on a patch of turf, my back against a tree. I was hot and tired from the ride and it was good just to sit. It was seven o'clock and I knew the circus did not begin until eight when it would just be getting dark.

The town was spread out in a long line below me, red roofs and pink, ochre and white walls. Over the roofs I could just see the edge of the thin strip of sand, and away to the right the block of buildings which was the Arago Laboratory and Aquarium.

It seemed a long time ago that I had gone in there and met Sophie. And a whole lifetime since I had met Drexel in Wales and sacrificed gladly the Songa Manara project. There was bitterness in that thought. Still the sacrifice had brought me to Sophie. Drexel I had lost. But there was Sophie now. . . . I loved Sophie. It was the easiest statement in the world, and the most difficult to understand. I didn't try to understand it. I sat there hugging it and, for a little while, not worrying about the circus or what I would do—except that somehow I was going to haul Sophie out of it.

A couple of men came down the path. They passed me with hardly a glance. In these parts there was nothing strange in the sight of a workman stretched out on the grass having a rest. Now and again a car hooted in the town below and far out on the dusky horizon I saw the lights of one of the Port-Vendres steamers.

I waited until a quarter to eight and then I went down. It was just twilight and dark enough for me to feel that I did not have to walk with my head down to hide my face. The circus was camped on an open space at the back of the town, not far from the Banyuls stream which was now a succession of dirty pools fringed with tall reed and bamboo growths. I joined a trickle of people moving towards the open space.

Against the paling sky I could see the silhouette of the big top and the hunched backs of the parked caravans and mobile cages. It was a small circus and the first few caravans I passed wanted repainting badly. There were one or two sideshows and a small roundabout for children worked by a man turning a wooden wheel. There was nothing impressive about it, not even the crowd which was sparse. If Gerard had anything to do with this affair, I thought, then he would have plenty of worry over the receipts. I could hear his voice fretting away back in that room in the chateau. . . . *Everything is falling to pieces and we have to take the cheapest.* . . . And what was it he had said on the stairs as he passed me? *Tonight we are as poor as crows. But soon.* . . . He didn't know it, and I certainly hoped it, but disappointment was probably walking up to his paybox at this moment.

Some children came dashing through the sprinkling of crowd, chasing a dog and, as I stepped aside to avoid them, I bumped gently into someone.

A familiar voice, but now a little slurred with drink, said, *"Monsieur, vous voulez les espadrilles?"*

I half-turned and there was Jean Cagou. He was not quite so brisk and glossy as usual. He swayed a little as he opened his case and his hair was ruffled and the smile on his face was slipping all over the place.

I shook my head and was going to turn away when he caught my arm, protesting:

"But, monsieur has not seen——"

Then he broke off, peered forward and up, as though I were an umbrella and he wanted to come under it, and nearly fell into my arms. He went on, tripping over his tongue, "But surely I know. . . ."

I grunted angrily and at the same moment gave his case a nudge which tipped some of his espadrilles to the ground. He gave a wail and sat down, gathering them quickly up to avoid their being trampled by the feet of the passers-by. I left him hurriedly and hoped that his tipsy mind would soon forget the encounter.

There was a queue formed at the paydesk before the large marquee and I joined the end of it. I had gone up about three places when I saw Dunwoody. He was standing a little apart near the paybox and looking down the queue. He saw me at the same time as I saw him, and with a nod of his head for me to join him, walked away.

I left the queue and went after him. He stopped in the lee of a flat-topped trailer and gave me a cheerful grin as I came up. I wasn't pleased to see him and I was at no pains to hide my feeling.

"What the hell are you doing here?"

"It's all right. Don't fly off the handle."

"But why are you here? What about the Colonel?"

"He's all right. I've locked him in and I've got his clothes in my saddle-bags. He can't move. Anyway he's dead to the wide."

"I still don't see——"

"You won't if you don't give me a chance to tell you. I got to thinking when you left. If anything went wrong down here . . . somebody recognized you or something. . . . Well, then, you ain't mobile enough. Now, with me standin' by—you got speed. The old bike's just outside the grounds. It's sensible, you know. Anyway, two heads are better than one."

I did not say anything for a moment, but I guessed I was not getting the full truth. He knew what I was thinking.

"What else?" I asked.

Dunwoody looked around at the parked caravans and trailers and said reflectively, "If your hunch is right, Jabal might be here. Plenty of places to hide him." He patted his leather jerkin. "We've both got guns. We might be able to lift him this evening. You couldn't do it alone."

I laughed. He might be pudgy and look like nothing, but he was game.

"You just didn't want to miss any fun?"

He nodded. "That's true. Albert's always saying I'm too impetuous. But if you're going to do a thing—do it quick, I say."

I gave in. "All right. Let's go in." I started for the paybox.

He held out his hand. "I've got the tickets. Two. I've an idea the old boy in the paybox is your friend Gerard. He might have recognized you."

He was right. The man in the paybox was Gerard. I went back and had a look from a safe distance. Even in the half-light and with the little of him that was visible there was no mistaking that scruffy, tufty hair and the thin tight-drawn face, cross-hatched with its anxiety lines.

Seeing him there, his head bobbing about and his hands scraping in the crumpled and dirty franc notes, did something for me, something that had been lacking for a long time. I came awake, came out of a dusty dream and everything became hard and clear. I was right. This was the place and these were the people. But more than anything else I knew that somewhere close at hand was Sophie and that no matter what happened I was going to see her. I was going to get her away and after that we were going to have Jabal. Everything was falling into place, everything was working for me and I knew my own luck well enough not to question it or to let any doubt in. This morning I had been in the doldrums. Now I was sailing.

Dunwoody and I went in. The real entrance to the big top was masked by a small marquee which held a menagerie. It was lit by electric light that came from a generator that thumped away somewhere in the near distance. The crowd going into the circus passed first through the menagerie. Dunwoody and I circled slowly round with them and it was not long before I recognized two old friends, I Myna and Golden-eye. The first was an Indian myna bird—it didn't look like 3,000 francs worth, not for size or colour anyway—and the second was a golden-eyed pheasant, a beautiful cock bird. We walked around the cages. It was a poor show; a few monkeys with worn coats, a jackal that went round and round its pen practising for the mile walk, a honey bear, curled in a ball, and smelling like a damp rug. I know there are people who make a good case for caging animals, but they don't count with me. When I meet an animal that puts up a good case for being caged, I'll listen.

Dunwoody led the way in and we took seats in the front row below a small band which was raised on a wooden tier some way behind us. The ring was larger than I had expected. I kept my cap pulled well forward, but there was little danger of being recognized for the lighting, except in the ring centre, was poor. We sat there amidst the chatter and hum of voices and the band played selections from Offenbach and Verdi with more enthusiasm than style.

And within an hour I had seen them all; Fargette, Paviot, Sarrasin and Sophie. But if I had not known them and been there looking for them I should not have recognized them. Any policeman watching the show and with my descriptions of them in mind would have passed them over. In fact there was a policeman, the local gendarme from Banyuls, sitting about four places away from me. He must have had their descriptions from Didier, but he was enjoying himself, unworried by professional cares.

There were the usual acts; the band blaring away while a couple of trampolinists bounced up and down on their good-tempered bed; the long roll of the drum for the high-wire and the trapeze artists . . . and then Fargette. He came in dressed in baggy clown's clothes and with a troupe of performing dogs. The dogs were all shapes and sizes, but there was a wolf-hound amongst them. His face was painted but there was no mistaking him and I saw that round his neck he wore an enormous celluloid collar like the one I had seen hanging in the toilet at the chateau.

He put the dogs through a series of antics which they carried out with a quiet brisk indifference as though they disapproved of the whole thing. It was funny and the audience loved it. But I was remembering how the dogs at the Villa Maruba had not barked, and also the noise of barking and laughter in the afternoons at the Chateau Minerve. Fargette must have been rehearsing, or training, a new act up there.

When the turn was finished the dogs went off but Fargette stayed behind, wiped his brow as though exhausted and reached for a cigarette. He stood against a property door and the spot-light isolated him from the surrounding darkness. As he reached to light his cigarette a knife flew out of the darkness and cut the cigarette in half. The knife thudded into the door. Fargette, clownlike, puzzled, reached for another cigarette, but again a knife came from the darkness and chopped it in half for him and then the spot-light swung away from him to reveal a man dressed in Mexican gaucho clothes, wide-brimmed hat, and a belt festooned with knives.

I leaned over to Dunwoody and said, "That's Paviot."

"Handy with a knife," said Dunwoody and I heard him chuckle.

Paviot *was* handy with a knife, as handy as anyone I had ever seen. As I watched him fling knives at Fargette, outlining him against the door, I thought of the chopped cigarettes I had picked up in the courtyard. Now . . . here, in the circus, seeing it all . . . it was hard to realize that I had been puzzled then.

Everything was clear now. Sarrasin came on with his tigers. The clowns tumbled in horse-play about the ring as the great cage was set up. Sarrasin was the man on the circus poster and he was also my Sarrasin, a big, splendid brute carrying his leopard skin more naturally than any clothes. He put his tigers through their paces and I could feel the power and the pride in the man and there was no doubt that he was enjoying himself. But that didn't make me like him any better. For Fargette I had some sympathy, for Paviot disgust, but Sarrasin drew hatred from me and I knew why. He had used his strength contemptuously against Sophie and against me. I thought of the day Sophie and I had lain together on the cliff and of the dark bruise on her shoulder. I lit a cigarette and for a while the great bowl of the ring was lost to me, no more than a maze of shifting colours. Sophie whom I loved, and Sarrasin whom I hated. Whatever else seemed fantasy, those two things were hard and real. Against them even my feeling for Drexel was wan and spiritless. Drexel had gone out of my life in a sense when he had mutilated our friendship. All I had for him now was a charity which I could not avoid, but which I knew set people apart.

It's not easy to get one's motives and reasons sorted out, perhaps it was impossible for me to come to real truth in this affair. I could only hang on to the easy things that emerged from my thoughts . . . my love for Sophie, my hatred for Sarrasin and my compassion for Drexel which I suspected drew its life from the other two. I wished I had a clear, cold mind that could cut through cant and deediness to truth. All I had was a hodge-podge of half-baked thoughts and the conviction that that was how most people were unless they were saints and could command a spiritual ruthlessness and logic.

Dunwoody touched me on the shoulder and said, "This the girl?"

I came alive and said, "Yes."

"Thought she had dark hair?"

"It's a wig."

Sophie's hair was silver. She was going round the ring a foot on each of the backs of two white Arab horses. They were lovely things, lovely with the movement and form that makes a horse not an animal but a divinity and on their backs was a goddess. For me, anyway. She wore a short, white, Greek-looking tunic with a green belt and her dark hair was hidden by a tight-fitting silver wig. She was straight from some grey and gold island held by a wine-coloured sea. The vulgar crowd fell away, the patched and stained canvas canopy rolled back and the velvet night was full of heavy stars. She seemed to float from one horse to another, part of a slow-moving, graceful arabesque; she was neither maiden nor youth but some wonderful equivocal being that an incautious sound, a rude movement would startle into invisibility. I sat there holding my breath, stupid with love and uncritical adoration. . . . It sounds adolescent but for me it was a poetry in the blood and I didn't care who knew it. Time stood still without any awkwardness and the world stopped rolling without jolting a pebble out of place. Round and round she went and my eyes never left her.

When she had finished and gone out, I couldn't sit there. I had to go to her. I stood up. There were only a couple of people between me and the aisle.

Dunwoody held my arm for a moment and said, "Where you going?"

"I'll be back in a moment," I said and I pushed my way towards the aisle. I don't know how I got outside, through some slit in the canvas at the back of the seats I think. It was dark and the air was cool after the tent atmosphere. I could hear the generator pounding away and over its noise the crash and thunder of the band inside. Little lights showed in some of the caravans and a big arc light cast a great cone of pale yellow down by the main entrance to the marquee. Gerard, I thought, could count his money by it. Stepping over the stout guy ropes I went round to the back of the marquee towards the performers' entrance. Through the wide doorway of a smaller marquee I saw a circus hand holding the white Arabs. . . . *Remember money due on Arab.* It came to me now from Gerard's memorandum. Poor old Gerard, even the horses weren't fully paid for. How he must have jumped at Drexel's plan for some easy money.

And then, some way from the marquee, I saw the flash of a white tunic and a figure go up the short steps to a small trailer caravan.

I stood at the foot of the steps. The door was half-open for coolness and Sophie was sitting at a narrow dressing-table littered with make-up pots and odds and ends. She'd taken her wig off and thrown a dressing-gown over her shoulders, and she had her elbows on the table and was looking at herself in the mirror. Her legs were pushed out to one side of her chair and the pose was the same almost as the one she had had that first time I saw her. The princess who had lost her golden ball. Not unhappy but empty of hope.

I went up the steps and when I was inside I closed the door behind me. She turned and looked at me and at first I thought she hadn't recognized me because of my cap and the overalls. I pulled the cap off and smiled, but there was no need for that. She had recognized me but she was not believing it. She stood up and the dressing-gown fell back loosely from her shoulders and slid to the floor. It curled and twisted round her feet, and it was green and yellow and looked like a grass mound decked with flowers. Her skin was very brown against the white of her tunic and her face was very still with a fine-chiselled grace and firmness. The dark eyes which had been clouded with that familiar apprehension suddenly cleared and were bright and sparkling as though there was distant candlelight behind them. . . . That's how she was for me.

I said, "Sophie." But it wasn't a name or word. It was the movement of love in me.

She came into my arms and she rested there, not trembling, not excited, a bird coming down from the air, settling its wings and feathers, coming home; and the breath from her mouth as she raised it to me was a sigh which expressed all happiness and yet, too, the gentle ease of a long fatigue passing.

*   *   *

She was back at her dressing-table and I sat at the foot of her narrow bunk. I could see her face in the small mirror as she leaned forward and absently repaired her make-up. For the moment there were no more words between us; just that tranquil silence in which she turned and smiled at me and reached back her hand to take mine. There was no world for me but this caravan, four hundred and fifty cubic feet of happiness, the chintz curtains tied with ribbons, an ivory crucifix above the mirror, a row of books, a blue and white stove and a curtain in a corner half-drawn back to show dresses, costumes and an untidy jumble of shoes.

Then she said, "At first they were all sure you would go to the police. But there was nothing on the radio, nothing in the newspapers. Gerard was worried and they quarrelled among themselves . . . all wanting to do different things, until last night when he came. Where were you?"

I sat there, not really listening to her words but to her voice with its faint huskiness and the odd, affectionate thought in my mind that when she had a cold it would sound like a croak. . . .

I said, "I didn't go to the police for a lot of reasons. You. . . . I wanted to find you first."

Her hand tightened on mine and she went on, "I was sure something terrible had happened to you. Otherwise, why should they have been so confident after he came? They wouldn't tell me anything today. I wanted to know but I daren't ask, daren't show what I was feeling. That's why when you walked in I couldn't believe it at first. Not after last night."

I came back from the mists and said sharply, "What are you talking about? What about last night?"

"I was in Gerard's caravan. I do the accounts with him and it must have been two o'clock when he walked in. They sent me away. But today everything was different. Gerard and the others like new men. . . . So confident. We've got a poor crowd tonight, and normally Gerard would be frantic. But he doesn't care."

I said, "Listen, Sophie, I'm at sea. Who is this he you're talking about? And why shouldn't he walk in and why anyway should it make you think anything had happened to me?"

"Who?" I saw the surprise on her face. "Haven't you been listening to me?"

"Of course I have. But you've just said he. What he?"

She stood up and I honestly believe she thought I was teasing her.

"Colonel Drexel, of course, David."

"What?"

I was on my feet in a flash.

I took her by the shoulders and I almost shouted, "Has he been here? Colonel Drexel? No—he can't have been!"

She said, "What's the matter, David? Why shouldn't he? He'd only gone to Paris they told me. Why shouldn't he come back?"

But her words now were only a wash of sound in my ears. Drexel had been here last night! I didn't get it. If someone had struck me hard between the eyes I couldn't have been more dazed. I stood there looking at her stupidly, but the stupidity didn't last. It exploded in a blast of anger that was almost physical. Drexel. The damned, black-hearted, devious snake! Here I'd been sweating my guts out and walking the edge for him and all the time. . . .

My face must have been an ugly sight for she suddenly shook me and said, "David, don't look like that. Tell me what is it? You make me feel afraid again."

"It's all right," I said.

It was the understatement of the century. But I couldn't go into it all with her now.

I stood there with my hands on her shoulders and she waited for me, afraid for me. And at that moment I am not sure that there was no fear in me. Drexel had been here the previous night. And then I saw it, saw how I had underrated him, under-estimated the devilry and the courage of the man. He had started to play for high stakes and when the game had gone against him he had staked higher. He had come out of his coma. He had recognized me all right, but he had gone on playing the invalid. . . . He must have enjoyed that. Me, sitting there, itching for him to come to his senses and he laughing, knowing that he was immobilizing me and waiting for his chance. And he had taken it last night. He must have slipped out, leaving Dunwoody sleeping, wheeled the motor-cycle down the drive and been away to Gerard. It was a hell of a risk . . . but just the kind of risk that delighted him. I knew now that I had not been mistaken when I thought I heard someone in the courtyard. It was Drexel, and he must have got back into bed only a few seconds before I looked in on him. . . . I swore to myself and couldn't help admiring the audacity of the man. This was the kind of thing which had made him a public hero. . . . And I saw it all. Last night he had made his arrangements with Gerard . . . and tonight, after the show, the whole gang was to come down on Dunwoody and myself and restore the *status quo*. But the plan would be a little different now. Neither Dunwoody nor myself would survive the ransoming of Jabal.

Sophie said, "You haven't told me a thing about what you've been doing or what you're going to do. Why are you here?"

I saw myself in the glass beyond her, tall, untidy in overalls, the cut on my forehead still raw-looking and my face was angry. I seemed to be staring at a stranger, a tight-lipped, angry-eyed being, tense now with an ugly but necessary resolution.

"Don't worry. It's all going to be fixed." And it was. I was throwing Drexel overboard. I was going to the police. It was the only thing to do. Minerva with the cold, stern face was the girl for my money. Doing the right thing would hurt Drexel all right—it would hurt me, too. But there was no other damned way out.

"I've never seen you look like this."

"I've never felt like this before."

"What do you mean? David. . . ."

"It's all right. What have they done with Jabal?"

"He's in one of the box cars. They keep him drugged, I think."

I said, "How much money have you got? Enough to take you to Paris?"

She nodded.

"Give me a pencil."

I found a scrap of paper and I wrote a name and address on it.

"You're going to Paris tonight. Take one of their cars and drive to Perpignan. You can get a train there. Go to this address. It's a friend of mine. Tell him I sent you and stay with him until I come. You're staying out of this mess if I can fix it."

"But I can't go."

"Yes, you can, and right away."

"But I've got another turn after the interval."

I thought that one over. I meant to go to the police and throw the whole thing in. But if Sophie cleared off before the end of the circus it might make them suspicious.

"Do your show and then go. I won't go to the police until you're well on your way to Perpignan. Do as I say, Sophie, and everything will be all right."

She was worried, I could see that. Too often in her life she had been worried and that dark look had lived in her eyes. Too long she had lived on the fringe of darkness and sunlight. Now she was coming out into the sunlight and I was going to be with her.

I bent down and kissed her gently. "Go to Paris after the show and wait for me. I can't explain more."

She stood up. It was hard for hope to take hold of her.

"You'll go to the police," she said "but they'll bring me back. The others won't let me go free."

"Nobody's going to bring you back. You're staying with me for good." I could do it, too, I knew. Behind Jabal there was power and discretion. Behind Drexel's coming disgrace lay my strength. The Foreign Office, the *Bureau des Affaires Etrangères* and the oil interests . . . they owed me something and I knew the price I was going to ask. Sophie's name stayed out of this. After all she had played a part she had never understood, forced into by fear. It was a small price and I knew they would pay it.

She said, "But they will bring me back. You don't understand." She was stubborn with the conviction in her.

"What can they do to you? What hold have they got on you?"

She looked up at me. "I'm not French. I've no papers—only forged ones. They got them for me when the circus came out of Spain, years ago, when I was a child. A word from them and the authorities would send me back."

"They wouldn't do that."

"They would. . . ."

I got it from her but it took some getting. Even to me she didn't like talking about it though when it came it didn't seem all that dreadful to me. But if a threat and a fear may have been held over you since you were a child and you've grown up with it, it becomes so much part of you that you can't shake it off or see its proper proportions. And every year that passes makes it more hopeless to contemplate ever being free of it. All her family, except her brother, were dead. They were from Barcelona and had got on the wrong side of the Falangists. Her brother still lived in Spain, an outlaw, a price on his head . . . working against Franco. If she was sent back she would be a wonderful hostage. They wouldn't care a damn what they did with her so long as it brought her brother in—and he would come; she knew that. He would give himself up to save her. And she was sure that the French would send her back because she had helped Gerard and Sarrasin to smuggle stuff between the two countries. She'd been useful to them on the French end, and they had a nice hold on her. . . . They were a prize lot, all right. They had brought her out of Spain and looked after her, given

154

her a job when she had been a destitute child and then had used her. Gratitude and fear, it's an ugly mixture, but it works.

When she had finished I put my arm around her.

"You're going to have a nationality," I said. "You're going to have mine as soon as I get to Paris." I kissed her and she was inside my arms.

"David . . . it can't be."

"Don't be a fool." I held her, driving out fear and warming hope in her. "You're not going back to Spain. You're coming with me to England as my wife. As for the rest of the stuff about smuggling and the French authorities—don't worry. No matter what Gerard may say about you, I can fix that. You'll have helped to get Jabal back. . . . God, they owe me something, too!"

But even while she was in my arms I began to think about Gerard and Sarrasin. They'd played on the fears of a child and built them up. . . . It was dirty, mean dirty, and I was sorry that I was going to finish them off cleanly by going to the police. They rated something less formal. . . .

"I'll give you an hour after the show is over," I said. "Then I go to the police. If you aren't in Perpignan on your way to Paris by then. . . ." I raised my hand, threatening her with love and for the first time she laughed, really laughed, a low, gentle sound that was music to me.

I went down the steps and she closed the door behind me. And I went back through the darkness and hoped I would not meet Gerard or Sarrasin because I knew I would not wait for the niceties of police procedure. . . .

When I got back the interval was nearly over. Dunwoody was twisting about in his seat with a strained expression on his face which I supposed was worry, but his habitual cheerfulness and twinkle wouldn't let it appear authentic.

He said, "Where the hell have you been? I began to think they'd nabbed you."

"I've been talking to the girl."

"The girl?"

"Sophie. I've never told you . . . but she and I are going to be married."

He stared at me with his mouth open and for once there was no twinkle in his eyes. Then slowly his mouth closed and he shook his head and blew out his cheeks.

"Either you like things to be difficult—or you're crazy."

"No, I'm not, I'm sane and I know exactly what I'm going to do. When this show's finished I'm going to the police. We're finishing with this game altogether." I put out a hand and held

155

his arm. "You've been a great help to me. But the best turn you ever did me was to sleep heavily."

"Sleep heavily? Look, save the riddles for some party. What is happening?"

I told him how Drexel had visited the circus the previous night. Sitting there in the front row with a gendarme a few places away and the ring hands smothing out the sawdust and tan bark for the last half of the show, I felt confident and my mind was clearly made up. When I had finished talking, Dunwoody said:

"If you're going to the police after the show, I know where I'm going now. I'm going back to the chateau. If Drexel really is all right he may not stay put. I've got his clothes and he's locked in, but that cove's a Houdini. You know that. He may get out and he'll find something to wear if it's only a couple of chair covers. . . . I'll be back there in an hour and I'll take up the gendarme from the village and we'll sit tight until we hear from you. You don't want the big fish to slip from you now. . . . Blimey, fancy him sneaking out on me like that! And he must have used my bike, too!"

I think this last must have been the bigger insult. I had to smile.

I said, "Yes, I think you should go back."

"No doubt about it. If he got out he might see that circus handbill in the kitchen. He'd guess what we were doing and he might warn these people. If Gerard and company knew we were in here they'd stop at nothing. Paviot would have a knife in us . . . or something."

"You'd better get going," I said. I felt that he was a bit cut-up that the Colonel should have slipped out while he was supposed to be watching him. That touched his professional pride. It was the kind of thing, I guessed, that his brother Albert would never let him forget.

He stood up to go and he said quietly, "Keep out of trouble."

"Don't worry." I nodded towards the gendarme. "When I get out of here I'm sticking to him. He's sure to go and have a drink somewhere. As soon as Sophie is clear I'm going to join him."

I could see the moment coming, a big moment for the gendarme and one he would talk about for years.

Dunwoody went and I was left alone. I slouched back in my seat, pulled my cap forward a shade more and lit a cigarette. There was only a little time left now. Jabal was going to be safe. There was going to be a hell of an awakening for a lot of people. I couldn't even guess what would happen to Drexel.

But at the back of my mind I had a feeling that international and oil interests might decide to keep the real truth from the public . . . it would be better that way. Whatever happened, though, it would be the end of Drexel. I could think of that without pity. The end of Drexel. . . . Prison for a while, maybe . . . then he would drift into a shabby obscurity, become a lonely, eccentric anonymity. . . . And for once I could find no compassion in me for him or any of the others. I was thinking of the child Sophie, her innocent simplicity warped by fears and threats . . . and, then, of the woman Sophie, waiting now to step out into the sunshine.

I THINK it was the spotlight which first made me uneasy. But I couldn't be sure of this. Maybe just waiting there, knowing that the end was approaching worked on my nerves and filled me with a growing impatience for the show to be done.

While the acts were going on the bowl of the ring was flooded with lights and the surrounding tiers of seats were in a half gloom, but every now and again a small spotlight from a box on the far side of the ring would detach itself from the other lights and the beam would drift gently round the sea of faces as though the electrician, tired of his real duties, was searching out some friend. This happened again and again. The light would come gently towards me. For a moment it would be full in my face and then gone. Maybe I was hypersensitive now but I got the impression that each time it reached me it paused for a moment and that somewhere a voice was saying, "Ah, there you are. Still there. Good."

I told myself not to be a fool, but my uneasiness persisted. I wondered if Gerard and company had found out I was in the circus. Maybe Drexel had got out and got in touch with them. But I could not believe this. And, anyway, I told myself, even if they did know there was nothing they could do. There were dozens of people around me, and a gendarme only a few places away. There was no way they could touch me. I don't remember much about the acts for I watched the gendarme most of the time. I didn't want to lose him. He was a big, capable-looking man, stolid and probably not very intelligent but comforting to look at.

But each time that spot came wandering across the seats and flicked over me, I stirred uncomfortably.

Sophie came on about half-way through the second half. There were two men with her and four easy-stepping, broad-backed grey horses. I wondered which were her favourites, the greys or the Arabs, and which got the bigger sugar ration. It was a curious sensation watching her turn somersaults, fly from one man to another and then, perched high on the pyramid of their shoulders, swing lazily round the ring. Out there she had a vitality new to me, her body quicksilver, every movement sure and fluid. I thought: I'm going to marry her. She's going to be my wife; a bare-back rider, a circus queen. When I went back to teaching it was going to be amusing. Mrs. David Bladen Fraser, late of the Grand Cirque Pyrénéen. The Board of Governors, the head's wife and the other women might look old-fashioned, but the boys would love it. . . . But was I going back? Could I go back after all this? And then, quite definitely, I knew I was going back. I liked teaching. Nothing had been changed for me. It was my profession and I didn't care a damn that there were no big money rewards . . . there were other rewards. Sophie wouldn't let me down. I knew that. Yes, I was going back. Drexel had always had me wrong. I wasn't pelagic; just a simple barn-yard creature. . . . I smiled to myself and the spotlight hit me full in the face and then was gone.

There was a great burst of hand-clapping and shouting as Sophie and her team went off. The band burst into a noisy fanfare and into the ring came tumbling half a dozen clowns and a crazy-looking motor-car which spouted flour from its horn and sent a jet of water shooting up from its radiator when the cap was lifted. It was all traditional, well-loved stuff. I watched them and I could pick out Fargette, and, I thought, Paviot and there was an enormous fellow in a battered top-hat and tight morning-clothes who I guessed was Sarrassin. But this was no surprise. In a poor circus everyone plays many parts. I watched them trip one another over, produce strings of sausages from inside their coats, pour water and flour about and, in their efforts to start the car, gradually shake the thing to pieces. Sarrasin did a strong-man act and failed to lift a great dumb-bell and then Fargette came along and lifted Sarrasin and the bar. The audience roared with delight. There may not be a touch of the poet in us all but there's a fair-sized slice of the clown. I laughed with the rest, but part of my mind was with Sophie in her caravan. She was changing now. She would pack a bag and soon be away. It was a long trip to Paris. I wondered what she would be thinking about all the way, saw her sitting in her carriage, staring out of the window while league after league of France flew by her. . . . Sophie moving ahead to a future whose strangeness I would have to temper for her.

The clowns now had given up the motor-car in disgust. In angry voices they were blaming one another and shouting that they must have a mechanic. With one accord they turned to the audience appealing.

"A mechanic! A mechanic! Is there a mechanic here?"

Voices called back to them and from behind me someone offered them fifty francs for the car as scrap.

But Fargette began to bounce up and down, his baggy check trousers ballooning, his great collar rising and falling about his ears and he shouted—

"Francois! There's Francois—he'll fix it." He pretended to recognize someone. Then, followed by the others, he began to run across the ring. They came straight towards me.

"Francois! Oh, the good Francois!"

"Francois!"

They came tumbling and running towards me. I had a suspicion of what might happen and I think I even began to rise. But the spot swung round suddenly and isolated me. There I was half-risen in my seat and I heard my own voice shout angrily, "No! No!"

Then my cry was swallowed in a burst of laughter from the audience as Fargette, Paviot, Sarrasin and another were on me. They grabbed me and hauled me roughly over the protecting bank into the ring.

"Francois! Francois!"

Laughing and pushing around me, they fought over my body. I was tripped and fell on my back. Someone squirted water in my face and I was half-blinded. I struggled up and swung out at them, but I went down again and my ears were full of the laughter and delighted shouts of the audience who saw in it all part of a carefully rehearsed act. I got to my feet and began to run back . . . back towards the gendarme. I must have looked a fool, not desperate, but funny. I shouted something but the next instant I was sprawling as Paviot tripped me and my mouth was full of sawdust. They jumped for me, picked me up by my arms and legs and carried me into the centre of the ring, swinging me stretcher fashion and chanting my name—

"Francois! Francois!"

They dumped me down and as I tried to rise, swearing at them, and striking with my fists, Fargette jumped on my shoulders and clamped his legs round my neck. I swayed upwards, nearly made it and collapsed. And now they just took me and sported with me. I could feel their blows no pantomime, no mockery. Sarrasin kicked me skilfully in the side and the breath went from me. I had no power to shout or resist. I was conscious only of the roaring crowd and this frenzied, dancing circle of clowns, their painted faces, red noses and weird clothes ringing about me.

They rolled me over on to a large tarpaulin, grabbed the corners and the next instant I was flying up into the air, arms and legs spreadeagled and the whole place reeling in front of my eyes. They caught me as I came down and up I went again, and I think I must have been weak, not physically, but with frustration. Right here, under the eyes of hundreds of people, they were carrying me off and only a few yards away was the security I had thought so certain . . . my gendarme friend, his red face convulsed with laughter.

It was a nightmare, the shouting, the blaring of the band, the flying up into space and then the slow dip back to earth, and the spotlights, coloured now, whirling and intertwining, the whole thing a mad, desperate medley. Once, as I came down and rested for a moment on the sheet, I saw Sarrasin's face leaning over me. It was painted with great streaks of red and yellow and his top-hat was cocked to one side, and I could see the quick heave of his throat above the tight hard collar, and he was smiling grotesquely through the grease-paint. No, not smiling, but laughing, roaring with laughter.

I think, in my confusion, the one thing I feared, if I had time for fear, was a quick knife-thrust from Paviot as I came down. But they had other plans.

I came down for the last time and lay for a second or two, so winded that I could not move. Fargette snatched up an enormous pepper-pot and sprinkled me with sand while another clown from an equally large container flicked white chalk for salt over me. Then with a great shout of triumph they suddenly rolled me over and over in the sheet. They screwed me up in it as a sausage is wrapped in a pastry roll. I was in darkness and half-stifled and then almost sick with giddiness as they began to swing me round and round.

I felt myself dumped roughly in the car, and then heard the spluttering roar of its motor. I was jolted and bumped about as it drove off. Someone sat on me heavily. I don't know what happened then. I was in darkness with only sensation for company. I heard the blare of the band die away and the roaring of the crowd thin to a faint murmur and there was only the clear, beating sound of the car. Then silence. Then voices. Something banged, a door clattered. I was lifted. I was thrown, flying upwards, and then, wrapped like a cocoon, crashed on to hardness. My head hit something and there was a galaxy of light before me eyes. A slow, irresistible tiredness swept over me. I didn't pass out, but I had no will or strength. I just lay there and groaned gently to myself against the nausea in me and idly wondered how long I would be able to go on breathing in this cocoon.

*   *   *

It was the regular jolting and the sound of the engine which brought me out of my stupor. I could breathe evenly and somewhere above my head and beyond me was a meagre light set in a glass bowl protected by an iron grillwork. I struggled to a sitting position and saw that the tarpaulin had been cleared from my head and shoulders but was still wrapped around my feet. I was on a wooden floor covered with a loose litter of straw.

A woman's hand came towards me, took my wrist gently and I heard Sophie say, "Are you all right?"

I said, "Yes," absently, and wondered what she was doing there. The floor jolted violently and I was tipped sideways. An arm held me and I turned my head to find that she was sitting beside me. Her arm held me firmly by the shoulder.

I said, "So you didn't get off to Paris?"

She smiled and put up a hand and brushed my hair from my forehead.

"No."

"Where are we?"

"In one of the lorried box-cages."

I pulled myself up a bit more and shook my head to get the bleariness from my eyes, and suddenly my mind cleared.

Sophie was sitting close to me with a raincoat over a blouse and skirt. I saw the plank-ribbed walls of the swaying box-cage and a little grilled window high up on my right. It came back then. Not only had I been taken, but she had been caught as well. That meant they knew about us. I said urgently, "How did they know about you? Sophie, what's happened?"

She gave no answer in words, but her eyes left mine and she looked towards the far end of the lorry. I followed her gaze and in the shadows I saw two men sitting on a long packing-case. They sat close together, their backs touching, both of them moving a little with the swing of the lorry. One was Fargette, still in his clown's clothes, and in his hand, glinting under the feeble light, I saw that he held an automatic. The sight of it reminded me of my own gun and instinctively my hand went to my overalls for it. It was gone.

But its loss hardly impinged on me. At that moment the second man swayed forward a little and the thin rays of the overhead light illuminated his face.

I couldn't believe it. I stared at him like an idiot and some-

162

where in my mind a voice was hammering away saying, "No! No!" and there was a vast emptiness inside me. It couldn't be! It damned well couldn't be! I almost shouted the words and at the same time some instinctive, rageful reaction sent me forward, trying to untangle the layers of tarpaulin from my legs.

Fargette raised his revolver and he said throatily, "Stay where you are, monsieur. If not——" The weapon swung towards Sophie, and, at that moment, her hand pulled me back.

"It's no use, David." Her voice was heavy with hopelessness.

I dropped back against the wall of the lorry, the jolt and bang of the boards beating against my shoulders. The man sitting by Fargette began to chuckle. The chuckle grew to a laugh. I could see the tears squeeze from the corners of his small eyes, and the rich shake of his plump cheeks. He raised the hand which was free of a gun and thumped himself on the chest to relieve the choking humour in him. The motion set his familiar toupee askew and his drooping Edwardian quiff trembled like the curled tail feathers of a drake.

"Oh," he choked. "Lord, it was funny! Funny. . . . If you could have seen yourself! Up and down, up and down and shouting your head off. . . . I'll never forget it. Not if I live to be a hundred!"

I said evenly, feeling small and with no advantage, hating to see him with all the honours, and hating the feebleness of my own words, "Don't laugh your head off, Dunwoody. One day I'm going to knock it off."

"Not you, chum. . . ." The bubble of dying humour was still in his voice and his tear-moist eyes twinkled as though they were set with brilliants. "Not you, chum. I don't like to say it, but you're the one who's going to be knocked off. You and the girl."

It didn't come through at once. Only slowly. Like ink dropped on to a blotting-pad, a small ugly spot and then spreading into an uneven, dirty patch.

"You and the girl." He said it again and the odd thing was that though there was no menace or force in his voice, just a plump old bastard with a shining face talking in a matter-of-fact tone, the words chilled me. Because Dunwoody meant it. The man was incapable of rhetoric. He meant what he said.

My hand found Sophie's and I held it tight.

"You're a bastard, Dunwoody," I said. "A dirty bastard. . . ."

"Naughty. . . ." He shook his head and I knew that I hadn't touched him. There was nothing there that I could touch.

And that filled me with a spleen that I wished I could have taken out on him. The words were there now, all the rich and pungent vocabulary that years in a Scots regiment had given me, but I let them lie. Not words, but action was what I wanted, and that was denied me.

"Don't try anything, Mr. Fraser," he said. "Keep in your little Jack Horner. If you don't we'll let the girl have it first."

I got myself in hand then. A lot of things were suddenly clear to me and I began to wonder that I could have been such an innocent. But then that is how one is betrayed; by one's own innocence, by the trust one puts in faces and words, by the blindness that keeps men's hearts shrouded. First Drexel, and now Dunwoody. I was getting my share this trip.

I said, "Mr. Greatheart Dunwoody. The heavy sleeper. The Dunwoody Detective Agency. . . . No wonder your card was dirty and crumpled. Did you only have one printed?"

He chuckled and shrugged himself more comfortably into his leather jacket.

"You take too narrow a view . . . uncharitable, I call it. I'm just doin' a job. My job. It ain't the kind you can do with love and kisses. But believe me I'm real sorry about what's coming to you and the lady. Real sorry."

I didn't believe it. Real sorry, where other people were concerned, was only a literary term for him.

"What have you done with the Colonel?" I asked.

His eyes opened a little wider. "Nothing—except a deal. You'll see him later, maybe."

"A deal?"

He nodded, and then flicked a fat finger towards the far side of the lorry. Lying in the shadows I saw something which had so far escaped me. A slight, curled-up form, a head cushioned peacefully on an arm. It was Jabal, apparently sleeping peacefully.

"Drugged," said Dunwoody a little severely, even disapprovingly, "and I hope they haven't overdone it because he's got a trip ahead of him early this morning. . . ." He chuckled and I hated to see him enjoying himself so much. "A nice little trip . . . back to Ramaut, by way of Spain, Mr. Fraser. And I'm real grateful to you. I am really. If it hadn't been for you I'd have never pulled it off. Lummy, it's odd, ain't it, the way things work out?"

He was like a man who'd won a prize in a sweepstake. Talkative and wanting to go back over it all, from the moment he'd thought of buying a ticket, what his wife had said and

164

how it was Wednesday the something, his lucky day and lucky number. . . . I knew how he felt. Right into his lap. Right into his broad, capable hands . . . the twinkling-eyed, chubby-faced bastard. But suddenly, beyond and above all this, came the lightning sear of panic. Jabal back to Ramaut. My head must still have been a bit muzzy for I heard myself in class saying, "'Jabal back to Ramaut'. Translate". And then the hesitant words, *"Jabal va vers sa mort"*. Oh, yes, and no mistake. Jabal back to Ramaut meant Jabal to his death.

"You're a Regent's man. You're a murderer."

"I'm doing a job. Didn't you ever send a platoon out knowing that some wouldn't come back? Death ain't so hard, not even your own if you get to thinkin' right about it. Anyway, you fixed it for him. I offered the Colonel a deal from Ahmed ben Fa'id ages ago, but he turned it down. Then you mucked him up. You did it, chum. If you'd sat tight in the chateau he'd have gone to the oil company and Jabal wouldn't be putting up his shutters. You——" He jabbed his forefinger towards me. "You, chum, fixed Jabal up. You gave me my chance to talk the Colonel round. And it was easy when he learned you meant to play guardian angel to him. Blimey, you should have heard his language. Come to think of it you did hear some. Remember the time you come in and said you thought you'd heard voices. Well, chum, you did. His and mine. Life's tricky, ain't it? The little ins and outs, I mean."

Life was tricky, all right. But it wasn't the little ins and outs as he called them. It was the people in life. People like Dunwoody and Drexel.

Dunwoody sat there, beaming, and I think he expected me to say something, to protest, curse him or even make some move. He was disappointed. But I didn't enjoy just lying there, jolted by the rapid progress of the lorry, feeling Sophie close against my shoulder and seeing Jabal curled up in a drugged sleep. It was no good telling myself that I could not be blamed if the things I had done from the best motives had inevitably brought them very close to death. . . . I couldn't believe it. Every breath we take involves us in some unexpected responsibility. I *was* to blame.

Drexel had the whole thing nicely planned. Originally Jabal was to be taken off and then ransomed to the oil company. No harm would have come to him. I would have been the scapegoat, safely out of it on my way to South America with plenty of money. Even if I had dared to come back, I could have proved nothing. The Chateau Minerve would have been empty and no trace of the people who had hired it. They would make sure of that. Gerard and company would be nicely hidden away in their circus, and Jabal's word would destroy mine.

But I had spoilt that by escaping and then holding Drexel. Dunwoody must have been watching his chance for a long time, and I had given it to him. My quixotic plan to save Drexel could not have been more convenient for him. Drexel must have come to his senses that first morning and he and Dunwoody had fixed the whole thing up. Drexel, now hating me, determined not to lose his chance of money, had gone right over. He had been forced into ruthlessness. He was selling Jabal right back to Sheikh Ahmed ben Fa'id and to cover himself he was prepared to see me and Sophie go under. It was the final passage in his deterioration. You made the first step, an easy one, but after that time and chance took over and there was no going back, no giving up, not if you had the stiff pride and hungry determination which marked Drexel.

At the chateau he and Dunwoody had fixed it all up beautifully between them. When the Colonel had gone to see Gerard he had, no doubt, given orders for Sarrasin and his boys to come up and take me. My coming to the circus must have put Dunwoody in a desperate mood. But not a hint of it had he shown me and, when I had told him about Sophie and my intention to go to the police, he had left me, slipped round and seen Gerard and they had worked out the clown act there and then. I could imagine Gerard's moment of panic and then the swift, capable decision to take me right under the nose of hundreds of people. If you play for big stakes you must take big risks—and they had not hesitated.

We were in the lorry a good two hours. We said nothing. Just the five of us. I had Sophie's hand in mine and I had the comforting feeling that she had found a new strength. She was no longer afraid . . . but I was, for her and Jabal and, frankly, for myself. Yet while we were in this shadowed, straw-littered world the real potency was slowly withdrawn from fear. Nothing could happen here so long as no movement was made. This was an interregnum. Real life, and the prospect of life's end, would come when we stepped out.

Fargette yawned occasionally and Dunwoody whistled very gently to himself. They were like a couple of night-watchmen, bored, waiting for the end of the spell. Looking at Dunwoody I could be coldly curious as to the kind of man that really lurked under that plump, cheerful exterior. He was a superb actor, and a man with a ready, unfaltering courage . . . it was odd that the qualities which made a hero went for a villain, too. Only that thin line of dedication separated them, the choice of a banner to fight under.

The lorry stopped and I was jerked forward. Somewhere outside I heard men's voices and then the bang of doors and the squeal of hinges. The lorry moved again and then stopped.

The doors at the back of the lorry were pulled back and as Fargette and Dunwoody rose, covering us still, I saw Gerard, Sarrasin and Paviot standing in a welcoming committee outside. Sarrasin was wearing a long, loose coat which I guessed covered his clown's clothes. Paviot had changed and both of them had wiped the make-up roughly from their faces. Gerard was in his wrinkled blue suit, his scraggy neck thrust forward as he peered into the lorry.

"All right? Is everything all right?" he fussed.

Fargette nodded and jumped down and Dunwoody followed lowering himself bulkily.

I stood up and Sophie rose with me. We walked to the end of the lorry and halted. The five of them stood in a tight semi-circle waiting for us.

So far as I could see we were in a large, barn-like structure, the lorry driven well in. A couple of hurricane lamps were burning on two cases near the wide open double doors and outside was a moonlit stretch of rough ground. Across the open space the corner of some farm-building, white, bone-like in the pale light, showed and beyond it I glimpsed a pewter-stretch of water and the dark plumes of poplars. There was a pungent smell and suddenly, from the darkness at the side of the barn, I heard the disturbed grunt of some animal.

"Come down and behave yourselves," said Gerard, and he might have been a fussy parent who had caught two children in some naughtiness. "Come down! Come down at once!"

We did not move for a moment. And in that pause, that moment of waiting, my eyes came back to their faces and there was that in them which was unpleasant to see. They weren't angry, they weren't resentful, they weren't anything but faces suddenly stripped of all feeling. They were looking at us and not seeing us as human beings. We were things, just things with which they had to deal . . . objects that were soon to be put away and forgotten, and maybe in their minds they had already disposed of us. Gerard, like an untidy sparrow, pursing his lips and impatient with our slowness; Dunwoody bland, patient, knowing his cards were good; Paviot, dark and shabby, full of a frayed energy and violence; Fargette, dwarf-like and with a simple, good-natured disregard of pain in others—and then Sarrasin. My eyes met his, and we spoke to one another without words, spoke our hatred of each other, and I could see that his had grown in pace with mine, and instinctively I knew that it was because of Sophie. Somewhere in him was a capacity for affection that was linked to Sophie. The nearer she came to me and disaster, the more he hated me as he acknowledged that he would do nothing for her.

I jumped down and then turned, reaching up a hand for Sophie. She joined me and they closed in around us. We were shepherded across the barn. The whole of one side was taken up by animal cages raised about three feet off the ground. Gerard opened the cage on the extreme left by the door. There was no point in protesting or fighting. There were too many of them. Sophie climbed up and I followed her. Gerard slammed the bolt over, padlocked it and they all stood back, looking at us. We might have been new animal stock, just arrived, and they watching us with an intense curiosity to see how we would take to our new quarters.

Then, as we did not move or speak, did nothing to feed their curiosity, they turned and left us. I saw Gerard hang his keys on a nail by the large doors. One of them closed and locked the back of the lorry with Jabal in it and they went out, swinging over the double doors behind them.

CHAPTER XVII

SOPHIE told me where we were. It was the farm which was used as the winter quarters and training establishment for the circus. It was looked after by Gerard's married sister and her husband. The barn we were in, a large corrugated iron affair, housed sick animals and those which were under training and not yet ready to go into the circus. The farm itself was about forty miles from Banyuls and well up in the mountains. The Franco-Spanish border was within five miles by a route, over very rough country, which Gerard and Sarrasin had used in the past for smuggling. The farm stood on the edge of a lake ringed about by the hills.

We sat on the bare boards of the cage floor and talked in low voices that echoed strangely about the cavernous interior. The cage next to ours on the right was full of birds. I could see them moving restlessly on their long bamboo perches. Our presence disturbed them. A large hornbill sidled up to the bars and stared at us magisterially. Somewhere in the far shadows there was a shrill cry and the beat of large wings, and then a thin, piping complaint. Somehow I was reminded of the dusk and lonely coastal flats and the weird sounds of unseen night birds . . . of the emphasis and menace that solitude can carry.

Further along the barn I could see the dark movement of animals, the occasional green glitter of eyes caught in the dim light of the hurricane lamps and hear the slither and rustle of straw as bodies turned restlessly. Once a monkey chattered and screeched indignantly and then was answered by the raucous, short growl of a lion.

"That's Karimba," said Sophie. "Sarrasin has four new lions and is training them. The far end of the barn can be turned into a large training cage. You're cold?"

She took off her raincoat and sitting close to me draped it over our shoulders. Then she looked across at the lorry which had brought us here. "Why have they left Jabal there?"

"He won't be there long." I tried not to think of what lay ahead of Jabal . . . and of us. But my mind refused to free itself of the thoughts. Somewhere the night wind rattled a loose sheet of corrugated iron—a shivering, apprehensive sound.

I said, "It's clear how they mean to take Jabal out. Over the

169

Spanish border. . . . God knows what will happen to him after that." I slipped my arm round her and she put her head against my neck and she was warm, strong and untrembling, but I knew what was in her mind. It was something neither of us had to speak about.

She said, "This farm was one of the first places I came to in France. I used to bathe in the lake, but even in summer the water is very cold. . . . Even now, you feel the night air is cold. Animals like cold, not draughts, but cold. It improves their coats. There is another barn near the farmhouse where we keep the horses. . . ."

It was hard to say whether she was talking to me or herself. . . . But I knew how she felt. It was hard to sit waiting in this gloom. I held her closer. My Sophie. . . . If it had been possible then I could have gladly had it that we might go back over the past days, never to have met, and me, never to have loved, that she might be free and in no danger. I remembered my moment of first seeing her . . . remembered the lumps of wrapped sugar spilling from her bag in the aquarium. We sat there and she told me about the early years she had spent on this farm, how under Gerard—who was wonderful with horses— she had been trained. But all the time she was talking part of me was away from her. Now and again I could hear Jabal turn over and mutter to himself in the locked lorry. A toucan, looking like a Jewish rabbi, sidled along its perch in the next cage and looked down its great nose at us. Karimba grumbled hoarsely in its throat from the far darkness. The place was restless, full of life, but none of it carrying any pity or under- standing for us. I watched a rat come out and forage along the bottom of some stacked bales of straw by the door. But time and again my eyes came back to the bunch of cage keys on a wire loop that hung on a nail by the large double doors. I had already tried the padlock and the bars of the cage but they were not to be forced. I looked at my watch. It was three o'clock. Soon now—if Dunwoody were right—Jabal would be taken off. An early morning trip. A trip from which he would not return and, after he had left, what would happen to us . . . or rather, how would it happen to us?

I held Sophie more closely and she was saying, "There's a little stream runs down behind the farm. This time of the year it's lined with arum lilies . . . a white pathway of them and the farm ducks lay their eggs amongst them so that you have to walk carefully. . . ."

I said, "We had ducks when I was a boy. But we never let

them out of the duck-house until eight o'clock in the morning. That made sure they always laid in the house."

She said, "These have no house." Then she was silent for a while and it was clear to me that her thoughts were back with those first days when she had been a child here. When time runs short one looks back on the good things and finds courage in them.

She went on, "Fargette came with me from Barcelona. . . . You know, he's not nearly as old as you would imagine."

I said, "I hate their guts. The whole lot of them."

Her hand tightened on mine and, very quietly, she said, "In their way they were good to me. When you're poor you can be good to people—and then cruel. I don't hate them. I just want to forget them."

I knew what she meant. People are good to you from their virtues, offer friendship and protection; and then, from their evil, from their own desperate needs, they are cruel. Why expect only the gifts of their virtues? If you take friendship, you must take the person who offers it, too. Very few jewels get a perfect setting.

She was saying, "Fargette is a good clown. . . . It is in his family. He fishes, too. There's a little boat we would take on the lake and he would fish and talk. . . . With grown-ups he is usually silent, but with children he talks. He used to tell me stories . . . all the tales from Perrault, and the Fables of La Fontaine . . . with a different voice for each animal. And he would tell my fortune. . . . Oh, David, you've no idea of the silly, lovely things he used to say. I'd be bruised and scratched from falling off the horses, convinced I would never be any good, and he would tell me what lay ahead. All the great cities of Europe and the wide tan-bark rings with thousands of faces watching like a spread of rice on the darkness and me going round and round and the whole world falling in love with me. I used to worry him for details. I was so young. Who would I marry and how many children would I have? And it would be an emperor with a row of stables so long that, as you looked down the stall-doors with the horses' heads hanging over them, the head of the last horse would be no bigger than a pea. And, standing by each horse, a child, a long line of sons and daughters. . . . We used to laugh until the boat rocked . . . inventing names for the children and the horses."

I said, "When you marry me, we'll be poor. It'll be one horse from a hackney stable at ten bob an hour." I wished I had not spoken. Though I wanted to keep it from my voice, there was

the note of angry despair in it which was my only answer to
the dimming brightness of the future.

"Oh, David . . . I don't mind. I don't mind. The other's only
a fairy story, and you, you're real and. . . ." I heard her voice
falter and, turning, saw her face. Her eyes were moist with
sudden tears and her mouth trembled. I knew that her thoughts
had caught up with her, and I cursed myself for the bitterness
which had been in my voice when I spoke last, cursed myself
for dragging her out of the comfort that lay in the past. She
came to me, throwing her arms around my neck, and she said,
"*Chéri . . . Chéri.* . . ." I held her, caressing her, trying to still
the trembling which was in her.

Momentarily she was all weakness and I would have given
anything to be all strength. I tried to be, tried to force courage
and hope from myself into her, and maybe I succeeded a little.
She lay still after a while, my arms around her, and the shadowed
enmity which seemed to wreathe about the barn receded a little.

The rat by the straw bales sat up and polished his whiskers
like an old colonel in a club window and took no interest in us.
We weren't human, no menace lay in us, we were just two more
caged animals. And I suppose the rat was right. What did we
have more than the animals around us? A little more intelligence
which, unfortunately, gave us a sense of the future. It would
have been better if we had not known what the word future
meant—for we had so little of it to come, and our intelligence
was turned to a frustrated restlessness and vain desire to escape.

Now and again, at the far end of the barn I could hear the
pad, pad of some animal circling its cage. Maybe a wolf or a
hyena. The darkness beyond the pale ring of light from the
hurricane lamps was pregnant with unseen life, the stir and the
cough, the sudden sharp snarl and the quick, shaking settle of
wings like small twigs falling. . . . And the warmth and smell
of the creatures was like a fog, harsh with ammonia, a dusty
rankness in the throat. After a time the atmosphere, the unquiet
gloom and the sense of futility and shortening time ahead,
began to work on the spirits until a brute dejection took one.
This was it. We were back where we belonged . . . with the
animals. What did we rank more than they, except a different
label on a strip of perspex outside the cage? *Homo sapiens,
European—male and female—presented by Colonel Francis
Drexel. Hyena crocuta—Abyssinian—presented by Monsieur
George Sarrasin. Felis leo—"Karimba"—African—female. (Pur-
chased out of the proceeds of smuggling penicillin over the
Franco-Spanish border.)*

But no matter how dejected I got, I didn't like it. Man's spirit doesn't take to cages. It was an outrage to the body and the mind . . . and I had a feeling that Sarrasin would appreciate this only too well. This was an insulting jest. . . . Somewhere down the row something began to shake at the bars of the cage frantically, chattering with a garbled fluency.

Sophie stirred and said, "That's a baboon we have. He cut his leg on a cigarette tin someone gave him. He has a very bad temper."

The rat sat and stared at us, undisturbed by our voices or the chattering of the baboon, a chattering that echoed strangely under the lofty iron roof. Then, in a flash the rat was gone. The baboon stopped cursing his fate and in the silence I heard footsteps outside the big doors. A small slip-door cut into the big right-hand door opened and a man stepped into the barn. He turned momentarily and called back through the moonlit rectangle:

"Get that mule over as soon as you can."

It was the voice of Colonel Francis Drexel, curt and full of authority. I watched him come towards our cage. My friend, Drexel; the man who had once saved my life and now, I supposed, felt he had the right to take it away. Logically it was a fair deal. He has given me more years of living than I had expected, a bonus paid from his own courage. It might have been comforting if I could have seen it that way.

He wore his tight-belted, shabby raincoat and there was a fullness of silk scarf about his throat. No hat, the iron-grey hair dark in the poor light, the trim, small body full of cut and thrust, he came right up to the cage and stood there looking in at us. His face was as grey as pumice stone and as rough, worn and old. But the eyes were alive and they had now a brightness I had never seen before, and he kept blinking as though there was sand in them. This was a new habit . . . and although it was a small thing, it changed him for me, made him febrile, uncertain and unpleasant. I had the swift impression that for the first time I was looking at the real Drexel, that for the first time in his life he had caught up with himself . . . that until now he had been playing a part which others had dictated to him. And because he was a stranger to me I had no words for him that came easily, either out of contempt or compassion. My Drexel had died years ago.

I don't know how long he stood there before he spoke. Sophie and I, close together, watched him, and it would have been hard to say what was in his mind until he spoke and then I knew that this stranger was an unhappy man, knowing himself to be the creature of his own evil, and obstinately determined to live with it.

He said, "You did wrong, Fraser. You did wrong." His voice was rough, overwrought. "You forced me and you know I'm not a man to be forced."

He waited for me to reply. But I had nothing to say to him. He had called me Fraser. I was a stranger to him, too. What was there for me to say? Argue with him? Plead with him? Beg him at least to let Sophie go and rely on her honour to be silent? He had nothing in him which would respond. I only had to look at him to see that.

Drawn by my silence, he said quickly, "I wish I'd never seen you. And when you're gone from here, I'm going to forget you."

He waited again and I could see that he hated talking to silence.

"Do you hear me? Say something."

I spoke then, but I wasted few words on him.

"That's right, Drexel. You forget us. Forget Jabal, forget Sophie here, and forget me. You'll find it the easiest thing in the world."

And moving gently from Sophie I drew cigarettes and matches from my overalls and lit a cigarette and ignored him. There was nothing between us. Exactly nothing.

I saw his shoulders move inside his coat and then with an abrupt movement he turned away towards the lorry. He went over and unlocked the rear doors and climbed up inside. As he did so I heard the sound of hooves clopping up to the big barn doors. The sound stopped and then there was the rasp of a wooden bar being pulled over. The doors opened.

Dunwoody and Paviot came in leading a mule between them. They took no notice of us. Dunwoody climbed up into the lorry and he and Drexel brought Jabal out. They lowered him over the edge to Paviot. Jabal stood there swaying on his feet, hardly able to keep upright and quite clearly unaware of what was happening to him.

Paviot held him until the other two were down and then they half-walked, half-lifted him across to the mule. He was hoisted up and sagged forward, his hands clasping the saddle-horn. Paviot squatted down and tied Jabal's ankles together under the mule's belly. The animal moved restlessly as this was done but Drexel hit it across the muzzle and quieted it.

Sophie and I stood there, watching them, listening to Drexel's quiet word of command. I don't know how she felt, but I guessed it was much the same as I did. I had forgotten myself, my own danger, for it seemed all to have been transferred to Jabal. He was more helpless, more innocent than we. He had done nothing active to ensure himself the role of a victim, done nothing except be himself and so excite the venality of others. A tallish, slim figure, dark-haired and young . . . little more than a boy, normally full of life . . . and he was going to be killed. I used the word bluntly to myself, for it was death that waited for him; maybe just over the Spanish border, maybe on some boat back to Ramaut or in one of the rooms of the palace of Sheik Ahmed ben Fa'id. He was going to die to feed the greed of others for the oil which was the blood of his homeland. The whole thing made me feel sick and angry.

Instinctively, I found my hands gripping the bars of the cage and the muscles of my body tensing.

Drexel said, "We shall have to watch him at first to see he doesn't slip. But once he's got some fresh air in him he'll come round enough to hang on."

He began to wheel the mule about and Paviot and Dunwoody moved at its flanks, a hand each on Jabal.

Paviot said, looking over at Dunwoody, "Your men better be waiting. It's not safe to hang about up there in daylight too long."

Dunwoody, in much better French than I had ever thought him capable of producing, said, "Don't worry. They'll be there —and with the money, too."

When they got to the door Drexel halted the mule. I saw him pause, saw the back of his hand rub slowly across his mouth in the manner of a man who has forgotten something and wonders if he shall return for it. Then he turned his head slightly and looked across to us. Dunwoody and Paviot followed his glance. I expected something to be said. But nothing was. There were no words in them for this moment. Just Drexel's eyes on me, his small, neat head showing above the bowed neck of the mule; Drexel going out and away from me, for I knew he was saying goodbye, and that in some odd way he wanted something from me if only an angry acknowledgment of the dead faith between us. But I had nothing for him.

He turned away. Dunwoody raised a hand gently, valedictory, and the beam and twinkle were in his eyes still and there was in him the ease and affability of single-minded roguery. He had put his conscience in store years ago. And I could respect him for it.

Paviot? Nothing, except the coldness of the moonlit morning

to match his inner coldness. He and the mule accepting the early hours and the work ahead, following their natures, and as indifferent to suffering in others as they were to the brute drive in themselves.

They went out and the big doors were closed and the bar dropped into place. And a moment after they were gone I found I was standing there, shaking at the bars, and swearing to myself. I wanted to be outside . . . to be after them . . . to be free to loose the animal ferocity which every moment in this cage drew from the black core of my anger.

Sophie took my hands away from the bars and, looking at my watch, pretending not to notice my mood, said, "Four o'clock. They will be over the border by eight. I know the path so well. . . . In the spring, at this time of year, it is a lovely walk. . . ."

*   *   *

I sat down with her. We talked quietly to one another for a while. But I could not sit still nor would my mind stay with our talk. I was restless . . . driven frankly by fear, fear for what lay ahead of Jabal and waited for us. When Drexel and Paviot returned, their money safe, our turn would come. I knew Drexel. Nothing would be done to us until the money was safe in his hands. One step at a time . . . the whole thing a neat military operation . . . 0400 hours move off with Jabal on mule . . . and so on until, possibly, 1200 hours . . . disposal of prisoners. Cold, inflexible planning.

I got up and walked around the cage. Karimba roared once and somewhere outside a cock began to crow. Time and again I stopped at the front of the cage and my eyes went to the length of wall by the big doors. The bunch of keys on its wire loop hung there; fifteen feet away which might have been fifty miles. I went over the cage again, tried the floor-boards and even climbed to the iron-barred roof, but there was no weak point, nothing that could be moved.

One of the hurricane lamps guttered and went out and the oil smeach of the smoking wick came across on the draught to us. The rat came back and started its foraging. I kept looking at my watch, greedy of time as a miser of gold, and the impatience from frustration began to kick in me as though it were a living thing.

"Sit down, David. There's nothing you can do." Sophie said it with all her love in her voice, but it was of no help to me. Women, after their first fears are curbed, are more resigned, full of a deeper, calmer courage than men.

"You'll wear yourself out, *chéri.* . . . Nothing can be done."

But I could not accept this. I kept seeing that mule, with Jabal on its back, picking its way up the mountain track, and the three men plodding with it. Somewhere up amongst the grey, pine flanked peaks was the border, and that to me became a symbol, a thick black band of mourning. Once across it I knew there was no power that could save Jabal. And when I didn't think of that, my mind went on punishing me. I looked at my watch and saw the slip of the seconds, and each one as it peeled off into limbo brought nearer the morning and the daylight and those last few moments when we, too, should take the beastly shock of not-life and slip away. . . . And how desperate my thoughts were I knew because the spirit refused to acknowledge the real word, the real act and called it "not-life," trying to coat the pill for the panic-poised child within me. At any other time I might have been braver; but there had been no Sophie then, no love, no eagerness for the future which went beyond my mere self. . . .

The baboon, sensing perhaps this uneasiness in a cage not far from him, had begun to chatter and now and again gave a queer half-strangled cry as though its body were charged with some strange agony. Its cries disturbed the other animals, for one by one they woke and protested and a bedlam of noise filled the barn. It would break out, rise to a mad pitch, and then suddenly stop and the darkness beyond the thistle head of pale light from the one hurricane would be thick with a low, urgent, breathing sound, and this was almost worse than the noise. It was a sequence which worked on the imagination, and set nerve and muscle on edge. When I held Sophie, I could feel it in her, and once when I kissed her cheek it was salt with the secret tears she had wept and wiped away.

Five times that awful noise coughed and barked and screeched and rasped its way to a crescendo, and each time we were held in the following trough of low, desperate panting and stirring, and then, as it started again for the sixth time, I could stand it no longer.

I swung away from Sophie to the side of the cage and grabbing the bars I shook them and yelled at the top of my voice:

"Stop it, you bastards! Stop it!"

It was odd. I don't know whether it was the ferocity of my voice, or because it was human and the human voice confuses all wild animals into silence; but they stopped.

Behind me Sophie laughed, an edgy, unreal sound. But I scarcely heard her, was not really aware of the effect my voice had had, for I was staring straight ahead of me into the next

177

cage, and my mind was suddenly cold and clear with hard shock.
I was drunk one moment and then, a bucket of water in my
face, standing sober, wondering where the idiot I had known
myself to be two seconds before had gone.

The birds in the next cage were restless, disturbed, shuffling
about their perches. It was these perches that held my attention.
They ran from side to side of the cage at different levels; long,
thick lengths of bamboo. My hands on the bars were now only
a few inches from the end of one of them. I looked at it and
saw that it was held to one of the horizontal cage bars by a
thin looping of soft wire.

I turned to Sophie and called her over. She stood by me and
I pointed to the perches, which were about eight feet long.

"Look, Sophie—if we can get three of those bamboos, we
can lash them together and then reach those keys on the loop
by the door."

Before I had finished speaking my fingers were at work on
the wire fixing nearest to me. It untwisted easily and by pushing
the bamboo up I got my fingers between the bars and had a grip
on it. The birds on the bamboo squawked and flew off. The large
toucan flopped to the ground and stalked away indignantly.
The end of the bamboo was attached on the far side of the cage
in a wire loop also. I pulled the perch back towards me to free
it. It would not come at first and I swore as I tried to get a better
grip with my fingers in the limited space between the bars. Then
suddenly it came away. The far end dropped to the floor of the
cage and I almost lost my grasp on the end I held. But I just
saved it and then I was pulling it through into our cage.
Eight feet of beautiful, smooth bamboo, marked here and there
by bird droppings. I could have shouted with joy.

Sophie called to me. She had climbed up the cage side a
little and was working at another perch. I went over and held
her and she made a better, quicker job than I had done because
her hand was smaller. The birds now were alarmed. Some of
them flew around the cage, their wings beating against the bars,
a dark, soft movement that sent up quick gusts of stale, dusty
air in our faces.

Very soon we had the three lengths we needed. And now
I was taking back all I had said about men and animals. The
cage had made us animals and stopped us thinking, filling us
with a desire for freedom and dwarfing our ability to conceive
a design for it. I was suddenly cocky, self-sure and elated . . .
hope was blossoming in me like a great red flower opening to
a new sun. I took the thin belt off my overalls and lashed two

of the bamboos together, giving them a good overlap to ensure rigidity. I poked one end out of the cage in the direction of the keys and set to work to lash the third bamboo on. For thongs I tore my large handkerchief into four strips. Then I pushed the long rod through the bars, keeping a butt of about two feet under my arm for steadiness. The rod reached the keys easily.

Sophie said, "You'll never do it. The end droops too much."

And she was right. The weight of the bamboos made the far end dip. I could get the end into the loop and lift it off the nail but the moment it was free it would slide down and off the drooping tip. And whichever way I turned the bamboo I could not get rid of the dip at the end.

"I'll do it." I was determined to do it. I pulled the rod back until the end was inside our cage. Then I lay down on the floor and pushed the rod out again at floor level and then up towards the loop of keys. The whole rod now sloped upwards at an angle of about thirty degrees until it was within two feet of the loop and then the dip, corrected by the long upward slant, evened out almost parallel with the ground. Once I got the wire loop on the far end of the rod all I had to do was to raise it higher and the keys would slide down towards me.

And they did. I got the end through the loop and then raised the tip. The loop came up free of the nail and half an inch back from the end of the rod. I shook the rod gently, raising it, and the next moment the loop was sliding down towards us, the keys swinging and touching off soft lights where the hurricane glow hit them.

We pulled the rod in and took the keys from it. I stood there, keys in my hand, and saw Sophie's face close to mine. All the anxiety which had been in my love went. It was a fighting, hopeful love now. I flung my arms around her, gave her a hug and a kiss and then swung round to the padlock. But I had to give the keys to her. Her hand was smaller and could go through the bars.

Quickly she found the right key and we swung the bolt back and then pushed the barred door open. We jumped to the floor. She would have moved at once to the small door in the big barn doors but I held her. We had to know what we were going to do once we were outside.

I looked at my watch. Drexel and his party had been gone nearly three-quarters of an hour.

I said, "How far is this place from a village or the police?"

"Ten or twelve miles."

"We'd never get any help in time. We've got to go after them ourselves. But they've got a big start on us."

Sophie was silent for a moment, frowning as she thought.

"You know the path," I said. "What chance have we got?"

She said, "They have to go right round the other side of the lake before they begin to climb. There's a rough road and they won't be travelling fast if they have to keep Jabal on that mule. If we could get a car we could drive round the lake. That would save time. Once we're in the mountains I can show you short cuts they won't take with the mule."

I looked over at the lorry. But she saw my look and shook her head.

"Too much noise . . . opening these big doors. Gerard has an old Citröen. It's usually parked in a shed round the back of the barn."

I said, "If there isn't that there must be the car Drexel came in. We've got to take a chance on it."

But I knew there were other chances as well. The party up in the hills was probably armed. Certainly Paviot would have a knife. Even if we could catch up with them and take them by surprise, the odds were with them. . . . I had to have something to bring down the odds.

"Come on," I said and I grabbed her wrist, making for the small door. I didn't say anything to her but I knew that if things were quiet outside I was going to go into the house and see if I could find something . . . a rifle, shotgun . . . something at least to give us a chance. By the time we did ten miles and found the police, a sleepy, obtuse gendarme who would be fifteen minutes coming to his senses and another fifteen getting in touch with anyone and then the whole palaver of a party getting up here. . . . No—there was no help there. Into the farm, I thought, and God help Sarrasin or whoever got in my way.

Maybe I prayed too hard that I should come by a rifle or a revolver. Anyway, my prayer was answered before I was ready to take it. That's the trouble with prayers—they usually get answered unexpectedly.

We were within four feet of the little door when it opened and George Sarrasin stepped into the barn. He was dressed in 'fancy costume'. Black sweater, the belt with the silver buckle, the tight breeches. In the pale light his face was large and ashen, a brooding, forceful head and some trick of shadows on it made me think of Nero . . . all he needed was a bayleaf crown. That was the mind, like a snipe never flying straight, but my body was already moving directly towards him. I saw his hand swinging towards the back pocket of his breeches and I knew he was getting my revolver for me. I hit him as he pulled it out. I hit him with my right shoulder and low down in the dirtiest tackle of my life—which for a Scot is saying something.

I heard the breath go from him with an anguished *sough*. He crashed back against the barn doors so that the elbow of the arm that was holding the revolver was jerked forward. We fell together, and I saw the weapon fly across in front of me. As I hit the ground, I shouted to Sophie. The shout was shortened in me as Sarrasin's foot came out and kicked me in the face.

CHAPTER XVIII

WE came up together and it was as though we moved in slow motion, as though the atmosphere itself had become glutinous and was seeking to hamper our actions. I felt the blood from my injured lips wet and warm over my cheek. He opened his mouth to shout and I dived forward, my hands outspread to catch his neck. His fist came up in a long swing and took me in the chest but my momentum carried me on, crushing down on him, and no sound came from his throat but a short grunt of pain.

We went down, rolling and rolling and striking one another, and we might have been tumbling on a cloud bank and we ourselves made of some insubstantial stuff into which fist and feet sank and then, when withdrawn, left our bodies without mark or pain. But dreamlike as the struggle might seem, I knew that what was in me was in him also. I didn't want just to fight and overpower him. I wanted to kill him. I wanted to destroy him because he had become associated in my mind with all the evil that had wrapped itself round me since I had come to France. I knew that in him there was embodied the apotheosis of all the potent desire of evil to flourish. But alongside all this in my mind raced the sharp, gutter-wisdom that all Scots have when it comes to a fight, the thing is bred from porridge, whisky and mist. I stood by no rules, since none was demanded. I kicked and gouged and bored. Fist, elbow, foot and, if I could have got a hold, I would have used teeth, for we were not men we were animals and in our wild slamming, rolling and pounding, we were watched by animals and over the suck and gasp of our breath I heard the savage, unhappy roar of animal voices, the frenetic chattering, and the beat of pinioned wings against bars.

I saw Sophie hovering round us, revolver in hand. But there was no chance for her to shoot or strike. We were one body. Many things I remember. The moment when we stood face to face and with a bestial chivalry just swung punch after punch at one another, turn and turn about, until my head reeled. I remember my face thrust deep into straw and his hands about my throat and the wet, mouldy smell of the barn floor. His belt came undone and my fingers clawed at his black jersey, ripping it so that the flesh underneath showed through like a great wound.

After that first attempt to shout he never tried again. He accepted the fight, accepted our isolation, and gradually I knew why. He was going to beat me, to kill me. He was stronger, bigger and impelled by an equal hatred. And I knew too that I didn't care who won. . . . Maybe I was a little drunk with the frenzy in me. I asked for no more than to go on fighting, win or lose, satisfied that the real consummation of the dark passion between us lay in struggle, not an end to the struggle. But even so there was still the little figure of my common sense, perched somewhere above us, that marked and feared and calculated. The animals were making such a noise that attention must soon be attracted from the house; Sarrasin himself, I was sure, had come because of the noise made by the unusually restless animals.

We slewed round on the ground and his foot slid out wildly and struck the packing case. I heard the hurricane lamp go over and a cry from Sophie. As I twisted sideways from under him, I saw the gloom shot with points of flame. Against the pale grey which filled the far doorway I saw Sophie stamping her feet on the tiny spurts and points of flame that ran like animated decorations up the side of a straw bale and among the loose straw on the floor. Then I saw no more of her for Sarrasin was astride of me and his enormous hands clamped themselves on my throat and I had only the vision of his great, overhanging face, lips drawn tightly back and his eyes dark with angry pleasure as he slowly throttled the life from me and held my leaping, straining body down with his weight.

From somewhere behind me the flames from the straw leaped higher and now his face was shadowed and lit with a constant movement. The roar of the blood in my own ears was mixed with the wild din the animals were making. His was the face of Nero over me, brutal with ecstasy as he watched me sink, a face that was pink, gold, black and white; the eyes shutting with a tiny movement each time he breathed and strained his hands against my neck.

Then blackness hit me. I went into the tunnel and suddenly the lights were out. Just the jostling and roaring and pounding of the wheels over the breaks in the rails. In a London tube when it happens the heart leaps sometimes and you say 'I've gone blind'. Dimly I heard myself say, 'This is death'.

*   *   *

When I came round Sophie was kneeling by me shaking my shoulders. I forced myself up a little on my elbows and she

183

called urgently, "David. Oh, David. Quick, quick. I can hear them coming."

There was a brisk, crackling sound in the barn and a pink and yellow glow was flickering over the walls. I saw that the fire had spread through the straw on the floor and across to the lorry. It was leaping around the wheels. Sarrasin lay a few feet from me, groaning.

Sophie put an arm under me and helped me up.

I said stupidly, "What happened to him?"

"I hit him with the revolver."

I swayed a bit and she held me and slowly my head cleared. I sucked at the air and it was like breathing burnt paper. I choked with the smoke. We stumbled towards the small door. Outside I heard voices calling and then through the open door ·I could see them. Three figures were running towards the barn and I recognized Gerard and Fargette, but not the other.

There was no time for us to get out. so I pulled Sophie aside with me, pressing against the big door and behind the shelter of the open small door. With luck they would come dashing in and past us. Not far away was Sarrasin on the floor and a ragged tail of flames curved part of the way round the lorry. If they were quick, I thought, they could get the big doors open and run the lorry out. The lorry was the real danger, for the building was of corrugated iron. I saw Sarrasin stir and then lever himself groggily to his feet. He didn't look our way. He stood for a moment with his hands against his forehead and then with a clumsy urgency he staggered towards the lorry.

Gerard and the others swept in through the door past us. I heard Gerard's alarmed call like the sudden yaffling of a woodpecker and he went, with arms upstretched like a prophet of despair, towards the flames and began to dance and stamp on them.

Sophie and I stayed for no more. We slipped around the edge of the small door and were outside. She took my hand and we began to run.

There was confusion in my mind. Nothing seemed clear and orderly. Life and time seemed to have reduced themselves to a postcard album that I was watching over someone's shoulder. They were flipping the pages over too quickly for me to get any lasting picture; only now and then a page stuck and I did see clearly.

There was the morning, a pearl stretch of sky. A row of poplars like angry cats' tails. And the spread of the lake, dull, tarnished tin-plate with a cold eddy of mist on its surface. A shed against the barn and a dust-powdered Citröen with its windshield wet with dew across which I drew my sleeve. The self-starter which complained and complained, whining under my foot.

There was the yard with a few early hens with fluffy feathers round their feet, as though their pants had slipped, pecking away at the dirt and then scattering as we came down upon them, the engine missing and coughing against the damp and cold. There was an open gateway and myself shouting suddenly to Sophie:

"Right or left?"

And hearing but not hearing her reply and turning right on to a rutted track.

The car kicked and bucked and something at the back went *bang, bang,* and further behind there were voices, shouting, angry, and then the sound of a shot. Suddenly, I was exhilarated and happy as though I had discovered the right way to live, in a postcard album with quickly turning pages, and I looked down and found Sophie's hand in the crook of my arm and I took my hand from the wheel and touched it.

Then slowly the pages stopped flipping and there was only one page, one postcard, and I drove into it, giving the car hell and not caring. A long stretch of dusty, bumpy lake-side track. The water a few yards away on our right was fringed by tall tufted reeds and enamelled here and there by green lily-pads.

To the left a slope went up gently through patches of grass and whitebroom and long slides of chipped rock into which pines had been stuck at careless angles, and ahead of us, far away round the lake, was the steep black side of a mountain, patterned with shadow as far as the tree line and then suddenly gleaming in the morning light and with a scalloping of snow along a smooth shoulder that ran to a pimpled peak.

Sophie said, "We keep along this track until we come to a quarry on the left. Then we must go up the valley."

"Track for the car?"

"For a little way. This is the road they used to bring the stone down."

I nodded. It was the kind of nod you give to a mildly interesting piece of information at a lecture, knowing you aren't going to remember it for long. Already my mind was ahead, beyond the quarry and up the valley. Somewhere up there, an hour ahead of us, was Jabal on his way back to Ramaut. . . . The cold morning air would have brought him round. He would know what was happening to him. Jabal who played *Smoke Gets in your Eyes* and *Frim-Fram Sauce* and whose

185

father had fought with Lawrence of Arabia. I thought of Saraj, noisy, dusty, sun-drenched, and the meat stalls on the quay with the long skewers turning over the charcoal braziers and the dark-eyed friendly boys who stole anything that was left around.

Out on the right a fish jumped and the ripples gave colour and movement to the dirty leaden surface. And I remembered Sophie talking about Fargette. . . . I looked across at her and she smiled at me. The sun lifted over a hill shoulder and the morning miraculously became tinged with gold and red and blue.

The car lurched madly over a hole in the track and Sophie was thrown against me. As she drew away, grasping the dashboard to steady herself, she said:

"I've put the revolver in your pocket. It's got a full chamber."

I'd got her, I'd got a revolver, and I'd taken up the chase. All I wanted for complete happiness was a pair of wings.

A stream came down the hillside and crossed the track to the lake. We went through it at speed and great sheets of spray rose like wings on either side of us, and I laughed because my prayer had been answered. A twist in the conformation of the lakeside brought us for a while into a position where just over my right shoulder I could look back and see the farm. It was small now and stood out on a flat promontory. From behind the barn, the open space hidden from our sight, a grey and tawny trail of smoke looped and swayed up into the sky. I guessed they'd got the lorry out. I wondered what they would do. Come after us or abandon ship? I didn't bother to think it out for them. That was their problem.

We reached the quarry. Running up from it was a valley, more a gorge than a valley, with a noisy, frothy, boulder-strewn torrent coming down full-pelt to the lake. Oaks and scrub reached down almost to the stream-banks. A narrow track twisted between the trees. I put the Citröen at the track, bounding and slewing in my seat and holding myself by the wheel. The outside mirror snapped off against a tree, a boulder took a long score down one side of the body, something snapped underneath but she kept going. We must have made nearly three miles before the end came. We topped a small rise and on the far side the track dipped away obliquely. The car slewed sideways and then, skidding back to the track, hugging it like a lover, jumped a rocky step and was suddenly foundered in the stony bed of a small stream whose far bank was studded with young larch.

We got out. Without a farewell to the car Sophie and I plunged into the larches, following a thread of path. She pointed once and I saw the marks of the mule's hooves in the soft ground.

The birds began to sing. Maybe they started because we brought them company and an audience made it worth their while. Behind us the sun slipped above some spur and the wood was full of green and gold haze. After a time the path steepened so that we were using our hands and I could see where the mule had been forced to take the slope on a zig-zag course. I followed Sophie, part of me taking pleasure in watching the strong, easy way she set herself at the climb, and another part of me worrying now about Jabal and the others. They had a long start on us and there was no guarantee that we should catch up with them. I kept that thought out of my mind. We had to catch them. My luck was running well so far. . . . I didn't care that in the past it had let me down . . . this time I was sitting it tight, ready for the sudden buck, the quick slip.

We came out of the trees and were under a broken shoulder of rock rising like a cliff from some Heronimus Bosch landscape through dark shadows to the pale blue sky touched with cloud-like wisps of morning sleep still waiting to be rubbed away. A nice simile, I thought; but as an Eng. Lit. master I would have slated any boy who had used it. However, this was hurried composition, and there was no self-criticism in me . . . just a mixture of happiness and racing anxiety to get ahead. And I knew what was happening to me; any climber would have recognized it. You put your body at a task and your mind swings free, like a ship at slack cable length, and half the joy of effort is the comforting, easy fantasy of thoughts.

The mule track ran away around the right of the buttress. Sophie said, "If we go straight up over we shall save a mile."

We went straight up over. It was like going up the Milestone Buttress on Tryfan, only four times as long and not quite as hard; no need for a rope, but every need for eye, hands and feet.

There were long loose patches of weathered stuff into which our feet sank deep and then a sheer rise in creviced and crannied steps, which I liked better because we made faster time. Once, waiting for Sophie to find the lead, I looked back and down. The lake was a long way below us and the sun had polished it now. There was still a plume of smoke coming up from the farm, and I could see that it came from the lorry which had been run out into the open yard. The animals were safe. . . . I thought of Sarrasin getting groggily to his feet and forgetting us as he went towards the lorry. Animals meant something to him. He was happy and at home with them. Tarzan of the Grand Cirque

Pyrénéen. But it was not a sneer. It was admiration . . . and because it was there I knew the bad blood was purged from me and old Father Compassion was back, smoking that pipe of his and being so damned wise and considerate that it was hard to make up my mind to kick him in the bottom and to remember all that had happened in the last weeks. You tell me, I said to the old boy, as I grasped at rocks and hauled myself after Sophie, what it is that makes us find something to like in the people we hate most. Perhaps it's gratitude for giving us a mark for a rare emotion . . . for hatred is vintage stuff and should be decanted slowly. Friendship—I followed the fancy, with Drexel in mind, as I squeezed behind Sophie up a narrow funnel—isn't even chateau bottled. I was going to suspect it for a long time and stick to hatred and love.

When we got to the top we ran along the edge of a plateau and then could look down into the twisting valley that snaked around the great mountain plug we had just climbed. We stood watching the break in the trees and rocks where the trail came into view. But there was no sign of Drexel and his party.

"They must still be ahead," I said. "How far is the border?"

Sophie pointed. Facing us was a long, broken line of crests cut with valleys whose lower cheeks held a faint stubble of trees. There's something about hills to be crossed which can depress you. They sprawl grandly across the edge of the sky, big, still insolent creatures, and if you worry about them they only irritate and exhaust you. The thing to do is to put your head down, keep your eyes no more than ten feet ahead and go on.

We started forward over the plateau at a gentle jog trot. After twenty minutes there was nothing gentle about it. But we kept on, Sophie and I, plugging forward and I was glad that she was ahead of me, for I loved every inch of her and every movement in her. She looked small and not up to it, but she had a strength inside her which I would never have suspected. She was no drooping princess over a pond now. The wind took her black hair and filled her blouse, wickering at it, and there were few words between us, but many a look and we both knew what was in one another's thoughts.

I don't know how long we were going. It may have been half a lifetime; but it seemed longer than that. I know I had time to get a new job, furnish a house and raise a family. I had trouble with the boys' names. The girls I left to Sophie, and I was old and inclined to bore my grandchildren with the tale of how I first met their grandmother. We splashed up the course of a stream that was as cold as all charity. I felt the sole of my right shoe flapping loose and a bunch of flies began to treat my cut lips as quick-lunch counters.

The head of the stream ended in a waterfall, a dark, slimy spout thick with moss and ferns. We stopped, our feet on the gravel bed of the pool into which the fall thundered, the water lapping above our ankles.

"Up there?" I said.

"That or around the slope which will lose us time."

"All right," I said, but I didn't like it. It was a wet, slippery, dangerous climb with a notch of blue sky two hundred feet above us.

Sophie made a move forward but this time I held her back. A quick glance had showed me that there were a few overhangs and ledges where she would need a hand coming down to her. I had more height and strength than she. I put a hand on her shoulder and pulled her back towards me. Her face came up to mine. God knows we had no time for it when every second counted, but I didn't like the look of that wall-face and my imagination painted a hundred ugly pictures. We kissed and for a moment there was warmth and tenderness and a velvet smooth oblivion about us. She had her hands on my back, gripping me, and her mouth against mine had a life of its own, drawing me into her. Her eyes were open and I saw the fine sheen of sweat on her eyelids, and her eyes weren't black but a dark steel-blue and their brilliance mirrored my face and also the changing colours of the small rainbows that salaamed above the white spume at the foot of the fall. The water could have risen six feet to our heads and I wouldn't have felt it.

I wasn't aware of beginning to climb with her behind me. A miracle must have separated us. It was like going up a cliff covered with wet sealskin. I dug my fingers and feet into the thick moss, tore it away and broke my nails uncovering the hard rock to give her firm holds. Once I slipped and came down three feet with a crack that should have smashed my ribs. The V-notch got wider and wider. The falling water drew away to our right and its spray was now only faint on our faces. We were soaked through and cold. Ten feet from the top I reached down for her.

I began to pull her up, but suddenly she slipped and her hand, wet and slimy with moss, was jerked from mine by her weight.

My heart turned over like a dolphin diving. I saw her falling and below her the long black drop with its ragged white ribbon of water smashing down to the pool at the foot of the cliff.

She slid three yards down the rock face and then her outflung hands grabbed at the stone. I jumped, marking a ridge below me, and went down the rock with my heels dug in. I hit the ledge with a jolt and grabbed her as she hung there, lying half over the edge. I pulled her up and clasped her to me. She was making a weird crying noise from shock. I could have killed the whole world in revenge for the fear that was still pounding in me.

I didn't care a damn about Jabal or anything then except her. I kept her there until the terror was gone from her body. I talked to her, not knowing what I said. And, sooner than I thought she would, she came out of it, and I loved her for her courage.

*   *   *

At the head of the fall we were on some kind of watershed; a long stretch of boggy grass that sang with hidden water as we started across it towards a patch of firs. Beyond the firs I could see another ridge rising and drifts of snow hanging in the lee of its spurs. We had only gone a few yards when I saw a movement against the far line of trees. There was the white flash of two faces turning towards us. Distantly I heard someone shout. I began to run squelching across the wet, cushiony ground, and as I went I pulled out my revolver. Behind me I could hear Sophie following closely.

Dunwoody must have been leading the mule and was already lost in the trees, but Drexel and Paviot were behind, standing at the edge of the trees. I had a feeling that somewhere on our climb they must have looked back from some vantage point and seen us.

To my surprise they did not wait for us or try to hold us off. They turned and ran into the trees, and we went after them. I had my revolver out and I was eager to get at them. But I was not so reckless that I was going to run into an ambush. I waved Sophie back and stopped when I was some way into the trees. Then I called her on, and I went forward another jump, watching every clump of scrub, every tree trunk. They were young trees and the trunks gave no cover. But there was no sign of Drexel and the others, Then I heard them ahead of me. One of them was shouting and I thought I caught the *clop, clop* of the mule's hooves, and the sound was oddly echoing and hollow.

I knew why a few moments later.

We came to the edge of the trees and before us was a stretch of open ground about ten yards wide that abruptly fell away to a long, curving gorge, a great fissure thirty feet across. The ravine stretched along the full length of the foot of the peak that rose on the other side. Across it was a thin, flimsy plank bridge. . . . But bridge was too fine a word for it, it was just a few slender pine poles and planks and a handrail that was rotten and broken away in places.

It was an ugly looking place, unwanted, barren, as though nature knowing it was a border area, neither France nor Spain, had let the whole thing go. The far hillside was untidy with shale and loose rock, and water from the melting snow patches glistened over it like snail trails. A cold wind came whistling along the edge of the trees and the black crack yawned and grinned like a gigantic shark's mouth with the bridge a toothpick that had got wedged between upper and lower incisors.

I took a step out of the cover of the trees and went back at once. Dunwoody with Jabal on the mule was halted on the far side of the bridge. Seeing me he raised his revolver and fired. I heard the bullet plug into a trunk not far from me. At that distance it was good shooting.

I pulled Sophie down behind a rock and then peering round the side of it saw what they were doing. Jabal had had his feet freed now and was sitting the mule upright and looking reasonably recovered. Dunwoody had the lead rein in one hand and a revolver in the other and he was watching our rock. At the far end of the bridge Paviot and Drexel were working. They were kicking away at the earth and pine pole ends. I saw the turf flying and then a plank went clattering down into the gorge. Paviot bent down and got his hands round one of the long poles and began to heave and strain. And I knew what was coming. They were going to dislodge the bridge and then there would be no crossing for us. It would take us ages to go down the length of the gorge and find a place across, and by that time they would be up over the crest and into Spain. On the far side of the crest Sophie had already told me there was a track good enough for a car. We'd get there in time to smell their exhaust fumes.

I got up on my knees and took a shot at Paviot, but it went wide, striking the ground somewhere near the mule and making it plunge. Dunwoody fired again at me. I ducked back into cover, cursing. It was dangerous to fire at them. I might hit Jabal. Dunwoody could keep me pinned down easily while the other two worked away.

I was saying 'Hell! Hell! Hell!' to myself stupidly. To have come so far, to have the whole thing practically in my hands and now to lose it all. . . .

Another plank went and I saw the crazy handrail sway and

partly break away as Drexel now bent to the other supporting pine pole. The two of them began to lift the bridge and work it sideways.

And then I knew there was only one thing to do. Not a thing you think about, but something the body starts doing without thought. I stood up and began to run forward, revolver in hand. I sprinted for the bridge and I was going to cross it before they slid it over into the gorge.

Dunwoody fired again and shouted, and the bullet might have gone right through me for all I knew about it. Drexel and Paviot looked up and across to me. I saw Paviot's right hand free itself from its hold on the pole and slide round to his pocket.

Behind me I heard Sophie shout my name. But I kept on running and, suddenly, this was another picture postcard, but an animated one; the blue sky, washed on a little carelessly, and a black splash of a buzzard soaring somewhere up aloft; the wet snow-water gleams and the tight clumps of rock-moss; Dunwoody trying to hold down the head of the restless mule; and Drexel heaving away at the pole and the end of the bridge now two feet in the air. And now, seen for the first time, a thin double strand of wire strung across the mountain flank marking the border line, and me running in a kind of lurching, dreamlike fashion, as though I had a whole pack of dogs about my feet to trip me.

Dunwoody fired again and this time I knew where it went. The bullet hit the ground a few feet ahead of me and a splinter of stone came up, whirring like a June bug, and dug itself into my right cheek, the pain filling me with fresh anger.

But I never reached the bridge. Paviot's hand came round full of the blackness of the gun he held in it; but beyond his hand I saw something else. Paviot became part of the landscape. I had eyes for no one except Jabal. Dunwoody shouted and Jabal swung sideways, kicking out with his foot. The revolver went spinning from Dunwoody's hand. The next moment Jabal had wheeled the mule round and was riding down on Drexel and Paviot. It was no wild charge, just an unwilling, lumbering movement that proved the mule had no sense of crisis. Jabal rode down and they heard him coming. It was too late for them to do anything. He drove the mule straight at Paviot. I saw the man lurch backwards, heard him yell, and then he went over the edge of the ravine. Drexel dropped his pole. The flimsy bridge crashed back and a cloud of dust went up from its rotten timbers.

I stood there, three feet from my end of the bridge, and there was no movement in me. Drexel twisted towards Jabal and tried to grab the lead rein. But Jabal flung himself off on the far side of the mule from Drexel and the next moment he was on the bridge and running towards me with Drexel after him.

I shouted "Jabal. . . ." I would have shouted more to warn him, for the disturbed bridge was as weak as cardboard; but the name Jabal was all I ever got out for at that moment the bridge collapsed with both of them on it.

Behind me I heard Sophie cry agonizingly. The bridge folded up slowly but with an ungodly cracking noise, and I saw white wood splinters fly off into the air like locusts. Jabal flung himself forward, grabbed at a piece of handrail and then slid back towards Drexel and out of my sight as the bridge dropped away.

I moved then, flinging myself to the edge of the gorge, and there the bridge was below me, hanging downwards from my side like a rotten stairway, the transverse planks at all angles like a wrecked xylophone. Twelve feet beneath me I saw Drexel hanging on to a plank with one hand. With the other he had got Jabal beneath the arm and shoulder and was holding him up. The youth's dark face was twisted with pain and there was a cut across his forehead. He was almost out and unable to help himself.

"Quick, David!"

But Sophie was late telling me, I was already on my way down the crazy ladder of the bridge. I hadn't realized until then how deep was the drop in the gorge. It went down like a black and angry wound into the flank of the mountain.

"Hurry, for God's sake!"

I saw Drexel swinging below me as the bridge swayed over the deep drop. Somewhere a timber broke away, hit the side of the gorge and started a clattering fall of rocks and sliding earth. A plume of dust swirled up into my face.

I climbed down, tearing my hands and ripping my clothes and then I could go no further. There was a gap in the planking about three feet long. I hung on to the side pole, not trusting the last transverse plank length, and I reached down. I got a hand on Jabal's arm and I began to pull him up. He was coming round a bit and made a feeble effort to help himself. I gripped him and I heaved but with only one arm it was a hell of a strain. Drexel saw this and he helped. His face tensed with the effort to push Jabal up. Slowly he came and then I got a firmer hold on him and his right hand came up and clutched at the plank by my shoulder. But I wasn't looking at Jabal. My face was only a couple of feet from Drexel's and, as I took the strain and Jabal began to help himself more, working up past me, Drexel's face relaxed. Jabal's weight went from him and

I saw his freed hand come towards his other hand to take a hold on the length of broken handrail he was grasping. But he was too late. The rail, rotten with wind and rain and snow, began to pull and crumble free from the clumsy great nails that held it. Drexel looked at me, and he knew he was going. Jabal was past me now, climbing upwards, and I could hear Sophie helping him, encouraging him. But they were in another world. There was only Drexel below me, and beyond him the dark gorge with Paviot lying twisted there somewhere far beneath. . . . I reached down a hand now to Drexel, shouting to him to take it. He could have taken it easily. But he hung on one-handed to the rail and his free hand—though it moved—never went out to take a fresh hold or to grasp mine. His arm came up in a slow gesture, greeting and farewell, and he was smiling, that damned, hard, spit-in-the-eye-of-the-world smile . . . the old Drexel. I couldn't bear to watch it because I knew what he was doing and I didn't want him to do it. I wanted to bring him up, to bring him back, to have it all over and forgotten and things to be the same between us. . . . I was the boy who wanted time to go back on itself. But he was a man and he was tired of time and he was wise enough, and big enough, to know that the score chalked up to our friendship could be wiped out now with only one payment.

He just said, "David." My name, his voice, his eyes on me, and everything the same between us, and the payment made. When I grabbed at him the rail went, or, maybe, he let go of it a second before it pulled away. I don't know. I only know that I shut my eyes. Not wanting to see his black silhouette turning over and over and dropping to join Paviot in the blackness below. I shut my eyes but his face was clear in my mind . . . and it was the face that had come back to me long ago when I had lain in the sand with the vultures up above and the flies bunching indecently about the wound in my leg. His face and that last valedictory movement of the hand which, had he raised it another three inches, could have grasped mine. And I knew then which was the true nature of Minerva, knew the truth about myself and Drexel, and the truth about the love in our friendship. . . . Nothing matters if you love. Nothing. Once it's there, it's there for good.

*　　*　　*

Dunwoody got away and I never saw him again. He went up the mountain on the mule, plump-bodied and, I'll bet, beaming even in disappointment. I fired the rest of my rounds after him hoping to wake some frontier guard and get him picked up. But it didn't work.

It took us a long time to get back to the farm and when we did we found Didier there with a party of gendarmes. Jean Cagou had recognized me in the circus, recognized, too, that I was no part of the clown act, but it had taken them all a long time, too long, to get round to the farm. Gerard they got, but not Sarrasin. He disappeared into some other jungle; and Fargette—and I couldn't help being glad about this—went with him, or maybe alone. Maybe, somewhere, he still wears a red nose, a large white collar and baggy checks and sets the children's voices shouting with laughter.

The Foreign Office fixed a lot of things up. What Drexel would have called their 'poops' went to work and the Press never had the full truth. It was all very gentlemanly, except that, a few months later, somewhere along the line Sheik Ahmed ben Fa'id died, probably not peacefully, in his bed. I think Jabal was there when he died. And Anglo-Media's oil concession still stands, renewed for fifty years.

Drexel? He lies on a hill above Banyuls with just his name and two dates cut into marble, and once every spring for certain the flowers against the headstone are fresh . . . and afterwards Sophie and I walk down past the Arago Aquarium and along to the *Café aux Bons Enfants* and have a drink. We never talk much over the drink. We just sit there, watching the old women burn the seaweed and after a while her hand comes out and is held by mine.

THE HIDDEN FACE

PROLOGUE

THE tide was full in. There was no wind or swell, and the sea had an oily, black look, all the life gone from it. The promenade lights had just come on and now the pier lights followed them, stringing a drooping necklace above the dark sea as though a salesman had flicked a collar of pearls over a velvet cloth.

I was driving a hired car and I had the hood down. Two hours to London, I thought; a bed at my club and the next morning would see me on the plane back to Canada. Back to work, back to a country where as Ross-Piper, with whom I had been staying, had said, "A man can fill his lungs with God's air instead of the State's." Ross-Piper was in London now and I had spent the last two days alone.

I drove slowly, enjoying the night air, my pipe and the movement of people and traffic. I was looking forward to getting back. The Company had started a new hydro-electric project and it was being handed to me, a responsibility which at thirty-two I hadn't expected but which I was privately vain enough to enjoy.

But when I got to the roundabout by the pier and should have turned left-handed through Brighton to the London road, I didn't. I kept straight on along the coast road. I knew then that I was going to Alfriston after all. For the time being I just sat wondering why the hell I was.

On my return from Canada I had wanted to go to Alfriston, but I had held the desire down. Ross-Piper had helped, telling me not to be a fool, knowing how I had felt about my father and fearing the violent, summer lightning anger which was in our family and which had landed me in trouble before. I said to myself, "It won't take ten minutes and then I'll go across country and hit the Eastbourne-London road."

Beyond Seaford I was driving fast. It was full dark now and the headlights bit into the night. I hoped perhaps that the speed would shake it out of me, but deep down I knew that I was in a hurry to get to Alfriston, to get it over and then to be free to go back to Canada with the whole thing out of my mind. I didn't know exactly what I was going to do. I thought in terms of a damned good hiding, of fists, and of putting the fear of God into him. One certain thing was that the thing which I thought I had conquered was with me, claiming me when I imagined I was most free of it.

I had to crawl through Newhaven. There was a lot of army stuff about on training manoeuvres. Outside the town I turned left up the river road to Alfriston. The May moon had come up behind my back. I could see the water meadows with a faint lacing of mist over them and away beyond them the black hump of the rising downs. Now and again my headlights hit the side of a cottage, a toothy stretch of palings bone-white under the glare, a cat's eyes suddenly bright from the foot of a hedge and then the grey length of the old stone bridge as I turned across the river towards Alfriston. There was a courting couple standing at the end of the bridge. I drew up alongside them.

"Can you tell me the way to the Maltings?"

The man took his arm from around the girl and came forward slowly and his voice was rich and full of Sussex.

"That's Mr. Hansford's place. Through the village and the first turning to the left down to the river."

The name was spoken for me and free now for my thoughts as I drove on. James Gurney Hansford. A man whom I had never seen. A man whom I hated.

There was a little notice-board with the house name on it stuck in the hedge at the top of the lane. A hundred yards away I could see the lights of the house. I left the car by the notice. I wanted to walk. . . . Maybe I had half a hope that I would still turn back. Maybe he wouldn't be there. He had a flat in London and only used this as a week-end and summer house.

It was a small Georgian house standing at the side of a narrow river inlet which had been banked with lawns and turned into a water garden. Where the garden met the lane was a low, red brick wall cut by an ornamental wrought-iron gate, now open. A flagged path led between two lawns to the front door, and as I went up to it I saw to the left a large French window. The curtains were drawn back and the room was full of light.

A man was sitting at a desk facing the window. I moved off the path and across the lawn. A large cedar tree with a wooden seat around it stood about ten yards from the window. I paused beneath the tree and watched. The man had a pile of letters and some parcels at one side of the desk. He kept reaching out to the pile, slitting a letter with a paper knife and then reading. It was like watching the beginning of a play, the curtain had gone up and there was this moment of waiting and wondering what was to come, all brightness, all interest, all silence.

Then, down by the inlet, a moorhen suddenly gave a quick *craik* and there was a shiver of broken moonlight on disturbed water.

In that moment my anger was abruptly cold and discouraging. The lower branches of the cedar reached down over me like a canopy and the moonlight etched their shapes in blurred shadows on the grass. I felt my body move to go. Against the power which had brought me here, another was working to take me away. But as my eyes were on him, a change came over the man sitting at the desk. He had been reading a letter and now he put it down before him on the desk, holding its edges as though it were a small tray, and his head and shoulders went back and he began to laugh. It was silent, it was deep, and it was grotesque. I saw his head and shoulders and his arms swaying with the power of the laughter that was in him and I knew that it was the kind of laughter that feeds on the agony of others. Even though the windows were shut and all sound was smothered between us I still knew that inside the room he was laughing silently to himself, laughter that belonged to the night, to the dark water that curved round the house and to the brooding, cavern-like shadows of ponderous, squat cedar trees . . . the laughter that rises from the helplessness of others.

I was suddenly ablaze with fresh anger and before I was aware of it I had gone swiftly forward to the window. I caught the handle and pushed it open. I stepped close to his desk and as I did so he moved. He pushed his chair back and his right hand went out to a side drawer in his desk. I beat him to it. I went round the side of the desk and knocked his hand roughly from the half-open drawer. I took out the revolver for which he had been reaching. It was a heavy, army-type Colt .45. I stepped back with it in my hand and he said, "What the hell does this mean?"

I said, "I'm Peter Barlow and neither of us will need this."

I put the revolver down on a small round table well away from the desk.

He sat there for a moment saying nothing. Maybe he was trying to guess what was in my mind, maybe he was content for the moment to let the fear ease from him. His face, when I had taken the gun, had shown the panic in him. He was probably in his middle forties; a big man, but somehow all out of proportion. He had a great barrel of a chest and his shoulders were wide and straight, but his arms were short and stumpy. Sitting back in his chair it was almost as much as he could do to stretch out and reach the desk.

"You're Hansford," I said.

He nodded, his eyes on me.

"And you're old man Barlow's son. Well——"

There was a lot in that last word. Relief mostly. He knew where he was. Maybe he thought he knew how to deal with me.

He relaxed into his chair and pursed his mouth, waiting for me. His lips were very red and his face had a high colour, a large smooth face, blown up as though it were made of rubber. Overall, he gave a feeling of weight and power. I wondered how much it would take to knock all that out of him, for that was what I was going to do.

I said, "Yes, I'm old man Barlow's son."

"He was a fine man. I was sorry to hear of his death."

He sounded genuinely sincere, but the words were false and I had all the trouble in the world to stop myself from going forward and knocking his teeth into his throat.

"You made the last three years of his life hell. You filthy blackmailer!"

Hansford stood up. There was an awkwardness about him that seemed out of place in this elegant room with its fine Sheraton desk, the Hepplewhite chairs and the fragile gleam of porcelain from a glass cabinet by the door. He had surrounded himself with good things. There was a painting of a white mare on the wall behind the desk which I was sure was a Stubbs and must have cost him a tidy packet—money he had taken from my father and others.

Hansford said stiffly, "I don't know what you're talking about."

"You blackmailed my father. In three years you had five thousand pounds from him." I was talking evenly but there was cold, black anger in me.

"Get out of here before I call the police!" He spat the words at me and I saw the wet flash of his thick red lips. His hand went out to the desk telephone and the movement freed some of the anger in me. I went round the desk and jerked the trailing flex from its fitting in the floor socket.

"We don't need the police."

He backed away to the end of the desk and I stood there with my hands trembling.

"You gave him three years of hell. I'm going to pack all of that into three minutes for you. When I leave this room you're going to wish you'd never heard the name Barlow. . . ." As I spoke my eyes were half on him, half on the desk. There was a fine silver inkwell, a framed portrait of a woman, a beautiful cut-glass desk lamp with hanging lustres, and a large alabaster cigarette box. My hand went out and I swept the top of the desk clean. The stuff went to the floor with a crash.

Hansford reached down, picked up the silver photograph frame, and threw it at me. I swung my head aside but not quite fast enough and a corner of the frame caught my cheek. He hurled himself at me and he was shouting and his face was suddenly blown up to bursting point, red with rage. I don't know what he was shouting. It was a high, incoherent spilling of sound, and in the fraction of time before I hit him I knew with a cold, rare pleasure how he could be hurt. Not through his body but through his possessions.

I hit him and he went backwards to the floor and knocked over the small table on which I had put his gun. I saw it go skidding across the carpet towards the french windows.

And at that moment the room door partly opened and a woman looked into the room. I saw her face, full of surprise and anxiety, the movement of a green skirt, and then one arm with the gold flash of a bracelet going up protectively as I moved threateningly towards her.

"Get out and stay out!" I shouted.

She backed out quickly. I locked the door and swung round to him. Standing by the china cabinet I put my hand on it. The wood was fine and had a smooth run, and the little figurines inside trembled gently at my touch.

He was on his knees, rising, and he knew what was in my mind and there was a devil in me that wanted to prolong every moment of his agony.

"Beautiful," I said. "Collector's pieces. They must have cost you hundreds—of other people's money."

"Don't! For Christ's sake, Barlow! Be sensible! We can talk this over."

He was up and coming towards me and his short arms were outstretched awkwardly.

I laughed at him.

"I'm going to smash them. Everything in this room! I'll go through the house and smash it up and then, if you call the police, I'll tell them the whole dirty story!"

He came at me screaming and I hit him again and he went down. Then suddenly I saw what was wrong with him, why he was shouting and incoherent and so easy to hit. He didn't know how to use himself. He didn't know what to do with his body or how to fight or protect himself. His arms and hands made clumsy, scrabbling movements and his fingers were widespread to scratch and not bunched to strike. He was like a woman, not a man. When he came at me again, I pushed him away. I couldn't hit him.

He stood away from me and I think he sensed the change in me.

"I'll do anything," he said. "Anything, but don't break the stuff up. That's Chelsea—in all the world you can't replace it."

"And in all the world you can't replace the hours of torture you've given people." My hand was on the cabinet, but I knew now I would never push it over. It wasn't me. It was only some ugly, primitive shadow of myself standing there.

"Be reasonable, Barlow," he said whimperingly, and the self-pity in his voice, the whole craven attitude of the man disgusted me.

"Don't whine," I said. "I'm going to be reasonable. I'm not going to touch you or your things. I'm going to leave you to live with yourself, with your rotten, dirty self. No one has to punish you. Just knowing what you are must be enough for you——"

He came towards me, grateful maybe, or still uncertain, and I pushed him out of my way. I walked past him. I couldn't get out of the room quick enough, away from the ugly shadow of myself. I went out through the french windows and I didn't look back. I wanted to forget him and forget the whole episode. The moorhen called to me from the water as I passed under the cedar.

At the top of the lane I sat in the car and I got out my handkerchief and dabbed at the deep cut on my face. My hands were trembling and I felt cold and empty inside and I wanted a drink. I lit a cigarette and sat there, waiting for the backlash of my anger to ease down before I began driving. A convoy of army lorries came roaring down the road, picking me up in their lights, and a motor-cyclist went by, his machine backfiring like a Chinese cracker. Then the noise of the traffic was gone and there was only the still night and the high serene moon and the jagged black run of hedge shadows.

And then, as I was about to move off, I heard someone running down the lane from the house; heavy, lumbering man's steps. Hansford, I thought. He's going for the police. I didn't care a damn what he did. And I didn't wait for him.

I drove into Alfriston and I stopped at the first public house and had a double whisky and asked the way across to the Eastbourne-London road.

I drove up to London slowly, left the car at its garage and then went round to my club and to bed.

It was a long time before I could sleep. I kept seeing Hansford's scrabbling, feminine frenzy of anger and the red, bursting-point face. If he'd been a man, coming at me hard, ready to hit and defend himself, I knew I would have gone on and smashed him and the house up. But against the frantic, fake figure he was I could do nothing. I was surprised that my father had been taken in by him. But at sixty-five he had been old and tired, and too full of pride, too full of pride to tell even me about it. Only Ross-Piper had known in the few weeks before my father had died. My father had owned a small shipping export and import business in London, but he had sold it about five years after the war. It was only after he had sold it that he had learned that in the last years of his ownership, when he had left most of the work to his manager, this man had involved the firm in a couple of illegal shipping deals. Consignments had been made out to India and had been shipped illegally to Poland through Gdynia. The cargoes were mostly copper and brass rods, prohibited exports to Iron Curtain countries. The old man had been furious but helpless. The firm no longer belonged to him and was now honestly managed. To inform the authorities would have been to destroy its goodwill. The manager had died and the old man had made restitution by paying into a war refugees fund all the money made over the two illegal deals; but the secret had aged and daunted him. And then Hansford had found out and had begun to bleed him.

I lay there, thinking it all over and blaming myself for some of the things that had happened. For years I had meant to come home on vacation from Canada, but the time never seemed right and one job had led to another. And then news of the old man's illness had brought me back too late.

*   *   *

Next morning I was sitting in the plane, waiting for it to move out on to the runway for the take-off, when the air hostess came forward to me.

"Mr. Barlow?"

"Yes."

"There are two gentlemen who wish to see you out-side."

At first I thought it must be someone from the company's London office with last-minute instructions. I went out without my hat and down the landing steps.

A man in a raincoat and soft hat and one of the airport officials in blue uniform waited at the bottom of the steps.

The man in the raincoat said, "Mr. Barlow? Mr. Peter Barlow?"

"That's me."

"Would you come along to the Control office with me, please? It's important."

Ten minutes later the plane was on its way, but I was still in the office under arrest for the murder of James Gurney Hansford.

CHAPTER I

THE small daughter of the house was watching me work at the blocked waste-pipe of the sink. She was about five years old, had a bright face, all innocence and health, a dirty pinafore and a pair of red sandals.

She said, "I put sand in the sink."

"I know you did. That's why I'm here."

"It's naughty. Mummy says so."

I asked her, "What's your name?"

"Marie Anne Louise Bockworth."

"It's a name I shall remember."

From the kitchen where Rington was taking a cup of tea with Mrs. Bockworth, he called, "Hurry up, Barlow." He had his eye on me, but his voice was friendly, and I knew that when we had finished I would be offered a cup of tea. They were always like that when you were on this kind of job. But the moment you stepped outside and set your face towards the tall red walls and the eyes of the world were on you, then the snap came back into the voice and the stiffness into their manner.

Because I was an engineer they had made me a plumber and motor mechanic. It had taken a long time and had needed patience on my part. Patience in the last two years had come hard to me, but in the end I'd mastered it and learned the art of waiting. You learn a lot of things in prison. You get an eye for detail that never lets you forget the pattern of Marie Anne Louise Bockworth's pinafore, an ear that can pick out the noise of blackbeetles foraging at night, and a sense of memory so acute that you can remember things you had no idea had entered your consciousness at the time. Sitting there under the sink with the smell of scullery damp in my nose, I could remember the exact background to the Stubbs' painting of a horse in Hansford's room. A pond with yellow railings, a couple of regency beaux in white doeskin trousers, the corner of a red stable block and a weather vane atop the pigeoncote with the arrow to the south-west. And that's where it should have been for the sky was full of rain clouds.

I got the waste joint back on and began to tighten it. When you have all the time in the world you think about yourself . . . about your own case. I'd spent hours going over the past. Why hadn't I told Ross-Piper I was going to Alfriston? Because I hadn't known. But it was a mark against me. Why had I gone in and out through the french windows? It looked bad and another mark went up against me. The fight with Hansford and the woman coming in. She'd seen him on the floor, seen my anger . . . her evidence alone would have been enough. House-keeper, she'd called herself; though no one believed that. . . . But worst of all my fingerprints on the Colt .45. Why had I grabbed it from the drawer ahead of Hansford and put my marks plainly on it? The courting couple I had asked the way to the Maltings—why did the man have to be in the public-house where I had called for a drink? Why did he follow me out and take the number of my car? I could hear his voice in the witness-box. "He looked kind of wild, sir. And there was this great cut on his face." Why, at the moment I was sitting in the car at the head of the lane, did an army convoy have to go by and a motor-cycle backfire to cover the sound of a shot fired by another man? The man who had come running up the lane as I had driven away. And why would no one believe my story of another man, another man who had put a .45 bullet through Hansford's head, who must have stood outside the windows and watched our quarrel and seized the chance the gods had decided to give him? The police had just shrugged their shoulders and my own counsel, I had seen, hadn't really believed me.

I finished wiping the joint, collected my tools and put them into the brown canvas bag. As I stood up Rington came to the scullery door.

"Cup o' tea?"

I shook my head. I wanted to get outside. I turned and for a fraction of a second I let my hand rest on the head of Marie Anne Louise. She had done me a good turn with her sand. But for that this might have been like any other day, a time for brooding, for nursing hope and gentling the impatience that reared inside me. Today I was going out . . . on my own and running hard. I went past Rington and stood in the narrow hall while he still talked to the woman. Inside I felt a little sick and there was a fine tremble all over me. It was a long, long time since I had been like this and I knew that the only cure for it was action.

There was a narrow, cheap mirror in the hall and I saw myself in it. A brown, shapeless jacket, pale grey trousers and a shoddy white shirt . . . prison uniform. The moment you put it on you lose identity. I looked brown and fit, but somehow I seemed shorter and my body looser, less co-ordinated. Fair hair and pale blue eyes and the lines down the side of my mouth grown deeper. I was watching the face of a stranger.

Rington came up alongside me and said, "All right, oil painting, stop admiring yourself and get going." His voice was still pleasant.

The woman called her thanks to me and I went out of the front door with Rington behind me.

The garden with its cracked concrete path was untidy with toys and the high winds of the past week had smashed down the tall lupins in the border. A loose trailer of rambler rose caught at my canvas bag and whipped back against Rington. The June heat beat up from the concrete path and the woodwork of the gate was hot under my hand as I pushed it open.

I waited for Rington to come through. We were in Nicholson Street—named after a former governor of Parkhurst Prison. Twenty yards away a green bus came slowly down Horsebridge Hill on the main Cowes-Newport road. The people inside looked hot and listless. The air was heavy with the smell of tar and gravel, and now and again came the faint wisp of hay scent. I could hear the sound of a cutting machine in one of the prison fields up on the hill behind the jail.

Rington gave me a nudge in the back and said, "Lead on!" The snap was back in his voice now. We were warder and prisoner. He'd forgotten my name and remembered only my number.

We started down the street, past the rows of warders' houses, away from the main road. In five minutes we would be inside the prison and he would turn me over to the warder in charge of the building party. I would be back on the wrong side of the red wall and ahead of me there would be—at the luckiest— thirteen more years to add to the two I had already done. Wakefield, Maidstone and now Parkhurst on the Isle of Wight. They changed you around and if there was reason in it, it escaped me. For two years I had nursed the hope of getting away, had wakened each morning knowing I was serving another man's punishment and trying not to think of the two weeks that had passed with a death sentence over me. When the reprieve had come to make it a life sentence I hadn't been glad or sorry or anything but possessed with the instant idea that I would get out and find him, the man whom no one except Ross-Piper believed in. After the reprieve I'd had a few words with Ross-Piper. "I'm coming out," I told him. "Nothing's going to keep me in. I'm coming out and I'm finding that man." And he had known I'd meant it. He'd nodded, and he didn't have to say

209

he was going to help. He was a man in a thousand, nothing frightened him. Thirteen years to go, maybe more; for a life sentence could mean anything, twenty, eighteen or fifteen. It depended on behaviour, and the years of strain and degradation made a man's behaviour uncertain. But not for me. I was going, and this was the day.

Walking ahead of Rington, because the moment was so close, my mind was confused with a hundred small details. Two years inside take the edge off one's clarity of thought.

We came to the end of the street and were on the edge of a large patch of ground that sloped down to the prison walls and the gravelled road that led to the gates. To the right the ground climbed through a strip of weary allotments backed by warders' houses. Through the gaps in the houses I could see the grey outer prison boundary wall, ten feet high and running with Roman straightness towards the far high crown of Parkhurst Forest. Just beyond the houses where the wall met the first of the prison fields was a sentry-box. A warder was standing a yard from it. And away, far away, I could see where the wall turned and ran along the edge of the forest. The lush green of young chestnut growths and the dark stance of firs were like metallic cut-outs against the pale blue sky.

A few months ago Gypo had come to me and said, "Any time between June the fourteenth and June the twenty-fourth." Gypo, big, white-haired, ugly, good-tempered and vicious and with more years in prison than out, was a man of power who had taken a fancy to me; and I had nodded and asked no questions. Gypo didn't answer questions. And today was the twenty-fourth of June. For two weeks I had waited and nothing had gone right. Usually I could have been certain of going out with a field party or of being sent to fix a tractor. But the days had gone by without hope and I had been stuck with the building party on the new cart sheds at the bottom of the prison exercise yard . . . within the walls.

Two young girls came running up across the open ground, shouting some rigmarole of song to one another and laughing. I was sweating and I put my hand to wipe it away. In a moment when I was running it would be hotter. Warder and prisoner, we went down the slope and I was repeating silently to myself Gypo's last message: "Highburn Bungalow on the main Cowes-Newport road. Come at it by fields at the back, through Pallancegate and Ridge Copse. And keep out of the bloody forest." I was seeing a dirty scrap of ordnance survey map which he had palmed to me weeks before. A scrap of linen-backed paper and every mark on it a mark on my mind. I looked up at the green bastion of the forest waiting on the skyline. Nearly everyone made for it, and once in they were trapped. But I was going into the forest. They must think I had gone in. I should have about fifteen minutes to get out before the roads around the woods were patrolled. Eighteen minutes from now.

The red main wall of the prison was close now. Beyond it rose the two principal blocks of the prison, tall, ugly red piles with great chimney-stacks, fork-tongued lightning conductors and little rows of barred cell windows. I could see the top edge of the gravelled exercise yard and the yellow line of wooden latrines. How many times had I gone round that yard?

A small saloon car had moved along the road at the top of the open space and was now coming slowly down the slight hill. I knew why the car went slowly—tourists, spending a day away from the summer beaches, fascinated by the prison and driving slowly around. Parkhurst was one of the show places of the Isle of Wight. I heard the thud of Rington's boots behind me. Their eyes would be on me, not on Rington. I was one of their chief exhibits. I saw that the car would reach the little stone bridge that spanned a ditch at the bottom of the slope at the same time as we would. It would happen then. Half a minute away. I changed my tool-bag from my right to my left hand. A trio of swifts came flighting down across the allotments, screaming their heads off. I raised my eyes to them and, in a moment of nervous elation, knowing the moment so close, I knew I was smiling. There they went fast and free. . . . Fast and free, Barlow.

We paused on the edge of the road to let the car go past. There was a young man and a girl in it. She had pale hair, boyishly cut, and a blue dress that showed her brown shoulders. Their eyes held me for a moment and then turned away, embarrassed. A whiff of exhaust gases swirled about me. I stood still on the road edge.

Behind me Rington said gruffly, "Keep moving."

I swung round and faced him, saw the large red-brown face glistening a little with sweat over the jowls, the soft brown eyes and the tight clamp of the blue serge uniform over his big frame. He knew what was coming before I began to move my arm. He grabbed for my shoulder but he was too late.

I hit him hard, my right fist driving into his adam's apple. He went backward, stumbled, and fell on his side and his peaked cap came off. He lay there groaning. Throwing the bag of tools on top of him, I turned and began to run.

I went up the road, heading for the last of the row of villas. A man in shirt sleeves was cutting the lawn in the end garden. The air was suddenly sweet with the fragrance of bean blossoms from one of the allotments.

I ran, waiting for Rington's whistle. If I could be over the boundary wall first I should be lucky.

Overhead the swifts came screaming back, chasing one another, cutting dark silhouettes against the heat pale sky . . . fast and free. And I was thinking to myself, somewhere out there, beyond the wall, beyond the island, out there in freedom was a man who should know I was running at this moment, should know that I was coming for him, that after two years I was starting to move instead of think. . . .

The man cutting grass saw me when I was five yards from him, sprinting for the wall across the rough ground. He turned and ran into the house.

Rington's whistle went when I was three yards from the wall. I saw the warder by the sentry-box look round, and then he was running towards me down the length of the wall. I looked back. Rington was lumbering up awkwardly from behind. The whistle went again. In the prison behind me I knew every ear would be cocked and that the cumbersome machine would grind into another gear.

I jumped with outstretched arms for the wall top. From the top of the wall I dropped into thick, two-feet-high meadow grass. Ahead of me the field sloped up to a small lane that ran in from the main road to border the north-east side of the forest. The easiest line for the bungalow would have been to go straight up across the field to the road, but I turned and began to run alongside the boundary wall towards the forest.

The long grass hampered my running and my feet cut a great swathe through it. The floury seed heads exploded in a fine dust around me.

I put everything I knew into that run for the forest. A fence came up at me, topped with barbed wire. I vaulted it and felt my jacket catch and tear. Then I was racing across an orchard and a flock of geese went waddling and hissing away from me. They were Embdens, big, burgher-like birds, annoyed at this intrusion of their afternoon peace. I was talking to myself aloud, part nonsense and part encouragement, almost as though the first air of freedom in my lungs had intoxicated me. I went across cropped pasture with white clover and buttercups and I knew what would be happening behind me, in the prison. Rington and the other warder wouldn't follow me far. They would go

212

back to report. They had the whole drill mapped out. There wouldn't even be much surprise, for this was the season for escapes; high summer, warm nights and good green cover. The working parties would be rounded up. There would be a harshness and snap in the warders' words, a covering of anger. "One away"—they hated it. And the prisoners would shuffle, go slow, but give no trouble, and there would be a triumph in them. *Who is it?* And by some magic the prisoners would know the answer before most of the warders. *Barlow's away. Bloody fool.* (But that was encouragement, not scorn.) *Barlow? Yes, tall, fair-haired cove in Thirty Party. Lifer. Bloody fool. Even if you get off the Wight they fetch you back in time.* (But not me. They weren't going to fetch me back. Most men run for home, but I had no home, so that there was nowhere for the police to look, no neighbour with a grudge to watch through the curtains. I was after a man who would have seen me rot for life.) The forest was coming closer. *Keep out of the forest.* But I was going in and then out. *Good luck, boy.* I'd get that even from men who disliked me. *Barlow, eh? Yes, scarpered after doing a plumbing job up in Nicholson Street.*

The edge of the forest threw its shadow over me. A wood pigeon came flighting out from a fir and swerved in mid-air as it saw my running figure. There was a sudden, sharp-lined picture in my mind of myself shooting pigeons in Norfolk with my father and a winter wind cutting in from the North Sea shaking the yellow grasses and larches. He was dead, and I should never have turned aside at Brighton for Alfriston. At the trial I had never told the exact details of the blackmail. It was blackmail, I said. What difference did the details make? Two years . . . and the hydro-electric scheme which should have been mine was already finished.

I was into the trees. Five minutes, and another ten to go before the patrol cars would be along the road between Noke Common and the forest. By that time I had to be out of the trees and across the road towards Pallancegate. Five yards inside the wood I turned right-handed and began to run parallel with its edge. The young bracken was just unfurling and the ground was covered with a litter of dead pine needles and leaves. I swerved deeper in, careless of the noise I made, to avoid the Forestry Commission gateway. I crossed the path leading down to it and for an instant caught a glimpse of the lodge cottage.

I was panting now like a heat-struck dog. A bramble caught at my foot and I almost fell. I came down a slight slope covered with faded bluebells and saw the ochre streak of the bordering road through the trees. A woman came cycling along it and I dropped flat. If she'd had prison ears she would have heard my breath pumping in and out. She passed and I was up again with twenty seconds wasted.

I pounded along now, close to the road, waiting for the opening that must soon show for Pallancegate. I knew it all on that scrap of ordnance map. I'd lived this run so many times in imagination that now I almost expected to come across each contour line as a physical feature. Yes, here was the gully with the little stream. The water flashed dark and cool beneath me as I jumped it. I edged nearer the road. A jay went shrieking from a tree ahead and I cursed its noisy interference. And then there was the Pallancegate opening, twenty yards ahead of me, and on the other side of the road. I burst through the hedge that bordered the forest and pulled up on the roadside, looking left and right. The road was clear. I raced across and as I reached the far side I heard the high, urgent whine of a car. I threw myself forward, rolling and crashing into the long ditch grasses. I lay there, my whole body shaking with its lust for breath. The car came speeding up the road.

I kept my head down, listening, waiting for the fall away of powerful sound, for the first squeal of brakes. . . .

The car went by furiously, shaking the tall lacy fronds of the cow parsley. I gave them a few moments' grace before moving, and then I crawled through the hedge and found myself in a field of young corn. Away to the left were the farm buildings of the Pallancegate turning, and further up the slope the trees of Ridge Copse. On all fours I made my way right-handed around the field, using the cover of the corn. At the top of the field I slid under a gate and was in a grazing field. A herd of jersey cows in the pasture raised their heads and gave me their slow, dowager looks and then decided that I wasn't worth knowing and ignored me. Beyond the field was the movement of buses and cars along the main Cowes road. From this point up to Ridge Copse was the bad stretch, all the way in the open.

I began to walk towards the trees, casually, holding myself down to a stroll while every muscle in my body ached to set me running. Far away to the right was a glimpse of the Medina river snaking down to Cowes. I remembered Gypo saying, "You're lucky to have someone on the outside to set it up for you." Prisoners had got off the island on their own before, but they had always been brought back. I knew the history of every escape in the last ten years. The most recent one had been in May of this year. The man had got down to the coast near Ryde and had tried to swim to the mainland. A destroyer going into Portsmouth had picked him up the next morning, clinging to a fairway buoy, half dead with exhaustion and sea-sickness.

I reached the copse and once inside the trees I began to run, following the line which I knew from my scrap of map. The edge of the copse came up with a fretwork of blue sky between the branches of an overhanging hawthorn tree. I stopped. Sloping away from me was a young orchard, reaching right down to the main road. There was a thin scattering of bungalows along the road, but I had eyes for only one which was immediately at the foot of the orchard. *Highburn Bungalow, thick thuya hedge, green and white garage.* And there it was with a red roof, white stucco walls and the thuya hedge which on the orchard side had been caught by frost and was now a rusty brown. To one side, with a creeper growing over it, was a green and white garage. Until that moment I had known it only as a tiny black mark clinging to the red artery of road on the scrap of ordnance map long since flushed down a Parkhurst latrine.

It took me half a minute to cross the orchard. I jumped the palings that backed the thuya hedge, pushed through the thick growth of foliage and stood watching the place. I was breathing heavily and soaked with sweat. The sun came back off the stucco walls in a warm wave of air. Little veins of grass grew in the cracks of the concrete path. The house looked dead.

I went up to the back door and knocked gently. I slid to one side and waited. Nothing happened.

I waited a bit longer, then I pushed the door open gently and went through to find myself in a kitchen. I stood there, alert and tense, holding my breathing down. Slowly, after the outside glare, the room came up into focus. On the kitchen table was a box of matches and a packet of cigarettes. I picked them up and saw that they had been resting on a white envelope. Words were typed across the front of the envelope. *Congratulations to the only man it can concern.*

I had to smile at that. Ross-Piper might have been in the room speaking. But I left the envelope where it was.

I lit a cigarette and filled my lungs. Then quietly I opened the inner door of the kitchen. A long passage led to the front door and the light came in through coloured glass panels, throwing distorted lozenges of red, green and blue over the floor. I went down the corridor, opening doors cautiously. There was a green-and-white tiled bathroom, narrow and dark and with a bath designed for pygmies; a dining-room with a tasselled red plush runner along the mantelshelf and a picture of an old paddle steamer above, and a couple of vases that looked as though they had been won at a fair booth, and then a bedroom, spick and span and dreary and the bed stripped to its mattress. There was another bedroom, facing the front garden, with the bed made up. A book lay half open on the bedside table.

The sitting-room, next to the kitchen, was peopled with the ghosts of summer visitors, and the carpet under the window was worn with the feet of people who had stood there pressing their noses against the window to watch the August rain and wonder what they would do that day. The furniture said sit on us, but don't expect any welcome or comfort. The whole place filled me with nostalgia from my boyhood holidays and I welcomed it. When you've lived in cells for two years a shack made out of potato sacks could seem like a palace.

Back in the kitchen I dropped into a cane armchair and reached for Ross-Piper's letter.

It was unheaded, divided into paragraphs and typed very badly.

1. Sit back and relax. God bless you, boy.
2. Beer and a bottle opener in the refrigerator. Whisky in the cupboard over the sink. Start on the beer.
3. Suitcase with your own clothes in the bathroom. Burn your other stuff in the boiler. Food in the obvious places.
4. Your name is John Allen. Driving licence in pocket of car parked in garage. Passport when we meet.
5. There's no house-to-house search and, as you know, they don't generally use dogs. But keep inside until you leave the place and then lock back door and put key under water butt.
6. Between seven and eight to-night the phone will ring. Answer it and if someone asks you if Jack is home, just say Yes.
7. Ordnance survey map of the Solent area on bookshelf in sitting-room. To-morrow afternoon drive yourself to beach at bottom of Grange Chine on south side of island. Leave car by farm and when it gets dusk walk along beach half-way to Shepherd's Chine and wait below Trig. Point 182. Around ten dinghy will come in for you. Signal: curlew whistle.
8. Drive across island in car is worst phase. May be police blocks, but your civilian clothes and car should take you through. Bottle of hair-dye in bathroom.

I smiled to myself. What a man he was. He had a position and a name to lose, but he was prepared to take a risk for me. I could only hope that he had covered his tracks so well that if anything went wrong nothing could be traced to him.

I got myself a bottle of beer from the refrigerator and for an hour I sat there drinking and smoking and trying to relax. But it wasn't a success. My nerves were on edge and I was listening all the time for sounds . . . any sound . . . the sharp rap of footsteps on a path, the noise of a car pulling up in the road.

A cheap clock on the mantelshelf struck five and I got up and went along to the bathroom, but before I went I put a match to the kitchen stove and I burnt Ross-Piper's letter.

CHAPTER II

THERE was a bottle of dark brown hair-dye standing on the bathroom shelf. I stripped to my pants and then, working over the hand-basin and scrubbing at my fair hair with a toothbrush dipped in the dye, I made the best job I could. When I had finished I looked like a bad snapshot of myself.

I had a bath then, principally to get the dye off my arms and torso, but also for the pleasure of being able to take my time about it. I found myself doing everything slowly, savouring each new luxury to the full. I was listening and wary still, but the caution in me had sunk to a lower level. I began to feel more like Peter Barlow than I had done for years.

I found clothes and dressed slowly, a clean white shirt, grey flannel trousers and a dark blue blazer. . . . My clothes, remembered clothes, and just putting them on did things for me. I wondered if I would ever walk into the pavilion at Lord's again and struggle for a drink amongst the masculine crowd at the long bar . . . or go to a London musical show and come out into the cool night, some new tune persisting in my mind, and walk into Soho for supper.

I was in a kind of dream . . . a man who was in the process of changing from one personality to another.

I went back to the kitchen and stuffed my prison clothes into the stove. Destruction of government property. I liked that. The whole outfit was worth about thirty bob. I watched the stuff burn and I knew that I had sloughed a skin, and I told myself grimly that I wasn't going back. I was out and I was going forward . . . but for the moment I didn't brood on what I was going forward to. Life in the next few days had to be lived in phases, each one self-contained so that the future was strictly parcelled-out. Right now I was looking no further ahead than the moment when I would get into the car and begin to drive.

I found eggs and bacon and cooked myself supper, and I did myself fried bread of a crispness unknown to any prison cook. After supper I sat on in the kitchen. I put my feet up on the table and settled back into a creaking cane chair. But there was not enough confidence in me yet to bring true relaxation. I was alert and wary. Close at hand was the whisky bottle and a glass.

It was Glenlivet—Ross-Piper seldom drank any other—and I paid it the compliment of taking it slowly. Before supper I'd fetched the ordnance survey map from the sitting-room. Already fixed clearly in my mind was the stretch of beach running from Grange Chine up to Shepherd's Chine. The little grey triangle symbol of Trig. Point 182, I knew, would be the end of the second phase. . . . But first there had to be the drive across the island.

It began to grow dark. I could hear the buses and cars going up and down the road, and as the shadows thickened about me in the kitchen I began to get the impression that I was going to sit here for ever in the gloom, suspended nervously between two lives.

The telephone in the hallway went with an unexpected clangour that made me jump from my chair so suddenly that I hit the whisky glass from the table and it shattered on the floor. In the few moments as I went down the hall I was angry with myself. Action was easy, but waiting was hell.

I picked up the receiver and grunted into the mouthpiece. A long way away, it seemed, a voice asked, "Is Jack home yet?"

I said, "Yes."

I waited. Then after a while the distant voice said, "Good." I heard the sound of the far receiver clicking into place.

I went back into the kitchen and sat down. There was a faint red glow from the bottom of the stove. It hadn't been Ross-Piper speaking. It sounded more like Drew, his manservant. Somewhere over on the mainland, at Southampton or Portsmouth, they would be together and they would have a launch of some kind. Maybe Ross-Piper would be using his own boat, the *Nestor*.

I sat there thinking how good it would be to see them both again. But more than anything I sat there thinking how good it would be to get off this island.

And then I heard the garden gate by the main road swing and click and quick footsteps sounded on the concrete path that ran around the bungalow. I was on my feet in a flash and moving to the back door when I saw the passage of a shadow across the window above the sink. The footsteps stopped by the door and for a moment or two there was silence. I moved noiselessly to one side of the door. I stood there, feeling my heart pounding, my mouth suddenly dry. The person outside was a woman; the quick steps had been a woman's. I wished I could have got the door bolt over, but I was too late for that. However, I thanked my stars that I hadn't put the light on. For this late caller there was no sign that the bungalow was occupied. I waited for her to knock and then eventually go away.

But there was no knock. To my horror, the door latch was pushed up slowly and the door swung gently open. A shadow came into the room and stood a foot beyond the door, a shadow among all the other shadows in the kitchen. Suddenly I heard the quick intake of breath, and I saw the shadow swing round.

I almost missed her, for she was as quick as an eel. I grabbed her arm just as she reached the door opening and roughly I pulled her back and pushed her towards the centre of the kitchen. Facing her, I reached out with my foot behind me and kicked the door.

As it slammed I said harshly, "Stay just where you are and don't make a sound, or I'll have to get rough."

My hand was still grasping her wrist and I could feel the hardness of a bracelet under my palm. I couldn't see her. She was just a shadowy shape in front of me.

Then she spoke.

"I'll do as you say. But you already are being rough. You're hurting my wrist." It was a young voice, sounding scared.

I let go of her at that and stood there, wondering what in hell I was going to do, knowing that this was the thing that happened in all plans . . . the sabotage that life works on the best of schemes.

Then slowly I backed away towards the kitchen window to pull the curtains across before I put on the light. My eyes were on her dark form all the time, but she made no move.

I groped behind me for the switch. I couldn't find it and said half aloud, "Where the hell . . . ?"

She laughed then, and I saw her shape stir a little and momentarily the vague oval of her face was faintly touched by the glow from the stove.

"It's on the other side of the door. You don't know this house." Her voice was cool and controlled now, and I was annoyed because I had given something away and more annoyed perhaps because she was so calm.

My fingers found the switch and for a second or two there was a reluctance in me to press it down. My mind was like a sea anemone, sensitive to the slightest change of feeling in the room. I had the odd feeling that the moment the light came on something would be started . . . that life would begin to get out of hand.

I flicked the switch. The naked bulb blazed above the kitchen table. The room came up, shabby and sordid; the crumpled tradesman's calendar on the wall behind the refrigerator, the cheap clock on the mantelshelf, a toby mug full of paper spills, my dirty supper plate, the whisky bottle and the broken glass on the floor . . . all ordinary everyday things, stirring nothing in the mind.

And then, at the side of the table, this girl. I wasn't ready for her. I stood there frowning and staring at her, and the only thing I knew was that it was over two years since I had been so close to a woman. She should have been plain or forbidding, with mousey brown hair and a thin, angular body that stirred no hunger. . . . But she was beautiful. She should have been old and ordinary and scared. But she wasn't. She was young . . . about twenty-five . . . and her eyes were clear and unfrightened. She had dark hair, so dark that it was full of light and left blackness behind as a word without meaning. It was cut boyishly and just untidy enough to give character to art. Somewhere in memory her face seemed to have looked down at me from some painting, a long, oval face, and there was strength in it, in the high cheek-bones that gave the faintest hollowing to her face, in the warm red mouth that instinct told me could relax to tenderness or tighten to a vigorous *damn-you*.

I was staring at her so that maybe she felt she had to speak and break the spell.

"In the dark," she said, "you sounded very rough. But you don't look at all fierce."

I said "Sit down." I nodded towards the chair on the other side of the table.

Never at any moment in my plans for escape had I laid down any procedure for this kind of moment. Nothing in my operation orders covered this. My mind was possessed by a waywardness I could not control. The thing was on me and I just had to go on with it. I wanted to hold her face between my hands, to feel the faint warmth of her breath coming from between those lips. I wanted so many things that had been dead in me for years. I should have been worrying about my safety, how her presence here would complicate my plans, but instead I was wondering what it would be like to put my hands on her hair, to touch with my fingers the line of her neck. . . . In my mind the words were all for physical things, the way she stood and moved, the set of her breasts, the line of her arms and legs . . . but beyond the words was the real thing. I wanted the thing which had been taken from me for so long, the right to be a man with a woman and to have the hope of a future to share. . . . To escape all this I forced myself to see her penny plain and not tuppence coloured. She was just good-looking I told myself. She seemed more because I hadn't been near a woman for so long. She wore a light summer coat, half open, and one of the buttons was loose, hanging by a thread. Beneath the coat she had a simple green dress with a narrow white belt, and as she sat down she began to pull off a pair of white gloves that could have been much cleaner than they were.

I sat down opposite her.

"Who are you and what are you doing here?" I asked.

She didn't answer at once. She looked at me and for a moment there was the shadow of a frown on her face and I felt that the frown wasn't for me but for something in her, something she was trying to work out for herself. There was an unfurled apricot-coloured rosebud in her lapel, a shiver of light reflected from one of her small gold earrings, and the collar of her dress was caught and turned up against the brown skin of her neck. In any other woman it would have been untidiness, the slight disarray of her hair, the loose coat button, the rumpled dress collar . . . but in her they became natural. The frown went.

"My name's Swinton," she said. "Catherine Swinton. And I was coming in here to sleep the night."

"But this isn't your bungalow. You've no right to come here."

She nodded and there was an almost childlike gravity about the movement and then with a smile she said, "That's quite true. However"—she paused and there was a quick flicker of light in her eyes—"I've got a feeling that you shouldn't be here either."

I sat up. "What the devil do you mean?" I didn't even begin to sound angry, let alone feel it. She was watching me and I saw how dark and deep her eyes were.

She shook her head. "You sit in the dark. When someone comes to the back door, you hide behind it. When you want to put the light on you have to be told where the switch is. If you really had a right to be here and you caught me coming in, you might pull me back and you might tell me to stand still until you put the light on, but you would not tell me not to make a noise. I'm not a fool."

She was as cool as ice, but not unfriendly. She had an advantage and she was riding it easily. But I was in no position to give anything away to her.

"This bungalow's been lent to me. I've only been here a few days and I haven't learnt where everything is, and as for telling you not to make a noise I didn't want you screaming your head off hysterically and rousing all the neighbours."

She began to laugh then, but I reached over and grabbed her wrist.

"Don't get funny with me."

She stopped and her face tightened with a quick anger.

"Take your hand off me."

Very slowly I let her wrist go.

"Thank you. Let's be sensible. You haven't been here several days. I slept here last night and you weren't here. Also on the table here last night was an envelope with a very curious inscription on it. 'Congratulations to the only man it can concern.'"

"You read what was inside?"

"Of course not. I don't mind borrowing a bed when I'm broke, but I don't read other people's letters."

She reached for the packet of cigarettes that lay on the table and helped herself to one. Automatically I found myself holding out a light to her. We didn't say anything. I suppose we were both of us wondering—she, what I was going to do, and me what the hell I could do short of cutting her throat.

After a while I said, "You know too much."

"Maybe I know, or guess everything. Before I came along here I went into a café at Newport. The waitress told me that one of the Parkhurst men had escaped this afternoon. The description she gave fits you, except for your hair, which should be fair. You've dyed it very well, but it's still damp and some of the dye has run on to your temples."

She reached out and with two fingers rubbed gently at the skin of my forehead. It was only for a second or two, but somehow that gesture and the sensation of her fingertips on my skin raised a hope in me that I had no reason to expect. But it was there, springing to life from a spontaneous, frank gesture which seemed to tell me so much about her.

I stood up. This was it. This was the point where things went wrong and a man was left without plan and forced to follow circumstance and rely on his own wit. I wasn't dealing with a scared woman. This girl had courage, and with it clearly went an independence and will which I would be a fool to cross. At the moment she had a certain amount of sympathy for me—but I knew how easily it could be lost.

I went to the kitchen cupboard, turning my back on her while I reached in for two glasses. I gave her time if she wanted it to make a jump for the back door.

I turned round and she was sitting at the table watching me.

"I can't offer you gin," I said. "But there's whisky. I think

223

we'd both better put our cards on the table. Maybe we can work something out."

She stood up and began to slip off her coat.

"You drink. I don't want any."

"Please," I said. "It's the first whisky I've had for two years and I need to share the pleasure."

She drank with me. I told her how I had escaped and what I meant to do on the following day, though without mentioning Ross-Piper by name.

I finished up by saying, "That's the position—and you've walked straight into it. I don't know anything about you yet. Maybe I can trust you. Maybe if you gave me your word not to say anything for a few days and I let you go I'd be perfectly safe. But I can't do that. I'm not in a position to trust anyone. So until I move off that beach tomorrow you've got to stay with me. If you won't do that then I don't know yet what to do. I could tie you up and leave you here gagged, or I could cut your throat. I'm serving a murder sentence. One more wouldn't matter. . . ." I watched her. In her position it could not have been easy to take.

She narrowed her eyes, almost as though she were trying to bring me into proper focus.

"A sentence for murder?"

"That's it. You're in the hands of a dangerous man."

I didn't tell her I was innocent. At the moment I wanted to convince her that I could be ruthless.

She got up without a word. She picked up the supper things from the table and carried them to the sink. Her back was to me and I heard the crockery rattle as she placed it in the sink. Just for a moment something about the way she stood, lost and abstracted while she thought, made me sorry for her. I didn't like forcing her, but there was nothing else I could do. She'd walked in on me and now she had to go along with me.

"There's no need to be scared," I said quietly. "So long as you do as I say——"

She turned round then and came to the table, facing me. She looked very young and I think she meant to look brave, but her hands gave her away. For a moment they played with the edge of the table and then she dropped them out of sight.

"I'm not scared now," she said. "At least, not so much. . . ." Momentarily there was even the ghost of a smile on her face. "You don't look——"

"Just do as I say and we'll get along. I don't want trouble and neither do you."

224

"What do you want me to do?"

"Stay here tonight, and tomorrow get into a car and drive across the island with me. If we're caught you can say I forced you."

"You're going to drive openly across the island?" She was more natural now and I thanked my stars that I wasn't dealing with a woman who would have screamed or turned hysterical.

"Yes. But it makes it easier with a girl by my side." I smiled and stood up. I wanted to put her at her ease. "All you have to do is to look as though you were going off to a picnic with your boy friend. . . ."

She really smiled then and I was glad that it was working out this way. There would have been no relish in me for playing a tough part.

"All right. . . . I'll try."

"Good . . . and thank you." Just for a second I reached out and touched her on the arm. Then, as I moved away, I went on, "The only problem is that someone—your family—may miss you. We've got to get that covered."

She gave me a little laugh. "No one will miss me. I'm alone."

"Alone?"

"Yes. And as well as being alone I'm hungry. Do you mind if I have some food?"

"No, carry on. It's all yours."

She fried herself eggs and bacon, and while she cooked she told me about herself. I listened to her and slowly the odd situation began to reduce itself to a natural pattern. She was in it now and she had enough common sense to make the best of it. It couldn't have been easy for her, and I tried hard to do nothing that would alarm her, and I think I succeeded. . . . At least she ate with a good appetite, which is more than most girls would have had at supper with an escaped murderer.

CHAPTER III

I DIDN'T intend to sleep that night. I sat in the sitting-room with the door open so that I could see across the passageway to her bedroom. Her door was half-open and I could see the bottom of the bed. I had offered her the pyjamas and dressing-gown which Ross-Piper had put in the case for me. She had taken the dressing-gown but not the pyjamas. In her coat pocket she had a nylon nightdress which she had pulled out as though it were the most normal thing in the world to carry about, explaining that she had left her suitcase with all her other things in the cloakroom of Newport Station.

She'd come down from London to take a job in a hotel, and on the second day she'd walked out because the manager's ideas of the off-time duties expected of a receptionist didn't fit in with hers.

She'd walked out with her case and about ten shillings in her pocket and had gone to Newport, where she'd wired an aunt who lived near Oxford to send her some money. She'd seen this bungalow the night before just as it started to rain and she had come up to the front porch to shelter. Then she'd gone round to the back and found the kitchen door unlocked and had walked in. The place didn't look as though it had been lived in for days, so she had helped herself to a bed. And the next day, when no money had come from her aunt for her at the Newport Post Office, she had decided to spend another night here. When I'd asked her if the aunt was likely to send her money she'd said, "She will when she gets my wire. But she may not be at home."

I sat there thinking about her. And that was good. If she hadn't been in the house I should have been thinking about myself—going over in my mind the things that might happen tomorrow. I smiled to myself as I remembered how several times during our talk she had laughed. . . . I liked her for her courage and for her laughter; a woman's laugh was something I hadn't known for over two years.

About three o'clock there was a quick shower of rain. I could hear it hissing down outside, splattering against the window. I felt as sleepy as hell and in order to keep myself awake I got up from my chair and went to the kitchen to get a glass of water.

As I came back she was standing in the doorway of the bedroom. The dressing-gown was pulled loosely around her, her feet were bare and she was standing with one on top of the other. Her eyes were warm and dark with sleep and she looked like some drowsy child. I'd have given a lot to put my arm around her, lead her back to bed and tuck her in with a good-night kiss. That was all I wanted, something warm and personal, the right to give and take affection. . . .

She said, "You look tired."

"I am."

"Then why don't you sleep?"

I didn't reply. She knew the answer as well as I did.

She shook her head, a small movement of impatience. "You can trust me. Don't be stupid."

"I can't do that," I said. "Look"—I reached out and took her arm—"if I told you that I'd been inside all this time because of a ghastly mistake, that I'm an innocent man . . . I wouldn't expect you to believe me at once. Isn't that so? And that's how I have to be with you."

She didn't answer for a moment. Then very slowly she put down her hand and took mine where it held her arm and then, still holding mine, she drew me into the bedroom. At the foot of the bed she half-turned towards me and she looked lovelier than any woman I had ever known.

"No, it isn't so," she said softly. "You meet some people, and you know about them at once. If you say you didn't do this thing, I believe you. I believe you even if you can't let yourself trust me. But even so there's no reason why you shouldn't sleep. Maybe one needs to be free in order to trust. Now"—she nodded towards her clothes, which were folded on a chair—"take those back into the sitting-room with you, and this." She took off her dressing-gown and, for a moment as she slipped easily into the bed, her body was like a flame in the blue nightdress. She tossed the dressing-gown to me. "Take them and sleep on them —I'm not going running off to Newport in the rain in my nightdress." She lay back and watched me, and I stood there with the dressing-gown in my arms and I felt like a fool. I dropped the dressing-gown on to the bed and I swung round and was out of the room without touching her clothes. I closed her door and went into the sitting-room and flung myself down on to the uncomfortable settee, and I lay there disliking myself for a long time before I went to sleep.

★　　　★　　　★

227

We ate breakfast together the next morning. Afterwards she washed the dishes and I helped her dry them, and then she went to make the bed. I was thinking all the time of the hours that lay ahead. I sat by the kitchen door and smoked, and I could see the long slope of orchard up to Ridge Copse. . . . Outside, out there, all over the island, a lot of people were concerning themselves with Peter Barlow, and I could feel it, feel their concern registering in every nerve of my body. It was a fine sunny morning after the night's rain. A few goldfinches were playing over the heads of the thistle clumps at the bottom of the grass strip. I watched them absently, knowing time was a weight on my hands and that the fine edge of impatience in me would not go until we were moving.

We had ham and salad for lunch. She went into the garden and picked the lettuce from a small plot. She made mayonnaise and, watching her beat up the eggs and feed in the olive oil and vinegar, I wondered at the apparent calmness in her. She was on my side, but if the police got me there might be a lot of trouble for her. I picked up a sharp knife and put it in my pocket. "If anything goes wrong, you must say I threatened you with the knife, that I made you sit alongside me and behave naturally, ready to let you have it the moment you caused trouble."

An hour after lunch, when I went out to the garage, I felt like a tortoise without a shell, and I seemed to move at tortoise pace, too.

The car was a bronze-coloured M.G. saloon, GFX 789. I had to push the driving seat back to get more room for my legs. I drove it on to the roadway and Catherine came out carrying a couple of towels and two old bathing costumes we had found in the house. She'd made up a picnic basket, too, from the food left in the house. My story was that we were a couple on holiday and going over to the Back of the Wight for an afternoon on the beach.

She put the stuff into the back of the car and I held the door open for her to get in. I noticed that she had sewn the loose button firmly back on to her coat and washed her white gloves. I couldn't remember her doing this during the morning, which showed how much my mind had been living outside the bungalow. She slid in beside me and gave me a little nod. Something about the movement sent a shapeless longing through me. It made me think of all the other natural movements and responses a man would come to know if he were to be with her.

I reached into the pocket of the car and found the driving licence. She watched me as I opened it and examined it. It was made out in the name of John Allen and he had held a licence since 1940.

She said, "Your friend thinks of everything." Then she reached into the dash pocket and pulled out a pair of sun-glasses which were there. "Put these on; it helps."

As I took them our fingers touched for a moment and I said, "You don't know how grateful I am that it was you and not someone else who walked into the bungalow."

I started the car and we pulled out, heading towards Newport, along the road which would take me back past the prison. It was the easiest and most direct route, and if there were road blocks, I had decided, it was better to be checked on a main road where they would be busy and not expecting me. The moment we started driving I felt better. I had a car, a change of clothes and a companion . . . few escaped convicts were ever that lucky. Peter Barlow, I thought, in a dark blue blazer, neatly creased grey flannels, his hair no longer fair and a pair of sun-glasses to confuse the character of his face, and a good-looking girl beside him. . . .

The bungalow was about three miles from Newport, and, driving not too fast, we were soon at the top of Horsebridge Hill. The road dipped and away to the left I could see the waters of the River Medina, a thin silver spill fringed with trees and brown mud and sand stretches. The tide was low. By the time Ross-Piper came for me it would be high. There was a warder's wooden look-out box in the road corner of a field half-way down the hill. The fields that side were only worked by prisoners almost due for release, but there were none out today.

Some cottages came up on the right and then a public-house set well back. Farther down on the right was the turning into Nicholson Road. . . . Yesterday, only yesterday, I had worked there. And then there it was dead ahead waiting for me, the great sprawl of ugly prison buildings, lofty chimneys thrusting into the sky and away, away up to the right the dark line of the forest.

A large green bus dawdled ahead of me and I longed to put my foot down, to get by the prison as soon as possible. Two years done, and certainly another eighteen now if I ever went back. I kept the speed down, choking my impatience and doing what all tourists did—driving slowly to watch the prison on the right. I wondered what the girl at my side was thinking.

We passed the gravelled driveway up to the main prison gates and then saw the new houses for warders on the left. The gardens were bare and unestablished, marked with grey concrete posts and wire strands, and today no working parties, no dark blue warders and men in shirt sleeves were digging or trundling earth in the old-fashioned prison handcarts. The bus drew in to a stop and I passed it. To the right now was the bowling green and the recreation ground. A warder was standing by the pavilion and a prisoner was rolling the bowling green turf.

I stepped on it then up the hill that rose towards Newport. I wanted the prison behind me. Albany Barracks came up on the right, a sentry at the gate in pipe-clayed belt and gaiters, and the barracks themselves neat and army-tidy, and bright with red-painted fire points and red and blue notice boards . . . 70th H.A.A. Regiment, R.A.S.C., R.E.

Catherine touched my arm and she said, "There's a police block ahead."

A policeman stepped out into the road and raised a hand. I pulled in behind two cars that were stopped in front of us.

For a while we were ignored while the cars ahead were checked by two policemen. I looked at Catherine Swinton. She was watching the policemen. And I thought, what man ever knows a woman's heart? She held me in the palm of her hand.

I said, "When they come, smile—every woman does that for the police."

She nodded.

The two cars ahead were cleared. Another car and then the bus drew in behind us. Life seemed to have gone into agonizing slow motion. My fingers beat a tattoo on the driving wheel. Catherine turned and smiled at me. I took my hand off the wheel. A policeman came down towards us and then I saw that with him was a warder, the familiar dark blue serge, the shining buttons and the silver swing of chain looping from the right-hand trouser pocket. I knew him, and momentarily my hand went up and fidgeted with the sun-glasses. John Allen, I told myself, driving with his girl friend for a picnic on a beach; not Peter Barlow. Faces meant nothing. They wouldn't see me. They would see both of us. They saw people as part of the group they made. Man and girl in a car. . . .

"Your licence, please, sir." The constable was at my door and he was looking at Catherine. And the warder was at her door. I thought, this is it. I felt suddenly sick and my body went hot all over. Then I heard her say, "What's the trouble?"

"Prisoner escaped, miss." The warder was looking at her. In that moment I knew that she was my best disguise. Who would want to look at me when she was sitting there?

The constable looked at my licence. The warder gave a glance

230

at the back of the car, at the towels and picnic stuff and then his eyes were over me for a moment.

"Where are you going?" he asked.

"To the Back of the Wight for a swim. Just touring round."

He nodded and his eyes came back to Catherine. Talking to me, but looking at her, he said, "Don't leave your car unlocked anywhere."

The policeman handed the licence back through the window. "You haven't signed the last renewal," he said. "Better get that done. . . ." He grinned at Catherine and then waved us on.

We drove a hundred yards in silence and then I heard the snap of a lighter and a cigarette was held out to me. I put it in my mouth and bent forward to the flame, not seeing her, my eyes on the road ahead.

"Thank you."

She said, "I don't think we'll be stopped again. They probably only have check points on this side of the island."

*   *   *

We went through Newport and then southwards over the downs to the coast which faced the English Channel. The country had a high June greenness, not yet dusty and tired. It was a rare feeling to have freedom spreading around me. For two years my horizons had been limited and I had begun to lose the habit of looking up and staring into the distance. Now I couldn't keep my eyes from the country, miles of it. I picked out the white scars of chalk pits on the downs, the hunched, seawind-shaped lines of thorn bushes, the thatched-roof stone cottages in the deep hollows and the chocolate-and-red and blue-and-gold inn signs like medieval banners. And then, cresting a hill, the great, glittering silver cloth of the sea lay before us.

We came down to it through narrow, twisting lines and then out on to a wide military road that ran the length of the lonely coast. The road ran across a red brick viaduct that spanned the stream running down Grange Chine to the sea. By a slate-roofed farm there was a turning off into a field. On the grassy slope of the valley through which the stream ran were a few caravans and tents. I parked the car by the hedge beyond the farm and we got out.

Carrying our stuff between us, we went down to the sea. There were sea pinks growing in the short turf and at the mouth of the chine the stream was partly dammed by a shingle bar. The water spread back from the bar in a wide pool, its surface littered with driftwood that the storms had washed over. A

231

few families and holiday parties were on the beach. We walked beyond them in the direction of Shepherd's Chine and found a place to sit on a small turf plateau at the foot of the tall, crumbling cliffs.

We sat there, not talking much, except about small things. And yet the odd thing was that I wasn't embarrassed or made impatient by the long silences between us.

At four o'clock we had tea. Catherine had brought a Thermos flask with her, and in one of the villages we had passed through we had bought some cakes, and also three or four daily newspapers.

Over our tea we read the newspapers. There was little in them beyond the bare fact that I had escaped and it was believed that I had taken to the forest. One of them—stuck for a fill-up, I imagine—carried a brief account of the Hansford murder and of my army career. Catherine read this, and for a while she talked to me about my service in the army. But my attention wasn't fully with her. I didn't like this beach. I didn't like sitting out in the open, knowing that at any moment the silhouette of a police-man or a warder might appear on the cliff-tops.

Suddenly she said, "When you get away, what are you going to do?"

"I'm going to find the man who really murdered Hansford."

"Won't that be terribly difficult? Or have you got something to go on?"

"Not a thing really."

She looked at me, puzzled.

"But you must have something to go on."

"Very little."

"Say the police catch you and put you back in prison?"

"Then I'll escape again."

She laughed at that. "You're a bigger optimist than I am."

"That's all I've got, optimism and my innocence."

"Well, I hope you succeed."

"You think I'm crazy?"

"Yes, I do. But it's the kind of craziness I understand. After all, needles have been found in haystacks. . . ."

As the evening wore on and the sun began to drop, I told her there was no point in her staying any longer with me. It would soon be dark. She didn't seem in any hurry to go. She was used to me now, and it wasn't difficult to see that in a way she was enjoying herself. But it wasn't only that. I sensed that she liked me, had sympathy for me and wanted to stay as long as she could.

When she was ready to go I walked down the beach a little way with her. She was going to take the car back to the bungalow and spend another night there. Just before we got within sight of Grange Chine she stopped and said, "Don't come any farther."

She held out her hand and mine touched hers for a moment. She stood there with the breeze stirring her hair, and she smiled, a nice, warm, natural smile, as though I had taken her out for the day and now we were parting . . . no longer strangers.

"I won't forget you," I said. "You've done me a damned good turn."

"You don't have to thank me. I didn't like it at first . . . I really was scared. But now it all seems very different."

"Bless you."

"And good luck to you. I hope you find that needle."

I watched her figure growing smaller in the dusk as she went down the beach. Then I turned away and walked back to the spot where I had worked out Ross-Piper wanted me to be. It was a point where the tall cliffs ran back, making a shallow cove.

I suppose I should have been thinking about Ross-Piper, about the chance of the police picking me up, about the needle I had to find in a haystack, but for half an hour I sat under the cliffs and stared at the sea and thought about Catherine. It was a pleasant half hour and it wasn't spoiled for me by the thought that perhaps the impression she had made on me was entirely due to the fact that she was the first woman I had met in two years and she had helped me. . . . No, I liked her for herself . . . for the way she handled herself, for her laughter, and for her sympathy.

The tide lapped towards a large rock that stood high and dry in the cove. By the time the tide was in the rock would have become an island.

Some time after Catherine had left, two men came strolling along the beach from the direction of Grange Chine. A small path ran up the cliff close to the point where I was sitting. They were deep in some conversation and didn't see me until they were a few yards off. Then they stopped talking and went by in silence. One was short, thickset, with very dark fluffy hair and a strongly wrinkled face. He wore a loose tweed jacket, grey trousers and white tennis shoes and swinging from his left hand was a long length of seaweed. Something about the way he walked, his broad shoulders, and the thin, slightly bowed legs, reminded me of a jockey. He gave me a glance and a slight nod. The other man didn't even look at me. He was taller, thinner, carried a stick and wore a dark suit and a white cloth cap. He stared ahead of him and there was a frown on his face. I watched them walk out around the far spur of cliff and disappear. I sat there and finished my cigarette.

Somewhere out at sea was Ross-Piper. As soon as it was dark enough he would head in for this cove. . . . It would be good to see him again. I began to feel impatient. The night came loafing down the Channel as though it were in no hurry to have the westering sun finish its display of colours. It occurred to me that if the two men came back and found me still sitting there they might think it curious, so I went up the little cliff path. I could stay on the cliff-top until it was dark enough for me to come down again. The cliffs at this point were fairly high, going up nearly two hundred feet. The path climbed through patches of loose, crumbly earth and chalk. About twenty feet from the top of the cliff it came to an end. Recently part of the cliff had fallen away and taken the top part of the path with it. A long slide of mud and loose stones dropped away to the beach, leaving about three square yards of turf platform with a couple of gorse bushes. Rising from it was a steep face of chalk overhung at the top by a sagging crust of topsoil and grass.

I sat down by one of the gorse bushes, and I was hidden from the beach, which was what I wanted. I didn't smoke. I just sat there and watched the darkness gather around me and heard the tide creeping up below. Some jackdaws were playing about the cliff to my right, and now and again I heard the scuttle of rabbits over the loose scree slide. The last light went from the sky and the evening brought a slight wind with an edge of coldness in it. Now and again I could hear the distant hum of a motor going along the military road and away down to my right, far down at the end of the island, the loom of St. Catherine's Point lighthouse began to show. The wind began to freshen a bit and long banks of cloud came sliding up from the south-west, hiding the stars and helping the darkness. At a quarter to nine it was dark enough for me to feel secure about returning to the beach.

I was on my feet, ready to start down, when I heard sounds of footsteps on the beach below. The sea was making a steady wash and gurgle over the shingle, but the rattle of displaced pebbles came clearly up to me. I looked down, but I could see nothing except the faint line of the breaking waves and another ring of foam some way out where the sea had now encircled the standing rock. The footsteps were louder now and there was more noise than one man would make. Then for a moment I caught the flash of a torch. It came on and off so quickly that within a few seconds I couldn't be sure whether I had really seen it, or had mistaken the wet gleam of a wave on some rock.

From the edge of the platform I looked down into the gloom, and a quick feeling of uneasiness rose in me. It could be the two men who had passed me coming back.

There was no sound from below now except the slow wash of the tide over the pebbles. I stood straining my eyes into the darkness, tensed and waiting. Somebody had been on the beach. I was sure of that. But there was no sound of them now. Gradually I began to believe that they must have passed on, the noise of their going covered by the sound of the waves.

A few seconds later I knew I was wrong. Quite clearly I heard the slide and scrape of feet on the path and the heavy grunt of a man who sets himself to a steep climb. A stone rolled in the darkness and there was the quick intake of a man breathing. The sounds came nearer, moving up out of the darkness, and there was nothing I could do to get away. Behind me was the steep face of the broken cliff. I moved slowly back across the turf until I was close to the cliff face, and then I dropped into the scant cover offered by a gorse bush on the lip of the long scree fall. In those few moments I was telling myself a lot of things which were meant to be reassuring. But their power was lost before a sharp intuition that trouble was coming panting and slipping up the path towards me. Holidaymakers, I told myself, anxious to be off the beach and taking the first path. They couldn't be expected to know that it came to a dead end. The two men who had passed me could have become suspicious of me, could have gone round the far point and then doubled back to watch me. They would know where to find me . . . where to send others to get me. I crouched there, angry with myself at having sat in a dead-end. I was a fool. If I'd carried on like this in the army, I wouldn't have lasted a month. Parkhurst yesterday, freedom today, and Parkhurst tomorrow. Well, that was a recognized escape routine. I was going to be just like all the others.

There were two of them, and they were the men who had gone along the beach. They came up over the lip of the platform and stood together five yards from me and the white cap of the taller man made an irregular blur in the darkness.

I didn't move. For all I knew they were not concerned with me or even aware I was there. I kept my face down and hoped that they would go back.

Their heavy breathing began to even off. Then suddenly the torch came on. Through the tangle of bush I saw the white cliff gleam a few yards to my right. For a while the torch rested there unmoving. The man in the white cap came forward a few paces, but it was the other who held the torch for the light remained still. Slowly the torch began to swing in an arc and the light was kept well down. It swept across the far gorse bushes, flashed against the chalk again and then was full on me. I sat there momentarily blinded and blinking at it.

Out of the darkness a voice said gently, "All right, stand up and don't give any trouble."

I stood up slowly and I said, "What's all this about?"

One of them laughed, a rough, awkward little sound, and the torch shifted, hitting the ground just ahead of my feet and throwing a more general illumination over the platform. The man in the white cap had the whole of one side of his body lit up by the torch, and he was stooping forward a little, leaning on his stick. The other man, the jockey-type, was still lost in the darkness behind the torch.

The man with the white cap moved his stick slowly, half raising it and pointing towards me. The way he did it made me think of some stroller in a pleasure garden pointing out a fine plant in an herbaceous border, easy, unconcerned and only mildly interested.

"Turn round, Barlow," he said, "and put your hands above your head."

"I'm not Barlow, whoever he is," I said, keeping up the bluff, but with little hope. "And I'm certainly not doing as you say. Who the devil do you think you are?"

"Turn round!" It was the other man. His voice had a deep, earthy rumble in it, and with the words the torch flicked up into my face and then down again.

With a show of indignation, I protested.

"But I'm not Barlow. You're making a mistake."

"Save it for later," said the short man. "And keep your hands well away from your pockets."

"But you damn fools——"

"Save it!"

To emphasize his words the man in the white cap gave an impatient wave of his stick and I saw that it was heavy and rough-cut.

"Turn round and put your hands up," he snapped, his voice hard and testy.

Very slowly I began to turn and raise my hands. My mind went quickly over the chances of getting away from them.

As I turned the torch came up and I saw the roughness of the chalk face and the grey top of the long scree, and I was trying

236

to remember what the drop had been like. All loose, broken stuff, I thought, with the heavy rocks and boulders right at the bottom. It was a hell of a way down, and if I did it, I thought, it would be better to have company and help in breaking the fall. I stood facing the cliff and the man with the torch said, "O.K."

I heard the other step forward, heard the rustle of his jacket as he moved. I swung round, and he was close to me and between me and the other man. The stick went up and his face was a grey mass beneath the white cap. I jumped for him and my arms went round his body. I deliberately let myself go with the momentum of the jump, swinging sideways and taking him with me. We hit the ground together and he tried to hold me and pin me down. But I arched my back, digging my heels into the turf and, carrying him with me, rolled towards the edge of the scree. The torch flashed over his face. Something kicked out at me and caught me in the side. The pain went through me like a blade and momentarily the dark-lined face of the man with the torch was lit up and then disappeared. I felt the edge of the scree give, heard the rattle and seeth of stones and then we were over, rolling and slewing downwards, and I held on to my man as though he were the thing I loved most in the world. I pushed my face into his chest and we went smacking down the long slope.

We fell through a darkness that was full of sound and viciousness. An avalanche of stones and loose chalk went with us. My hands and arms rasped across the rocks and loose stones, and with each turn of my body the ground came up and smashed into me. Then suddenly we dropped through space, over a ledge or shelf, and as we hit the ground again he was torn from me and I rolled free, numbed and dazed. A grey shape came sweeping up towards my face and I put my hands out and felt the bite and rasp of sharp stone across my palms and then the thump of my body crashing into some boulder. It was a noise and sensation that seemed to be happening far off and unconnected with me. I just lay there, stupid with the blow and listening to the diminishing, almost musical, settling of the loose scree stuff above me.

CHAPTER IV

I LAY there, looking up at the windy night-sky that had cleared in places to show a few stars. I could see part of Orion and there was a foolishness in my head, for I was impatient for the clouds to move so that I could see the whole constellation. My body was so battered that there was a kind of comfort in it, but I knew that the moment I moved the comfort would go.

Somewhere up aloft part of the Orion constellation came loose and began to dance down towards me. I knew then that the star flickering down from Orion was a torch coming down the path towards the beach.

I struggled to my feet, and as I did so a great stab of pain shot through my left side. I pressed my hand against the bottom of my ribs and the pain eased off. I took a couple of steps awkwardly down the foot of the loose scree. To my right I picked out the white blur of a cap, but I could see no sign of the owner. The torch flashed high above me and a voice called loudly something which I couldn't catch.

As quietly as I could I went down the slope of the beach towards the sea. The torch dropped lower and I heard the sharp rattle of shingle as someone reached the beach. A voice called heavily, "Rance! Rance! Where are you?" And then, after a pause, "Hell!"

Making a lot of noise, the man began to move along the top of the beach towards the scree foot. The torch went out. I edged backwards towards the sea, trying to match my steps with his, and every move I took sent a jab of pain into my left side.

The man at the cliff-foot stopped moving suddenly. I stopped, too. The torch came on, flashing over the broken slope. Abruptly there was no sound except the slow wash and break of the sea behind me. I waited, knowing only one thing—I had to stay on this part of the beach until Ross-Piper came and I had to avoid these two men.

Then, as I stood there, I became aware that I was not alone. Somewhere close to my right a few shingles rattled gently. There was silence and then the shingles went again, but this time closer. I half turned, peering into the gloom. On the night breeze I caught a trace of perfume and the next moment a voice whispered close to me, "Peter. . . ."

I reached out. The shingles stirred once more and then my hand was on a shoulder. I drew her close up against me, and then, as she started to whisper, I touched her mouth for silence.

At the head of the beach the torch flashed round in a half circle. Quite clearly I saw the sprawl of a body in the dim light and then its movement as Rance began to sit up. The torch went out and voices came down to me, blurred and echoing softly against the cliff front.

I had no time to waste wondering why she was back. All I knew was that she couldn't be left here. If these men got her she'd be in trouble.

The torch flashed again and stayed on, and now there was the steady grind and crash of beach stones as the two men began to move forward, the torchlight swinging to left and right as they combed the beach for me.

Taking advantage of the noise they made, I stepped backwards towards the sea, and I drew the girl with me. Where I went she had to go.

"Stick with me," I whispered, and then we were backing into the water. We moved out, away from the advancing torch, and the water rose around us. When it reached my armpits I dropped back gently and we began to swim. My clothes filled with water, ballooned around me with trapped air for a while and then began to drag. The pain in my side seemed to have gone.

Fifty yards out and just ahead of us was a greying in the night which marked the meagre surf that played tonsure-like around the standing rock which had now become an island.

I pulled myself on to it, hauled Catherine up, and then we slid along a little ledge and lay there with the water running from us. Alongside me I heard her move, twisting over to free herself of her long coat. I reached out a hand and helped her, but my attention was on the beach.

The torch kept moving to and fro, going out and coming on, and over the sound of the waves I could pick out their voices. I glanced seaward. There was nothing to be seen except a grey and black cloth.

Catherine shivered gently. In a whisper which the noise of the surf about the rock covered easily I said, "What the hell were you doing back here?"

Her voice came to me a little breathless with the cold in her, "The car was gone when I got to the farm. . . . I didn't know what to do. So I came back along the cliff-top so far. I watched you for a while. . . . Then I came down to the beach when it was dark——"

"What on earth for?"

"I don't know. I think maybe I just wanted to make sure you went off safely. . . . I don't know. Then I heard all the noise. . . ." Her words finished in a spasm of shivering and I put out my arm and drew her close up against me.

On the beach the torch was flickering along the water's edge, and now and again I saw the reflection in the water of two uncertain figures. I prayed that they would not have noticed this rock.

I don't know how long we lay there. All I know is that the two men never gave up. They widened the area of their search and they went back over the scree fall. One of them even climbed down it with the torch, thinking, maybe, that I was lodged unconscious part way down it. After a time they became a pattern of light and sound remote from Catherine and myself.

And then, after ages it seemed, I heard it. It was some way out and very faint, but it was unmistakable—the long, fay-like rise and fall of a curlew call. I put my head down and listened, and distantly I thought I could make out the sound of oars echoing against the shabby curtain of the night. The call came again, and this time the men on the beach must have heard it, for I saw the torch come swiftly down to the water and heard the urgent grind of pebbles under feet.

I gave Catherine a tug and we slipped into the water. I saw her reach up for her coat and there was an unexpected affection in me for her. A coat was a coat and cost money. I took it from her and wrapped it round my neck. And then we were swimming, side by side, known only to one another by the slow break of ripples and the quiet gasp and drive of our breathing.

We'd made about twenty yards when the call came again, and to our right. I trod water and whistled gently, and as I finished I heard the clear splash of an oar and the swirling sound of water.

We swam on, and then right over us was a darker darkness against the night.

I said, "Here."

The shape came round and I made out someone sitting in a pram dinghy. I swam alongside and hung on to the stern.

A familiar voice, but not Ross-Piper's, said, "Strewth! It's Mr. Barlow."

"It bloody well is."

"Yes, sir. But there was no need to swim out, sir. You'll never get into this nutshell from the water."

"There was need to swim, Drew. And don't bother about

our getting in. We'll both hang on to the stern and you can tow us out." Catherine came alongside me as I spoke and I saw Drew peering forward.

Surprise in his voice, he said, "Us, sir? Are there two of you?"

"Yes, Drew."

"Very good, Mr. Barlow. And if I may say so, welcome back."

"Thank you."

He pulled on the oars and we began to move out. I hung on to the stern with Catherine and I kicked a little with my feet to help, and I was smiling to myself. The last time I had seen Drew was on the evening I had gone to Alfriston. Ross-Piper would have only men servants and Drew was an old naval stoker of the most exemplary dignity when on duty. His off-duty life was confined almost entirely to race-tracks and public bars.

*   *   *

The next morning there was a grey, silvery haze over the water, a thin, swaying succession of mist veils through which the sun would soon break. A little swell was going, hardly more than a slow, untroubled heave and fall of the sea. I sat by the wheel with Ross-Piper, holding a mug of coffee and smoking a cigarette. From below there was the sound of Drew clearing up the galley and the breakfast things. Catherine was still sleeping in the fore-peak bunk.

For me it was a different world. I was among friends and for the time being relieved of all tension. Nobody was going to come round a corner and recognize me. There was no need to watch every move I made or weigh every word I uttered.

Both Ross-Piper and Drew had a way of reducing excesses to quite ordinary proportions. Ross-Piper was the kind of man who had he turned a street corner and met a charging rhinoceros would have side-stepped and passed on, his keen mind at once paring the fantasy down to its logical explanation. He'd told me once that as a brain surgeon—and there were few of his eminence in England—he lived so much among miracles that his sense of surprise had become atrophied. But not his sense of enjoyment. He was a man who enjoyed life.

His welcome the night before had been typical. He had helped to haul both of us on to the deck of his motor launch, the *Nestor*, and as I had stood there he had put his arms around me and hugged me, saying, "Still doing things the hard way? Welcome, boy, welcome." Then stepping back he had turned to Catherine and held out his hand. "If you're from Parkhurst, too, then there's nothing wrong with the English penal system." Then, with a

241

great laugh, he had carried on, "Get below and change, both of you, while I take this tub out. Drew, whisky, rum, cocoa, whatever they want. What a moment this is! Wouldn't have missed it for a lakh of rupees!"

Later, when we were well out, he had come down and joined us. My left ribs were hurting me and my hands were cut and scratched from the fall. He strapped up my ribs with a long, tight bandage. "Might have a couple cracked." He had fixed a cut in my hand with plaster while I told him about our trouble on the beach.

He sat beside me now, chewing at an old pipe, one hand resting firmly on the wheel. Two years hadn't seemed to have changed him or his clothes. The last time I had been on the *Nestor* with him he must have been wearing the same blue sweater, the same patched serge trousers. I could convince myself that I recognized the same old oil and paint stains. He was a big, comfortable, heavy man, somewhere around sixty, and his hair, which was crisp and springy, was the colour of tow and fuzzed out behind his ears. He had the bluest eyes of any man I've ever known and his face was shaped to a forceful bluntness, all valleys and plateaux and peaks. He was full of common sense, but because of the strength and exuberance in him, impatient of conventions and authority and, though he seldom showed it, he was a dedicated man; for him there was nothing in life so important as his work as a brain surgeon.

We both sat there while the *Nestor* moved gently up the Channel and I knew he was waiting for me to speak. There was a sudden gleam of morning sun through the mist curtains and the moleskin sea was peacock plumage. I jerked my cigarette over the side.

"Where are we heading?"

"Rye Harbour. In the last couple of years I've taken to running up and down the coast between there and Southampton. Nobody thinks it odd when I come and go—but June's the only month I get free."

"You've taken a hell of a risk for me."

"If I hadn't helped you'd have tried to do it on your own. Anyway the risk isn't so great. We've been careful. You had the sticky end. The only snag is this girl. She's bound to find out who I am." His face was ponderous, the whole look that of a man considering a diagnosis.

Meaning it, knowing it to be true, I said, "You don't have to worry about her. You can trust her absolutely."

"You'd better tell me."

242

I told him everything then and he sat there listening patiently. Only twice did he interrupt. When I explained how Catherine had gone back to the car to find it had disappeared, he said, "That was part of the plan. The moment you'd finished with it our man was to take it away. He was in Portsmouth with us yesterday. He took the car away and he's closing up the bungalow and taking the keys back to the agent. There won't be anything to trace from that end."

And later, when I described how the two men had tried to capture me on the beach he whistled gently and then said, "Hell . . . I don't like that. From your point of view it's better that the police should think you are still on the island. That was a bit of bad luck."

When I had finished he was silent for a while. Drew came on deck carrying an armful of damp clothes and spread them in the bows. He went below and I heard him talking somewhere forward to Catherine.

The sun was strengthening now and there was a large patch of blue sky overhead with a couple of gulls caught in the middle of it, wheeling round and round.

Ross-Piper slewed himself towards me and for a moment his hand rested heavily on my knee.

"All right, Peter. Now you listen to me. I'm not going to worry about myself, or about the girl. I'll take your word for her. But I'm worried about you. I'm an old man and that gives me an advantage over you. I've learned that few questions are answered by a simple yes or no. And few problems are black or white. You've got a problem on your hands and you've got to find an answer. I've helped you to get out because I know you're an innocent man and because I knew that you meant to get out and would go on trying until you'd brought it off. You're the kind of stubborn bastard who usually gets what he wants. I felt that I had to help you. But the thing is what are you going to do now?"

"There's no problem there," I said sharply. "I'm an innocent man and I mean to prove it."

He rolled his eyes.

"As simple as that?"

"No, I don't think it will be simple."

"Nor do I. If only you had one concrete thing to go on, but you haven't. You're looking for a needle in a haystack and the field the haystack is in is cordoned with police. Do you see what I mean?"

"Yes, that the whole thing is going to be bloody difficult."

He straightened up.

"Bloody impossible. Take my word for it. No, no, listen." He put out his hand as I stirred sharply. "It's your choice eventually, but just for now listen to me. The police are after you. They're not fools and their filing system is the best in the world. When you go ashore you're going to have to watch every step you take. When you blow your nose you've got to hide the laundry mark on your handkerchief. You're going to walk a tightrope. You're going to have to watch yourself every second because somewhere there are a lot of people watching for you every second. If this depresses you you can change that mug of coffee for a large gin."

I laughed. "But I know all this."

"You think you do. You look at it as though it were one of your army jobs. But in those days you belonged to a side. You could go back to base. But not today. You're alone."

"What are you getting at?"

"You know as well as I do. I can sympathise with your wish to prove your innocence, but in the last six months I've decided that it's idiotic, impractical, dangerous and a waste of living time. You look surprised. . . . Well, I don't blame you. It's not easy for me to give this advice. I was brought up in the days when the impossible was always possible, when the world still had a few edges to fall off. High adventure, the British Rajh, Treasure Island, whisky sixpence a nip and virtue triumphant . . . Peter, those days are dead if they ever existed. You carry on with this caper and you'll be back in Parkhurst within three months."

He meant it, I could see that. I didn't want to admit it but I had to. He could never say a thing he didn't honestly believe even if he knew people were going to hate it. And I was hating it at this moment.

"What else can I do?" I sounded a bit bad-tempered and I was sorry for it. I avoided his clear blue eyes, turning from him and looking forward, seeing the bows of the *Nestor* rising and falling gently, hearing the steady drone of the engine and the spit and gurgle of the exhaust over the side.

Ross-Piper laughed, but there was no unkindness in it, only a deep charity. "You remind me of Tom," he said. Tom was his son, long dead. "Any time I advised something he didn't want to do he used to put on the same mahogany face that you've got just now. Face it, Peter. You've got to clear out of England altogether. I've got a passport for you. You've got a new name. I can fix you a passage. You're still young, and you've got a

244

profession and you can start somewhere else. With each month that passes, it'll be easier. You'll never be Peter Barlow again—but that's only a name. But at least you'll be a man, outside, free, and with a lot of full years ahead of you."

"And always have this secret hanging over me?"

"Most people have some secret, some shame—and the majority reach the grave with it. You've had a bad deal, I know that. So have a lot of other people. Injustice . . . we all have to take our share of it. The great thing is to learn how to play your bad cards, not to complain about the deal."

He was silent then, waiting for me to speak. I could see his point of view. What chance did I have of finding the real murderer of Hansford? A snowball's in hell. But he himself had said that life was full of miracles. Maybe one would come my way. I could even ask myself whether it was justice for myself I wanted or punishment—yes, vengeance if you like—for an unknown man. It didn't matter. The important thing was the drive deep down in me. And that drive had taken force and vigour now that I was out.

The mist was lifting fast now, sucked up in quick swirls from the face of the water. I heard Catherine laugh with Drew down in the cabin. And I thought how good it would be to laugh, to be free of this grinding ache, this soreness of the mind . . . but running away wasn't going to cure it, not for me.

Ross-Piper said quietly, "You've a right to feel hard, you've a right to consider yourself unfortunate. I meet people like you every day of my life. Under sentence of death from cancer and a dozen other things. Injustice . . . but they have to take it. Just consider whether it wouldn't be better for you to take it, rather than start on a course which may well put you back in prison for the rest of your life."

I stood up.

"I was born Peter Barlow," I said, "and I'm going to stay Peter Barlow. I don't want to be John Allen in Buenos Aires who's afraid to go to bed at night in case he talks in his sleep."

Behind me I heard him sigh, a deep, parental sigh marking resignation and unwanted wisdom. I saw his point so clearly; but I still had to be myself.

"You're a stubborn bastard, Peter. However . . . I had to say it. I won't ever mention it again. But I hope that sometime before it's too late you'll come to me and say I was right and ask me to fix it for you."

I turned, looking down at him. The square, blunt face was

smiling, but the smile had a sad tolerance in it. It was the face of a man too old and too wise to be surprised.

I said, "Maybe it will come to that. But first of all I've got to try the other thing. If I went away without trying I'd all the time be wondering . . . blaming myself for taking the easier course."

I took a few steps forward to the companionway and then back to the wheel to ease the ache in my left side. Drew appeared on deck at that moment and came over to us. He was almost as old as Ross-Piper; a stiff, crab-like figure, an ancient red woollen cap pulled down to his ears. He had a way of standing that was vaguely gorilla-like, his arms well out from his long body. His face looked as though it had been cut from chalk and was the same colour. He only needed rings around his eyes and a big red mouth and he would have been a clown full of sad humour.

With the familiarity which existed between the two on the boat, Drew enquired, "What's he decided to do?"

"To stick his neck out," said Ross-Piper. "I'll give him two weeks."

Drew nodded. "It was bad luck you were spotted on the beach. Now the police will know you're away, sir. And the girl, too . . . it isn't good to have women mixed up in this kind of affair." Then with a look at Ross-Piper, he asked, "Will we still make for Rye? There might be a reception committee waiting for us."

"We'll put him ashore before we go in."

They began to discuss how they would get me ashore and I sat there listening to them. They would do everything they could for me, but the moment I was ashore I should be on my own. It wasn't a moment I was impatient to meet.

CHAPTER V

ALL day we moved up Channel out of sight of land. It was a blue, gold and silver day with a gentle wind and no kick in the sea. Part of the afternoon I sat up in the bows and trolled for mackerel with a scrap of red rag on a hook, but I caught nothing.

Catherine came and sat by me and she was in a cheerful, gay mood, like a girl on holiday. Drew had fixed her up with a pair of canvas trousers, a white sweater and she wore one of Ross-Piper's silk scarves round her neck. Behind us on the deck our clothes were drying rapidly.

"You must be cursing me," I said.

"Why should I? I'm enjoying it." She lay back on the deck. "I haven't been on a boat for ages."

"I can think of better ways of coming on board."

"But not more exciting."

She knew all about Ross-Piper by now, and they got on very well. When we reached Rye she was going to take herself off to an aunt who lived near Oxford . . . and that was that.

She sprawled on the deck, her hands under her head and stared up at the sky.

"You might as well give up fishing," she said. "There's obviously not a fish within miles. And anyway, your bad luck's only making you look more glum."

I turned at that, surprised.

"Have I been looking glum?"

"Terribly. Are your ribs hurting you?"

"Not too much."

"Then what is it? It's a beautiful day. You're with your friends. And at least for twelve hours you don't have to worry about a thing."

She reached out for a cigarette from the packet between us and I struck a match, cupping it in my hands for her as I bent towards her.

"Twelve hours is a very short time."

"It's a long time. Anyway, you don't have to spoil it by thinking ahead."

"That's a damned easy thing to say."

"Now you're cross as well as glum." There was no sharpness in her voice. She turned on one elbow and looked at me and

247

then went on. "Is it something Ross-Piper has said? You were talking for a long time this morning. That's why I kept below."

She was right, of course. It was because of Ross-Piper. His attitude towards my affairs hadn't come up to my expectations and I suppose I was suffering from plain disappointment. I knew I could rely on him and his loyalty. But the thing I really wanted was his approval, and he was too honest to give his blessing to a wild goose chase which might land me in danger.

I told her what Ross-Piper wanted me to do and also how I felt. She listened and for a while her face was grave and I had the uncanny sensation that she was putting herself in my place, seeing and feeling the problem as though she were me.

"What do you think about it?" I finished.

She sat up and crossed her legs. She squatted there, bulked out in the big sweater and the baggy trousers and she managed to look absurd and beautiful. The sun on the side of her face showed up the faintest bloom on her skin. The wind whipped at a loose end of the red scarf and her dark eyes on me were very still.

She said, "I can see his point of view."

"Well, I don't. I'm not running away." My voice was hard and there was a greater disappointment in me now.

"It's not running away. It's accepting facts. The longer you stay in England poking around, the more chance there is of your going back to prison." Her hand came out and rested on my arm. "You've had an awful time, I know. But it's over. You could go away and begin to live, write the whole thing off to experience."

"And somewhere, all the time, there's the man who really murdered Hansford laughing his head off . . . walking free!"

Her hand on me tightened, and there was a warm concern in her voice as she said, "Why bother about him? Do you think anyone escapes punishment? You'd risk going back to prison . . . just for the flimsy chance of finding this man!"

"Yes, I would."

She relaxed then, drawing her hand back and giving a little shake of her head.

"Why are you shaking your head?"

"It's the only thing to do. You've made up your mind, and nothing's going to alter it."

"That's right."

She grinned.

"Stubborn, that's you."

"You don't like that?"

"Oh, but I do."

"But you said you agreed with Ross-Piper."

"I said I could see his point of view. It makes sense—but not for you." She sat up. "That's all that matters. You must do what you feel you have to do. Even if it sounds hopeless to other people."

"Thanks."

I must have sounded dismal for she suddenly began to laugh, and then I found myself laughing with her.

*   *   *

When darkness came Drew took over the wheel and Ross-Piper, Catherine and myself sat in the cabin and he explained to me what lay ahead. We were to run into the entrance of Rye harbour around four in the morning and while it was still dark I was to be put off in the dinghy. To take me right into the harbour moorings would be too risky. The Customs people would note the launch's arrival and I might be seen going ashore. I was to row the dinghy on the top of the tide to Camber Sands, about a mile up from the harbour cut entrance. It was a light affair and I was to haul it into the dunes where Drew would collect it later. On the other side of the dunes was a golf course and a road. Drew would bring a car round to a point near the golf club-house and I would take it over and drive to Canterbury where a room had been booked in an hotel for me under the name of John Allen. In the car would be a suitcase with clothes and other things I wanted and about five hundred pounds in notes.

Catherine said, "Why can't I drive the car round for him? We could go on together then to Canterbury. From there I could get a train through to London and so to Oxford."

Ross-Piper looked from her to me and said, "It might be better. Drew's known around here and if anyone sees him handing a car over to you at that hour of morning they might be curious. He could go round and pick up the dinghy later."

"If Catherine doesn't mind," I said.

"I'd like to."

"Good," said Ross-Piper. "Then that's settled. From Canterbury you'll be on your own, Peter." He paused for a moment, rubbing the bowl of his pipe against his nose and looking at me. "I'm going back to London. If you change your mind—you can always call me at the hospital or my flat."

"I'm not going to change my mind,."

He shrugged his shoulders and half smiled at Catherine.

"Maybe he'd listen to you?"

She shook her head. "I've tried it."

He reached back to the bookshelf behind the bunk on which he was sitting and took a large brown envelope from between two books. He tossed it across to me.

"There's a passport in there. Now you'd both better get some sleep. How about those ribs? Are they easing up?"

"They'll be all right." They were hurting me still. Also my head was aching and now and again I shivered, as though I were in for a bad cold. But I kept all this to myself. I didn't want to give him any chance to hold on to me . . . any chance to weaken my determination to carry on with my plans.

I didn't sleep much. I lay in my bunk and a hundred different thoughts chased through my mind. In a few hours I would be ashore. Then Canterbury, and I would be on my own. I could take nothing and no one for granted and I had enough sense to see that it was going to be a kind of loneliness which I had never known before; a loneliness exaggerated by the fact that I was doing something opposed to the advice of two people who meant a lot to me. The police wanted me . . . I was going to walk a tight-rope, and the damnable thing was that it seemed the right and reasonable thing for me to do. It had to be. It was all very well to be logical and count chances, but there was a higher logic than this every-day stuff other people pushed at me. I was the one who was right. Not Ross-Piper or Catherine.

Just after three Drew came down and made some cocoa in the galley. He laced it with rum.

"We'll be going in soon, sir."

Catherine came aft, wrapped in an oilskin over a pair of Ross-Piper's pyjamas. She took a mug of cocoa with me, but we didn't talk much. We just sat there under the swinging oil lamp, with the sound of the sea running outside and the occasional splatter of a wave flicking on to the deck and I wished with all my heart that she could have been a hundred per cent for me. Three o'clock at night is a dead time and I felt the need for one person at least to be absolutely on my side.

Before I went out of the cabin she said, "You're sure you can make the row with your ribs? Drew says it's a long pull."

"I'll make it." I reached back and for a moment I held her hand.

I went up on deck. We were about a mile off shore now and I could see its bulk against the night sky. Ahead of us and off the port bow Ross-Piper pointed to a red light. It marked the mouth of the river cut running up to Rye Harbour. There was a small, choppy sea going and now and then a tail of water slapped over the bows. I remembered how once on just such a night I had gone up the Adriatic coast to go ashore above Ancona, to go ashore to danger . . . but leaving friends to go ashore and find new friends even in the midst of danger. This time I was on my own. Ross-Piper had said that. Without a side.

The red light came slowly abeam of us and Ross-Piper cut the engine down to a low grumble and we gradually ran up the coast until the light was almost astern of us. Then he eased the *Nestor* round. The sea was grey, silver and dark blue. The few stars seemed tarnished and weak and Ross-Piper's face in the pale binnacle light looked washed-out and seemed to have lost its strength. It was a comfortless moment, no colour, no warmth, and I think if Catherine and the old man had set on me then they might have talked me round.

Drew went aft and began to haul in the dinghy which we'd been towing. I pulled the belt tight of the raincoat which Ross-Piper had given me. As I turned to go past the wheel I saw Catherine's face framed in the square of the cabin opening and she raised a hand to me. I returned the wave and then Drew's grating voice was saying, "The tide's running strong, sir. But it's with you. Only you must get into the sands before it takes you down to the river mouth. The other side of the river it's all steep shingle and a hell of a place to haul a boat out. And no cover come the morning."

I went over the side and Ross-Piper held the painter ready to cast me off. His face was above me, just a grey shadow. I began to say something, to try and thank him but he stopped me.

"Save your breath for rowing, boy. God bless you—and good luck. You're a damn fool—the kind that believes in miracles."

I fancied that there was even a reluctance in him to let me go, that he could wish he were coming with me and taking his share of damn-foolery—for no matter what wisdom age and experience had given him, there was wildness in him which must have been a constant challenge to the regulated life which he and so many others were forced to follow.

He dropped the painter into the bows and the dinghy fell away. I saw him a shadow against the sky for a while and then the night swallowed the *Nestor* and all I could see was her greying line of wake and the shine of her navigation lights growing smaller as she headed down coast towards the harbour mouth.

I put the oars over and I began to row inshore, cutting across the tide and being taken with it. The sea was more awkward than it had looked from the deck of the *Nestor* and I soon had a couple of inches of water swirling over the floor boards. It was hard work, too. I crabbed in, turning now and again to mark my progress against the low silhouette of the dunes but not daring to stop for fear the tide should take me down too far. And every pull I gave on the oars sent a sharp jab of pain through my left ribs. I hadn't worried about them before, telling myself that I was only bruised. But now I cursed them, setting my teeth against the tearing drag of the pain and feeling the sweat break out cold on my forehead. I missed my stroke once because of a sharp pain jab and I went over, half-backwards and twisting, and there was an agony of searing ache in my side as I slipped from the thwart.

Tide or no tide, I had to sit and get my breath and let the pain ease from me. Then I set to rowing again, taking short, half-hearted strokes. I don't know how long the trip took. Much longer than it should have done, and when the keel grated on sand I was much farther down than I should have been. I drove the dinghy in as far as I could and then climbed out. For a moment I was tempted to let her go, to drift away, but *Nestor's* name was on her and an abandoned dinghy might raise questions. I dragged her up the sands, panting and grunting and wincing with each step I took. I found a hollow among the marram grass and I left the dinghy with her oars under her. Ross-Piper had told me that the beach by day was full of holiday folk and the dinghy would excite no curiosity for people often left their own boats there during the season.

I lay back on the sand by the dinghy and I lit a cigarette. As long as I was still I had nothing more than a dull ache which I could put up with. I finished the cigarette and found I wasn't looking forward to the moment when I would have to move. There was a steady wind blowing over the dunes, sweeping the sand along so that it made a continuous chittering sound as it hit the stems of the marram grass. The whole place seemed alive with tiny voices. Most of them seemed to be telling me that I was a damned fool.

Away to the East, up-Channel, the sky began to lighten and that was the signal for me to move. I got up and, like a man walking with an open basin of water on his head, fearful of slopping it, I went tenderly across the dunes. I pulled so many faces, wincing and grimacing, that the muscles of my cheeks began to ache.

I found the golf-course and picked out a place on a dune side above one of the greens where I could sit in the cover of a clump of tamarisk bushes. I lit another cigarette and I hoped I would never have to move again.

Somewhere out in the flat meadows beyond the dunes the larks began to rise and sing, and I watched the morning light break sluggishly over the marshes, the whole landscape being slowly developed before me; the shabby holiday bungalows along the road, the long planes of green meadow cut with ditches and marked with the spasmodic movement of sheep and, in the distance, the rising ground of the Weald of Kent. A few starlings came and dug holes for leatherjackets in the smooth green below me.

I watched the world wake, a labourer on a bicycle coming down the road, an early lorry showing its back along a distant main road, a milk van working like a vole from bungalow to bungalow and, away behind the golf club-house, the roar of a tractor starting up. Another day, but the same kind of life for most people. Another day for me, but I knew that from the moment I went on to the road I would be going into another life. I wasn't really going to be John Allen or Peter Barlow. I was only going to be the shadow of a man. . . .

CHAPTER VI

In Rye a policeman held us up while an enormous milk tanker came round a corner. The sight of the dark blue uniform made me stir uneasily. When he turned and waved us on with a smile, I grinned back at him.

Catherine said, "I wonder what you really look like?"

"How do you mean?"

I lay back against the seat and shut my eyes. There was a wicked throb and ache playing around my ribs.

"With your hair fair.'"

I opened my eyes to find her looking at me with a little frown of concern.

"You had a bad time rowing in?"

"I'm bruised. It makes it awkward to move." I felt as though I would like to lie down and not move for a couple of months. And I was a bit disgusted with myself for giving so much attention to my state. I had other things to think about.

We were early and Catherine was taking a roundabout route for Canterbury. We went from Rye across the marshes and up the slow slope of the Weald and into Tenterden, a small country town bordering a long graceful street. Here we stopped at a café full of horse brasses, warming pans and rough hand-made pottery that grated on the fingers, setting the nerves on end. We had breakfast and when the coffee came Catherine took a small silver flask from her coat pocket and poured some brandy into mine.

"Ross-Piper," she said. "You're lucky to have a man like him."

"You and him," I answered. "I'm lucky all round."

Before we drove off again she walked to a newsagent's shop and bought the morning papers. I read them as she drove. There was no photograph of me and the general feeling was that I was on the Isle of Wight though out of the Forest. That was for the press, but I guessed that the police were alive to the chance that I was well off the island. The two men must have made a report.

The brandy had given me a lift but it didn't last long and after half an hour I was feeling like death. Catherine must have known it for after a while she passed the brandy flask over to me. I took a swig and handed it back.

"You're in no shape to be alone," she said. "I've only got to look at you. You're as white as a sheet. You'll faint in the hotel . . . and then you'll have everyone fussing around you. What you want is a bed and a place where you won't have to bother with people."

I should have resisted, fought to have my own way, but there was nothing in me to put against her. The countryside was swelling and contracting as though I saw it all through turbulent heat waves.

"You're not going to Canterbury. You're coming with me."

I let it go then. With anyone else I would have stuck my heels in. I'd been in worse shape than this before and had had to go on alone. But this time I didn't have to force myself. She took everything right out of my hands and I had to admit that I was glad to let her do it. It had never happened to me before, to abandon myself to someone else, and maybe it couldn't have happened then if it had not been Catherine.

The next six hours passed in a queer, febrile dream state. She stopped the car once and I saw her in a red telephone box.

We drove on and sometimes I was talking to Catherine and sometimes I was half asleep. I don't know what I said and I didn't care. . . . I began to build up for myself a picture of a room and the most important thing in the room, the bed. It had to be a big bed, with space to toss and turn, with deep cool linen corners where my legs could reach down and ease the heat of my skin, and a mattress so soft that I would sink into it, sink far into it and away from the drumming in my ribs. I knew I had a fever and I remember thinking that they were right then, the people who said that once you'd had malaria it hit you again sometime. This was the first time it had come back to me . . . if it were malaria . . . and I remember saying to myself childishly that it wasn't fair, to get out of Parkhurst, to have a job to do and then find myself with fever and this bloody hammering at my ribs. Then later there was a cottage, a long low thatched place like a calendar illustration, wistaria growing over the face of it and sparrows quarrelling in the reed thatch and Catherine taking me up the path with her arm in mine. But the great joy was the bed. It was there just as I had imagined it, better even, for the sheets had a lavender smell which I hadn't ordered and I didn't care about anything. There was Catherine's voice, the voice of another woman and a man's voice. I let myself sink away from it all and it didn't worry me that somewhere inside me the man who used to be Peter Barlow was watching it all with impatience and near contempt, saying, "Hell, what an exhibition! A crack on the ribs and a touch of fever and you let yourself go like a sick sheep. No guts."

*   *   *

It was two days before the fever left me. When I woke on the second morning I felt limp but my head was clear. There was a tighter strapping of bandage round my ribs than the one Ross-Piper had put on and there was no ache or throbbing, just an area of stiffness as though my side was made of dried chamois leather.

The sun coming through a low window hit the bottom of the bed and the sparrows were still quarrelling in the thatch outside. The floor was broad, polished oak planks, covered with hand-made woollen rugs. The ceiling was oak beamed and strong enough to hold up a church vault. There was a knitted sampler of the Lord's Prayer on the far wall, and on the others, coloured prints of wild flowers. The curtains were chintz, an Elizabethan print with strange pomegranate and lotus growths, and the wardrobe sat fat and aldermanic by the door defying anyone to say how it had been got into the room. I liked it but I knew at once that it was the kind of place where I should have to walk with my head between my shoulder blades to avoid stunning myself to death.

The door opened and Catherine came in with a breakfast tray. For a moment I felt awkward and embarrassed as though I were seeing her for the first time. I sat up in bed and she fixed the pillows behind me.

"You can move," she said. "There's nothing broken. The fever was the worst thing. You talked a bit but you didn't give anything away."

"You had a doctor to me?"

"Of course. But you needn't worry. He's known my aunt for years. He knows nothing about you."

"So that's where I am. At your aunt's?"

She nodded and then went over to one of the windows and opened it. The morning air came in full of the scent of cut hay. She came back towards the bed looking fresh and cool in a white dress and she poured out coffee for me.

"You know," I said, "you shouldn't have involved her—or yourself."

"I didn't involve her. She's not the kind of woman you can involve. I told her who you were and all about you——"

"You told her!"

256

"Of course. All she had to do then was to say yes or no. She said yes."

"You're both crazy. What would you have done if she'd said no?"

"I have another aunt, and an uncle. They'd have said yes, too, only they live rather farther away. One's in Cornwall and the other in Paris."

"What about Ross-Piper? Have you let him know?"

"No. Now get on with your breakfast. The doctor says that in a couple of days you'll be O.K. except for a certain amount of stiffness."

And there I was in this small cottage somewhere, I gathered, between Oxford and Bicester, and while I felt unhappy about the risk it meant for Catherine and her aunt there was nothing I could do about it. I could only be grateful to them both and glad that I hadn't been left to keel over in the lobby of some hotel.

After breakfast I was left alone. I slept for a while and then read the morning papers which Catherine had brought with my breakfast tray. I was out of them altogether.

At first I had imagined that I should enjoy a day of complete laziness, but after lunch I began to feel well enough to be impatient. I got up and in a dressing-gown walked gently round the room. My side was still stiff chamois leather, but it was softening up and I could move fairly normally, though my legs were a bit weak. I found my suitcase in the large wardrobe.

Inside were a couple of changes of clothes and a neat brown-paper parcel in which were wrapped five hundred one-pound notes. They were new and crisp. I had money of my own in a London bank, and as I flipped through the fresh notes I wondered what the legal position would be if I walked into the bank and wanted to cash a cheque. Would the cashier refuse when he recognized me? The clothes I had worn from Rye were hanging in the wardrobe, too. I couldn't stay in this cottage long out of fairness to the two women, but while I was here it seemed a good opportunity to settle my line of action.

The photograph in the passport was a good one, though the hair had been darkened. Ross-Piper had told me that it had cost a hundred and fifty pounds. Looking at it I remembered something Gypo in Parkhurst had once said to me, that it was easy to get out of prison if there was someone on the outside who was prepared to spend money. But money wasn't all. Once out, a man had to have somewhere to go . . . where the police or his friends would never think of looking for him. The trouble with most prisoners was that they made for home, where they could get help—and found themselves soon picked up. I saw from the passport that in the last three years I had been to France, Italy and Germany and each time on a business man's travelling allowance. It was a good hundred and fifty pounds' worth.

The trouble about a line of action for me to take was simple. I hadn't got one. The only thing I did have was a kind of Micawberish faith that something would turn up. I knew a lot about James Gurney Hansford from the facts that had come out at the trial, and also from some work which had been done for me by a detective agency while I was in prison. I sat on the edge of the bed going over it all in my mind, and Catherine came in and scolded me for being out of bed.

She stayed on and I found myself telling her about Hansford and my trouble.

She listened very carefully, and somehow it raised my confidence to have her there.

James Gurney Hansford, I told her, had been born at Looe in Cornwall in 1910. His parents had kept a small hotel there. He'd gone to Exeter College, Oxford, and finished up with a pass degree in arts. From 1934 until 1939 he had held a number of jobs, finishing with a partnership in a small timber importing firm which had gone bankrupt. For five years before the war he had been a territorial in the Honourable Artillery Company, and when hostilities broke out had early been commissioned in the Royal Artillery. His army service had seen Dunkirk, North Africa and Italy, and then finally the Second Front. Later he had joined the Allied Control Commission. In 1945 he was still with the A.C.C. in Germany, and here he had run into trouble and been court-martialled.

"I could never find out why," I said. "I wanted to during the trial, but my defence counsel said there was no help in this. The prosecution's main point was that I had killed Hansford because he was a blackmailer. If we blackened his character further it only strengthened their hand. . . . But I've always felt that there was something funny about his army career. Perhaps, maybe, that there was something in it which would give me a clue to why he was killed. . . . In prison, you know, you live by hunches, not by reason."

After his court-martial he left the army and lived in Paris for a while. But by the beginning of 1950 he was back in London and, so far as I could find out, without any visible means of support except a small antique dealer's shop in Bond Street. But he seemed to have plenty of money, keeping a flat in London and his house at Alfriston, and he travelled widely over the

Continent. His housekeeper-cum-mistress, a Mrs. Carla Lodi, who had seen me in his room the night he was killed and whose evidence had been most telling against me, had disappeared since the trial. My detective agency had been unable to trace her.

"And that's all I've got, Catherine. I'd like to know more about his time in Germany, and I'd like to find Carla Lodi. But just how at this moment I've no idea. Sounds hopeless, doesn't it?"

Catherine nodded, but it was an absent little nod, and I could see that her thoughts were far away. Then she turned to me and said, "He could have been murdered by someone else he was blackmailing."

"He could, but he was a methodical man and kept his accounts in order. We found details of all his transactions with my father in a rather simple code. But there was no suggestion that he was doing it to anyone else. No, what I want is details of his court-martial and to talk to someone who knew him in Germany. Or failing that, this Carla woman. . . ."

Catherine stood up and looked down on me gravely. She was very still and very lovely.

"Or failing that?"

"I'm not thinking that far ahead yet." I answered sharply.

When she was gone I got out of bed again. I found it eased my ribs up to walk a little. I sat in a chair by the window and smoked. Catherine was right, of course. The whole damn thing was hopeless. But I wasn't going to accept that. Not yet, anyway.

The door opened behind me and I turned, thinking it was Catherine again. But it was an elderly woman who I guessed was her aunt, Mrs. Lovell.

"How are you, Mr. Allen? Feeling better?"

She held out her hand, and as I took it she gave me a grip which squeezed my fingers.

"Thank you, I am. I want to say, too, how grateful I am that you let Catherine bring me here. As soon as I can I will clear out. Maybe tomorrow."

"You'll go when I say you're fit. As for being grateful, nonsense. What are you doing there, brooding?"

I laughed. "No, I've just been thinking of the man I'm supposed to have murdered and wondering what my chances were of finding the real culprit."

"What an old-fashioned word. Culprit. I should say your chances were very remote. If I were going to murder someone—and I could make quite a list of candidates—I'd take very good

259

care not to leave stupid clues around. I don't care what people say, the mechanics would be easy. It's the will to murder which is difficult—unless one is in a passion, of course, and then it's just savagery, and one is almost always caught. You'll come down to dinner, of course? You look fit enough for it, and I know how men hate eating off a tray in bed."

As she spoke she was moving around the room, and I got the impression that her thoughts were only half with me, her eyes and her hands were for ever being attracted to the things around her. She tapped the knitted sampler as though it were a barometer and told me that Catherine's mother had knitted it. "Blood, sweat and tears and she the most irreligious of my pagan sisters. The word *hallowed* is spelt wrong, you'll notice, but she refused to unpick it."

I watched her, fascinated and amused. She was a tall, gaunt woman, with a great beak of a nose and warm, iron-grey eyes, and her hair, which had been fair, was now the colour of old end-of-winter snow and drawn back tightly into a large rosette kind of bun at the back of her head. She stalked about like a great crane, and for all her awkwardness, which suggested that at any moment she was going to fall forward on to her nose, there was a certain elegance about her movements, particularly of her hands and arms. She straightened my bed cover, picked up a couple of newspapers from the floor and gave me a passing lecture on tidiness which somehow jumped to the information that her own husband, now long dead, had once been a foreign correspondent for Reuters. Then going to one of the windows, she took a pair of secateurs from the pocket of her shapeless brown cardigan and began to snip off long lengths of wistaria blooms.

"I've entertained a great many distinguished people in my time," she said, turning, her arms full of the pale blooms, "but never an escaped convict." She stopped talking, and for a few moments she was very close to me and very still, and there was no escape from her steady, warm eyes. Then she said, speaking much slower, "Your two years in prison must have taught you a lot. A man should always be grateful for any experience . . . that's how life is made up. Experience—good and bad."

"And now that I'm out?" I had a feeling that she was deliberately inviting the question, and I suppose that because with me it had become so important I couldn't resist putting it to her. "What should I do?"

"You don't want me to tell you. You know already. Truth is the only thing that matters in life. Truth and justice. And if you kill yourself going after them, well, you kill yourself, and it's as good a way of dying as any."

I don't know what I said, or whether we did go on talking, or how finally she was out of the room. All I knew was a deep sense of comfort and support.

CHAPTER VII

Two days later I went to London. I felt better and I could walk normally. The stiffness in my side was softening up, and so long as I made no violent movement I could even forget it.

Catherine drove me to the local station, Blackthorn, which was about three miles away, and I took a third-class return for London. Catherine wanted to come with me, but I was adamant about going alone. She had taken enough risk and trouble for me already. In fact, without the trouble she had taken, I would not have been going to London. The day after I had talked to her about Hansford she had gone off to London on her own. An old friend of her aunt's, a Major Rawlings, was on the staff of the War Office. He was an elderly man, and she had bullied him into taking her out to lunch. Looking at her in her London clothes as she had told me her story in my bedroom, I knew that no man, no matter how elderly, would need much bullying. He'd given her a good lunch and she had pretended that she was going to do some free-lance work for a newspaper and wanted information about Hansford's army career for a topical article on my escape. The major had taken her back to the War Office and got Hansford's court-martial file. He hadn't let her look at it, but he had told her that Hansford had been court-martialled for the illegal sale of captured enemy equipment. There had been another charge which had been dropped, but he had refused to say what it was, explaining that he wasn't sure at the moment that it was material which could be cleared for the press. She had got from him the name of Hansford's commanding officer at the time of the trial. This was a Lieutenant-Colonel Drysdale. And he lived at 27A Kew Green, Kew. He was the man I was going to see.

I was at Paddington station just after eleven, and I went into a telephone booth and looked up Drysdale's number. A woman answered my call, and she told me that the colonel would not be back until after seven that evening.

After that I was stuck with the whole day on my hands. I got on the Underground and went to Piccadilly Circus. I came up into a blare and swirl of traffic that for a while confused me. I crawled around the circus like a beetle afraid of being stepped on, but by the time I reached Leicester Square the prison man was fast going, and I began to feel at home. I was bare-headed and wearing a light raincoat over a dark grey suit. I was John Allen, not Peter Barlow, and I tried to walk as though I had as much right to the freedom of the pavements as anyone else, but I knew that at any moment I had to be prepared for disaster. Someone might turn and catch a glimpse of my face, memory might be stirred . . . this fear was in my mind constantly.

In the Square I went into another telephone booth, and I called Ross-Piper's flat, which was near Covent Garden. When the receiver was lifted at the other end I just said, "Drew."

There was a silence for a moment and then Drew's voice answered, "Blimey . . . Peacock in half an hour." The receiver clicked down.

From Leicester Square I walked through into Covent Garden, and then to the Peacock public-house in Maiden Lane.

Within half an hour Drew came in, very stiff and angular in a dark blue suit, hard white collar and wearing an old-fashioned bowler hat. He looked for all the world like a detective from a farce. We drank separately for a while and then came together at the bar.

"We've been having kittens about you, sir."

I told him that I was staying with Catherine and that I was on my way to see Colonel Drysdale at Kew. He wasn't very interested in all this.

"The guv'nor's away in Hertfordshire. Won't be back till late tonight. He'll be glad you're all right, sir. We had the police around to the flat a couple of days ago, but the guv'nor didn't have any trouble with them. They feel he's too big to have monkeyed about with anything like this. And if you'll pardon me, sir, I think he is. You ought to get out."

I knew how he felt about Ross-Piper. He would have done anything for him. I thought about Ross-Piper down at the hospital and clinic he ran in Hertfordshire. . . . I knew he spent a great deal of his own money on it and that his work there on diseases of the brain and brain surgery meant everything to him. . . . One careless word from me could land him in trouble. For a moment I came near to agreeing that I ought to get out. I had no right to involve other and innocent people in my troubles. The thought made my beer taste bad.

After Drew had gone I had a snack at the bar, and then I went out and sat in a cinema. I saw the whole programme round twice, and when I came out it was half past six and raining. I walked to the station and got on a train for Kew. The last of the office rush-hour was on and the carriage smelt of wet mackintoshes and stale tobacco.

The only time I'd ever been to Kew before was when I was twelve and my mother had taken me to the Royal Botanical Gardens. I didn't remember it very well. I got out of the station and walked across Kew Bridge to the Green. It was large and triangular-shaped, surrounded by trees, and on two sides by old houses still wearing a faint look of surprise that they should be allowed to carry on their village existence in London. I walked up the right-hand side, past a couple of pubs, towards the black and gold main entrance gates to the Gardens. The rain was a gentle drift now, giving the evening a faint purplish haze against the far green of the trees in the Gardens. Behind me the buses roared over the bridge. Some small boys were playing a muddy game of cricket, oblivious of the rain. . . . It was everything an English summer evening should be, damp and peaceful.

Number 27A was about half-way up the road; a little white-faced Queen Anne house with a green ironwork balcony roofed in the shape of a scallop-shell on the first floor. It was cramped in between other houses, a bed of polyanthus roses in front of it and a small side entrance down a narrow alley. I went up to the front door and rang the bell.

Nothing happened. I rang the bell again, and this time after a while I fancied I saw the curtains of the bow-shaped window on my right shake a little. I waited.

Then suddenly, without my hearing anyone come to it, the front door opened.

A short, elderly man stood with one hand on the door. He was wearing a shabby velvet smoking jacket, slack dark-grey trousers and carpet slippers. He had the stance of a terrier waiting for the move of a rat, tense, alive, shoulders square, his head forward a little and the whole of his small body tight with a controlled muscular readiness. His eyes were very much alert, but they weren't unfriendly. They just took everything in and reserved judgment. He had a pugnacious, well-worn face. Yet over all this there was something else, a seediness and looseness that seemed to be wearing down the alertness. His mouth had an occasional nervous little tremble. He gave me the impression of a man forcing himself to some effort and knowing all the time that he wasn't succeeding.

I said, "Colonel Drysdale?"

He said, "Yes." And then his eyes were looking past me, watching the street and the green, as though it were someone else he was expecting.

I said, "I'm from the Press, the *Daily Record*." He didn't answer, so I went on, "We're doing some stuff about this man Barlow who's escaped from Parkhurst. We want some information about Hansford—the man he killed. You were his C.O., weren't you?"

"Yes." There was no welcome in the word.

"We'd pay, of course, for anything you gave us. Personal impressions, you know. Human angle." Money. It worked.

"Come in," he said, and there was warmth in his voice.

I went in and he shut and bolted the door behind me, and the action made me look at him questioningly.

He said, "Don't want to be disturbed, do we?" For a moment he smiled, and it was a good smile, but he chased it away quickly and nodded towards a door on my right.

It was a long room with a desk near the window, small tables and little china cabinets sprouted from the floor and walls. The curtains were drawn almost full over and there was a green watery light over everything. Any wall space left free from the cabinets was covered with photographs and small pictures in heavy gilt pouting frames. Near the window was a wing-backed chair, its tapestry worn and shiny, and a tray attached to the arm. On the tray was a whisky decanter, a glass and a plate of biscuits. Everything was old-maidish and fussy, and shabby and dusty; a green cave from the floor of which pie-crust occasional tables grew like dark toadstools.

Colonel Drysdale nodded to a chair by the fireplace, which held a spread Japanese fan across its mouth.

"Sit down, old man," he said, and now there was a curious, forced bonhomie in his voice. "Sorry to have been so cagey about letting you in. Fact is most of my visitors aren't welcome. Bailiff types, people who want money. . . . You know how it is these days. What?" He laughed. Then he sat down and poured the last of the whisky from the decanter into his glass. And at once he was embarrassed by his action. He was on his feet and saying, "You'd like a drink, old man?"

"No, no, don't bother. Allen's the name. I only——"

"Course you must have a drink. I'll get another bottle." He was out of the room before I could say more, and I sat there waiting for him. He was gone a long time, and when he came back I noticed that he was now wearing shoes. The whisky bottle was wrapped in white tissue paper, and I guessed that he had gone out of the side door and down to one of the pubs for it.

"Damn cellar light fused. Couldn't find it. . . . Still, here we are at last."

He poured whisky into a glass he fetched from one of the cabinets, and I saw his hand shaking as he set it down near me. I didn't know what to make of him. He looked like a man going to pieces, but fighting it, and if that touched my sympathy there was an occasional stiffening of his body and a passing stillness in his eyes which gave me a queer feeling of having to deal with two men at once.

"My paper would like to know something about Hansford, particularly his war experiences in Germany. I've been to the War Office and they've given me some bald facts about his court-martial."

"Oh, who'd you see at the War House?"

"A Major Rawlings. He suggested that you were the man to see."

"Rawlings. . . . Don't know him. Still, I'm out of touch these days. Right out of touch. . . ." He dropped back into his chair as he spoke, and he seemed very small, lost almost in the shadows. He shuffled his feet a little, and I noticed that around his chair various papers were scattered on the carpet. They were racing papers. "Remember Hansford, though. Uncertain sort of squirt. Never really cared for him. He was court-martialled for the sale of captured enemy equipment to a set of German black marketeers."

"What kind of equipment?"

I had out on my knee a notebook and pencil which I had bought before coming out here.

"Lorries mostly. Hansford was the type who never missed a chance of making money." He broke a biscuit with a quick snap of his fingers and then munched it noisily. "Women, too. Not that I blame him for that. But with other things it all adds up. Even so, the man's dead. He had his good points."

"This Barlow's always maintained he was innocent of the murder, you know. That's what makes his escape interesting. My paper wants to go into that angle. If Barlow didn't kill him because he was blackmailing his father, then somebody else did —and for what? Was there anything in his war record that might help there? This other charge, for instance, that was dropped at the court-martial?"

He sat forward suddenly, and the change in him was very marked. He had his eye on me as though I were an old offender in the orderly-room, not unliked, but not to be trusted.

"What do you know about that?" It was a bark, and I suddenly saw him as he must have been years before, a real terrier, hard and efficient before whisky and debts began their work.

"Not much. Major Rawlings was a bit embarrassed because they seemed to have lost part of their records at the War Office. That's why he suggested my coming to you."

"Lost their records, eh? Damned lot of incompetents. However, if Rawlings sent you to me, I suppose there's no harm in my telling you about it."

"It'll be a great help, and, of course, my paper likes to pay for its information."

He nodded and dusted some biscuit crumbs from his trousers. He then poured himself another whisky.

"All right. But it'll cost your paper twenty pounds. Don't like to be mercenary, but the Press can afford it, and retired pay wouldn't keep a cat alive these days. . . ."

He started to go off into a long diatribe about the difficulty retired officers had in getting civilian employment and started some story about an admiral he knew who was working as a farm labourer. It was easy to see that he was a man who liked to be busy and had nothing to occupy his mind but horse racing and whisky. With difficulty I brought him back to Hansford.

"It's all ancient stuff now, old boy. He was court-martialled over the lorry deal, but the other charge was suppressed in the interests of public security."

"Why?"

His answer was more than I ever expected, and I felt something like a small electric charge go through me.

"Because it had to do with the German forgery and distribution of Allied currencies during the war. Believe me, old chap, this wasn't something we wanted made public at the time."

The forging of Allied notes. I sat there and the smoke from my cigarette went up straight and thin in the cool, still room, and I felt the first tremor of real excitement and hope stir inside me. I didn't interrupt him. I listened and, while I took in his story, I watched him and wondered about him, because now he seemed to have shaken off his waywardness, seemed to have come to a decision and to know where he was going. . . .

He had been a colonel in the Intelligence Corps, and the problem of the German forgery of Allied notes had been his main concern. For most of the time he had been seconded to an American S.S. unit engaged on the same work. The story he told was new and fascinating to me.

Early in the war Heinrich Himmler had created an organisation whose aim was to undermine Britain's economy by the counterfeiting and distribution of bank-notes on a tremendous scale. The man who'd really handled the job was an S.S. Major Bernhard Kruger, who took over in 1942. Most of the outstanding printing technicians in Germany were Jews, and were already in concentration camps. Kruger had them rounded up and taken to a concentration camp near Berlin. In the camp printing plants were set up and plates were engraved. After many trials the Hahnemuhle paper concern of Brunswick succeeded in reproducing Bank of England paper with all its elaborate water-markings. The notes turned out were put into three grades according to their degree of perfection. Grade One notes—the best—were used in neutral countries, Grade Two in occupied countries, and Grade Three were stored to be dumped by plane at the right stage of the war in Great Britain. Fortunately, by the time enough Grade Three notes were ready the Luftwaffe had been driven from the air over Britain and the plan never came off. The most famous victim of the Grade One notes was the Albanian professional spy, Bazna, valet to the British Ambassador in Ankara during the war, who received three hundred thousand pounds' worth of the notes from the German Intelligence Service for secrets he filched from the Ambassador's safe. When Berlin began to be heavily bombed Major Kruger had the plant and the men moved to an underground factory in the Austrian redoubt. It was April, 1945, before the new plant was in operation. By that time American troops were already closing in on the redoubt.

"We know now," said the colonel, "that when Kruger knew the end was near he got orders from Himmler for the whole set-up to be destroyed. Notes and records were to be burned, the plates and the dies to be sunk in Lake Toplitz nearby the new camp, and all the workers to be taken to another camp and killed. Actually not all of this happened. Some of the plates and dies were sunk in the lake and some of the notes burned, but a lot of stuff was taken away and hidden. Kruger himself disappeared towards Switzerland with a fortune in Grade One notes and has never been heard of since. Fortunately, too, the poor devils of printers and so on were not killed. They weren't even transferred. . . . We got there in time."

"We?"

"The Americans. But I was with them, and so was Hansford. He'd been attached to me as an Allied Control Commission officer in charge of the immediate welfare of refugees and our own nationals released from the camps. There was a camp at the mouth of the underground gallery where all this business went on. Redl Zipfcave it was called. We found all these technicians there. We recovered a lot of the stuff, but there was much more that never turned up. Kruger turned out in his time notes to the face value of about a hundred and forty million pounds sterling. Later, of course, the Bank of England brought out notes with the metallic strip in them."

I watched his face as he told all this. He was a different man. Maybe he was back in those years when he had been doing a useful job. Even his manner of speaking was different. Direct. No "old boys." Again I had a queer sensation of watching two men rolled into one.

"And where does Hansford come in this?"

"He found a batch of notes and sold them off at the same time as the lorry deal. Also, though this was never established, I believe he got hold of plates and dies. . . . However, we got rid of him under the lorry charge. The other thing at that moment was too delicate to broadcast."

I said, "Could he have got dies and plates back to England?"

"In those days it was easy. You could pack a case with anything and send it through the Military Forwarding Officer, or get a friend in the R.A.F. to fly stuff back. You think he was killed because he was in some forging set-up here and became a nuisance?"

I was surprised that he had put it so bluntly and quickly.

"He could have been."

"True."

He sat down in his chair and, holding his hands together, began to crack his knuckles. The sound put me on edge. I sat there and I told myself that the thing was reasonable. I looked at this man, at the iron-grey hair, the still grey eyes and the unhealthy colour of his face.

I said, "Did you ever know Hansford after the war?"

He got up and, coming over to me, poured a little more whisky into my half-empty glass.

"Never, old boy. I read about his murder, of course. Was abroad at the time. Had a job in Spain. Manager of a heather root factory. You know . . . briar pipes. Didn't last long."

He went back to his seat and raised his glass to me. I pulled out my wallet and began to count out twenty notes. I could see him trying not to watch my movement, and he said:

"Interesting job, yours. Haven't got a vacancy for a racing correspondent, have you?" He laughed, and, putting his glass down, glanced at his wrist-watch.

"Tell me," I asked. "Do you think Hansford was the kind of man with enough nerve to set up a forgery outfit over here?"

"Nerve? Why, my dear chap! He had enough nerve to steal the Crown Jewels. Drink up and have another."

I drained my glass, but I refused another. I had a lot to think about and I wanted to be on my own. I left the pound notes on the table at my side. Although I could see he made no shame of his need for money, I just couldn't feel I could hand them across to him. He wanted me to stay and have a few more drinks. He was lonely, too. I said I had to get back and reluctantly he let me go.

"Do you mind going out of the side door, old chap?" he said. "I don't like to advertise when I'm at home. Otherwise they keep knocking at my door with writs and God knows what. No peace for the indebted. Anything else I can do for you just let me know."

* * *

As I went out into the rain a clock somewhere was striking the half-hour. I was telling myself that if Hansford had come back to England and set up as a forger, then he would need help. It wasn't a one-man business. And somewhere along the line he could have quarrelled with his helpers. Why? I had no answer to that. But something could have gone wrong and Hansford had been killed.

I crossed a narrow strip of garden and opened the door in the wooden palings that lined the side alley. As the door clicked behind me two men who had been waiting outside, one on each side of the door, closed in on me.

I had no time to turn and get back into the garden. One of the men was tall, wearing an army raincoat and with a grey cloth cap pulled well down over his forehead. The other was short and plumpish.

They came at me like a couple of watchdogs. I passed three of the most surprised seconds of my life: not because of the unexpected attack, but on account of the tall man who was bearing down on me. I was so damned surprised that I was too stupid to move for a moment. The tall man was one of the two who had tried to pick me up on the beach on the Isle of Wight, the one called Rance. He threw himself at me, and this time he had no stick. His hands grabbed me by the throat and at the same time the other man jumped on me from behind and clamped his arms around me, pinning my elbows down. The whole thing was done so suddenly that I had no time to shout or struggle. I walked through a door and the next moment I was helpless, hands about my throat, digging into my skin, and a weight on my back and my arms pinioned helplessly. I strained to free myself, but I might have been encased in lead. We just stood there in an agony of grotesque statuary. Rance's face dipped closer to mine. A beading of rain dripped off the peak of his cap and I saw the hard line of muscle down his jaws as he pressed on my throat, and then slowly his face began to dissolve into a watery haze that was shot with black and silver streaks. The great hands tightened on me like a vice and I heard a harsh, animal, desperate sound grating from my throat. I was going, and I knew it. In a few minutes my heart and lungs would burst and I would dip into a great blackness . . . and with the thought there was a phase of clear, high vision . . . of seeing myself dragged down the alley, dumped among the nettles on some waste ground . . . seeing and beginning to understand. . . . And in that moment of clarity I wondered what else Colonel Drysdale had done when he left the house to get whisky, and whether he would stay tight in his house and coolly face the police when they asked him the routine questions that would be asked of every householder round about after my body had been discovered. . . . Colonel Drysdale, who could afford to tell me so much of the truth because he knew I would go out through the side door. . . .

And then, leaning forward against me, all his strength dedicated to throttling the life from me, Rance slipped on the wet ground, and for an instant his hands were slightly relaxed to seek a better hold. In that instant I had air, and it was like breathing flame, but the flame brought with it life and fury. I was suddenly full of a black, violent desire to live. . . . I jabbed forward and smashed the top of my head into Rance's face. At the same time I kicked out and felt my right foot jar against the boniness of his leg. He went back from me, his hands still on my neck, but their grip slackened and I breathed. I kicked again, and this time my foot caught his knee and a grimace of pain contorted his face and his hands slipped from my throat. He staggered back against the wooden palings. I swung sideways and bent forward, body and mind moving into the routine which had been hammered into me by sergeant instructors in unarmed combat. The man on my back went over my shoulders untidily, like a clumsy sack of potatoes, his hands seeking still to keep their grip on me. He fell from me and I slumped back against the palings, my throat whining with the torture of breathing. I saw Rance come forward, blood running from his nose where my head had struck him, and he seemed twice as large as life. I thrust myself off the palings and went for him, and he seemed deliberately to push out his head for the blow. I hit him on the side of the neck with all my strength and he dropped backwards awkwardly. There was a great smack from his body as he hit the ground, and I saw his head jerk forward sharply as it hit the bottom of the palings. He lay there, unmoving.

I turned. The other man was rising now. He was half on his knees, crouched like a sprinter on a mark. As he came up I saw his right hand whip back and forwards and something flashed through the air towards me. I threw up an arm in instinctive protection. There was an angry rip of raincloth under my arm and then the dull bite of a knife going into the wood of the palings behind me.

I didn't wait for more. A man with one knife may have two. At any moment someone might turn into the alleyway and shout, and the last thing I wanted was a crowd and the police.

I ran down the alleyway. A car passed me, going up towards the Botanical Gardens. A few people were moving through the rain around the green. I looked back. Rance was lying on the ground still, but the other man was up, and I saw him jerk the knife out of the palings and then start towards me. He wasn't running. He came up towards me, walking steadily, and there was something in his gait, in the way he moved, that filled me with an angry frustration. I couldn't turn and fight him. I couldn't call for help. I couldn't do anything but seek some escape . . . and that now was not so easy. These people intended to pay little attention to caution. On the bus or train or in a crowd . . . the knife would find me.

I turned to the right and at a little jog-trot I went past the front of Colonel Drysdale's house and up towards the entrance of the Royal Botanic Gardens.

At the black and gold wrought-iron gates I paused. Through the ironwork I could see the long stretch of asphalt walk, flanked with lawns and great banks of azaleas and rhododendrons, and beyond a green, damp vista of trees and shrubs. There were very few people about, for the rain had driven them from the gardens. I looked back. Coming after me was the man with the knife, a short, thickset, powerful-looking figure. Then beyond him I saw two other figures. One was Rance, about a hundred yards behind the first man. He walked slowly and was holding a handkerchief to his nose. And beyond him, not moving for the moment, but standing outside his house, was Colonel Drysdale. He stood there, staring up towards me, a small, inquisitive figure in a light raincoat, a green pork-pie hat on his head. Three of them, I thought. And I knew it was no good sticking to the streets, or trying to get a bus or hoping to disappear into the crowd beyond Kew Bridge. . . . I had to shake them off. I had to go to ground somewhere.

The rain played a fat tattoo on the shoulders of my raincoat. I went through the gate and paid threepence at the turnstile to enter the gardens. The attendant moved slowly and grudgingly as though he disapproved of anyone entering the place so late. As he handed me my ticket he said, "It's getting on for eight. We shall be closing soon, sir."

I nodded. "I know. I'm walking straight across to go out by the other gate."

I went in and up the main walk and suddenly from a tree a blackbird began to sing, a lusty, boisterous sound in the wet evening, and it did nothing to cheer me at all. The rain slashed down and the rhododendron leaves had a fat, oily, polished look. Underneath one of the bushes a couple of moorhens were raking in the soft ground for grubs. I remembered the moorhen that had called on the night Hansford was killed. And grimly I acknowledged that one of these might well call on the night I was killed.

CHAPTER VIII

I TURNED left at the top of the walk. An attendant in a shining black cape passed me. Then ahead was the soft, trailing green of a great weeping willow tree and the dull glint of a lake. I cut across the grass towards a group of trees on my right, and as I did so the first man moved into the walk behind me. I went into the trees, and then on the far side I found a large iron-framed glasshouse. I flanked it and at its entrance saw a sign—Water-lily House. I moved a little way inside, but I saw at once it was no good to me. I wanted a place to hide until darkness came. It was hot inside and there was a great spread of red and white lilies on a circular pool. But apart from the pool there was only a narrow walk around the house.

As I came out somewhere in the gardens a bell began to ring, and I remembered a notice at the main gate announcing that a bell would be rung a quarter of an hour before closing time.

A path led through rose gardens, the scent hanging heavy and concentrated in the rain. A great shower of raindrops cascaded on me as I brushed by a shrub hung with purple flowers. Then I was on a broad path again. And at the far end was Rance. I moved away from him and out on to the lakeside. Beyond the trees on the far side rose a dark, Italianate-looking tower, and at the top of the lake, raised on a wide terrace, was an enormous glass structure, a great cathedral of glass. I hurried towards it. Away to the right I saw Rance's companion coming across the grass. A family of ducks kept pace with me along the lake edge and a few gulls swooped over the water. Somewhere behind me the bell rang again. A woman went by quickly, pushing a pram.

I hurried up the path, past the great glass structure. The moment I was beyond it and out of sight of Rance and his friend I began to run. I went down the back of the glasshouse and then up a flight of steps and along a path. A notice-board said *Palm House*. There was a small door at the far end, and it was open. I slipped inside, unseen by my followers. A young man and his girl were standing by the door, looking at a great tangle of creeper from which hung strange-shaped gourds. I went past them into a wide, green, glass-roofed vault.

I came out of the wet English summer evening into a tropical forest. Great palms and green growths soared up to the roof. The air was hot and steamy and there was a warm, rich, fruitful smell of damp earth. The place was about a hundred yards long and in the centre the roof rose to well over sixty feet. Between the walks there was a green tangle of vegetation, strangely curved and fronded leaves, and slim soaring palm trunks and creepers. It was difficult to see clearly for the rain and cloud outside filled the place with gloom and the glass itself was patina-ed with a faint brown growth. There were four doors to the place, but only the one by which I had entered seemed open. At the far end a party of three girls and a woman stood admiring a long festoon of yellow trumpet-shaped flowers that fell from the branches of a small tree. I passed them, and I had no eyes for the plants. I wanted a place to hide. As I moved round to the far side an authoritative voice called from the door:

"All out, please. All out."

There was an attendant at the door. The young couple standing there moved by him and the party of schoolgirls drifted down towards the door. I let them pass me, and then, out of sight of the attendant, I stepped off the walk and pushed my way between great tubs into the green heart of the plants and trees. A frond of starry wax-like flowers, deep orange in colour, brushed against my face. I crouched down, and four inches from my eyes was a label—*Clavija longifolia*. It meant nothing to me. The extent of my botanical experience was mowing lawns. And my interest at that moment was all outside, where Rance and the others would be looking for me. I heard the heavy tread of the attendant coming round the building. I lay down, coiled between three tubs, my face close to hard, wet gravel. Through a fretwork of leaves and stems I saw him go by me and then come back on the other side.

A few moments later the door slapped over and a lock turned. I sat up. I couldn't see very much, for it was growing darker in the place every moment. The rain hitting the glass roof filled the house with a continuous crepitation that gradually worked into the senses and became a sort of silence through which I could pick out the steady drip, drip of moisture from roof and leaves. It was hot now and I unbuttoned my coat and wiped my face with my handkerchief. I shifted a little so that I could look over the lake and gardens. It was like looking at a world flooded with green water, everything blurred and indistinct. I saw the distorted figure of the attendant moving along the lake terrace.

As it got darker and I knew I couldn't be seen from the

275

outside, I changed my position. I found an empty tub between two small trees that had great leaves shaped like elephant's ears, and I made myself comfortable on it. I smoked a cigarette, cupping the glow in my hands, but I got no comfort from it, for my throat was sore from Rance's grip. And now that I had time I could sort my thoughts out. I was locked in here for the night. That didn't worry me. When the place was opened in the morning I could hide and then slip out. I was safe here, and for the moment I had thrown off my pursuers. They would have to get out of the gardens as the attendants cleared it. I didn't overlook the chance that they had seen me come in here. They, too, could hide and come back for me.

But my chief thought was of Rance. There was no doubt that he was the man with whom I had gone over the cliff slide. And here he was again! The two men on the beach had known I was going to be there. They had gone for me not to send me back to Parkhurst, but to finish me off. Someone had known I was coming out and didn't want me out. That thought gave me more hope than I had ever had before. And now by going to Drysdale it seemed that I had walked straight into the heart of the mystery. I'd sat calmly in his room while he'd gone out to whistle up his thugs. And he'd felt so sure of finishing me off that he'd been prepared to tell me about Hansford and the forged notes.

I sat there full of a sustaining excitement. The fact that I was free was worrying someone enough to make them anxious to kill me. It was a strange kind of good news, but I accepted it almost with pleasure, and with the proviso that in future I should have to watch every step I took.

*   *   *

It was almost midnight. I'd shifted my position once or twice and had finally settled for a place on a length of flat wooden banking where I could lie down. I even dozed off once or twice.

In the great sweeps of vegetation the shadows were more defined. Outside it had stopped raining, and looking up at the glass vaulting I saw that the clouds were clearing and there was a pale slip of moon sliding in and out of the grey banks. Then I thought I caught the sound of footsteps.

I moved slowly down the house until I was in the tall, wide transept at the middle. I went to the door at the end of the transept and looked out. There was the grey glint of the lake and the blooms from a sweep of irises looked paper-white and ragged under the pale light. There was a heavy, faint-breathing silence around me. I could almost hear the giant leaves and creepers drawing in the damp air. The steady drip of condensing moisture from the wide leaves and arrowed fronds was like the soft sucking sound of greedy fish lips. And then, quite distinctly, I heard a noise from the door at the far end of the house. It echoed sharply under the glass roof. I moved back from the door into the shadows of the palms in the centre of the transept until I was in a position to see part of the door at the far end. There was a swift gleam of moonlight, and framed against a knife-edged frieze of leaves, I saw a dark figure outside the door.

The figure strained at something low down by the door lock, and then, abrupt in the long reaches of glass roofing, there was a loud screech of sound and a dying whimper of echoes. The door swung open and the shape of the intruder merged with the shadows inside the door. From his size I knew it was the man who had thrown the knife at me, and I guessed what had happened. I had been seen entering the house and they had checked that I hadn't come out. Now they were back, with a jemmy or bar to break the door. I had only seen one figure enter, but I knew there would be another, Rance, tall and determined, waiting outside to stop my escape.

I moved back between the tubs, treading softly until I reached the far side of the transept. Here there was an iron-runged ladder which went up towards the roof of the transept to a small railed platform. I had noticed this when I first came in. It was used, I guessed, by the attendants when they wanted to get on the roof or to attend to foliage and growths high up. I went up the ladder as far as the platform and then lay there, watching the shadows below me.

Suddenly, away by the door and for a while seen only through the intervening glass, a long, thin pencil of light from a torch began to flicker from side to side, peering and probing through the jungle growths. Slowly it worked its way along the house. It was used intelligently. First low across the ground among the shrubs and tubs and then reaching up each tree, missing nothing . . . a narrow beam of light like a long white stick feeling and prodding. It came across the transept and now was close under me. I could just make out the blur of the man's shape. He halted and I waited for him to move away into the far wing of the house. But he stayed where he was and the torch went out. I could feel my face and body wet with sweat and the hot steamy air was stale in my throat. There was no sound or movement from below and I knew he was standing there listening. Behind me another run of ladder went up to more platforms and a gangway, but I had no chance to move now and go higher without being heard. As though to point my danger, the light came on again and for a moment or two I saw a hand illuminated by the light and in the hand the black shape of an automatic. No knives now. No silence once the quarry had been found. This man would mark me and fire, and the crash of echoes could wake the world as far as he was concerned, for he would be out of this place and running, and there would be a dozen places where the walls could be climbed and the safety of the streets found. My only hope was that he would pass on, up the far wing and, not finding me, think that I had long gone or taken the chance hours ago of shouting for an attendant to let me out.

I lay there with my head peering over the edge of the platform, watching the torch. It swept round in a slow circle, away from the ladder and then back. It stopped, and looking down, holding my body in a tensed immobility, I saw why it had stopped and cursed to myself. On the wide, flat rungs at the bottom of the ladder the light was shining on the wet marks my feet had made on them as I climbed. I knew I was lost then, knew there was no virtue or safety in hiding and that my only chance lay in swift attack. His feet scrunched on loose gravel as he came closer to the steps. Then, as he reached the bottom of the ladder, I was up and down four feet towards him. The torch angled upwards and the light struck me full in the face as I came flying down the ladder. I threw myself outwards and downwards into the light, and I knew that if I didn't hit him I would finish with a broken neck.

I hit him. My outstretched hands found his shoulders. His quick cry was cut short by the shock of our meeting bodies. He staggered backwards to the ground and I crashed on top of him. The torch flew away to the left, a wheeling spoke of light, and then hitting the ground went out. At the same moment he fired and the shot woke a thunder of echoes in the place. I felt the hot breath of the report close to my face and high above us there was the splinter and smash of glass. I was thrown from him as we hit the ground, but I came back, groping at him in the dark, and my hand found his wrist and my fingers were on the revolver. He groaned and panted as he fought against me. I twisted his wrist back and there was the clatter of the revolver over the paved stones. We rolled over and over. He reached out to pull himself up by a tub and for an instant I saw him in a passing wave of moonlight, dark and squat above me. I rose quickly and drove at him and we stumbled together into a thick mat of creeper. There was the wet flap of leaves and branches, the swift rich smell of earth and blossoms, and then, slamming wildly with my right fist, I felt the jolt of soft flesh under my knuckles. He dropped away into the darkness. He must have crashed into a shrub, for there was a tearing, snapping sound. A spatter of fat water drops cascaded on me from high leaves. Then silence.

I jumped back on to the stone walk, and as I did so I heard someone running towards the transept from the far end of the house. It could only be Rance coming to see what had happened. When from the sound of his steps he seemed to be half-way up the house, I began to move down the far side of the opposite walk. He passed me, twenty feet away, and I saw a torch come on and begin to flicker through the thick growths.

A moment or two later and I was through the door and in the open. The night air, cold after the heat of the Palm House, struck at me like a douche of icy water. I jumped over a balustrade, was on the lake terrace and then running hard and right-handed towards a dark line of trees. From far away on the left I heard voices calling and saw the distant flash of a torch and I guessed that some attendant had been wakened by the shot and was coming to investigate.

I came to the garden wall and somewhere along it I found a railed space full of great piles of boiler coke for the hot-houses. I climbed the rails and then mounted the coke until I could reach the top of the wall. The street outside was still and deserted. A lamp burned fifty yards away. I swung myself over and dropped to the pavement.

CHAPTER IX

On the other side of Kew Bridge I found an all-night café, and I sat there for an hour and finally got a lift in a lorry going up to town.

I walked through Covent Garden just as dawn was coming up. The place was crowded with lorries and porters and the air sweet with the smell of cauliflowers and oranges. Ten minutes later I was in Ross-Piper's flat.

Drew made us coffee, and walking up and down the large sitting-room with its view over the London roofs, I told Ross-Piper all that had happened. He sat by the window in dressing-gown and pyjamas looking like some ruffled, sleepy old lion, but his eyes were alert, his face serious.

"Those two men on the beach weren't just casual passers-by who happened to recognize me. They were waiting for me. I haven't made any mistake about this man called Rance. Somebody knew I was coming out and they meant to finish me off quickly. But it misfired. Then I walked straight back into it when I went to Drysdale."

Ross-Piper came from the window and began to pour himself some more coffee. "You're getting into deep water."

"That's what cheers me up. I came out of Parkhurst knowing nothing. But now things have happened."

"You could go to the police . . . tell them about Drysdale?" suggested Ross-Piper.

"Not yet. I haven't got enough. He'd deny all knowledge of those two men. And they'll keep low. But the Rance character . . . I've been thinking about him. A man on the beach waiting for me. I see now I wasn't going to be handed over to the authorities. He was going to finish me off."

Ross-Piper nodded. "Someone was afraid that if you got out you could cause trouble."

"That's it. And I want to know how the news of my plan to escape leaked. How many people were in on the arrangements for my escape?"

Ross-Piper smiled. "It's not something you can keep in the family, you know, Peter. It was a long, slow business. The passport and the driving licence I did myself through a friend who's seen better times. But he didn't know anything about you. Drew and I fixed the bungalow and the car . . . all under false names. No one could have got anything from that. The most likely place for a leak would have been during the passing of messages to you in prison."

"Who did that?"

"Drew found the man."

"That's right, sir," said Drew, who was standing by the door. Since I'd come in he had changed into his dark-blue suit, and he stood there now very stiff and still and full of disapproval for this early morning visit.

"He's an ex-convict," said Ross-Piper. "He cost us a hundred quid and guaranteed to get the stuff in to you. How he did it we don't know. But I don't think he did it himself. He came down to Portsmouth, and he's the one who picked up the car after you left it and also locked up the bungalow."

"He knew you were going to meet me on the beach?"

"Of course. He had to pick up the car."

I looked over at Drew. "What about him, Drew?" I asked. "What sort of man is he?"

It was some time before Drew answered. He knew I was impetuous. He was afraid I was going to land Ross-Piper in trouble, and now, maybe, another of his friends might be subjected to the same danger.

"Tell him," said Ross-Piper suddenly. "If the police ever do pick Mr. Barlow up we know he'll keep his mouth shut."

Drew obviously didn't think that was very safe, but he said, "He's a small crook, sir. A bit of everything. The race-tracks, confidence tricks, and now and then burglary. He's a nice quiet little man, sir. Looks more like an insurance clerk than a crook. I wouldn't want to land him in trouble."

"Don't worry," I said. "I won't bring him any trouble—unless he's the man who started the leak. What's his name?"

Drew fidgeted a little. I could see he didn't want to tell me, his loyalty moving him to protect his friends. He looked appealingly at Ross-Piper.

Ross-Piper waved a large hand impatiently.

"You can tell him, Drew. It'll be all right."

Drew said reluctantly, "Arthur Fisher."

"Where does he live?"

"I don't know, sir."

"But you must."

"No, sir. He just moves about. I always used to meet him at the Freemason's Arms at the bottom of Hampstead Heath. He's in there most lunch-times when he's not working the tracks. Got a spotted dog, Nell, that's always with him."

"Did he pass the messages into Parkhurst himself?"

"I don't know, sir."

"How far would you trust him?"

Drew shrugged his shoulders. "He helped us for money, sir. A man like that can be bought both ways."

I knew what I had to do. I had to see Fisher. Drew went back to the kitchen to prepare breakfast, and Ross-Piper went off to dress. Whilst they were gone I telephoned Catherine because I knew she would be worried about my non-return. I told her that I had been held up and had spent the night with Ross-Piper, but I could sense that she did not believe this. However, I couldn't go into details over the telephone. I promised her that I would be back that evening.

After breakfast I had a couple of hours' sleep. Ross-Piper came in to me before he went off, and I could see that he was worried and concerned for me. He walked about the room in silence for a while and then he said, "I wish I knew what to do about all this, Peter. We've gone to a lot of trouble to get you out. It's going to be a stupid business if you now go and get yourself killed. . . . I know"—he raised his hand as I made to speak—"you've got the bit between your teeth and my sympathies are with you. But, you know, there's a lot of sense in the proverb that discretion is the better part of valour. I'm not asking you to change your mind . . . but I wish you would."

"I can't stop now," I said vigorously. "You must see that."

"Yes, I see it. But I don't like it. However. . . ."

He left the room and I lay there knowing that I would do anything for him except give up trying to find out who had murdered Hansford.

*   *   *

I got off the bus near the Hampstead Heath station, and I hadn't gone twenty yards before a policeman saw me. Until that moment I had kept my eyes open for policemen and had crossed the road to avoid them or turned aside to stare into a shop window until they had passed. But this policeman I couldn't avoid. He was standing just inside the entrance to the station and I was level with him before I saw him. Just for a second or two our eyes met. He looked at me, another man in the crowd, and then I was past him, but in the last fraction of time before our eyes parted I fancied I saw something in his face. You can't say what it is. But it is there; boredom, suddenly coloured by interest or doubt.

I didn't hurry. I kept my pace going up the gentle slope and heading for the Freemason's Arms. I didn't look back, but I had a cold feeling in the centre of my shoulders and I knew this was the kind of moment I had to learn to handle. This man had read my description, memorized the details, knew that it was a million-to-one chance that he would ever see me . . . and knew equally well that for someone the long chance must turn up, so why not for him?

I stopped and lit a cigarette, and with the movement I turned a little and looked back. He was coming towards me, leisurely, bulkily, and he might have been carrying on with his beat or following me. I couldn't tell.

I crossed the road. Two turnings up on my left was the Freemason's Arms. I knew the district fairly well, for just after the war I'd had a year in London with my home office and had often had dinner with a friend who lived at the top of the Heath. I took the first turning on the left. As I moved into it I saw that the policeman had crossed the road and was still coming after me, like a ponderous barge making slow progress against a strong tide. As the corner cut me off from him I reckoned that I had about thirty seconds.

Against the curb just round the corner a small saloon car was parked. As I came up to it I saw that the ignition key was in the lock and that the window on the driving-seat side was down. I walked out into the road and stood by the driving door. I tried the handle and the door opened. I pulled it a little towards me. The dark-blue bulk came round the corner and I knew that it had to be done right or I would be for ever lost. He had to think that it was my car and I was driving away innocently and unaware of him. I let him come five yards up the pavement towards me while I kept my hand on the door. Five yards and five seconds and the whole thing an eternity of time and suspense. A group of sparrows were quarrelling noisily in one of the roadside trees. A man in a garden across the way was spraying roses with some frothy mixture from a syringe. Further up the road a barrel organ was giving a sound thrashing to a song which was popular in Parkhurst . . . something about "Once I had a secret love, but now my love isn't secret any more. . . ." Only they sang different words to it. If I went back now I wouldn't see Parkhurst. It would be the Moor, and no man had ever beaten the mist and the bogs of Dartmoor. I didn't want to go back and break any records. I just wanted to stay out.

I got into the car and started it, and then, with a prayer that the owner was well away and would not see or hear, I turned the car out from the pavement. But I didn't go up the road away from the policeman. I had to convince him that whatever suspicions he had were false. I swung the car across the road, backed and filled once, and then, as he watched me from the pavement a few yards down, I drove back to the corner past him without a look in his direction. I stopped at the corner, waiting for a lorry to move by and in the rear mirror I saw him watching me. And then as I edged out into the road the bulky body relaxed and with a slow swing of his arms he began to walk away.

I went down past the station to the bus stop, made a circle around the traffic island and then came back, driving as slowly as I could. I stopped outside the station and checked him on my watch, in imagination following him up the side road until he should be out of sight. I gave him five minutes and I had to fight myself not to cut it down to three.

Then I drove the car back into the turning. There was no sign of the policeman. He had gone up the road and disappeared. I parked the car where I had found it, and three minutes later I was in the Freemason's Arms.

"Whisky. A double," I said to the barman. I took it with me over to a table and sat down. I felt as though I had run a mile. There was a tiny flick of nerves in my right arm and it was some time before the whisky began to take the knots out of me.

It was just after twelve when Arthur Fisher came in. He had the Dalmatian dog, Nell, with him. He went to the bar and got a drink and then carried it to a table some way from me. He sat down and began to read a morning newspaper. Nell squatted at his feet, very still and statuesque, her muzzle raised, her eyes blinking now and again.

I went to his table and sat down opposite him. He looked across at me and I nodded and said:

"Good morning, Mr. Fisher."

The paper came down slowly to the table. He wasn't hurried or confused. He was thinking and he was watching me. He put out a hand and picked up his glass, and before he drank he said:

"Good morning."

He had a nice, quiet, grey kind of voice, like a worn piece of flannel; and he was a nice, quiet, grey kind of man. About forty-five, I thought, going bald back from a narrow forehead, a white face with a faint stippling of beard shadow around the mouth and chin. He looked, as Drew had said, like a clerk; negative and a little frayed from the steady wear and tear of uneventful days. In the breast pocket of his navy blue suit was a row of fountain pens and pencils and the stiff points of his starched collar had worn his shirt thin on each side of his dark tie. Somebody had strengthened the weak places with very fine darning. And, just as one might have expected from an under-paid, disregarded clerk, there was a hint of sadness and frustra-tion about him, particularly in his eyes, which were a moist brown.

I said, "You're probably wondering who I am and why I've come over to you."

He nodded, and then drank. After he'd put his glass down he tidied up his paper, folding it into a tight baton.

"I've come to thank you," I said. "And also to ask you a few questions."

He cocked his head a little and one hand dropped and began to tease at Nell's ears.

Then he chuckled and said, "You've got a nerve. Yes, you've got a nerve all right—if my guess is correct." And then the smile was gone and his eyes were around the bar. There were only a few other people in the place.

"I felt I had to thank you personally for helping me. I'm very grateful to you."

"I've been paid, Mr. B. I've been paid. That's the main thing. Don't think I've got a suspicious nature, but I imagine it was less your gratitude than the questions you want to ask that brought you here. It doesn't sound very nice, does it? But I live a make-shift life. . . . Oh, very makeshift. No time for fine sentiments. Let's have the questions."

"All right."

He was looking me up and down, and before I could go on he smiled again and said, "You don't look like a man out of you know where, I'll admit. You look easy. But then the great art is to look like you aren't. You know, one of my dreams every time I go inside is to escape. Not that I think it would do any good. They always get you . . . at least they do us professionals because we haven't got anywhere to come back to except the place we come from. But you always dream about it, making a hero of yourself like. Sorry." The smile went and suddenly the brown eyes were fixed steadily on me. "The questions."

Nell moved forward a few inches and put her head on my knee. I teased at her ears gently and she wriggled her muzzle into the palm of my hand, asking for more affection.

"Have you ever heard of a man called Rance?"

"No, Mr. B." And then, with a glance at his dog, he went on,

"Taken to you, hasn't she? Unusual for her. Usually very reserved."

I said, "You know something about me. Why I was put in. You know why I'm out?"

"No."

"Because I want to find the man who really did murder Hansford."

"Didn't you do it, Mr. B.?"

"No, I damned well didn't."

"Well . . . well."

"What is more, the man who did it, or his friends, knew I was coming out and they tried to stop me."

He sat there, dowdy and still, while I told him about the attempt on my life, and my conviction that somewhere along the line there had been a leakage of information. "You had some-one," I said, "who passed messages in to Gypo at Parkhurst. I'd like to talk to him. I'd like to know how you got hold of him."

He stirred then, rather uncomfortably.

"You're asking a lot, Mr. B. If you get picked up, the less you know the better. In a way it's unethical of Drew to have given you my name. Very unethical."

"Somebody," I said vigorously, "tried to murder me. I'm not dealing in ethics. I want facts, because I want the truth. You can help me."

"Oh, sure I can. But it isn't easy. Ethics is ethics, you know, in this business. For instance, this man who got the messages into Parkhurst. Well, you know how it is. I go round to one or two of the boys, drop a word in a pub here and there that I want someone. . . . Nothing happens for a long time, and then one day he turns up. I don't know him personally, but I know about him. What you've got to understand is that by the time he starts work a lot of people know you're on your way out. You can't keep that kind of thing secret in my parish."

"But you can tell me who he is and where to find him."

"I could. But say you go to him. He's going to be offended. And you know, Mr. B., the people in my parish don't just sulk when they're offended. Next thing I'll know is that I've been razored up at Ascot. And, Mr. B., I can't afford that."

"The racing in Ireland is just as good. Why don't you go over there for a couple of months?" I knew what he was after, but I could see that he had to be persuaded.

"It could be. The Irish have got some very fine horses."

286

"The best in the world," I said. "I think a trip to Ireland would be good for your health."

He thought it over, and while he did so I slipped out my wallet. Luckily I'd come to London with plenty of money. I didn't know what the rate was for mending broken hearts in his parish, but I thought fifty pounds might cover it. His eyes moistened with a sad satisfaction at the sight of the crisp notes, and I think I overpaid. He took the fifty, and then, fishing one of the pencils from his breast pocket, he tore a corner from his morning paper and wrote on it. The moment he handed it over to me I could see the uneasiness spread through him. He was regretting it almost at once, and anxious to be gone.

*   *   *

The name was Daiken, Henry Daiken, and the address 213 Matfield Road, Poplar.

I had a snack at the bar of the Freemason's Arms, and I was in Matfield Road by three o'clock. I used the underground and buses and kept off the pavements as much as I could.

It was a street of neat little houses, backing right up against the wall of the Millwall Docks. Over the house roofs I could see the stiff necks of cranes and derricks and the banded funnels of cargo boats and steamers. Each house had a neat plot of garden and a thin privet hedge. Number 213 was right at the end of the street and flanked by an open piece of ground that, unlike the other houses, left room for a small drive-in to a wooden garage at the far end of the garden, right up against the dock wall. In the downstair window was a coloured plate taken from some magazine of the Queen. All the ground-floor curtains were blue, those on the top floor white and the front door was painted red. Fisher had told me that Daiken was a versatile and reasonably successful crook—he'd only been in four times— who was ready to turn a dishonest penny at almost anything. From the house decoration I could see that as well as being a crook he was a patriot. A real Empire-building combination.

The woman who answered my knock at the door didn't like me from the start. She was blonde, about thirty, and had the hardest-looking eyes I'd seen for a long time. Her face was made up too much and her hair was set in brassy waves. As she spoke a cigarette bobbed up and down between her dark lips with nervous life of its own. She wore a white lacy blouse. Below her waist she was a working woman—a thick black skirt with a piece of sacking round it and shapeless carpet slippers on her feet. Her hands were wet and red with soap-suds.

287

"Henry Daiken," I said. "I'd like to see him."

She wiped her wet hands on the piece of sacking. "Oh, you would. And who might you be?"

I gave her a smile, hoping to soften her, and said, "I'm a friend of his in a way."

"In what way?"

"Do I have to fill out an application form? I just want to see Henry, for old times' sake. We went to the same college together."

She understood at once and moved back into the house, saying, " 'Arf a mo."

She went to the foot of a narrow flight of stairs and shouted, "Henry, someone to see you. Friend of yours, maybe. But 'e ain't got no name, or 'e's forgotten it."

I couldn't catch what was shouted down to her, but she translated for me.

"He don't want to see no one without a name. 'Is health ain't very good this morning."

"Tell him I'm from Gypo."

She shouted this up and I could see the cigarette in her lips jerking. The voice answered her and she translated again for me.

"O.K., come in. Top of the stairs first on the right. You'll excuse me, I'm sure, but I got to give the chauffeur 'is orders and see cook about dinner tonight."

She went off in a cloud of cigarette smoke and cheap scent and I went up to Daiken.

It was a back room and from the window the chief view was the grey rise of the dock wall. Daiken was lying on the bed in his trousers and shirt and the place was littered with papers. There was a bottle of Guinness and a glass on the floor by the bed and a saucer full of cigarette ends. Daiken was small and built like a jockey—wide, strong shoulders and thin legs. He was about fifty and his face looked as though it were made of some dark-coloured india-rubber. Even when he wasn't talking it moved about gently all over the place, nose down to his upper lip, his cheeks corrugating and creasing, eyebrows rising and falling, and a moving bulge where he ran his tongue along the inside of his cheeks. He seemed to be fascinated by the things he could do with it. His darkish hair was like a collection of carpet fluff and his eyes were brown and bright like a puppy's.

I stood just inside the door and he looked me over calmly, his face simmering gently. He gave no sign of recognition. Neither did I, which made the two of us good actors, but I had a feeling that he was better than I could ever be. I had unexpected luck in my hands, and for the moment I didn't quite know what to do with it. Henry Daiken was the second of the two men who had attacked me on the beach. Daiken and Rance. There was no doubt about it.

He said, "You from Gypo?"

I nodded and pushed the door behind me. The puppy eyes were alert and missing nothing.

"How is the old tyke? Time he died."

"He's very much alive. He suggested that you might be able to help me."

"Can't help myself much this mornin'." He pulled a wry face. "Hangover," he explained. "Celebrating last night. Me birthday. I'll never see fifty-one again. Matter of fact, first thing this mornin' I didn't think I'd ever see again. . . ." He grinned and then winced against some pain in his head.

"That's too bad," I sympathized. "Still, I only want a few words with you."

He was a superb actor, for he knew me, and not by any shadow of a look or falter in his voice had he declared it. He reached over, and ignoring the glass, took the Guinness bottle by the neck and helped himself.

"Only thing what keeps down the pain," he explained as he lowered the bottle. "Too bad I ain't got a bottle of champagne to mix with it. Nothing like black velvet for the after-birthday blues. So you're from Gypo, eh? Nice chap, Gypo, even though they call him a menace to society. . . . Some of these judges is pretty insultin'." He suddenly laughed, and then stopped, raising one hand to his head with a pathetic groan.

It was an odd thing, but although I knew this man had tried to kill me, I couldn't help liking him. I moved closer to the bed, and half smiling I said, "All right. Now let's cut out the comedy and get down to business. You impress me, but you don't deceive me. You know who I am and I know who you are. We've met before on a beach."

Just for a moment his mouth narrowed to a long, thin slit. Then he made a puzzled face, his apple chin bobbing about like a fishing float and one hand going up and teasing at the fluff on his head.

"On a beach, mister? When would this be?"

"Less than a week ago, Daiken. On the Isle of Wight."

"Not me, guv'nor. Haven't been out of London for weeks. You know something, mister? I think you're wastin' your time with me."

"No, I'm not. You were there with a man called Rance. I'm very curious about both of you, and more curious about the people who employ you. If you don't feel like talking, maybe I could persuade you. In a way, you could call me a desperate man. . . ." I heard my voice hardening and felt the patience running from me. "I could smack you about a bit and perhaps jog your memory."

The threat didn't touch him. He slipped one hand under his pillow.

"John and Mary, jogging along behind the old grey mare." He sang the line, regretted it and winced. "You can't jog nothing, mister."

His hand was now withdrawn. It held a revolver which he cradled absently on his midriff. He seemed hardly aware of it. It just lay on his shirt and he patted it, and I saw how long and well formed his hands were. Jockey's hands, strong and sensitive.

"Nobody jogs Henry Daiken," he said. "Least of all Mr. Bloomin' Peter Barlow. I'm surprised after all what I've done for you. Blimey——" he gave me a warm, friendly smile; "I was slow on that one. I got nothing to do all day but read the papers, and I see your photograph, and naturally I got my interest in you—and a little touch of dark dye on your hair puts me wrong." Then in a serious tone, with an echo of sympathy in it, he said: "You must be crazy. This is London. The Metropolis. The heart of the whole stinkin' world. Every copper with a description of you—and you walk in here!"

"Why don't you shout for the police, then?"

"Who, me?" His eyes widened with surprise. "Why, none of the boys would ever talk to me again if I did that. Besides, I helped you get out. Who really give you my name?"

"Gypo gave it to me before I left Parkhurst."

"Then he shouldn't have done. Next time I'm in I'll have a word with him."

"Come on, Daiken," I snapped sharply. "You helped me out, but you also tried to kill me. All right, you were paid for it. But I'll pay you, too. I want to know who employed you and Rance. Was it Colonel Drysdale?"

"Never heard of a Rance," he said stubbornly. "Nor no Colonel Drysdale. And haven't I told you I wasn't on the Isle of Wight?"

One hand still on the revolver, he reached for the Guinness bottle again. He finished it with an appreciative convulsion of his face. He tossed it to the floor. Then, shaking his head at me, he said sadly: "You're up a dead-end. I can't help you, but I like you. You did it nice, real nice, coming out of Parkhurst.

290

You must have brightened the hearts of all them boys back there. But you're a fool to hang around London."

I turned away from the bed and went to the window. I looked out into the back garden, and I wondered what the devil I could do. To make him talk would take more time and privacy than we could ever hope for together.

"Take my tip and sling your hook," said Daiken. "You got good friends in England. They'll fix you up abroad where the coppers would never think of looking. But you stay around London and you're askin' for it. Either from the police or them beach-boys you worry about. . . ."

It was the kind of good sense I'd heard before, but I was in no mood for it. Finding him had been more luck than I had expected, and I knew I had to go along with it. Luck was an uncertain horse unless you used the whip on it. I stood there and Mrs. Daiken came into the garden, carrying a tin bath full of wet clothes. She put the bath down and went to the garage. She was inside for a while, and through the open door I saw the green bonnet of a car with a chromium-plated mascot on top of the radiator. It was a jockey on a racehorse. I wondered how long ago Daiken had lost his jockey's licence. Poor Henry Daiken, I thought. Poor enough to own a car. Or maybe he'd stolen it. His wife came out of the garage carrying a clothes-line and a bag of clothes pegs. Cigarette in mouth, she swayed like a chorus girl from some third-rate musical comedy towards the tin bath.

I turned back to Daiken.

I gave him a grin. Inside I was hard with determination.

"All right, Daiken. Keep your advice. I went up for a job another man did. I was damn nearly hanged. Now I'm out and somebody doesn't like it. I don't blame them either, because when I catch up with them I'm not wasting any time being polite."

He played his part well. He shrugged his shoulders slowly and said regretfully, "Cheerio, chum. I wish I could do more for you." He might have been refusing his best friend a loan, but more than that, his voice was full of quiet insult. This man and Rance had tried to kill me, and the sight of him lying there confident and smug infuriated me. I reached out and suddenly whipped the revolver from him and tossed it out of the window. He wasn't afraid. He was off the bed in a flash, reached to the floor, and was coming for me with the Guinness bottle raised as a club.

I smacked him on the jaw, and the satisfaction in me was a

kind of bliss. As he went down I said, "That's for pulling a gun on me."

He came up with the bottle still in his hand, and he slung it at me. I ducked, and it went through the top half of the window pane with a crash. I heard his wife shout from the garden. Then he was on me like an angry wild-cat. I fended him off and hit him again, and he stumbled back against the bed and then rolled to the floor.

"Oh, my 'ead! My bleedin' 'ead," he moaned.

"Tell Rance and Drysdale and any others who might be interested that I'm not easily put off and that I lose my temper quickly. . . ."

He made no move for me. He just lay there holding his head. I backed towards the door, and at that moment it opened and his wife came rushing in. She took one look at Daiken and then she was on me. I side-stepped her rush and decided to leave. There had been satisfaction if not great sense in hitting Daiken. I wasn't anxious for any exchanges with his wife. She went by me clawing and swearing, and then I was out of the room. I slammed the door and twisted the key in the lock. Inside they sounded like a couple of mountain cats arguing over a kill. I ran down the stairs and went to the front door, which was still ajar. But I didn't go out. I slammed it loudly, staying on the inside, and then I went quietly along the passage, and into the room on my right. Upstairs I heard them beating at the bedroom door. After about half a minute there was a crash and I knew they had broken it open.

CHAPTER X

IT was the front room of the house, the one with the blue curtains and the picture of the Queen. Just to my left beyond the door was an upright piano with a lace runner along the top and a framed photograph. The photograph showed a group of men, bottles and glasses in their hands and rosettes in their caps, standing at the back of a motor-coach. Daiken was there, bottle in hand. It looked like a dart club's outing or a football party. Standing next to Daiken at a football match, I guessed, would be an education.

I had the door closed, leaving only a crack through which I could see part of the stairway. Following the crash of the door upstairs, Daiken's wife came running down. She passed me, and then I heard the front door open. After a few moments it was closed with an angry bang, and she came back. Daiken moved down the stairs a few steps towards her so that I could just see his feet and trousers. He was groaning and grunting to himself.

"He's gone!"

"'Course he's gone, you useless lump," he snapped, bad-tempered. "Think he was going to stay and do the dishes for you? The bastard, he's goin' to cause trouble. You got to go and phone."

"Do it yourself!" she shouted.

"You want the back of my hand? Oh, my 'ead! I ain't in no shape to go out."

"You shouldn't drink like a pig——"

"You get going. . . ." He swore at her with angry fluency for a while, and then finished, "You phone the *Boutade* and tell 'em Barlow's been here."

"Luvaduck, was that Barlow?"

"It weren't the flaming Angel Gabriel! And don't use his name over the phone. Say Gypo's friend, or the island boy. They'll get it. And bring me back a packet of fags."

Sliding back to the crack of the door, I saw his legs begin to retreat up the stairs. The woman was standing only a few feet from me, the back of her blonde hair burnished bright.

"What's the phone number?" she called.

"Strewth," he groaned. "Don't you never remember nothin' but the names of film stars? Gerrard 47593."

I repeated it to myself. Gerrard 47593.

As his legs disappeared he shouted, "And don't be all day."

She turned away from the stairs and called irritably, "I ain't goin' to run, if that's what you mean."

She disappeared down the passage, grumbling to herself. The tap stopped running and I waited. After a little while she came back past the door of the front room, and she was humming to herself.

The front door slammed. From behind the curtains I watched her go down the garden path and out into the road.

I gave her two minutes by my watch, and then I went out, opening and closing the front door carefully and glad that Daiken was in a back room. I turned up the street away from the direction she had taken. Fifteen minutes later I was in a telephone booth. There was no trouble. *La Boutade*, restaurant, with a Soho address and the number Gerrard 47593. I put three pennies in the slot and called the number. I booked a table for dinner at seven that evening.

*   *   *

I spent the rest of the afternoon in the warm, dark security of a cinema. I sat there in deodorised sanctuary and I went over the past and all I knew of Hansford, and all that had happened to me, looking for some chink of light, some lead which might help me. Daiken was a hired man, and so possibly was Rance. Pay their price and they did your work. I wasn't sure about Drysdale. The thing that had to be answered was who "they" were who had to be warned at the *Boutade*.

That it was "they," and not "he" or "her" supported my feeling that somewhere there was an organisation or group . . . and among them there had to be the man who had murdered Hansford.

When I came out from the cinema it was dark and a light summer shower was falling. I turned up my coat collar against it and, hands in my pockets, walked from the Haymarket to Soho through the rain-polished streets, admiring the movement and colour. Inside prison all movement becomes slow-patterned and monotonous, and colour loses its spirit; dull greys, browns and reds. . . . I revelled in this kaleidoscope of greens, yellows, blues and scarlets and for at least half a minute I watched a Coca-Cola sky-sign with the simple interest of a child. I went up Shaftesbury Avenue trying to recall how Keats' line went on from "beaded bubbles winking at the brim. . . ." I didn't have much success. I'd always been on the mathematical side. An engineer, not a literary man. Long ago, when Tom Ross-Piper and I had been working our way through France to Spain, I remembered we'd had an argument about poetry as we lay in some woods all day, waiting for night and the chance to hop a train. I'd maintained that there was true poetry in mathematics, that figures, not words, could best express man's dreams. Tom hadn't agreed and we'd never finished the argument, for he had been shot dead four days later and I had come on alone.

The restaurant was at the top of Greek Street, near Soho Square. There were three steps up to a half-glass door with a black frame, and across it in gold running script the name *La Boutade*.

An ancient, crabbed, dried-up man in a waiter's suit took my raincoat and hung it in a vestibule.

I went through into a small bar that curved across one corner of a long room, a soft, plush, red velvet cave with gilt trimmings. Farther down the room there was a silver lattice-work with artificial pomegranate blooms twined over it and beyond that a glimpse of tables.

I ordered a dry martini and looked with a great deal of interest at the rows of bottles behind the bar. I had a lot of different drinks to taste again after two years. I could see that I was early. The business in here was done at lunch-time and between half-past nine and midnight. There were signed photographs of theatrical and film celebrities around the bar and the place had an expensive, well-breeched feeling; the kind of place where at its busy periods neither love nor money would get a stranger a table.

A few of the tables beyond the lattice screen were occupied. Some waiters fussed and scurried and others leant half hidden behind a screen or service door gazing out into a secret landscape of boredom. The barman filled a dish with olives and slid it towards me. I watched the faces of the waiters, but they were just waiters. Nobody took any notice of me. I finished my drink and went down the room.

A head waiter, his face as white and featureless as his shirt front, manifested himself gravely from behind a desk near the lattice-work. He checked the false name I had given in his register of tables and then handed me over to another waiter who took me through into the far part of the cave. He settled me at a corner table, where I had small room for my legs and the table-lamp with a huge parchment and velvet shade obscured most of my view.

I pushed the lamp aside and the waiter left me with a menu and the problem of selecting my first considered meal for two years. It was one of those large menus which when opened was almost as big as the table itself. A careless movement with it and I could have knocked the lamp over. It was written in purple ink in a small, flourishing continental hand very difficult to decipher. I was certain then that the place was going to be expensive; a small table, an over-large menu, and not enough leg room. I noticed that the name of the proprietor was given at the head of the menu. Giulio Latti. I felt I would like to know Giulio.

However, for the next few minutes I decided to forget him and concentrate on the purple menu. What, I wondered, would the Wine and Food Society, or Monsieur Brillat-Savarin have recommended as the right meal to mark the end of a two-year prison diet?

I had an omelette du Baron de Barante, full of pieces of fresh *cèpes* and shredded shrimps, then saddle of lamb with a bottle of Musigny, and finished off with a piece of Camembert, which was at the right stage of deliquescence, and coffee. And the whole time I was eating no one took the slightest notice of me except the waiter. There were about eight other tables occupied. A young man with the kind of pale fair hair that I'd once had was sitting two tables away from me with a very pretty girl. Their heads were close together in one of those Soho low-voice colloquies which range from the soul to ski-ing holidays. There was no room in their world for anyone else, and the same seemed true of all the others dining there. Yet this was the place Henry Daiken had told his wife to telephone.

When the waiter came to pour me more coffee he asked me if I had enjoyed the meal, and he said it as though he really wanted to know. I told him I had, so much that I would like to tell the proprietor so myself.

"I'm sorry, monsieur," he said, and the little shrug he gave was full of regret, "but Signore Latti is away for a few days. But I shall convey your pleasure to the chef."

It crossed my mind that Giulio Latti might be recovering from the rigours of a trip to Kew.

After that there was nothing I could do except light a cigarette and take my time over the second cup of coffee.

For a while I played with various ideas . . . extravagant ideas, like leaving the place and then trying to find some way in after it had closed so that I could have a look around . . . but to be on the London streets after midnight seemed unhealthy. I had a train to catch to Blackthorn . . . Catherine and her aunt would be worried if I didn't turn up. What could I do? Nothing, I decided, except maybe come back in a few days if I were still at liberty, and have a word with Giulio Latti.

A few more people were drifting in now. I stared at the decorated panels that lined the walls. From where I sat in a corner I could only see two of them clearly on the left-hand wall. They were done in an attractive manner, a maze of thin, confused black outlines and washed over here and there with blue, reds and yellows. They reminded me of the work of Felix Topolski. Each one was concerned with a definite subject. The panel immediately on my left was Agriculture, showing a great tractor, its radiator almost filling the panel, and then the towering bulk of the driver against a wind-whipped sky full of gulls. The other one I could see represented Drama, a writhing crowd of faces and costumed figures packed into a theatre interior whose columns and proscenium arch sprouted strange jungle-like growths. Many of the faces I recognized as famous actors and actresses. There was a movement and vigour in the thin lines which seemed to suggest that the artist was a man of over-flowing energy, talent and impatience.

When the waiter brought my bill I asked him, "Who did the panels in this place?"

"I don't know his name, sir. They were done about five years ago, when the place was opened. He was a Hungarian or Polish gentleman, I think. Signs himself Sava."

The meal was as expensive as I had thought it might be—but worth it. I gave him a good tip and he pulled the table away from me as I rose to go as though he were opening the gates of a palace for a prince to pass through. Half turning to slide out from behind the table, I saw for the first time the painted panel in the wall above my head. I felt my muscles stiffen suddenly as though someone had unexpectedly struck me. Standing out from the crowded scene was the figure of James Gurney Hansford.

It was so fantastic, so unexpected that for the moment I had the confused, irrational impression that it was real, that this was Hansford. I stood there, staring at the wall panel, caught up in a moment of isolation which seemed to hold threat and promise. . . . There was no mistake, no accident about this. This was Hansford drawn by a man who had known him. The thick red lips, the high colour of the cheeks, that large, smooth, blown-up apple face balanced on the too thin neck, the wide shoulders and the barrel chest and the short, stumpy, dwarf-like arms. . . .

"It's very impressive, isn't it, monsieur?" said the waiter behind me.

I turned away from the wall. "It certainly is," I said.

As I passed down the room to the trellis-work I saw that there was a woman sitting inside the little pay-desk by the service door. She was middle-aged, with the full-blown good looks of an Italian. At seventeen she could have turned any man's head. Now she had a faint dark line above her lip, a pair of comfortable bosoms, and the faint suggestion of a third chin. She didn't look at me, but I knew her. The last time I had seen her she had been standing in a witness-box giving vital evidence against me. She was Carla Lodi—Hansford's old housekeeper-cum-mistress. As I went out I was telling myself that any Italian restaurant proprietor who was married more than likely had his wife in the pay-box.

In Greek Street I picked up a taxi. I got the driver to take me as far as Hyde Park Corner, and there, in case anyone were following me, I paid him off and got on the Underground for Paddington.

All the way back in the train I was seeing the panel. Impressive. It certainly was. Its title was clearly Liberation. It showed the gates of a concentration camp, plainly German, for the warning notices were in that language. But the gates were open and a crowd of miserable, emaciated figures were struggling out to be greeted by a small party of American and British military figures. There was a jeep, and behind it a couple of weapon-carriers, and in the far distance a range of tall mountains. Standing up in the jeep was a man in British battledress waving his right arm, and, large in the foreground, already out of the jeep and moving towards the camp was Hansford. He, too, was in battledress, his army cap off and held in his right hand. Hansford the liberator, I thought grimly. Germany. Hansford in trouble for the illegal sale of equipment. The German forgery of Allied currency. Some Hungarian artist named Sava. . . . And all this at La Boutade. It came to me then that I wanted more than anything to talk to Signore Giulio Latti. . . .

When I got out at Blackthorn Station it was gone eleven and Catherine was waiting for me with the car.

"I've met the last three trains," she said. "How are you feeling?"

As I settled beside her I said: "Fine. I'd forgotten all about my ribs."

She turned towards me, and in the glow of the panel instruments I saw that she was looking worried. I suddenly realized what might have been going through her mind as she had waited for train after train. But I understood more than that. I knew what I should have felt had I been waiting for her . . . and just imagining it evoked the emotion in me, and with it came the sharp movement of the thing which suddenly belonged to us both . . . which was claiming us both.

I tried to hold it back, to kill it now swiftly, but it was away from me, alive and free and not to be denied.

As though it were the most natural thing in the world, as though it had been waiting there serenely for one or the other of us to give it life and movement, and this was the right and proper time and setting, I put out my arm and she came towards me and we kissed. A simple, unhurried caress between us, but for me, as I knew it must be for her, full of the strength and permanence which rest in simple things.

In the darkness of the car, the night beyond us marked only by a dim station light, we held each other, without words, almost now without the movement of caress. The two of us very close, and very still. And I knew that this was the moment that breaks for everyone at some time: that it was here for us now, choosing not our time, but its own.

After a while we separated.

I heard my own voice, stiff and strange.

"I'm sorry I'm late. But you shouldn't have worried."

"I couldn't help it."

She put up her hand and touched my face as we drew apart and I caught at her fingers and carried them to my mouth, kissing the palm of her hand.

"This is crazy," I said. "Crazy for you and impossible for me."

"Nothing's impossible."

"I love you. . . ." I had to say it, even though I knew I had no right.

"I wanted you to say that."

"Look," I said, fiercely now to control my feelings. "I'm an escaped prisoner . . . I've got nothing. Nothing, you understand. . . . We must forget the whole thing. . . ."

But she wasn't even listening. She started the motor and began to drive off, staring ahead at the road and smiling.

CHAPTER XI

OFTEN I'd wondered how it would be. Often I'd tried to deceive myself that I had seen it. But now the reality made all the wishful fancies of the past seem pale and false. Here it was, and there was no escape. A moment not of fierce, racing ecstasy, but of warm, frank truthfulness which needed no words and only the simplest of movements. This was love, as humble and faithful as a pilgrim, and not to be turned aside.

I woke early the next morning. It was a little after six and the rain had gone. I dressed and went out. At the back of the cottage was a meadow through which ran a small stream. I walked along this to a point where it broke over a narrow weir and then widened into a great pool almost a hundred yards broad. There were some mandarin ducks swimming about below the weir. Farther out the smooth surface was dimpled by the rise of small dace and roach to a hatch of flies. I sat down below a pollarded willow and smoked. A whitethroat kept skirmishing out from some reeds to pick off the dancing flies, and I thought how good it would be if things were really simple. How good it would be if I were just staying with Catherine and her aunt and there was nothing before me but the laziness of a summer day, the promise of love, and the prospect of ordinary days ahead to strengthen it. But now, what had seemed simple began to force itself upon my conscience and intelligence as impossible. So long as I inhabited the no-man's land between law and violence, I had no right to ask anyone to share that existence. Already Catherine had moved within its fringe to help me. If I stayed with her the moment might soon come when she would be exposed as openly to danger as I was. That was something I could not tolerate. So far I felt that I was safe, but there was no knowing when my security might be broken. I knew so well that a man can never tell when he has given a hostage to misfortune; that at the moment when he feels most confident he reveals some weakness. Catherine had to be away from me when that happened. Or rather I had to be away from her. And until this whole business was cleared up I had no right to offer or accept the gifts we had both discovered and wished to share.

I smoked three cigarettes while the whitethroat, gorged with flies, sat on a reed mace and made plaintive little cries, and I knew what I had to do.

I stood up to go back and there she was coming along the side of the pool towards me. The sunlight was on her dark hair and she was all colour and light and movement, the warm brown of her arms and legs, the yellow of her dress, the wetness of dew on her shoes that made red redder and beyond her a great sweep of blue and white sky against which she seemed to float. . . . She came up to me and my arms went round her and her face was raised to mine and there was nothing in me then to deny. We stood there, close together, closer than I had ever been to anyone. As we kissed I felt the simpleness of our love break free and take our bodies with a trembling power that passed to a fierceness. . . .

After a time we walked back to the cottage for breakfast. Later, as we sat in the garden, I told her that I was going.

"I'm well enough to be on my own. Every moment I stay here is dangerous for you and your aunt. And as for us . . . I tried to say it last night. I'm not going to try again. You know what I should say. You know what I must do. But if a man can do it—I'll come back. I've got to come back!"

She didn't say anything. She took my hand, and I knew that she understood. Anyone else, maybe, might have shown some compromise, but not Catherine. Only one thing she said:

"Don't go today. My aunt is going to be away all day and we shall be alone. I know you've made up your mind, but I would like to have this day free with you. You don't have to explain anything. I know why you're going. It isn't necessary because anything that happens to you also happens to me. But I can understand that this won't make you change your mind. But I want you today."

So I agreed to stay. We sat there and I told her all that had happened in the previous two days, and when I had finished she said she would telephone a friend of her aunt's whom she knew in Fleet Street. He might be able to tell her something about *La Boutade*, Giulio Latti and the Hungarian artist Sava.

"I can do it without making him curious."

She went off, and after a while her aunt came out to me. She was too good a gardener to come straight down the path. She stopped now and then to pick off a dead flower, to stir the earth around a favourite plant with a small hand-hoe she carried and once to firm the stakes around a great clump of peonies. She was dressed in a well-cut grey suit, but the effect was spoiled by a pair of old gardening shoes with enormous soles.

As she stood in front of me she saw me glance at her shoes. "I'm going to London for the day. Needless to say, I shall not be wearing these shoes. I put you in charge of the hot-water boiler. It's a beast, but I shall accept no excuses if you let it out. Catherine's hopeless with it. But I fear the worst."

I smiled. "I don't see why you should. Boilers are my line of country. In fact I'm something of an expert on heat conservation and fuel economy."

"Then I fear the worst for two reasons. One because you're an expert and this boiler delights in humiliating experts."

"And the other reason?"

She pulled a piece of raffia from a thick skein of the stuff which she had draped round her neck like an Hawaiian lei, and began to tie back a trailing branch of rambler roses.

"Have you ever been in love before?" She might have been asking me if I'd been in London before.

"No."

"I'm surprised. Most men of your age have minor attacks. However, since you're such a novice, let me explain to you that when you're in love it's inclined to drive really important considerations like keeping boilers alight, feeding the cat and watering the tomatoes from your mind."

"You want me to do all those things as well?"

"I do."

"I won't fail you."

"I hope not. But, more important, I hope you won't fail Catherine."

"You can be sure of that. But, anyway, how did you know?"

She came back from the rambler rose, stooping like a great heron, and there were wrinkles of laughter around her iron-grey eyes.

"She's often said she's been in love before. But this time it's different. She's got an appetite like a cart-horse, but she's eaten practically nothing since she came here. She's a girl who can look after herself, and she pays other people the compliment of thinking they can do the same. Yesterday she was as fussed as a hen with one chick."

"Don't worry. I'm going away tomorrow and I shan't come back until I'm free."

"A fine sentiment, but you've got a lot to learn. If you're in love you'll come back, free or not. That's what it's all about, making and claiming sacrifices. Doing damn silly things and

302

having as much control over yourself as a piece of thistledown in a westerly gale. It really is one of the most wonderful things in the world, and completely without logic. Irritating, too, at times. And I'm thankful I don't have to go through it all again. However, don't let me depress you and don't forget to shut the greenhouse door after you've done the tomatoes."

Half an hour later she drove off in her car. As Catherine and I walked back from the gate the telephone in the house began to ring. She answered it while I went and watered the tomatoes, remembering to shut the door when I had finished.

She came out with a basket to pick peas for lunch, and as I helped her she told me the call had been from her friend in Fleet Street.

La Boutade had been opened five or six years previously. Until its opening the proprietor, Giulio Latti, had run a smaller, far less successful restaurant near Victoria Station. At the moment *La Boutade* was one of the top eating places in London and very popular with the theatrical world. Giulio Latti was a Sicilian who'd been in the country twenty years. He was married, but had no children. He was apparently a shrewd business man and, though this was generally unknown, in addition to *La Boutade* he ran a chain of coffee stalls for lorry-drivers on the roads around London. He'd been in trouble once with the police over a row with a waiter. Giulio had picked up a knife in rage and slit the man's arm. The damage had been slight and he had been bound over to keep the peace.

"And the drawings? This Sava man?"

Catherine shook her head. "He didn't know much about him. He came from Europe after the war. There was a paragraph or two in the papers about him when *La Boutade* was opened and he was simply referred to as an artist friend of Giulio's. My friend checked the art galleries, but they know nothing about him and it seems fairly certain that he's never had a London showing. My friend wanted to know why I needed all this."

"What did you say?"

"I thanked him and told him to mind his own business."

"And will he?"

"I think so."

I went on picking peas.

Catherine said, "It doesn't help much, does it?"

"I don't know. . . ."

"What will you do?"

"I'm not sure yet."

303

The things I could do were limited and quite clearly full of risk. I wanted to know more about Sava. To do that I had to find Giulio. Also I wanted to speak to Colonel Drysdale again. Sava, Hansford, Drysdale and the German counterfeiting plant at Redl Zipfcave—at last I really seemed to be getting somewhere.

*　　*　　*

It was a happy morning and afternoon. Apart from being in love and being with Catherine, it was full of things which I hadn't done for years. I picked peas and podded them. I stoked a boiler and helped to wash and dry dishes. I mended a broken chair and sat on a kitchen table with a glass of beer and a cigarette, talking while Catherine grilled a couple of steaks. Her appetite, I saw, had revived. We went for a walk across the fields, keeping to ourselves and moving for a long time in a blissful silence, just holding hands. We came back and had a swim in the pool. We lay in the sun and she told me something about her father and mother. Her mother had been born in Buda-Pest. Her father had been an attaché at the British Embassy in Rome for a long time. Catherine had been born in Rome and spent many years there. Then there had been trouble between her father and mother and they had separated. One way and another she had shuttled between them and a succession of aunts and uncles all over the place with the result that she had become early self-dependent and—though she didn't even hint at this—starved of any real and lasting affection. As far as I could make out she'd had a bewildering number of jobs from teaching Italian at the Berlitz School of Languages to washing dishes in a holiday camp, and none of them had lasted very long.

I rolled over on my elbow and watched her face as she spoke. The sun through the trees at the pool side flecked her warm skin with a gold dappling. If I could I would have made the moment last for ever because my love for her was like a fine pain inside me. And momentarily I was angry, angry that I was not free to bring to her all that she so clearly wanted and had missed. I was caught up in a dirty web and until I was free of it there was nothing I could do beyond acknowledging our love. We had these few hours together and because they were so good I swore to myself that I would come out of the darkness which surrounded me and find my way back to her. Not only justice for myself impelled me now, but—even stronger —the angry determination to merit and ensure other days like this . . . to bring to her a life to which all men and women had a simple right.

I leaned over and kissed her and she ran her fingers through my hair. Somewhere not far away the whitethroat gave a little trickle of song and then was silent as though even his comment on this golden day was inadequate.

That evening, with all my chores done and the boiler still burning well, we walked into a small country town about five miles from the cottage. We had dinner at an hotel on the main square. Going into the town brought back the alertness and caution in me. Among people I found myself full of distrust. Maybe this strained my imagination. Just before we went into the hotel a car drove past us and for a moment I could have sworn that the man in it was Colonel Drysdale. I said nothing to Catherine. But, imagination or not, an uneasy feeling began to possess me.

After dinner we found the local cinema and sat together in the darkness and I wished that this was how it would always be—uncomplicated, just the touch of a hand now and then, the look across a table, the dark velvet anonymity of a cinema and the presence beside me of another person who banished all other people from my thoughts; that I would go out presently into the night and walk home, talking, content with small things. . . .

We came out and the night sky was full of stars, more of them and much brighter than in any child's drawing, and we began to walk home. On the outskirts of the town we had to wait while a goods train moved over a level crossing. It went away into the darkness with a red eye winking at us. Then we were alone on the road. A dark river ran under a grey stone bridge. The road began to rise and there were tall elms to our left and to the right a long hill slope pale with the great expanse of young corn.

A car went by us very quickly up the hill, its headlamps whitening the ears of corn in the field and turning the lower branches of the elms to a vivid green that reminded me of pantomime scenery. It stopped at the top of the hill and I saw it back into a gateway and then turn out and face towards us. For an instant we were walking in the full glare of its headlights. They clicked off and there were only the two dull yellow eyes of its sidelamps, beady, reptilian-like eyes squinting at us. It squatted there on the rise of the hill. As we neared it the uneasiness I had felt in the hotel was with me again.

We were ten yards from the car when I heard the door slam.

305

In the same moment the headlights blazed up. Catherine and I halted, held by the light. Her hand in mine, I felt her fingers grip more tightly. Fantasy stepped from the shadows and became reality.

A figure slid round into the lights and his shadow was thrown long and ink-black down the road towards us. He was joined by another man and their two shadows were blurred stains that spread across the cone of light. They moved forward side by side and as they did so the car behind them followed, rolling silently down the slope to keep pace with them.

I didn't stop to know more. I jerked at Catherine's arm and pulled her round. No words were needed between us. We began to run. And there, three yards behind us, lit full by the headlights, was Rance, who must have left the car before we arrived and had moved down the shadow of the hedge to come behind us.

"Get back, Barlow!" he cried and I saw a great stick in his hand go upwards and in the hard light he was like some ancient prophet full of wrath, his face twisted and lined, his gaunt arms seeming to fill the sky with the force and shape of angry power.

"Run! Keep running!" I shouted to Catherine, and releasing her hand I threw myself forward in a low tackle. I hit his knees with my right shoulder and we both went down in a long rolling fall. Then I was up and past him, seeing Catherine a few yards ahead of me on the road and hearing the others coming after me from behind.

We went down the road held by the light. I heard the car start up and come swiftly after us and our shadows danced and swung on the road ahead. And as we ran I was full of an angry disbelief. It couldn't be happening. It couldn't. How could they have traced me? And then, sweeping aside all that, a greater anger because of the girl at my side and the danger which she had to share with me.

The car was almost on us when I saw a break in the hedge to our left. I swung aside and pulled Catherine with me. She went through the gap first and as I followed she was three yards ahead and breaking a great swathe through the knee-high corn. I caught her up in the midde of the field and glancing round saw two figures moving into the path we had made.

I ran beside her, heading for a clump of trees on the far side of the field.

"We must separate," I panted. "When we reach the trees you go to the left and I'll keep to the right in the open. It's me they want, not you."

306

She made no answer, but when we reached the trees she swung right-handed with me and I had no time to argue with her. We raced through the trees and the ground was soft and damp underfoot and there was a sudden smell of wild garlic on the night air. The trees fell back to reveal a great spread of night sky and a long slope of meadow-land, sepia and grey in the starlight and broken with a mad confusion of grass-grown anthills and tall, archaic thistle growths. Away at the foot of the meadow gleamed the long snaking line of a river. Far to the right a few lights showed from the town we had left.

I knew then what it was to run without hope, to run without purpose, not knowing where to go or what to do, making of running itself a virtue. Savagely I remembered what Ross-Piper had said about having no side. Any cottage we turned into would give us shelter for a while, but explanations would be demanded and truth would come crawling into the open. If I wanted the help of the police, the protection of ordinary men and women, then I had to declare myself sooner or later. But no matter how helpless I was, I knew that it was better to go back to the houses, to the people of the small town and to find escape there rather than to stay out here and be cornered in some field where even a shout born of despair would shred away into the night air.

A fox barked away to our left. Catherine stumbled over an anthill and I caught and pulled her up. The two men came out of the trees and made down the slope after us. Rance was not with them. Neither of them was tall enough for that.

We came down to the river by a long row of willows and the ground under our feet was rough and pock-marked. The gloom suddenly broke and swirled with a crazy motion of dark shapes. Waves of sweet cattle odour filled my throat as a herd of young bullocks rose from their resting place and charged, kicking and snorting, out into the field.

"There's a bridge a little way up," Catherine said as we ran. "We must get into the town."

The banks of the river fell away steeply and the water swirled by, its surface marked with little swirls and eddies. A hundred yards higher up we hit the bridge, a rough wooden structure made for a cattle crossing. Our feet thundered on the boards, and then we were over and moving up the far bank. Almost at once it seemed I heard behind me the hollow stamp of other feet on the bridge.

I don't know how long it took to get back to the town. Half an hour, maybe more. Sometime while we were running I heard a church clock strike midnight, long, self-satisfied booms that echoed out across the fields. We stuck to the river for a while. I saw a rat swimming, a wavering V-line across the black surface. Then there was gravel under our feet, the draughtsman-like curves of steel tracks ahead of us, and suddenly a cube of light suspended in the sky. From inside the cube came the warm glint of polished handles. A man in shirt sleeves leaned with his back against a window reading a paper. A few yards beyond the signal-box was the level-crossing and the road to the town. As we took it I saw on the road beyond the river bridge the slow movement of a car crawling along with its headlights dipped. Away down the track were the dark shapes of the two men still jogging along after us.

As we passed the grey concrete face of the cinema, I caught Catherine's arm and pulled her down to a walk. If we ran now we might attract the attention of a policeman.

At the corner of the town square there came the flicker of headlights sweeping across the house-fronts. I glanced back. The car was coming up the road behind us.

We slipped round the corner into the square. The place was deserted. It could hardly be called a square, just a broadening of the road. There was that deadness about it peculiar to all country towns at this time of night. High up in the sky the gilt hands of the church clock marked the quarter after midnight. Running away from the church a row of old cottages hung their frowning brows over the pavement in heavy sleep. The unlit windows of the shops had a cold, remote look as though life had deserted them a hundred years before. The front of the hotel where we had dined showed no light except for a single bulb above the transom of the closed door. A cat moved out of a doorway and stalked across the square, ignoring us.

A car swept into the square and we were full in the headlights. I turned and ran with Catherine towards the other end of the square. As we reached the far pavement a door suddenly opened in a building to our immediate right.

A great rectangle of yellow light broke itself into strange geometrical shapes down a length of steps and in the frame of the doorway a man and woman were silhouetted sharply. I heard voices and laughter and then, above and beyond this, the sound of violins and accordions, a high market-pig squeal of vigorous music.

We halted at the foot of the yellow flood of light. From the doorside a poster flapped advertising an old-time dance. I looked back. Coming across the square were three men. They came slowly, unhurried, sure of themselves, sure of us. . . .

I would have pushed Catherine up the steps towards the dance-hall and turned back, but her hand clamped itself around my arm.

"Don't be a fool," she said urgently. "They can't touch us inside. At least we shall have time to think."

We went in, without paying, merging into the hall as though we had just been outside for fresh air. It was another world, a world of light, of music, of people and movement. The band was playing and the floor was untidy with people making up sets for a square dance.

Someone called to us to make up a set and we were on the floor, far away from the door.

The music died away, a figure in a red-black-and-white checked shirt moved to the microphone by the band and shouted something I couldn't catch. I stood in the made-up set with Catherine on my right, our hands touching lightly. She smiled and there was something about the smile which went through me in a spasm of anguish. A man by himself can take what comes. I wished bitterly that I had left her that morning.

The band broke into life. High above the music I heard the voice of the caller.

"Honour your partners! Honour your corners!"

As Catherine curtseyed to me I saw from the corner of my eye that far down the hall Rance had come through the doorway and was standing close to it against the wall. His eyes were going over the crowd searching for us. The caller began to sing, the violins and accordions squealed and the floor was a maze of coloured movement. Catherine and I became part of the movement.

> ". . . All join hands and form a ring
> Now forward to the centre and don't be slow
> Spread out wide and away we go
> Break and trail along that line
> Your lady in the lead and the gent behind . . ."

The last time I had square-danced was in Canada; an age ago, in the days when I had been free and confident and perhaps a little overpleased with myself for the progress I had been making in my work.

CHAPTER XII

THE hall was full of young people in gay dresses and coloured shirts, dancing as though their lives depended on it. And that was the wrong way about, because we were the only ones in danger of our lives. We'd come in looking hot and exhausted but this gave no one a moment's concern for all there were hot and exhausted. I went round and round with Catherine and the place was a maze of patterns and the air was hot and stuffy. And all the time Rance stood by the door.

The band squealed and clashed, the boards echoed to the stamp of feet and the voice of the caller sang hoarsely above it all.

> "*Post oak crook and an elbow hook*
> *The more you swing the better you look . . .*"

And Catherine looked wonderful. At this moment, more wonderful to me than ever. She smiled at me as we swung round together, and the touch of her hand on mine, the way her body moved, spirited and graceful, sent a thrill of longing through me. Just for a moment I could imagine that we were isolated from everything except our love and the pleasure of dancing together.

> "*. . . Big white horse and little red wagon*
> *Rear wheel's off and the axle draggin' . . .*"

Round and round we went and then over her shoulder I saw that Rance was still standing by the doorway, smoking, and watching us.

The dance finished and we sat down near the band. I gave Catherine a cigarette and lit one myself.

"We've got to get out of this place somehow."

"The dance finishes at one," she said. "I saw it on the poster as we came in."

"That means we've got about half an hour."

The floor began to fill for the next dance. The band started to play an old-fashioned waltz. We swung round and round and Catherine was in my arms. I leaned forward a little and my lips brushed her hair. I was going. As soon as I could leave her I was going out of the hall. It was the only way. Rance wanted me. He could have me so long as Catherine was left in safety.

As we passed close to the door I saw Rance clearly for the first time. He wasn't so tall as I had thought. He had a leanness which made him seem tall, and his face had, even in repose, an angry forcefulness. He looked like a man quietly and deeply obsessed by some disturbing idea which was like a physical hunger in him. The kind of look I'd seen in some priests and scholars. As he smoked he leaned on his stick and this tipped one shoulder down a bit and gave the whole of the top part of his body the stance and malevolence of some gargoyle. If there was one thing I didn't have to be told about him it was that he was a man without pity. He kept his eyes on us and he waited.

Catherine looked up into my face. Maybe at that moment some intuition told her what was in my mind.

"We'll find some way . . . I don't want you to go . . . either to them or back to prison." Her hand tightened on mine. "You're here with me," she said fiercely. "You're staying with me."

I pulled her closely to me so that she could not see my face.

The music changed and we found ourselves going round the hall doing the *Gay Gordons*. We passed close to Rance, but he looked at and through us as though we had no existence for him, nor would have until the right moment came. And on the wall above the door the hall clock marked the ten minutes to one.

When the *Gay Gordons* came to an end we found ourselves on the opposite side of the hall. We began to cross to our seats and were in the middle of the floor when the band started playing again. Before we knew it we were caught in a great ring of couples doing a barn dance. After the first few moments I lost Catherine, for in a barn dance the women move up and the men move back, changing their partners and working slowly round the great ring. This was the moment I had been waiting for. As she moved away from me her place was taken by a red-faced girl in glasses and I was caught up in the moving circle. We went round the hall gradually and I saw that Catherine would reach the door where Rance stood about eight partners ahead of me. When I got to the door I would break away from the dance and go through and face Rance and the others. . . . They would have their hands full dealing with me and have no time for Catherine.

I turned and swung and clapped my hands and the faces of my partners passed me in a haze. There was only movement and colour and the door drawing nearer each moment, and Rance leaning there and myself knowing that in a few moments

311

I would be with him . . . and there was a savage gladness in me at the thought.

I saw Catherine draw level with the door, saw her step sideways in the dance so that she was only a dozen feet from Rance. And he ignored her. His head turned a little my way as though he knew I were the one, as though he had already guessed what I meant to do. His head turned over his shoulder and he gave a little nod to someone behind him and out of sight. It happened then.

Every light in the hall went out as someone threw the main switch which must have been by the hall door. The band went on playing; there was a pandemonium of shouts and laughter and the shuffle of feet through the darkness. People blundered against me. I pushed them away and, possessed by an urgent fear, I tried to make my way forward. A pair of hands clutched at my arm and a girl giggled close to me. . . .

The lights went up suddenly and a great surge of laughter echoed up to the roof. It was a joke played by some dance-happy youth. . . . No one minded and the great circle still swung round. I'd lost my place in the dance and I stood a few feet from the door. Rance had gone. Looking round the ring of dancers to where Catherine should have been I saw that she, too, had gone. She had been only a few feet from Rance and ten seconds of darkness had been enough for him.

I ran through the doorway and down the steps into the night. Fifty yards back along the pavement a car was drawn up. Standing alongside it was Rance and with him another man. Between them they held Catherine by the arms. As I moved towards them the door was opened and Catherine was pushed in. The other man got in after her, but Rance stood by the side of the car and he turned and faced me as I ran up the pavement.

As I came up to him various things were registering in my mind. The car was my own, the one Ross-Piper had provided me with at Rye. They must have stolen it from the cottage while we were out. And moving across from the parking place now was another car which drew up behind mine. As I reached him, Rance said sharply, "If you start anything, it'll only bring the police. And, anyway, the girl will be gone."

He stood there, his mouth twisted in a sour smile, one knuckly hand bone white on the head of his stick as he leaned his weight on it. There was a grudging admiration in me for him. He'd taken the situation and made himself master of it. He'd worked more coolly and efficiently than I had.

Catherine was sitting in the back seat. I couldn't see clearly the man sitting beside her. For a moment our eyes met. She was scared, and her face showed it. But for an instant she smiled. I hated myself for dragging her into this.

"Let her out!" I swung round on Rance. "Let her out or I'll shout and bring the police here."

"Shout your head off, Barlow," he snapped. "You'll bring the police for yourself. We shouldn't wait—and the girl would go with us."

Rance said nothing more. He faced me and he waited, and then the man in the driving seat slid across and opened the front door and his head was cocked up at me a little.

"You'd better get in, chum. There ain't a thing you can do. It won't even help you to start runnin'—which is a Godsend because we've had enough for one evening."

It was Henry Daiken.

Rance raised his stick and tapped the side of the door and he might have been giving a signal to a dog to jump in.

"Get in, Barlow," he said.

Angrily, I shouted, "Let her out and then I'll get in. You don't want her."

"We want you both," said Rance slowly. "Get in. There's nothing you can do, and you know it."

He was right. As long as they had Catherine I was helpless. I got in alongside Daiken. Rance closed the door on me and then he slid into the back seat so that Catherine was between him and the other man.

The car drove off and I saw that the one behind was following us.

I sat there beside Henry Daiken and he whistled gently to himself as he drove. He went out through the town and on to a main road which I didn't know. I watched the lights wash across the faces of the cottages and the road shadowed like sealskin and inside me there was a great apprehension. . . .

Daiken after a while said, "You ain't said good evening to all your old friends, yet." His face turned towards me, screwed up, the chin and nose working, and he nodded backwards.

I half turned. Beside Catherine there was the stir of a pale face in the shadows and the glint of light on the clips of fountain pens and pencils in a breast pocket. There was no mistaking who it was.

I said bitterly, "You should be in Ireland, Fisher."

His voice came out of the darkness, low and a little sad, a sound like the passing of a rough hand over coarse material. "I'm sorry, Mr. B. But this wasn't any of my choosing. This isn't my line of country at all. No, Mr. B., I don't like it but I had no option. I told you what they were like in my parish."

He sounded genuine and I believed he was.

Daiken said, "Gypo could never have given you my address. He don't know it. So when we needed an extra man we knew where to look. Don't you worry, Fisher boy, you can go to Ireland when this is over."

He began to whistle "In Dublin's Fair City where Girls are so Pretty," and suddenly swung off the main road down a side lane.

I said, "How did you know I was out here?"

Nobody answered. We sat there in silence bumping down the side road and then suddenly Rance began to laugh to himself. It was a queer, half-choking sound.

I swung round and said, "What the hell's so funny?"

He stopped then and he leaned forward until his chin was resting on the crook of the stick between his legs and his face a few inches from mine.

"Life, Barlow," he said. "Life, that's the funny thing. This stinking life where all the wrong things are important. 'No, Mr. B., I don't like it but I had no option'." For a moment his voice had the sad whine that belonged to Fisher, and then it changed and was his own, harsh, unwilling as though he had to drag the words from himself. "Of course he doesn't like it. Perhaps none of us do. But each in his own way has no option. As for your address, Barlow—you told us where it was. You went into *La Boutade* and were recognized. In the pocket of your raincoat, like a damn fool, you leave a third-class return ticket to Blackthorn station. Satisfied?"

I turned back, swearing to myself. A small thing, and I should have thought of it. All they had had to do was to send a man to the station ahead of me. As I had come out to be greeted by Catherine he must have been around. Dimly I seemed to remember that there had been another car following along the road behind us for a while. A slip of cardboard in my pocket and now not only me, but Catherine was caught up in this dark movement through the night.

Without turning I said, "You can't possibly want to do her any harm. Why can't you let her go? You've got me. Isn't that enough?"

"No, it isn't, Barlow. If you'd wanted it that way, you should have kept it that way. Once you ask other people for help—then they share the risks with you."

"It's common sense, chum," said Daiken.

"Don't bother with them, Peter," said Catherine.

I turned to her and she gave me a smile.

"That's right, miss," said Daiken cheerfully.

We drove for another ten minutes and then the car swung off on to a farm track, moving down between tall hedges. Now and again the ditch growths swished against the sides and the car lurched and jolted. In the mirror I saw the other car following.

Our car stopped. Three yards ahead a field gate shone brightly in the headlights.

"All change!" said Daiken cheerfully.

"Right, Fisher," said Rance.

Fisher got out and opened the gate and our car went through and stopped a few yards inside the field. For a moment before the headlights went off I saw the whole scene clearly. We were at the top of a field slope, smooth green meadow that dipped sharply downwards. At the bottom of the slope was the sharp line of a bank and beyond it a wide stretch of river, a black, oily smear lined on the far side by tall poplars, dusty in the headlights.

Daiken got out and came round to my door. He opened it and motioned me out and I saw that he was holding a revolver.

None of them spoke and it was clear that each knew what to do, the whole thing long planned. Rance, a great, stooping, monkish figure brought Catherine out of the back and his hand never left its grasp on her arm until she was sitting in the front next to the driving seat. He flicked the handle lock on her door and slammed it tight. She raised her face to me . . . the face of a woman to whom I had brought love, and now this. . . .

Fisher shuffled around like a shabby mole. There seemed no air to breathe. A great moth blundered into the front of the car and the smack of its body against the glass was sharp and vicious. Fisher took a bottle of whisky and two glasses from the back of the car. He spilt whisky over the driving seat, then corked the bottle and tossed it in at Catherine's feet. He threw the two glasses after it and one of them hit the bottle and smashed. Behind us in the lane the other car waited and the driver was only a blur, hunched over the wheel, apparently unconcerned, waiting patiently to drive them all away when it should be done.

"Round the other side." Rance jabbed my back with the revolver. He and Daiken now flanked me, crowding in, their eyes on me. I didn't have to be told what they wanted me to do. I would go round to the driving seat and I would sit behind the wheel. Maybe before I slid in, the stick or the revolver would

315

crash down upon my head. I'd slump behind the wheel, unknowing, and Catherine alive and knowing all at my side, and then Daiken would mount the running board, release the brake and ride down with us, hand on the wheel until the car was a few yards from the bank. . . . And I would go over, unknowing . . . but Catherine would know.

"You filthy swine!" I shouted. "You can't do this. Let her out."

My voice echoed against the far poplars. They crowded me and made me move, the revolver hard against my side, the stick half-poised. I held myself in check. The moment had not come yet.

I looked at Fisher. "You can't stand by and let them do this to her," I said. "She's done nothing."

He mumbled, not words but a dry sound in the night, and I knew he was as helpless as I was. And I knew, too, that as much as I had done this thing to Catherine, so I had done it to him. I had dragged them both in. . . . Dragged them in because I had wanted justice for myself, and I thought then of Ross-Piper and his advice to give the whole thing up.

They had me round to the driving side now; Fisher, his sad spaniel eyes turned from me . . . maybe longing for the thing to be over, for time to sweep on and help him forget; Daiken, his face working like an old man having trouble with his false teeth, a face with so much written on it that nothing could be read; and Rance, full of anger and bitterness and some private darkness of the spirit. . . . Fifty yards away the steep bank and the drop to the deep river, and all around us the hot summer night rested heavily on the smooth meadows. The whole sleeping world around us . . . and when it woke we would have become another of the stupid tragedies to paragraph the breakfast silence and the morning ride to work . . . a man and girl, a car drawn up in a field after a dance, the whisky, the embrace, and then the accident of a brake lever released as they kissed. The rushing, panic-filled last moments blurred by whisky and love . . . an accident, and even when it became known, if it did, that I was Barlow, still an accident.

We stood there and the night and the horror held us all.

Then Rance said gratingly, "Turn round."

I turned and through the open door of the car I saw Catherine. Behind me the stick was being raised and I knew that this was the moment. Catherine was looking up at me. Suddenly I called fiercely to her, "Let the brake off!"

I turned and Daiken was behind me, the revolver raised. I

smashed my fist into his distorted face and as Rance hit out at me with the stick I jumped sideways. The blow caught me on the shoulder but I was away from them. I saw Catherine reaching out towards the brake handle on my side. For a few seconds my body hid her from the view of the others. She jerked the brake off and the car began to roll forward. Rance came at me, but I dodged aside.

I heard a shout behind me, and then I saw the car rolling down the meadow slope and the flash of the swinging door. Catherine was still inside. I went after it, but I had no hope of catching it. The door swung forward and back and then forward again. There was the movement of an arm, and I knew that she was fighting to get across, to be free of the door. . . . The car raced silently towards the black strip of water, and then, when it was less than four yards away, I saw her jump out of the door. She fell and rolled down the slope. The car reached the bank, seemed to rear like a frightened horse, and a red tail-lamp winked for a moment against the far stars. A great spout of water rose as the car hit the river and the spray of cascading drops swept against my face as I raced for her. She was on her knees a foot from the bank, struggling to rise.

I caught her up and we began to run. I could hear her fighting for breath where she had been winded by the fall.

I looked back. Black against the pale star-littered sky were the three shapes as they came down the meadow slope. A frieze full of silent malevolence.

"We must get across the river. . . ."

We slid down the bank and the water came up around our ankles and the mud sucked at us. Catherine threw herself out and the splash made a great curving sheet of silver wing. I went after her.

We were fifteen yards out when the men reached the bank. They halted and I saw Daiken's arm go up with the revolver. But Rance caught at him, and I heard the word "Fool!" rasp across the water. Then slowly the night eased itself back into it old shell, a soft, balmy summer night with the hawking flash of bats above the water, a thick hedge of reeds that rustled like heavy silk as we grasped at them and pulled ourselves up, and the smell of rotten leaves as our feet plugged through mud.

We were as wet and slimy as a couple of water-rats. We half ran, half jogged and I kept my hand on Catherine's arm. Once when she stumbled I held her, swung her round to me and our lips met. She clung to me and I felt her body trembling. I knew then, after the horror of the past hours, what it was to love.

CHAPTER XIII

WE walked into the kitchen just before seven o'clock looking like a couple of tramps.

Catherine's aunt eyed us severely. "Where on earth have you been? Where's your car? I didn't hear it."

"At the bottom of the river," Catherine replied.

"And we're lucky not to be in it," I added.

She was silent for a moment and then said quietly, "You'd better go up and bath and change while I get some breakfast."

I stayed in the kitchen while Catherine bathed first. I told Mrs. Lovell all that had happened and what I now intended to do. I'd discussed this with Catherine on the way back. I was going to telephone Ross-Piper and get him to fix me up a room in London. I would go up that morning. I had to get away from the cottage and from Catherine. The longer she stayed with me the more dangerous it became for her. I didn't want her to stay at the cottage either, and she had agreed to come on the train with me to London and then go and stay with some friends of hers in Kent. We should part at Paddington Station.

Mrs. Lovell was busy cooking while I talked, but when I had finished she came to the kitchen table.

"You mean to go on with this business?"

"I have to now."

"Has Catherine tried to persuade you to give up?"

"No."

I knew what was in her mind. If I went on I was going straight into danger. I might get killed or find myself back in prison. I still had the chance to clear out of the country—and there wasn't any doubt that Catherine would join me.

"I see. . . ." She hesitated for a moment. Then, turning back to her cooking, she said over her shoulder, "Well, in that case you'd better be properly equipped. When you go up to bath you'll find an old chocolate box at the back of the airing cupboard. There's an automatic revolver and some ammunition in it. Take it. My husband bought it years ago when he first went to Turkey. I could never think why he felt he would need it more there than in England."

When I went up to bath I took the morning paper with me. I lay soaking and reading. I was back in the news again. My photo-

318

graph had been shown on television. There was a certain grim amusement in reading the list of places where I had been reported. There were half a dozen districts in London and about nine provincial towns as far apart as Plymouth and Newcastle-on-Tyne. Also the paper carried a symposium on the question of my guilt or innocence of the murder of Hansford. Ross-Piper's name was amongst others. His comment was brief—"Barlow is innocent and has a right to be free. Good luck to him wherever he is." The eminent brain surgeon they called him, and there was a paragraph about his establishment in Hertfordshire. There was a line or two from my old boss—"He'll be hard to catch. Personally I think he's out of England by now." A celebrated author, a woman columnist, an Italian actress and a Socialist member of Parliament all had their little say. The woman columnist spoke of a meeting with me at a cocktail party four years before which I thought was strange since I had been in Canada at the time up to my neck in snow and mud.

As I dressed I made my plans. It seemed obvious to me that *La Boutade* was the centre of things. But no matter whether it was Drysdale, Giulio Latti or Rance who directed operations, I could see no future in a frontal attack. More and more I was becoming convinced that the man I wanted to talk to was the artist, Sava. He had known Hansford in Germany and was a friend of Giulio Latti's. Somehow I had to find him.

Before we left the cottage Catherine telephoned Ross-Piper's flat for me. Ross-Piper was out of town on a consultation and would not be back until that evening, but Drew promised to get a room for me. He knew his way around and would understand the kind of place I wanted. He told Catherine to telephone him again when we reached Paddington and he would let her know where the room was.

"He didn't sound very friendly," Catherine said.

"I know. He worships Ross-Piper and he's afraid I may get him into trouble. He's absolutely right to feel like that. My name may mean trouble to anyone helping me. You know that."

"I don't mind trouble."

I knew she meant it, too. But now I had my teeth into something and I had to handle it alone.

Mrs. Lovell drove us to Blackthorn station in her car and we caught a small branch train that would take us to Princes Risborough, where we would change for the main London train.

We had an end compartment to ourselves. The first thing that met my eyes after I'd swung our two suitcases on to the rack was a view of the Isle of Wight. Catherine made a far prettier picture.

She sat by my side in a grey suit with a touch of white lace at the throat and the smallest bit of white nonsense on her head for a hat. She looked cool, lovely and altogether too precious to lose and I wondered if I was a fool even to be taking the risk. I could cut free now and go away with her. If she'd asked me to do that then, I think I would have agreed. But she didn't, and I knew why. She understood the stubborn spirit that was in me. The only thing she was likely to ask was to be allowed to stay with me and share whatever came. But I'd already given my answer to that.

I sat there with her hand in mine, watching the countryside go slowly by, and we didn't talk much. We were both too full of thoughts and conscious of the moment soon to come when we would part.

The train clacked its way along, in no particular hurry now that it was supported by the State, through a rich green countryside, fat and growing from a wet July. We stopped at a little station with its name spelt out in white stones across a bank of blue lobelia and I heard the rattle of milk churns being swung aboard the goods van.

We were not long out of the station when a man came along the corridor outside our compartment. He stopped with his back to us. I felt there was something vaguely familiar about him. Then he turned and looked in at us. It was Colonel Drysdale.

My hand left Catherine's and was in my pocket grasping the revolver. But I kept it there. Drysdale stood outside looking at me and there was an anxious, nervous smile on his face and a quick, occasional tremble to his lips. He wore a green pork-pie hat and a shabby tweed suit.

I said to Catherine, "That's Drysdale out there."

Her head turned and we were both looking at Drysdale. He kept his eyes on us, but his body moved in a kind of embarrassed shuffle.

"He looks harmless enough," said Catherine. "Anyway, they wouldn't try anything on the train. There are plenty of people in the other compartments."

"I'm not trusting him or anybody."

At that moment Drysdale put down his hand and slid the compartment door over.

"Hullo, old boy," he said, and the friendliness in his voice was strained and false. "Mind if I come in?" He slid the door shut and then sat down. He bobbed his head at Catherine and said with a touch of his hand to his hat, "Good morning, Miss Swinton."

I said sharply, "Sit where you are, Drysdale, and don't try anything funny." Just for a moment I pulled the revolver from my pocket enough for him to see it.

"Good Lord, old boy, you won't need that."

I couldn't tell whether his surprise was genuine or not. In fact I couldn't tell anything about him.

"What do you want?" I snapped.

"Well, as a matter of fact, old chap. . . ." He broke off, ran a finger around the inside of his collar, and then went on hesitantly, "Well, it's damned difficult. . . . Don't quite know how to put it without giving the wrong impression. . . . Mind if I smoke?"

His hand was going to his pocket when Catherine said, "You'd better have one of these." She opened her bag and held out her case. He took one and she snapped her lighter for him.

"Very kind of you. . . ."

"Come to the point," I said brusquely, "and don't keep up this nervous old-boy act. You ought to know that doesn't wash with me now."

"I can't help being a bit nervous. . . . Matter of fact, if things weren't as they are I wouldn't dream of doing this. Shows what you can come to when the shoe pinches. . . ."

"Listen, Drysdale," I said impatiently, "it's hard for me to sit here and talk to you. After what you fixed up for me at Kew, and what you were prepared to have happen to Miss Swinton last night, it's all I can do to hold myself back from beating you into a pulp and throwing you off this train."

He looked at me then with so much astonishment that I didn't know what to make of him. Either I had him wrong or he was deeper than any man I'd ever met before. He sat there lost and perplexed. The morning sunlight was full on his worn old whisky face, showing up the slight sag under the eyes. All the vigorous, terrier stance of his body was gone.

"I don't know what you're talking about," he said.

"Yes, you do. You know who I am, don't you?"

"But of course. That's why I'm here, old boy. You're Barlow. It came to me the moment you left my house."

"It came to you a damned sight earlier than that. Early enough for you to have two men waiting for me outside. I suppose you'll say you weren't down here yesterday either?"

"Well, yes, I was. But I don't know anything about any two men. Honest, old chap, you're talking in circles. Perhaps I'd better put my cards on the table . . . though it isn't very easy in front of Miss Swinton."

"Don't mind me," said Catherine.

Drysdale was silent for a while. I could almost see the effort he was making, or pretending to make, to pull himself together and put over what he had to say. I'd seen him do it once before when he had begun to talk about the German forgery affair. This time it looked just as genuine.

"It's like this, Barlow," he began, and the hesitant voice began to firm up and find some of its old authority, "a few minutes after you walked out of my house I realized who you must be. But I was too late to get after you."

"Somebody else was doing that!"

"Well, as far as I was concerned, I wanted to see you again very much. The next morning I telephoned the *Daily Record*. They confirmed they had no reporter called Allen. Then I got on to Major Rawlings at the War Office. I told him that I'd had someone from the press asking me about Hansford's court-martial and the German counterfeiting business. I wanted his clearance. It didn't take me long to get from him that Miss Swinton here had been to see him, and he very obligingly gave me her address. I put two and two together and took a chance that you might be connected with her, and I came down here yesterday by car. I saw you leave the cottage in the afternoon. You'll understand that I wanted to see you alone, Barlow. So I waited around, but you never came back. Slept in the car all night, and then this morning I spotted you going off to the station. I didn't want to scare you off, so I drove along to the next station and got on the train as it came in. . . ." He paused momentarily and then sighed. "Well, I'm glad that's off my chest. You understand, of course, why I did it."

"That's just what I don't understand. Why did you do it?" I was watching him closely as I spoke.

"But surely you understand, old chap?" It was back, the old bonhomie and nervousness. "The money . . . I'm hard up, you know that. And you're Barlow. I've only got to pull the communication cord and . . . well, dash it, do I need explain more?"

"I don't think so," said Catherine before I could speak. "If Peter doesn't buy you off, you'll go to the police."

"Reluctantly, yes. And believe me, I don't like it, old man, any more than you. But I really am stuck for cash. Wouldn't dream of doing it otherwise. The Lord knows what the chaps at the club would say. . . ." There was a pathetic, weary note in his voice as he finished.

Curtly I said, "How much?"

322

Rather diffidently he said, "A hundred and fifty pounds." And then added, "Notes, of course. No cheques."

It was some time before I answered him. The train rattled over a bridge and I caught the flash of water and the tall white-ribbed side of a mill-house bright in the sun. I looked at Catherine and then at Drysdale, and no man was more uncertain than I at that moment.

Then I said, "You must hate yourself for doing this."

He didn't answer. He just squirmed.

At my side Catherine said softly, "Peter . . . don't."

But I knew what I was doing now. "All right, Drysdale," I said. "I'll pay you a hundred and fifty. I've got it in notes in my suit-case on the rack, but I'll save you from earning it the way you meant. You can get it another way."

"How?"

"By selling me some information."

"Glad to, old boy." He was reviving.

"Do you know a restaurant called *La Boutade* in Greek Street?"

" 'Fraid not. Can't afford to eat in that kind of place."

"Well the wall panels are decorated with drawings, allegorical drawings . . . industry, medicine, war, drama, and so on. One of them stands for Liberation. . . ." I watched him closely as I went on explaining the scene and how the artist had portrayed Hansford moving towards the group of prisoners. His eyes never left me. "There are mountains in the background and American troops. At a guess I would say the scene comes from——"

"Redl Zipfcave?"

"Yes. And I'm naturally interested in the man who drew the scene because he must have known Hansford. Sava's his name, and faces live in his mind. Hansford's did. It lives in my mind, too, because somewhere there's a man who murdered him and would have let me hang for it. I want to know all about Sava."

The train blew for a crossing. Drysdale smiled. It was a warm, satisfied smile, and it might have meant anything. He rubbed his hands together, and I noticed that the nails were chalky and brittle.

"Oh, I know Sava," he said eagerly. "I know a lot about him. He's a Hungarian Jew. The place must be Redl Zipfcave. He was there. He's an artist, but, more than that, he was a very fine engraver. That's why the Germans made him work for them. And what is more, he and Hansford were great friends. I see

323

what you're driving at, old man. Jolly decent of you to put it this way, too."

"Where's Sava now?" I asked.

"Yes, I see what you mean." He was following his own line of thought still. "You think Hansford started a forgery business over here. . . . And he could have done. But he'd need someone else like Sava for new plates and new designs——"

"Do you know where Sava is now?" I asked sharply.

He dropped his cigarette end on the floor and crushed it with the toe of a well-polished but well-worn brown shoe.

"I'm not sure. Two years ago I heard from him at Christmas. He sent me a small water-colour he'd done of Snowdon. He's in Wales somewhere. I didn't keep his letter, but so far as I remember it was near a place called Capel Curig." He cocked an eye at me. "Do you know it?"

"It's near Snowdon. I used to climb around there with my father. What kind of a man is Sava?"

"I only saw a little of him. He was forced into that forgery business by the Germans. He was a scruffy, scraggy type . . . full of gratitude to me and Hansford. . . . He used to start crying at the drop of a hat. Death warmed up. He went through a lot, poor devil. About my age. . . ."

I stood up and reached for my case, dropping it down on to the seat opposite. I opened it and hauled out my bundle of notes. As I counted a hundred and fifty I didn't look at him. I wanted him to be exactly as he appeared, a broken-down officer so hard up that he had to do this for money. I could take him that way. Even like him. But the dark suspicion had already come into my mind that I wasn't half so shrewd as I had imagined. Drysdale might have played me exactly as he had planned, as he and the others with him had planned. Maybe they wanted me in Wales. Sava might not be there, but I would . . . and there were wide-open spaces and no onlookers but the mountain sheep and the ravens.

I handed the wad of notes over to him and he stuffed them in his pocket without looking at them. The train was just pulling into Princes Risborough and we all had to change.

Drysdale stood up, and for a while the old spring and tautness was back. Maybe the money in his pocket was like fresh blood in his veins . . . better than a dozen tots of whisky. He slid the door back. "I'll leave you here. I'll have to get a train back to pick up my car. And as for the money, old man . . . I'm glad to have been able to help. One day the horses will run right and I'll pay you back. Good luck. Good day, Miss

Swinton." He flicked his hat and was gone down the corridor.

I looked at Catherine and she smiled at me. I didn't know whether to grin or frown.

"What the hell do you make of him?" I asked.

She laughed. "I like him and I believe him. And I'm sorry for him. I hope the horses do run right."

"Well, I'm damned if I know. I believe he wants me to go to Wales, and I'll bet Sava's nowhere near the place."

"Of course we must go to Wales, and today."

"We? You're for Kent, my girl."

"Wales," she said stubbornly.

"Kent," I said equally stubbornly.

CHAPTER XIV

THE argument continued nearly all the way to London. But there was nothing I could do. Catherine's mind was made up. She was coming to Wales with me. It was no good telling her that I didn't want her, that it was dangerous . . . her mind was made up. I even tried getting angry with her, but it was no good.

"I'm coming," she said stubbornly. "And don't try to give me the slip at Paddington. I should just go to Capel Curig on my own."

I didn't try to give her the slip then. But as an idea I pigeon-holed it for the future.

I telephoned Drew myself from the station and told him that I wouldn't want a room in London as I was going to Wales.

"Wales?" he queried. "What on earth for?"

"To find an artist called Sava. He lives somewhere near Capel Curig."

I heard him sigh at the other end of the line. I think he was getting pretty fed up with me. "Tell Ross-Piper when he gets back tonight that I'll get in touch with him if I find anything. And don't worry, Drew."

"Yes, sir." There was the gloomiest note in his voice.

Catherine arranged the hiring of a car and we started after lunch.

It was dark when we got to Capel Curig and at the first two hotels there were no rooms. It was July and the holiday season. We were lucky at the third—the Bryn Tyrch Hotel. With a certain amount of Welsh reluctance they provided us with a late meal. As there was nothing we could do that night we spent the hour before bed having a leisurely brandy with our coffee. For the first time that day I relaxed. As a boy I'd often spent holidays in the Snowdon district with my father, and already the smell and feel of the place was closing around me. I sat there, watching Catherine leaning back in her chair and thought how good it would have been if we were just two ordinary holiday people . . . imagining that when tomorrow dawned we should put on thick boots, stuff a rucksack with a change of socks and two unappetising sandwich lunches and go off together.

When we went upstairs she came into my room to say good

night. I stood by the window with my arm around her. Beyond the road was a low water-meadow and a glimpse of the Capel lake with dark sedges like a smudge of smoke around its shores. There was a moon behind the hotel somewhere and the country lay very still, the long valley of the Nant y Gwrhyd held peacefully in the cradle of the dark hill shapes. Somewhere away up to the right was Tryfan, the Milestone Buttress and the great cliffs of Pen yr Oleu Wen . . . places my father had loved. All that was a long time ago. He was dead, and Hansford had hastened his death, and Hansford's death had caught me up in a dark tangle which was still close about me, from which I might never be free. . . . My arm tightened about Catherine and her face was turned up to me. I kissed her, gently at first. Then with the thought chasing into my mind that everything I did included her, and that the passion in me for truth might destroy her as well as me, the kiss became a hungry fierceness between us. The closer we were the more danger we held for one another. And at that moment there was born in me a ruthless conviction that our survival depended on my being alone. I hadn't been able to stop her coming to Wales with me, but every step I took now had to be made alone. I could risk myself, had to risk myself, but Catherine had to be kept apart from it all.

*　　　*　　　*

I found where Sava lived more easily than I could have hoped. It was a lovely morning with high white balls of cloud rolling across the blue. A warm wind was coming in from the west, just strong enough to set the trees about the river shaking and tossing. Our waiter at breakfast said it might turn to rain later in the afternoon.

As we walked up to the village post office where the road divided for Bangor and Llanberis the sun was warm on our backs. Great cloud shadows slid across the long flanks of Moel Siabod and the air was full of the sound of calling sheep and the hurrying river. It was Catherine's idea that we should inquire for Sava at the village post office. She waited outside while I went in.

The woman inside told me all I wanted to know. Sava lived near Beddgelert. The house was just off the main road close to Lake Dinas, and its name was High Firs. Sava was not married and he lived alone and his real name was Kostavitch. Sava was how he signed his paintings.

But when I got outside with Catherine and she looked at me

inquiringly, I just shook my head. From this point I was going to work on my own. And, as though the Fates wished to demonstrate my wisdom, a small black saloon car came slowly up the road at this moment and turned down by the post office. It was going so slowly that I thought it was going to pull up, but when it was a few yards away it accelerated. As it went by I saw that the man driving it was Colonel Drysdale. He did not seem to have seen me. Catherine's back was to the car and I said nothing to her.

We walked back to the hotel and we got the car out. I had to keep up a pretence with Catherine until I could shake her off. We drove down to Bettws-y-Coed and I went into the post office there. But I asked no questions and contented myself with buying a packet of cigarettes. By twelve o'clock we were in Llanberis and I had pretended to ask at four or five post offices for Sava and each time, so far as Catherine was concerned, without success. And now, judging that I had confused the source of my information enough, I decided to abandon her. I didn't like doing it, and I knew that although she would understand my purpose she would also be furious. But it was the only thing to do. I had no doubt in my mind that the moment I went to Sava I would find a reception committee waiting. It was an interview I wished to carry out alone.

We went into a pub for a drink and sandwiches. I was hardly inside before I said to her:

"Damn it, I've left my cigarettes in the car."

But it didn't work. She pulled a packet from her bag and I had to sit there and smoke and drink and try to kill the impatience which was rising in me. I was worried, too, that she would sense what was going on in my mind. She was no fool and might well be aware of my intention to give her the slip.

We sat there with the bar to ourselves, talking, and my impatience to get away was like an itch in me. I know that at one time, in answer to some question she put, I found myself telling her of my adventures while travelling across France as an escaped P.o.W.

"That's how I came to know Ross-Piper," I said. "His son Tom was with me. Afterwards, when I was back home, I went to tell him how Tom had died. . . ."

Telling her about it made it seem even longer ago, a life far in the past and not easily related to the Peter Barlow I was at this moment. Secretly I'd always reproached myself for Tom's death. The old emotion reviving gave this moment a poignancy which made me more certain than ever that I must keep Catherine out of trouble. Tom, another man and myself had got as far as Cahors in the Dordogne, where we had been given the name of a resistance man to contact for the next leg of our journey—and also the information that he might not be too reliable. I decided that we had no choice but to try him. We went down to the town from our hiding-place in the hills above the river Lot and walked straight into a trap. Tom was killed, but the other man and I got away. When I had told Ross-Piper that I blamed myself for Tom's death, the old man's eyes had blazed with anger in his grief-drawn face. "Don't ever say that to me again! Never!" And I never had. And after that he had always spoken of Tom as though he were still alive, but somewhere far distant.

"Of course you couldn't blame yourself," said Catherine, and for a moment her hand was on mine. What she didn't know was that, right or wrong, you can blame yourself, and that when two people were as close as she and I were it became even harder to avoid the moments which might carry misfortune.

I got up and said I was going into the wash-room. A few seconds later and I was outside. I let the car move down the slope of the road for fifty yards before I started the engine. Then I was away driving through the town and the great scars of the slate quarries were black in the sun across the lake on my left. I was running away from her and I knew it was the right thing to do. If things went wrong I would go on running and never come back.

I drove up the valley towards Pen-y-pas and Snowdon came up on my right in a great shoulder of green, grey and purple and with the smallest tonsure of cloud ringing its peak. All the way down to Beddgelert I was trying to work out how Sava should be approached. If he were entirely innocent and uncon-nected with this affair there would be no danger for me. But I had a strong feeling that Sava was the bait in a trap being set for me.

I went down towards Beddgelert, past the grey crags, the jade-green spills of lakes, the boggy hillfoots and the steep patches of woods. I found the house easily enough. It was some miles short of Beddgelert, facing across the main road to Lyn Dinas. From the road I couldn't see much of it through the trees. It was three floors high, built of stone and with a dark slate roof, and it sat ugly and awkward in a patch of fir and oak trees, with a long curve of yellow gravel drive going up to it. It wasn't only an ugly house; it seemed surly, hunched with its back against the steep hillside, its windows glowering out at the lake.

I drove a mile past it and then parked the car in a field entrance. Then, climbing up the hill, I began to work my way back to it across country. I went up through an oak wood, then over a couple of steep hill fields, and finally through a young fir plantation and out on to a stretch of bare mountainside. Far below on the right I could just see the shimmer of the lake between the trees. A buzzard came low down-wind to look at me and then went away across the valley in lazily mounting spirals.

I found a place at last where the hill thrust a bare, rocky shoulder out above the trees, and I could look down on the house. I was hidden by a bulwark of grey, yellow lichened rock on one side and a thick screen of gorse bushes on the other. Between myself and the house was a steep drop dark with stunted oaks, and then an open break covered with rising young bracken that sloped down to a narrow fringe of tall red pines. Through the pines I could see part of the house and the drive. Somewhere away to my left I could hear the brawling of a stream and across the valley there was the slow mite-movement of sheep on the high pastures.

I watched the house for an hour, and there was no sign of life from it. After a while I changed my position, moving farther round and dropping a little lower, but I did it slowly, using all the cover I could. Standing well back from the blank windows of the house, a dozen men could have been inside watching the hill slope. I wanted to see but not be seen. From my new position I now had part of the drive in view. Backed up against the hill and separated from the house by a wide courtyard was a smaller, lower building which I thought might be a garage or a studio. All I could see was the roof and one side pierced by a wide window.

I lay in the cover of some bushes and overhead grey clouds began to thicken and drop lower, threatening rain. For a time I debated an open approach. I had a revolver. I could walk boldly to the door of the house. I could—but there was no knowing whether I would ever reach it. These men were not only ruthless, but showing something of desperation. One shot from a window could drop me as I walked, and that was all they needed. Looking down at the yellow drive, I seemed to see myself crumpled there. I didn't like the picture at all. I preferred to be the centre piece of a brighter composition.

The rain began to fall, heralding a typical Welsh change of weather. It was a soft, gentle rain killing the wind. I lay there with the water beading my clothes and down below was the house. Dead and waiting. Now and again I heard a car go by on the main road.

*   *   *

I went down. It was raining harder now and the light was getting bad, which was a help to me. I moved farther around the hillside until I was directly behind the house and above the small building that backed the open courtyard. Here I found the stream whose noise I had heard all the afternoon. It channelled down a mossy, boulder-hung chute about four feet deep. There was little more than six inches of water in it. I dropped down into the gully and began to work my way down its course. The stream left its gully at the foot of the hill about twelve feet from the side of the garage building. Here it moved for a while between two lawns and then disappeared into the tall, dark mouth of a culvert which, I guessed, carried it out of the garden and under the main road to the lake. From the foot of the gully I should be without cover. But twelve feet away was the side of the garage which would hide me from the house.

It took me half an hour to get down the gully. At the bottom the stream cascaded into a little pool. I stood there pressed against the green, slimy rocks and a few feet away was the side of the garage building and a long run of window. Across the way the windows of the house covered the courtyard.

I had no choice of moment for crossing the open space. I counted ten, and then I was out of the cover of the rock and sprinting for the side of the window.

I stood there and waited. Nothing happened.

I moved along to the window and cautiously looked in. It was a small room full of odds and ends, three or four deck-chairs, a couple of wooden crates, one of those old-fashioned wire-frame dummies on which women used to fit dresses, a bicycle and a set of wooden apple storing racks. In the far wall was a door slightly ajar.

I tried the window. It was an old-fashioned affair and unfastened. I got my fingers under the lower pane and began to raise it. It went up without noise.

I hauled myself over the sill and dropped quietly into the room, and as I stood there I took out my revolver. There was no sound from the other room.

I crossed to the door, which was open a little way towards me. I was looking into a studio, a large airy room with a great slope of north lights and a long run of window facing away from the house. There was a long table with artist's materials scattered

331

over it. Close by was an easel, and stacks of canvases were leant against the wall. On the floor were piles of magazines, a trunk, a few vases and bowls. I pulled the door open more and the room widened out before me, bringing into view a stuffed monkey sitting on a branch fixed to the wall, a collection of fishing-rods standing in a brown earthenware tub, a book-case with the books all over the place and another easel with a charcoal sketch of a landscape blocked out on it. Nearer me, almost in the centre of the room was a low, flat-topped desk with a man sitting at it, leaning forward with his face resting on one arm as though he had fallen asleep.

I walked up to him, my revolver ready, and he didn't move. And I didn't expect him to move. Death has its own look, and I'd seen it too many times not to be able to recognize it even from the back.

I didn't touch him. I went round the desk and faced him. I knew then that one thing I was never going to do was to talk to Mr. Kostavitch. "A scruffy, scraggy type. . . . Death warmed up. . . ." I remembered Drysdale's words. This was Sava. A thin, scraggy-looking man in a worn navy-blue suit, the pale skin of his scalp showing through his sparse hair. He sat there with his face on his arm turned a little towards me, and it was a face which even in death had gained no tranquillity. He looked worried, nervous and afraid . . . the only positive expression was an angry, stiff twist of the mouth. Somehow that look filled me with compassion. It was written all over him, the face of a man who all his life had found himself holding the dirty end of the stick. There was no room in me for disappointment because his death might make things harder for me. . . . I was just sorry for him for what I guessed life had done for him.

There was a glass on the desk with a trace of water in it, and close to it a small bottle holding three or four white tablets. I leaned forward and smelt the glass. It was an unpleasant smell. I must have touched the desk, for he slipped a little awkwardly in his seat and his face fell from his arm. Underneath his hand I saw three or four sheets of closely written paper. I went round behind him and looked over his shoulder. I couldn't read what he had written. At a guess I thought the language was Hungarian, his native tongue, and that made things more certain for me. I touched his face. It was still slightly warm, so that it could not have been long ago that he had killed himself . . . maybe even while I was deciding to come down the stream gully. A man kills himself because things become too much for him . . . the sheets of writing I meant to take with me. Although

Sava was dead he might well still be able to speak to me.

And then I noticed something very odd. The fingers of his right hand on the desk were stained and marked with colours . . . red, green and black, and the stuff on them had smeared the desk blotter and showed clearly in his prints on the glass. Down the side of his shoulder, too, was a long wet streak of yellow, like a squirt from a toothpaste tube. I touched it and smelt it. It was printers' ink.

Outside the daylight was going. Through the wide windows I could see a far bank of trees and the smooth, wet shine of rhododendrons flanking part of the drive.

I turned back to Sava. Across the floor from the desk were long ink trails leading to a small stairway in the far corner. It was made of plain white pine and down the handrail was a long smear of red and black printer's ink. I stood at the bottom of the steps. I had a feeling that Sava had been waiting for me, and that he meant me to follow the marks of printers' ink.

I went up the stairs. I was in a long, low attic-room with a small window, shrouded in cobwebs, that gave a view of the house across the courtyard. But I had eyes for nothing except the wall opposite the window. A large, rectangular section of the brown matchboarding which lined the wall was swung back, revealing a dark entrance which ran straight through into the hill against which the building had been erected. It didn't need any great observation to see that when the matchboarding was swung shut there would be no sign of a door in the wall.

From the dark opening came a warm, sweet smell of ink, and far down it I caught a faint yellow glow of light. Five minutes later I understood the angry twist of the mouth of the dead man. It had been the anger of determination, of revenge.

There was a narrow passageway about five yards long and then a low, wide chamber that had been hollowed out of the hillside, an enlargement probably of a natural cave. It was lit with two powerful overhead lights. I stood on the threshold of this chamber, and everywhere I looked showed the signs of Sava's last frenzied act. On the floor a yard from me was a large sledge-hammer, its handle marked with ink.

He had gone through the chamber like an avenging demon. Pieces of machinery were scattered over the floor, the bright scars of fractured metal catching the strong light, long tubes of ink lay like squashed caterpillars about the place and the coloured smear of their entrails was over everything.

I picked my way forward slowly. A scattering of notes like a fall of autumn leaves covered the ground by a machine which

I took to be a press of some kind. Ink and oil were splattered over them. I picked two of them up. One was an English pound note and the other an American five-dollar note. I stared at them for a while and then let them flutter back to the floor. Farther down the chamber great sheets of paper had been dragged down from a high shelf and lay defaced and smeared like dirty tablecloths. Another machine close to the end wall with a small rotating drum had been smashed and hammered until it was a confusion of metal, and on a small stand at its side were five or six engraved plates, cracked and splintered. Sava had gone through the place like a whirlwind. Crates were broken open, a drum of oil had been punctured near its base and the viscid fluid was still spreading in a black pool over the floor, and a small desk near the passage entrance had been battered and hammered so that it now lurched to one side, drawers gaping. Letters and files on the floor were soaking up the oil in which they lay. There was nothing here which could be repaired. Before another counterfeit note could be produced everything would have to be renewed . . . and without Sava there was no hope of renewing the precious plates from which the notes must be struck.

I went back down the passage, and I was a different man. The whole tragic story took shape for me. Sava had been forced by the Germans to use his genius for their forgeries, and then Hansford had come along and Sava had found no escape. In return for freedom in England he had still to go on using his talents to serve Hansford. And when Hansford had been killed there still had been no escape. The others had taken over. And then I had come out. Maybe when he had been told to sit tight and be the bait in the trap which would finish me off, the whole thing had got too much for him. Hansford's murder he could accept, had to accept . . . but to play a part in another that had been asking too much and finally he had escaped. The wreckage he had produced could not be ignored. I had as much as I needed now to take me into the open, to send me to the police.

As I stepped through the doorway into the top room I heard a telephone ring down in the studio, and I remembered that on the desk there had been a house-phone. The telephone went on ringing and ringing. If it weren't answered someone would come over from the house. I crossed to the head of the stairs, and as I did so the bell stopped ringing. It left behind it a heavy, oppressive silence and in the silence, from the studio below, I heard someone move. I halted. I could only see the run of the stairs and a small part of the studio, and the light was bad with the fast approach of evening. There was a rustle and scrape of footsteps below and then the quick slam of a door. At that moment I heard a shout from the house. I drew swiftly back from the stairs and, revolver in hand, I ran to the small, dirty window that commanded the courtyard.

From the back of the house and running hard across the open space towards the studio were two men. One was Rance and the other was Henry Daiken. They were halfway across the courtyard when I heard Rance shout and point to his left, and they swung away towards the little lawn through which the stream ran towards the dark mouth of the culvert. And then I saw Catherine. She came into view, running fast down the stream towards the road, and I realized that she would never make it. The two men were halfway across the lawn now and heading her off. I saw her look towards them, then turn and race back towards the hillside that rose behind the studio. I didn't wait for more. I spun round and rushed for the stairway.

CHAPTER XV

The thing I had dreaded was happening and in everything I thought and did there was a feverish, agonizing urgency.

I went down the stairway in three leaps. Sava was still at his desk, but he had rolled sideways and his head hung towards the floor now. I stopped for a second, intending to take the papers from him, but they had gone. I didn't search for them because I knew Catherine must have them. And as I dashed for the side room and the open window which would take me on to the lawn I was remembering that she had told me her mother had been born in Hungary, and that she herself spoke the language fairly well. While I had been in the printing chamber she had probably stood by Sava and read what he had written.

Outside the rain had thickened and there were low veils of mist laced between the trees. To my right and beyond the stream I could hear the crash and shouts of the two men as they went after Catherine up the slope. As I followed I saw the long smears made by their feet across the rain-dewed grass. I went after them, and there was a wild anxiety in me. I was in the open now, and I didn't have to think about anything except Catherine and myself. I didn't have to hide any longer from the police and the rest of the world. My hand tightened round the revolver.

As I reached the first of the pines and the rising ground, there was a shout from behind me. I looked round. On the lawn by the culvert-mouth a man was running towards me. He was too far away for me to fire. It was Colonel Drysdale.

I went into the trees and breasted the slope, crashing through the young bracken, following the trail left by the others whom I could still hear ahead of me.

I plugged up through a grove of small oaks, my feet slipping on the wet leaves and then over broken boulder-strewn ground, and as I crested a shoulder of hillside I saw them. They were well ahead of me, three small figures blotted out now and again by the sweeping curtain of rain and mist. Catherine was about two hundred yards ahead of the two men and running hard. Between myself and the two was a long gap which I set myself to close up. I ran desperately. A soggy bog-patch brought me to my knees once, mud and slime sucking at my feet, and then a great blanket of rain closed around me and I was panting forward, burrowing into the heart of a great grey blanket. And always ahead of me on the short, rain-beaded turf were the long marks left by the running men.

The track went up, always climbing, but slowly bearing away to the right, and I guessed that Catherine was trying to made a wide turn which would bring her back eventually to the road. She hadn't got a chance. The sweep was too big, and gradually, for all her fitness, I knew the two men would wear her down.

I don't know how long I ran. I seemed to have been running through all eternity, and keeping pace with me was the fear that I would lose them, that Catherine would be left alone with the two men. . . . If I lost her, nothing that remained to me was of any value. To be free again meant nothing unless she was there with me.

The mist and rain were all about me, a damp, blinding cloak, and suddenly there were no more tracks on the turf. I went on and my feet were on loose small stones. Out of the mist ahead three sheep sprang from the shelter of a rock and leaped away into the greyness. I stopped then, listening, and the only sounds I could hear were the thump of my heart and the slow hiss of the rain.

Desperate, I raced on blindly, going upwards. The loose stones turned to hard rock, and suddenly on my right the mist rolled back a little and I saw the ground falling away to a sharp, black drop. I was on the edge of a ridge. I tried not to think how easily one could come racing up to the drop in the rain and go over.

I stopped again, and then, above me, I heard a shout and the swift click of feet on hard rock. I put everything I had into it then. There was a small sheep track along the edge of the ridge and I went along it like a madman. The ridge began to rise more steeply. Once I had to use my hands to climb a long gully, and I was lost in a world where there was only the wet rocks, the steady drip of water and the swirl of mist and rain.

I came out of the gully on to a stretch of turf that broke away on my right to the ridge-drop. On the grass were the marks of feet. And then, close ahead of me, I heard a shout, an angry, exultant shout.

A great breath of air came whipping across the ridge, and for a while the curtain of rain was swung aside like a heavy theatre tab being looped back.

Fifty yards ahead of me the turf ended in a sheer black rise of rock and at the base of the rock was Catherine, and closing in on her were Daiken and Rance. I saw her back away from them, saw them lumbering forward and heard Daiken shout. They were above me, and their figures seemed to have swollen until they filled the little world encircled by mist. Rance rushed at Catherine, and I saw his hand go up and in it the great stick he always carried. She stepped back from him, her arms raised to protect herself. As she did so the short turf at the ridge-edge broke from under her. She went over, and from my sight, and her voice came echoing through the rain, no words, just sound, a high, sharp cry that went through my heart like a dagger.

In the few seconds that followed there was murder in me. I was shouting and swearing aloud, and as I ran I raised my revolver and fired. The two men swung about to face me. I saw Daiken stagger back and clamp a hand to his shoulder. I fired again, not ten yards from them, and there was a great spark from the black rock where the bullet struck a couple of inches above Rance's head.

They didn't wait for more. They turned and ran down the slope away from the ridge and into the mist. I followed them and fired two more shots. Then I pulled up, and I could feel my body trembling and there was a roaring blackness of savage anger in my mind.

*   *   *

The first fifteen feet from the ridge was sheer drop, and beyond that I could see nothing because of the mist and the fast-gathering darkness. I went down it, using hand- and foot-holds and found myself on a sharp slope of bare turf and whortleberry bushes, and I could see where Catherine's body had rolled across this. The turf slope ended in a long slide of loose scree stone, fifty yards of it, which I jumped down, digging my heels into the soft rubbish, and it was at the bottom of this that I found her.

She was standing up, swaying a little, and as I came up to her I caught her arm just in time to stop her from falling. I held her to me, and for a while there was nothing except the sense of wild relief that possessed my mind, and my voice repeating her name.

But there was no response in her at all. She lay in my arms and I could feel the limpness of her body. She didn't say anything. Now and again her shoulders shook with a fierce spasm of shivering.

I made her sit down, and she obeyed me like a shocked child. There was a large cut and a livid bruise mark high up on her left temple. I tied my handkerchief round her head as a bandage. Her skirt was ripped and part of the jumper she wore had been

338

torn right across her back. I let her sit there for a while, talking to her. She wasn't with me. She looked at me, but her eyes looked through and beyond me, and I guessed that she was suffering from concussion.

I let her sit for a while. I took off my jacket and put it round her shoulders. After a while she seemed stronger, and I decided to try and get her to the road. To leave her alone while I went for help was more than I could risk. I got my arm under her shoulder and brought her to her feet, and very slowly we set off through the rain and darkness. She walked, stumbling and sometimes falling forward so that I had to hold her up. I gave her all the strength and help I could, and as we went I talked to her, hoping to bring her back, to let her know that I was there and that she was going to be all right. I don't know how long the trip took us, but I do know that throughout those agonizing minutes I learned what love really was and the power and misery there could be in it. Nothing existed for me except Catherine. Sava, Hansford . . . all the mad, nightmarish events of the recent past slid from me.

Slowly we went downhill and finally struck a narrow track that followed a noisy stream full of froth-covered pools and waterfalls. It grew so dark that the track was hard to pick out. Once we both fell and I cursed myself for my clumsiness. When I tried to bring her to her feet again there was no strength in her. She just sagged against me.

I got my shoulder under her and I carried her in a fireman's lift. Desperately I wished myself back in Parkhurst, wished that we had never met . . . would, if the miracle could have happened, have wiped out all these days and have been content to sit out my time in gaol.

The track ran into trees. Every little while I had to put her down and rest, but in the end I reached the road, coming out on to it through a field gate.

Ten minutes later the lights of a van came up through the misty rain. I stopped it and explained to the driver that Catherine and I had been out walking and that she had had an accident.

The driver was an old man and his only comment was, "There's nasty these hills are when the weather turns bad."

He helped me lift her into the back and I made her as comfortable as I could. He was going through Capel Curig, and I told him I wanted to reach the hotel there.

He drove off, taking it as easily as he could, and I sat close to Catherine, my arm round her shoulder, trying to spare her from the jolting and swaying.

Only once during that drive did she give any sign that she knew I was with her. We'd been going about ten minutes when she stirred and opened her eyes, and she raised a hand to the neck of her blouse. I saw that she was reaching clumsily, feebly for something and I heard the rustle of paper. I reached over and found tucked inside her blouse Sava's letter. As I pulled it out I felt her body shudder and her voice came to me, broken and very faint.

"Oh, Peter . . . Peter . . . it's there. . . . He tells who killed Hansford. . . ."

"Don't talk," I said gently. "Not now."

But I felt her stir and sensed the effort in her.

"But, Peter . . . you must . . . you must. . . ."

And then her voice trailed off and I could almost feel the collapse in her. Her head dropped back against my arm and there was nothing I could do except sit shielding and holding her and loving her and hating myself for bringing her to this.

The old man helped me carry her into the Bryn Tyrch hotel and we laid her on the sofa in the hallway. At once the place began to seethe and hum as guests and staff gathered round. As I straightened up from laying her down I saw what was for me the most welcome sight in the world. Coming out from the lounge was Ross-Piper, tall, bulky in tweeds, and a slow smile on his great face for me.

"I'm a doctor," he said, elbowing his way forward. "What's happened?"

Even in this moment he was thinking of me, not revealing our relationship, and I admired him for his coolness.

"We were out walking and she fell over a ridge," I said.

He took charge right away. He had her carried up to her room and I went with him. I stayed there while he examined her and when he had finished I could see that he didn't look too happy. He opened his medical bag which he had brought up with him and began to prepare a syringe.

"She's in a bad way?" I could hear my voice shaking.

"Fairly. What happened?"

He bent over her and rolled back the sleeve of her blouse. Her face was white and the dark hair trailed over her forehead.

"The whole Sava thing blew up in my face," I said. "I tried to keep her out of it . . . went by myself, but she must have followed me. . . . I don't know. But they spotted her, chased her up into the hills, and she fell over a ridge. . . . Sava's committed suicide. She read his last letter, knows who killed Hansford. . . ."

340

He pressed the plunger.

"Steady, Peter," he said, and his face came round to me, warm and comforting. "She'll be all right. But I'm going to have to operate. She's had a blow on the temple that's fractured the bone and driven part of it in. We've got to do something about that right away. Now don't panic. . . ."

He stood up and for a moment his hand was on my arm.

"There's a hospital at Bangor and the surgeon there is one of my old students. I'll phone him to get things ready and they can send out an ambulance. I'll operate myself. . . ." He shook his head. "I came up to see if I could help you, and a damned good job I did. You stay here with her while I go down and fix things up."

He left me with her and I sat on the bed and held her hand. She just lay there, far from me, and there was a great loneliness inside me.

Ross-Piper was back within ten minutes. He had everything fixed. The ambulance would be out within the hour. He brought with him a large glass of whisky, which he handed to me.

"Now, there's nothing we can do until she's at Bangor. Tell me everything that happened."

It was hard to concentrate on other people. The only person I was interested in was lying on the bed, and for all the confidence which Ross-Piper inspired, I could not force back the fears which rose in me every time I looked at the still figure of Catherine.

I explained to him what had happened when I had gone to see Sava.

"When I ditched Catherine she must have guessed what I was up to. I don't know how she found out Sava's address. Perhaps she phoned the Capel Curig post office, or maybe she got it for herself in Llanberis. He's well known. After that it was easy for her . . . a bus, or a hired car. She did exactly what I didn't want her to do. You know what she's like."

"She's tough. She couldn't have made the trip back with you otherwise. Don't worry about her."

"She was in the studio while I was upstairs, and she must have read Sava's confession. She knows the language. She knows who killed Hansford. . . . But I'm not interested in all that now. She's the only one who means anything."

"Still . . . the police must be told. They must get down there."

"That can wait. The ambulance will be here any moment, and I'm going with you. I've got Sava's confession." I patted my pocket. "There won't be anyone left in that place if the police go there. Damn it . . how long do you think that ambulance will be?"

I was pacing restlessly up and down the room.

"It'll come, don't worry. When we reach Bangor you must get on to the police there. The local constable here wouldn't be much help."

The next hour went by in a slow agony for me. Ross-Piper fetched me another whisky and then left me alone with Catherine while he went downstairs to explain things to the manager of the hotel. I stood by the window and watched the road outside the hotel for the arrival of the ambulance.

It was raining hard through the mist now. A fierce, slashing downpour. It was gone eleven and the ambulance was somewhere fifteen minutes ahead of us on the road. I had wanted to travel in it, but Ross-Piper had made me come in his car. There was a nurse with Catherine in the ambulance and I wasn't needed.

I sat there listening to the monotonous *chunk, chunk* of the windscreen wipers and watching the blurred forms of the hedges and road ahead. Now and again Ross-Piper spoke, but I hardly heard what he said. My thoughts were all of Catherine, travelling with her on the road ahead.

Drew was driving and we two were sitting behind. The faint light from the dashboard picked out Ross-Piper's bulky shape as he lay back in his corner, solid, dependable and full of confidence. If he said Catherine was going to be all right, I told myself, then she would be. He was the best authority in England on this kind of thing. He was staring straight ahead of him, his lips drawn tight and his face full of thought, and by some trick of light his heavy brows filled the hollows of his eyes with dark shadow. He turned to me and said:

"You're a lucky man, Peter. Some people are. They go for the things they want and there's no particular reason why they should get them—but get them they do. The gods still have favourites, it seems. You'll go to the police and clear yourself. Catherine will be all right . . . and you'll go back to Canada."

"I'm not thinking beyond Bangor at the moment."

"You don't want to worry about that. Catherine will be all right. You can go to the police while I operate. You've got Kostavitch's confession with you?"

"Yes."

"Good." The word was almost a sigh. It was a deep, easy sigh . . . full of repose and security. The rain drummed on the roof and slashed at the windows, streaking the night outside with silver scars in the headlights. I moved slightly and felt the crinkle of Sava's letter in my pocket. Being free wouldn't mean much to me if Catherine. . . . I shied away from the thought, and then there was a picture of the dead Sava in my mind, crumpled across his desk. Sava . . . Kostavitch . . . I sat there and the two names beat in my mind.

Ross-Piper grunted to himself in his corner, and then with a chuckle said, "Yesterday one of the daily papers offered a thousand pounds reward for anyone giving information leading to your capture. . . . You're a valuable young man."

"It's too late now," I said.

Ross-Piper nodded. "Yes . . . too late." Then, after a pause, he went on, "Let me have a look at it."

"At what?" I said.

"At Kostavitch's letter. I know a little Hungarian. . . ."

I reached into my pocket. But my hand stayed there. Sava . . . Kostavitch . . . the words were still beating in my brain.

And very shortly I knew why. The thought crawled out of the darkness like some repulsive insect. Kostavitch. Ross-Piper had asked me if I had Kostavitch's confession. Something was wrong there. . . . I went back over all I had said to him and a disturbing certainty grew in me like a great coldness.

I sat forward, half turning to Ross-Piper. I found him watching me, and it was like seeing his face for the first time . . . not large, warm and comforting now, but a mask of shadows and grey lights, the deep eye sockets full of darkness and the broad mouth drawn tight as though he were suppressing some inner turbulence.

I turned away from him, not believing myself, even telling myself that strain and anxiety were playing tricks with my mind. This was Ross-Piper, old enough to be my father, who had known my father and shown himself my friend, risking himself for me.

"What's the matter?" he asked.

"Nothing. . . ."

"You've got the letter, haven't you?"

There was no mistaking the faint note of anxiety in his voice. And inside me a voice was crying out that it couldn't be. But I knew it was. I had never mentioned the name Kostavitch to Ross-Piper. Always, yes always, I had referred to him as Sava. Yet even now I wouldn't let myself believe it—it was fantastic, horrible.

"How did you know his name was Kostavitch?"

The words came from me in a rush—and I was desperately anxious for him to prove my suspicions absurd.

"You told me, Peter . . . back in the hotel. . . ."

"But I didn't!" I cried.

"Don't be a fool!" And he couldn't have given me more

344

proof. His words were angry and savage and I saw his great bulk stir quickly.

In front of me Drew said, "That's right, Mr. Barlow. I heard you." He leaned forward, and putting up a hand rubbed at the mist forming on the inside of the windscreen. And now I knew that both of them were lying. Drew's hand proved it to me, for as he rubbed at the glass the long length of the car's bonnet showed more clearly. With a cold thrill of apprehension inside me I was back in a stuffy bedroom, with Daiken lying on a crumpled bed and myself watching his wife cross a yard to his garage.

There, clear, black cut against the headlights as I stared past Drew, was the tiny figure of a jockey on a racehorse perched on the radiator cap. This was Daiken's car. Ross-Piper had no car of his own. He didn't keep one in London. If he wanted to come to Wales suddenly he would have to hire one or. . . . I don't think even then I was believing it myself. Because the man meant so much to me I wanted to find a way out. It couldn't be.

I sat forward farther in my seat and turned to him again. He was still watching me, but now the large, still face was thrust forward from the square shoulders and he was smiling in a way I had never known before, and as he smiled he shook his head gently. There was no doubt in my mind now. I felt sick, and each word came from me as though it were something obscene.

"You and Drew," I said. "You've been behind this all the time. This is Daiken's car. In God's name, what does it all mean?"

It was some time before Ross-Piper spoke.

"Now or later . . . it had to come," he said slowly, and his voice was full of a reluctant satisfaction. "You were quick to get it. That's the trouble with you . . . you get things even when you shouldn't. The gods play for you . . . in a way they never played for Tom. Yes, I said Kostavitch, Peter. I've known him for years."

From a terrible icy calm inside myself a hardness of spirit rose to meet him. "I've got it," I said. "And a horse and jockey on the radiator of this car. Daiken's car. But there's so much I don't get."

He dropped back in his corner then, and with the movement I saw his large hand slide from the pocket of his tweed coat and I knew what he held.

"There was nothing I could do," he said. "Tom's death made it easier. Rightly or wrongly, I could blame you for that. Yes, that made it easier. When Tom went and I had nothing left but my work—it came to mean everything to me. I even taught myself to hate you. It wasn't hard."

From the front seat, without turning his head, Drew said roughly:

"Shut up, guv'nor!"

"Not now, Drew. Not now. He deserves to know it all. You shouldn't have gone to Hansford that night, Peter. . . . All this would never have happened then. . . ." He laughed, a dry, painful sound. "I killed Hansford, Peter. Not because he was blackmailing your father . . . I never knew about that until it was too late . . . but because he was becoming dangerous to me, to my work——"

"You killed Hansford!" For me the nightmare of this day was starting again.

"Of course. Hansford and I met in Paris after the war. You always understood I was a wealthy man. So I was until the war, and then it all went. But Hansford had a way to make wealth. And I needed money to go on with my research, to keep my clinic going. When Tom went it was all I had to live for. . . . You've no idea how much money can be spent on a place like that. . . . And Hansford showed me how to get it."

"But you killed him——"

"He was an impatient man, Peter. He wanted to market our stuff too quickly, too dangerously, for the rest of us—so he had to go."

"And you'd have let me hang!" I said savagely.

"It troubled me. . . . I'm not a monster. But I told myself that what I was doing was more important than your life. I could afford to throw away one life if others were saved. . . . But there was always the thought of Tom in my mind. But you weren't hanged, Peter. The gods were on your side. And when I knew you were determined to escape I feared your luck. And, damn you . . . it held. Yes, it held until now." He laughed a little to himself, and it was an ugly, remote sound, almost lost in the beat of the rain. "It's a bad night, Peter. Rain. A filthy night. Your gods are asleep again. They won't hear you. And they won't hear Catherine."

"What the hell do you mean?" I jerked forward, but his hand came up and I knew there was nothing in his temper to stop him firing if I provoked him.

"That she must go the same way as you. If she's read Kostavitch's confession she knows I killed Hansford. Only she and you know. Afterwards the mess down at High Firs can easily

346

be cleared up. . . . Sava had the right of any man to commit suicide. We can replace him eventually."

"You mean you won't operate on Catherine?"

"I mean I will. There's nothing wrong with her. Just concussion. Normally she would be out of it in twenty-four hours. But I shall operate. No one will question my diagnosis, and she'll die on the table . . . regrettably, and a little later than you."

Drew said, "Shut up, for the love of Mike, guv'nor. There's no need for all this." And then, still without turning, he went on, "Sorry, Mr. Barlow, sir. But it's as he says. There's nothing you can do. I got nothing against you personally, but I'm for the guv'nor. Why the hell didn't you clear out of the country when you had the chance?" He leaned forward, changing gear, and as the car began to climb I saw a fork road and the white flash of a signpost. It was a familiar signpost, and I knew that we weren't on the road to Bangor. We were going back to High Firs.

"He wouldn't clear out because it wasn't in his nature," said Ross-Piper reflectively. "No, a man must do what is inside him. I helped you to escape, and I meant to have it all end on that beach . . . but it didn't. You've given me a lot of trouble since then. Still, there's an end to it now. . . ."

I sat there and I shut my eyes against the horror of the whole affair. And one thought hammered and hammered in my mind. Catherine was going to die. Catherine was going to die . . . and I was helpless. I only had to move and Ross-Piper would shoot me without a moment's hesitation. Things had gone badly for him, but I saw how they could still be saved. I would disappear. He could say I had telephoned him to come to Wales to help me out. He had come to persuade me to give myself up, and had found me with Catherine . . . a girl who loved me enough to share my risks. On the way to the hospital, knowing she was seriously injured and might die, I had jumped out of the car and had disappeared. . . . I sat there, seeing how he could cover himself . . . how it would all fall into place. . . . I was so desperate that I even doubted the reality of the moment and told myself that soon I would wake and find this all a beastly dream . . . but reality was there, inescapable; Drew driving, the car snaking down the long hill to Lyn Dinas, and Ross-Piper sitting away from me, saying nothing, heavy and implacable in his corner and part of his mind eaten and rotten with a long, slow madness that had risen from his grief for Tom and the fanatical love of his work. . . . And when I was gone the reality would still be there. Daiken and Rance and Giulio

347

Latti . . . and *La Boutade* and a chain of good pull-ups for drivers where the counterfeit notes were passed to the public. . . . And there was nothing I wanted to do for myself. Only one person counted, and that was Catherine. If Ross-Piper went to Bangor she would die. If he never reached her she would live. And I meant her to live, even if it meant the end of me. I could say it to myself simply and honestly, because the truth of it was inside me like a great warming flame, driving out the chill and horror which Ross-Piper had put there.

I watched the road ahead and I tried to remember how it went. It was all downhill past the two lakes of Gwynant and Dinas, and almost at the end of Dinas was the entrance to High Firs.

Drew said bitterly, "I always said we should have let you stay in Parkhurst. You'd have never got out alone."

"He would. He's the kind." For the first time there was the edge of anger, hard and vicious in Ross-Piper's voice. "Look at his luck. What other man would have found *La Boutade* and Drysdale, and got on to Kostavitch . . . ?"

"Isn't Drysdale in this with you?" I'd forgotten all about the man until then.

"No. He's a wretched half-pay officer who saw a chance of making a little money. . . ."

"But he's up here."

"If he is he's read about the reward and is trying to make up his mind to turn you in. I'm not worrying about him. He can be bought or silenced."

"You're mad!" I cried.

He didn't say anything. A car came up the hill and passed us. Its lights filled our own car with a bright glare for a few seconds, and in that moment of time I saw on the seat between Ross-Piper and myself his large black leather medical bag.

We were running downhill still through great curtains of rain. Away on the right, somewhere out in the darkness, was the long stretch of Lake Gwynant. I shifted my position slightly and let my right hand drop to the seat at my side. With my finger tips I could just feel the side of the black leather bag. What did a doctor carry in his bag? Stethoscope, syringes . . . I hoped it would be something hard, something metal that reinforced by the tough leather of the bag would deflect a bullet. I slid my fingers slowly under the bottom of the bag. It was no good hoping I would have time to grab the handle and raise it. It had to go up with a jerk of my hand from underneath. I had my fingers well under it now and I waited. . . .

Drew was driving fast and well, solid and silent ahead. Time seemed to withdraw from me so that I lived in a vacuum.

Ross-Piper stirred in his corner, sitting a little more upright. I could see the revolver clearly now, his hand resting in the lap of his coat. He spoke and I knew then that he, too, had been going back over the past and that underneath his hatred for me some faint regret or compassion had stirred, though it carried no hope.

"When you didn't die on the beach," he said heavily, "I took it as a sign that your luck would run. That's why I offered to get you abroad, to put you out of my life. . . . You should have accepted the chance. . . . That way we should both have been content."

I didn't answer. I had nothing to say to him.

We were off the hill now and travelling fast towards the top of Lake Dinas along a practically level stretch of road. Through the rain I caught a glimpse of the rising ground on the right and the black strokes of pine trunks on the left marking the verge of the lakeside.

The car swung right-handed fast and the tyres bit and screamed a little against the wet road surface. As I swayed towards him I jerked the bag upwards and into his lap and I threw myself on him. He fired once and shouted, and I felt a long finger of pain probe through my leg. Then all was confusion and noise and the wet, searing sound of the car swaying across the road. I was on him, sprawling across the seat, my hands fighting at his wrists, his face close to mine and his warm breath beating into my eyes. We struggled and twisted in the cramped space and I heard Drew shout, "Hold him, guv'nor!"

He fought like a maniac, swearing and shouting to himself. I smashed at his face with a free fist and the two of us were locked in desperate savagery. He jerked his hand free and fired again. The flame lit the inside of the car briefly, and I felt a long score of scalding pain across my cheek. We rolled together off the seat and he was beneath me. I heard Drew's voice, agonized and suddenly frightened, cry, "Guv'nor . . . guv'nor . . ." and then choke to a queer child-like sob. At the same time the car began to sway and snake. The last bullet had hit Drew.

What happened then was pure nightmare, the climax of the dreadful day. I wrenched the revolver from him. I struggled half up and saw Drew slumped over the wheel, which twisted and swung under his body, shaking his limp shoulders. In the headlights a great barrier of tree trunks smashed towards us like a dark palisade, and I had time only to raise my hands to my face.

There was a crash and then a madness of angry sounds, splintering glass and the squeal of tortured metal. Everything fell away from me. I was taken by a great hand and thumped and beaten and my ears were full of a grinding and smashing. I was flung up and down and not for one second did the noise cease or the great hand stop driving into me . . . and then I dropped away as the world exploded in a wild roar around me.

*   *   *

I came back to life once and everything was very clear and still around me. It was a world of rain and shining tree trunks, some of them fanged white in the light that streamed down from some high point. I was lying on wet turf and my body was one long ache. A face moved in the light above me and I recognized Colonel Drysdale, and behind him three other faces and the shine of silver buttons against blackness. I tried to struggle up, but his hand came down gently and held me and he said something which I couldn't catch . . . just sound, but with a deep gentleness in the tones. I dropped my head sideways and away to my left on the wet, silver-flecked turf I saw the still blackness of two other forms and beyond them the smashed car, tilted grotesquely with its rear wheels high in the air.

I said, "Catherine . . ." and then floated away, but I was still saying Catherine to myself.

It was my impression that I went on saying "Catherine . . . Catherine . . ." to myself. All eternity was wrapped around me and I was quite content to float for ever in a soft vacuum so long as I could say her name.

*   *   *

It was four days before I came out of that vacuum, and when I did she was sitting by my bed. She was holding my hand, and when I opened my eyes she smiled. I didn't say anything. I was content to look at her. She sat there smiling and then she leaned forward and kissed me.

*   *   *

After that she was always there when I opened my eyes, and, although it's a long time ago now, I still remember those days, every moment of them treasured while she helped me to come back, to come back from darkness and pain to the point where we could talk, to the day when I could sit up and then get out of bed and walk.

Drew and Ross-Piper were killed in the car accident. I knew that before she ever told me. Rance, Daiken and Giulio Latti and his wife Carla were all found . . . but little Arthur Fisher must have gone to Ireland and stayed there. And Colonel Drysdale . . . I had him wrong. He was my friend. In his own way. The reward, which he'd read about after leaving me in the train, had drawn him to Wales.

"All that money—it was a hell of a temptation, old man," he told me. "I was in a cleft stick. You see, I was heavily in debt, being dunned all over the place. I couldn't make up my mind what to do . . . until I saw you and Catherine go chasing up that hill and I lost you in the mist. After that I went to the police. We heard the sound of the car crashing from High Firs. . . ."

Ross-Piper had said I was born lucky. My luck held that night, for if they had not heard the crash of the car I should have lain out there for hours and slowly bled to death from the bullet wound in my leg. There would have been nothing for me . . . no freedom, no future, no return to Canada, and no Catherine with the bright dark look to share this all with me.